The TV Detective

The TV Detective

Simon Hall

Based on 'A Popular Murder'

Published by Accent Press Ltd – 2010

ISBN 9781907016059

Printed and bound in the UK

Cover design by The Design House

For Jess

Acknowledgements

All my detective and medical friends, as ever, for their advice and patience, John Bainbridge, Rob Steemson, and Alec Collyer for helping me to finally, at last and eventually find the elusive Ted Hughes memorial (it really is there, and I'd thoroughly recommend the walk that Dan, Kerry and Rutherford follow), our wonderful libraries and their even finer staff and readers who have supported me so well, and the Isles of Scilly, that beautiful archipelago of pure inspiration where the idea for the TV Detective series first nudged me (and isn't a bad place for a wedding either). My thanks to you all!
SH, Exeter, the freezing Winter of 2010

Chapter One

THE WOMAN WAS SHELTERING in the long doorway of what must once have been a club, or dance hall, eyeing each car that passed. The rain was thundering into the road, pavement, windscreens and rooves, the kind of rain that hurls itself at the ground with all its mighty force, creating a misty spray of rebounding raindrops that adds to the dense fury of the downpour.

Sitting in the car felt like hiding inside the drum kit of a particularly energetic percussionist, the relentless beat of the storm filling the dry haven with a chaotic beat.

Another car drove slowly past, tyres slicing through the standing water. The woman took a step forwards, placed her hands on her hips and performed a perfunctory wiggle which looked about as alluring as a minefield. The car accelerated on.

'The trouble is,' Dan said, projecting his voice above the pounding of the rain, 'that in this weather, everyone's kerb crawling. There's no choice but to drive slowly.'

'Yeah,' Nigel replied. 'And, anyway, are you sure she's a prostitute?'

It was a question Dan had already considered. Walking up to a woman and raising that very issue was unlikely to go down well if she wasn't. But he'd found reassurance in the incongruity of her attire. Everyone else who'd been forced to venture out on this miserable Monday evening was wearing a coat, collars turned up and pulled tight; sheltering under hats, umbrellas and briefcases too. The woman was wearing a tiny mini-skirt and a cropped top, her only concession to the bite of winter a fake and tatty fur coat resting open on her shoulders.

December 14th: the Millbay Docks area of Plymouth. The city's red light zone in the run up to Christmas, hardly abounding with festive spirit. The darkness suited the area, like one of the last drinkers in a seedy nightclub, it could only benefit from a lack of revealing light. At least a third of the buildings was vacant, some tumbledown and boarded up, decorated only with graffiti. Sodden strings of weeds wilted from walls and doorways. Soggy and forlorn litter lined the pavements and guttering.

The glowing clock in the car said a quarter to five. *Wessex Tonight* was on air at half past six.

'We're running out of time,' Nigel said helpfully.

'Thanks. I had noticed that.'

'So what are we going to do?'

'We'll have to go and talk to her.'

'I was worried you were going to say that.'

They'd been waiting for a break in the weather, but the downpour must have been a trainee of its kind. It felt young and keen, eager to pass its exams and qualify to become a major storm, perhaps a hurricane or typhoon, and seemed delighted to keep beating away at this small portion of the planet with all the gusto it could muster.

Which was, to put it mildly, considerable.

'What are we doing here, anyway?' Nigel groaned, his breath fogging the windscreen.

They'd been through all that. The newsroom was caught in the pincers of an awayday team-building exercise and an epidemic of illness, conveniently timed for Christmas present shopping before the high streets suffered their final annual frenzy. Dan, the station's Environment Correspondent, had spent the day researching various different stories, happily avoiding being called on to cover any of them – until the news broke of another attack on a prostitute.

The woman had been repeatedly slashed around the face with a knife. She wasn't critically injured, but she would be scarred for life. It was the third such attack on a prostitute in the last fortnight; the police had reluctantly released a statement to the effect that "it must be considered, given all the material circumstances, a person, or persons unknown, is, or are, at large in the city, harbouring some form of grievance against female workers in the sex trade which has ultimately manifested itself in violence."

Translated from the verbal morass of police speak, the cops appeared to be trying to say that there was a madman on the loose with a serious grudge against prostitutes.

Lizzie Riley, manic whirlwind of a News Editor, had demanded full coverage, but there was one problem. All the reporters were either unfit for duty, learning to become happy members of the great newsroom team, or out on other stories. The Crime Correspondent had taken voluntary redundancy six months ago, and the only journalist left in the newsroom was Dan.

The cross hairs of fate were settling on his chest.

His protests about the stories he needed to set up were ruthlessly overruled. A spate of otters being killed by cars in Cornwall was discarded. The plight of the Exmoor pony, an endangered breed, was ignored. Dan's search for the Ted Hughes memorial, Dartmoor's secret monument to the late Poet Laureate would have to wait for another day, as would the danger of erosion to the south-west coastal path, even the urgent need for more flood defences for towns and villages threatened by climate change. None registered even so much as a blip on Lizzie's interest-meter.

Her vision was more telescope than tunnel.

'I want a story about prostitutes being attacked, I want it good and I want it now. I want the cops, I want the girls themselves, and I want it all on tonight. Go!'

Dan went. He jogged down the stairs to find Nigel, his cameraman, in the canteen chatting to some engineers, and they drove down to Charles Cross police station, in the city centre, to interview a superintendent about the attacks. After ten minutes of patient questioning and bumbling answers, Dan had just about managed to coax a comprehensible response from the man. But that ordeal was the only easy part.

To make the report work, they needed to hear from the people who were most affected by the attacks. And as the latest victim was inaccessible in hospital, it meant speaking to some of her fellow prostitutes. So here they were, and the time was ticking mercilessly on.

'Let's get on with it then,' Dan muttered.

'How?' asked Nigel, with his usual logical practicality. 'I've never even spoken to a prostitute before, let alone tried to film one.'

From some men, you wouldn't believe such a claim. But not Nigel. A little older than Dan; although greatly experienced in the dark arts of news, he remained a gentle, kind and persistently optimistic man. A robust professional with a real zeal for the job, he was also a quietly moral Christian. The closest they came to arguing was when Dan pulled one of his little tricks to get a story.

Nigel also had a point. This wouldn't be an easy interview to secure. And time was ever more against them.

'Pull up alongside and I'll try to talk to her,' Dan said.

Nigel put the car into gear. The woman eyed them warily, but took a couple of paces forwards. Dan hopped out, skirted the bigger pools and puddles of water, ran to the shelter of the doorway and wiped some of the rain from his face.

'Err, hello there,' he said, as cheerily as he could.

'Who's in the car?'

'Err – my friend.'

She started backing off, her high boots sliding on the wet steps. 'Yer touch me and I'll scream. I mean it. There's cops everywhere now, and …'

Dan held up his hands. 'I don't want to hurt you. I'm trying to help.' He fumbled in his wallet, found his press pass, held it up. 'I'm a reporter. I want to talk to you about the attacks.'

She took a couple of steps forward and squinted through the gloom. 'Yer a reporter?'

'Yeah.'

'Who for?'

'The TV.'

'The telly? What yer want with me then?'

'I want to talk to you. About the attacks. About what's been happening. Did you know any of the other women who've been hurt?'

She pulled the coat around her body and shivered. Even behind the fur it was obvious that the woman was gaunt, almost emaciated. Her hair was a white blonde, but dark at the roots and she smelt of a potent mixture of strong drink and cheap perfume.

'I'm scared,' she said, and her voice was thin, tremulous. 'We're all scared. But we gotta keep working. We ain't got nothing else.'

She sat down heavily on a step, fumbled for a cigarette, cupped her hand against the wind and lit it. A swirl of rain invaded the doorway, but she didn't react.

'I want to help you,' Dan said again. 'I'm going to report what happened on the news tonight, and ask if anyone might have seen the man, or if someone knows who he is to come forward and tell the police.'

She snorted. 'Yeah, right. Fat chance. The cops don't care about us. We're nothing to them.'

'What's your name?'

'Rose.'

'Did you know any of the women who've been attacked?'

She nodded. 'Yeah. I knew Amanda, poor cow. The one who's just been done.'

'The one today?'

'Yeah.'

Dan took out his notebook and she flashed him a frightened look. 'It's OK,' he said soothingly. 'I just need to write this down. It's important we get your side of the story. If I can't speak to Amanda, then talking to people who knew her is the next best thing. What's she like?'

'Young. Only about twenty.' A lungful of smoke was whisked away on the wind. 'Not like me.'

It was impossible to tell how old Rose was through the mask of make-up. She reached in another pocket, brought out a quarter bottle of cheap whisky and sipped at it, her hand shaking.

'She said she was only doing it fer a couple of months, to make some money. She just needed a few quid to get out. To go abroad somewhere, she said. She was popular with the punters. Fresh, she was.' Rose laughed unpleasantly. 'Fresh meat, yer see. They love that.'

'And what was she like?'

'She was kind. Always talked to the rest of us. Shared her fags, and her booze too if she had any.'

A distant clock struck five. It was ten minutes back to the studio, and the report would take an hour to cut. They were running out of time. This interview would make the story, a woman who knew the latest victim, who could talk about her and the fear amongst the prostitutes about the attacks. Ideally, Dan would spend longer talking to her, try to get her to relax, persuade her to speak out, but he didn't have the time. News could be a ruthless industry.

Behind his back, he beckoned. The car door opened and Nigel got out, walked around to the boot, took out the camera.

'What's he doing?' Rose asked sharply.

'Don't worry, he's only going to do a few pictures of the area,' Dan said loudly, so Nigel would hear. 'We need the shots to show the viewers where the attacks happened. He'll shelter under here to keep out of the rain.' To distract her, he added, 'Tell me about yourself. Are you a local girl?'

She wasn't, she'd come down to Devon from London almost ten years ago, after the break-up of a relationship. It was a familiar story. The image of the sunshine county as a promised land still endured. She'd struggled to find somewhere to live, met a man who'd bought her a drink and something to eat, been kind, suggested there was easy money to be made working in a sauna and massage parlour he knew. Nothing dodgy, he'd reassured her, just rubbing some oil into old men's backs.

It hadn't worked out that way.

Nigel filmed while they spoke, shots of the boarded up buildings, the road, the sweeping headlights of the cars and the cascading raindrops. After a few minutes he gave a subtle nod, took the camera off its tripod and came to sit down beside them.

'Well, we'd better be going,' Dan said, holding out his hand to shake Rose's. Her skin was tough, heavily lined, ingrained with dirt and the yellow tinge of nicotine. 'There is just one more thing, though. How do you fancy saying a few words? About Amanda, and what it's like for you all, knowing this attacker is out there somewhere?'

She flinched. 'I ain't going on the TV.'

'It might help to catch him.'

'No way.'

6

'Come on. It'd make people understand what it's really like for you. It might make them care.'

'Or paint a frickin target on me for him, more like. I ain't going on no TV.'

'It'd really help, honestly. It'd make the story much stronger. Make more people take notice.'

'No bleeding way. No chance.'

She was adamant. Some people, when asked for a television interview, would say no, but start glancing at themselves in a mirror, begin adjusting their clothes, hair or make up. Not Rose. This was a no which meant no, a rare phenomenon in a vain world.

'You sure?' Dan tried again. 'It really might make a difference.'

'Not a prayer. Now go on, clear off. I've got a living to earn and yer putting the punters off.'

Dan got to his feet, Nigel too. They had enough for a story, could use some of the pictures of the area and the interview with the Superintendent, but it would be bland, lacking the main ingredient: a dish with no flavour. And they had no time to try to find another prostitute to speak to them. Rose was their only chance.

Dan took a step towards the car, stopped. 'Do you mind if I ask, Rose – just for my curiousity. How much does it cost? Sex, with you?'

She took a long draw on the whisky. 'Interested, are yer?'

'Just for the story,' Dan replied hurriedly.

'Depends, don't it? About a hundred.'

'And you, err …' he struggled to phrase the question. 'You do other things too? For the right price.'

'Yeah.'

'Just about anything?'

'Yeah.' Another snort, a noise which in a single second communicated the ancient collapse of self-respect and hope. 'Yeah, just about fricking anything.'

'So – how about an interview? For the right price?'

Beside him, Dan heard Nigel draw in a breath. A taxi rumbled past, slewing waves of water towards them. Rose stubbed out her cigarette, lit another, then said, 'What kind of price?'

Across the road, an engine started and a car drew off, the driver watching Dan carefully as she slipped away into the obscurity of the evening.

A traffic jam meant they didn't get back to the studios until a quarter to six. Dan jogged up the stairs to the edit suites and found Jenny, his favourite picture editor waiting. She grabbed the tape and spooled through it to get an idea of the shots and interviews. Her dark hair nodded as she quickly took notes.

Dan had written the script as Nigel drove. He sat with the camera on his lap, playing back the material they'd gathered, noting down the best pictures and which sections of interview to use, constructing the report around them. Experience taught you a range of tricks, and every second saved could be vital in beating a looming deadline.

How to put the story together presented an interesting dilemma. It was an axiom of TV news that you started a report with your best pictures. But in this case, they didn't have any meaningful images, just shots of the place where the latest attack had happened. Their best material by far was the interview with Rose.

Beginning a report with an interviewee was generally frowned upon, seen as more radio than television, the mark of an amateur TV reporter. But prostitutes didn't often speak out and her words had been compelling, so that was how it was going to be.

In addition, he thought, they might as well get their money's worth.

It must have been one of the strangest haggles in the history of commerce. It was patently obvious she wanted the money, but had no idea how much to ask. And he wanted the interview, but had equally little idea of what to offer. In the end he'd used the newly discovered benchmark of a hundred pounds for sex, argued that an interview couldn't possibly be as taxing, messy, or take as long, and so they'd settled on seventy-five pounds.

All was well. Now it was just a question of getting it through on an expenses claim. Rose had, unsurprisingly, not been able to provide a receipt.

'I said – what quotes do you want to start with?' Jenny asked, for the second time.

'Sorry, I was just thinking,' Dan replied. 'It's been an interesting afternoon.'

He directed her to Rose's first answer, when she talked about Amanda, her youth, her friendliness and her hopes for escaping from the street. Then it was a few pictures of the area, while Dan wrote about the spate of attacks, followed by another clip of Rose.

'We're living in fear,' she said. 'We know what could happen to us, anytime. I know a lot of people'll think we're just old tarts, but we're people too, y'know. We don't deserve this. If anyone reckons they've seen this guy, or knows who he is, please tell the police.'

Next they added the Superintendent, speaking about how violent and degrading the attacks were, and the police's commitment to catching the man. Then it was a couple more shots of the area, with Dan giving the *Crimestoppers* number for anyone who had information to call.

The report was finished by twenty past six. Jenny checked it back, nodded approvingly.

'Good piece. Simple, but powerful. You want to watch out.'

'Why?'

'They're talking about appointing a new Crime Correspondent. Since Mike left we've been missing lots of big stories. The ratings have gone down a fair bit. People like their crime. The word is the bosses are starting to reckon it was a false economy not replacing him.'

'Thanks for the tip, but there're no worries on that score,' Dan replied breezily. 'They've already asked and I said no way. I love environment and I'm sticking to it. Give me the coast and countryside, and ponies and otters over attacks on prostitutes any day.' He made for the door. 'Speaking of which, I've got to sort out a story on Exmoor for later in the week and I reckon I might just wangle an overnight stay in a lovely little pub with it. An ideal treat for the run-up to Christmas.'

Dan walked out of the edit suite, straight into Lizzie. She was at battle stations, arms folded, thin lips pursed. She didn't say a word, just beckoned with a sharpened fingernail and headed off towards her office.

'Care to explain yourself?'

Long experience of his editor had taught Dan the danger of the open-ended question. It was an invitation to blunder into a trap, to give yourself away, and he was having none of it.

'I have no idea what you mean.'

They stared at each other across her desk. Dan hadn't even been asked to sit down, a bad sign. A firing squad was hardly known for making its victim comfortable before the dispatch.

'I think you do.'

It was like a painful and unproductive dance. Dan held his editor's stare, then looked away at a single ribbon of red tinsel which had been stuck to the wall of Lizzie's stark office. As if sensing the atmosphere, it wasn't even bothering to sparkle.

'Well, I'll say it again then. I don't.'

'And I'll say it again then. I think you do.'

Another silence. The clock on the wall said twenty-five past six. Five minutes until the programme. That gave Dan an advantage. Lizzie always scrutinised each passing second of *Wessex Tonight*. Whatever she had to say would have to be quick.

She picked up a piece of paper and started reading from it. "I have to complain in the strongest possible terms about one of your reporters. He was seen, this very afternoon, paying a prostitute for an interview. I cannot believe an allegedly responsible news organisation such as yours could stoop so low. You have broken the law, and encouraged, aided and abetted immorality and illegality. I demand instant action, and unless punitive action is taken, will be putting my complaint to the police, the local councils, my MP, and your governing board."

The temperature in the room rose.

A knock on the door broke the silence. It opened a crack, but a dismissive hand waved the unseen visitor quickly away before he or she could make any further progress.

Lizzie dropped the piece of paper on her desk. 'It goes on, and at quite some length too, but that's the gist. So then, what have you got to say for yourself?'

'I, err …'

'Is it true?'

'I, um …'

'I'll take that as a yes, then. You paid company money to a prostitute for an interview.'

'Well, I … I needed the interview, and that was the only way to get it.'

'Sit down.'

Dan sat.

'I was only doing my best you know,' he said. 'We had to have that interview to make the story work.'

She scanned through the rest of the letter. There were a couple of pages, and the handwriting looked oddly familiar. Dan could see some of the words had been crafted in meaningful capitals.

"DISGRACEFUL … DISGUSTING … APPALLING … SCANDALOUS …"

The plastic chair suddenly felt very uncomfortable.

Lizzie looked up, said quietly. 'Our complainant wants you sacked.'

'Oh, come on. It's hardly a sacking offence. All I did was …'

'Break the law. Sully our name. Drag us through the dirt. If this gets out, it'll be all over the papers.'

'Come off it. I do what it takes. It's what I always do.'

'You went too far. Far too far.'

'Since when did you get all moral? What would you have done if I came back without the story?'

'You went too far,' she repeated.

'You were a reporter once. You'd have done the same.'

A stiletto heel grated into the carpet. 'But you broke the golden rule. You got caught.'

'All right then, discipline me. Tell me off in the strongest possible terms, as Mr Pompous Complainant wants. Write back that you've done it, and that's it, sorted.'

'That's not going to be enough.'

Dan shifted in his chair, could feel a prickling sweat spreading across his back. 'Not enough?'

Even to him, his voice sounded strangely thin.

'Yes, not enough. I have to take real action. So I'm changing your job. You're off environment. You clearly need to learn more about the law, so in future you're doing crime.'

'What? But I ...'

'You're on crime.'

Dan tried not to sound panicked but wasn't at all sure he succeeded. 'But I was trying to help! Make sure the story was good. Get the interview we needed. You'd have done the same. Any decent hack would. I was only ...'

'It's crime or nothing.'

Dan took a deep breath. 'But I've been doing environment for years. I love it. I know all the stories, all the people. I'm on top of all the issues. I get all the exclusives. I've got a lovely load of stories all ready for the Christmas period. I'm not just giving it up.'

'Someone else can do all that.'

'But it's ... it's what I do!'

Lizzie glanced at the clock.

6.29.

'It's what you *did*. Now it's crime or nothing. You've got until we go on air to decide.'

'And this is nothing to do with you needing a new Crime Correspondent, I suppose?'

She didn't reply, instead kept her face impassive.

Dan tried to ignore the spin of memories flying through his mind. The visions of sun-blessed days filming Dartmoor's rugged tors, soft autumn rains on pristine Cornish beaches, wading through crisp and crystal rivers on Bodmin Moor. Watching wintering birds peck their hungry way along the mudflats of the Exe Estuary, hiking the heights of the crumbling cliffs of the Dorset and Devon Jurassic Coast.

And now knife attacks on prostitutes. Run down streets in tumbledown city centres. And murder, rape and robbery. And who knew what else.

The great encyclopedia of human inhumanity. Gift-wrapped, and all his.

And as welcome as rain at a wedding.

The title music of *Wessex Tonight* boomed from the television. Dan picked up his satchel and headed for the door.

'See you tomorrow then,' Lizzie called after him.

In reply, all Dan could manage was a sulky shrug, the like of which the most recalcitrant of teenagers would have been proud.

A long night was in prospect.

He would sit on the long blue sofa, flick through some television channels, watch a minute or two of a couple of programmes, turn the set off again. He'd pick up a book, read a page, then realise he hadn't taken in a word, reach for a newspaper, try the crossword, not manage to solve a single clue.

It was well after half past seven before Dan noticed he was hungry. He trudged into the kitchen, found some half stale bread and made beans on toast, ate one slice, then slipped the rest into Rutherford's bowl.

The Alsatian chomped his way through the unexpected treat, pawed the bowl around the floor to check there were no tasty remnants lying hidden anywhere, then padded back into the lounge.

'Life's changed, dog,' Dan told him. 'See what you get for trying to help? I should never have agreed to do that story, and I should never have paid that woman for the interview. I did what I thought was best for the programme and this is what happens.'

Dan got up from the sofa again and walked over to the pictures on the mantelpiece. They were the nearest he had to family photos. One was a shot of him, taken by another walker, standing on top of Dartmoor's Hay Tor, sweating, but grinning with the achievement of scaling the great granite rock. Another captured Dan and Rutherford at Land's End, the vast extent of the shimmering ocean behind them, the finale of one of their walking holidays. A smaller shot showed him and Nigel filming in a flood in the Cornish seaside town of Looe, Dan up to his waist in water as he told the camera about the havoc the spring tides were causing.

Each picture was a memory from his years as Environment Correspondent.

From what was now a previous life.

Dan stared, then gently laid them face down.

'Life's changed,' he told Rutherford again.

He walked over to the bay window and watched the clouds fleeing across the night sky. The rain had eased, just a misty drizzle now, the distant rooftops shining damp in the orange streetlights. The central heating in the flat grumbled as it switched itself back on. He stretched out a foot and traced patterns in the pile of the carpet.

Dan paced into the bathroom, gave the sink a wipe, thought about having a bath, ran the tap awhile, decided against it. He wandered into the spare bedroom and checked through the line of shirts on the clothes rack. Which was the style a crime correspondent should wear? Nothing fancy, just plain, sober and sombre, to match the stories he would be covering.

A series of knife attacks on prostitutes. What a lovely start. He wondered what the next delight would be.

In his bedroom, Dan picked up a discarded sock from the floor, smoothed the sheets, puffed up the duvet. Rutherford followed, looking puzzled. Dan gave him a brief, understanding smile. The dog had never before seen his master take such interest in domestic chores.

Back to the lounge, a check through the CD rack, nothing he fancied listening to. The time ticked on to eight o'clock. Dan flicked some dust from a bookcase, scanned the lines of jackets and blurbs. There was nothing he wanted to read. He sat back down on the sofa. Rutherford stretched out at his feet and yawned.

'What shall we do, old friend?' Dan asked him. 'I can't seem to settle on anything.'

The dog sat up and nuzzled into his master's arms. Dan ruffled his fur, thick for the weather of winter.

'How about a walk?'

Rutherford let out a quick bark at the sacred word and Dan almost smiled, but the expression wouldn't quite form. He fumbled the leash from the hallway cupboard and they walked across the main Eggbuckland Road, quiet now, and into Hartley Park.

It was deserted, unsurprising for a damp, Monday evening. Most people were content to spend the night in, the achievement of having survived the start of the week sufficient for the day. Dan let Rutherford off his lead and the dog sprinted away, across the grass to the line of oak and lime trees which marked the park's boundary and began sniffing his way along. In the distance, a police siren wailed.

'I'll be with you in a minute,' Dan muttered to himself. 'Don't solve whatever crime it is before I get there.'

He started walking fast, striding hard, feeling his heartbeat pick up with the effort. Rutherford ran back over and jogged beside him, occasionally stopping to nose at a fascinating patch of grass. Unseen in one of the trees, a wood pigeon freed a forlorn call.

Dan waved an irritable hand. 'Leave me be,' he called to the bird. 'You're yesterday's news. I'm trying to give up all that environment stuff.'

The grass was soaking underfoot, the turf wrapping around his shoes. Muddy water started to seep its chill. A motorbike roared past, its engine gunning.

'Well, look on the bright side,' Dan panted to Rutherford. 'At least I've still got a job. There's no danger I won't be able to afford to buy you dog food, or have to give you away to an animal home. And that turkey I promised you for Christmas is still going to happen. I know it's your favourite.'

One of the streetlights at the edge of the park flickered and blinked off. Shadows shifted across the grass.

'And maybe it was time for a change, anyway,' Dan continued. 'I've been doing environment for five years. Perhaps I am getting a bit stale. Maybe this is the new challenge I need.'

Rutherford stopped, began sniffing at a tump of grass, cocked his leg and left the traditional calling card.

'Classy, old friend,' Dan scolded mildly. 'But we were talking about me, and I'd appreciate your attention. As I was saying, perhaps the change will do me good. And it can't be so difficult, being a crime correspondent, can it? OK, so I won't have any contacts to give me the inside track on whatever's going on, and all the other crime hacks will. I won't know any of the details of police procedures, or detective work, or the running stories. In fact, if we're being honest, I won't know a bloody thing.'

Dan walked on, whistling to Rutherford, who trotted over. The drizzle was gathering its strength, turning to a light rain.

'Maybe we'd better stop this conversation,' Dan told the dog. 'I don't think it's making me feel any better. Let's go home and have a whisky instead.'

He put Rutherford back on his lead and they headed for the flat. In the darkness of the hallway Dan noticed his mobile was flashing with a message. Four missed calls, one answer-machine message. That kind of insane insistence could only mean work.

It was Lizzie, and sounding more excitable even than usual. Her voice fizzed and crackled from the phone's speaker. A man's body had been found in a lay-by, just outside Plymouth. The circumstances were what the police, with a great bound of insight, and the application of considerable analytical skills, were describing as suspicious.

The man had been blasted to death with a shotgun. The whispered word amongst those who knew had it that the victim was a well-known local businessman. Well-known perhaps, but far from well-liked. The talk already was of a revenge killing, for any one of an impressively long list of notorious misdemeanours.

Lizzie Riley, Editor of *Wessex Tonight*, wanted her newly appointed Crime Correspondent on the scene instantly, if not sooner. He would be fully briefed up and comprehensively knowledgeable, and ready to cut a report about the killing for the late news.

It was proving to be quite a day.

Chapter Two

THE RAIN HAD REGROUPED its forces and pounded down with renewed fury. Dan squinted through the gloom. Red tail lights blurred in the cascades of water washing over the windscreen and a film of mist fogged the windows. The car hadn't yet warmed up, and he shivered.

It felt like a perfect night for a murder.

His flat was in Hartley Avenue, just outside the city centre, and only five minutes from the dual carriageway A38, the main road between Plymouth and civilisation. The lay-by was just a few miles to the east. It shouldn't take long to get there.

His first story as Crime Correspondent.

He'd expected it to come tomorrow, maybe the day after if he was lucky. To have time to sleep on the idea, to grow accustomed and acclimatised to the new world. And, more importantly, to read up on police procedures, research the running stories.

Not to be cast straight into the fire.

Perhaps it was better this way. Get stuck in, don't procrastinate with too much thinking, allow the nerves to grow. Just learn as you go.

He didn't come close to convincing himself. Dan wasn't surprised to find his eyes watering. He dabbed at them with a sleeve.

He wondered how wise it had been to leave behind the bottle of pills, hidden at the back of the bathroom cabinet. He'd taken it out, stared at it, even opened the lid, been tempted to take one, maybe more, but stopped himself. They hadn't worked before. There was no reason to think they would now.

He turned on the radio, twisted the volume up loud. This was no time to let it take him.

A big story, his first in the new job.

Dan flicked the wipers onto maximum speed, their frantic arcs forcing back the torrents of rainwater. The car had reached the edge of the city's sprawl, the lines of concrete and brick, the

17

beacons of the streetlights falling behind. Darkness lingered, punctuated only by rushing white headlights. The wheels slewed through the wash of the road.

Now the glowering sky changed colour, tinted with strobes of blue.

Dan indicated, turned off into the lay-by and pulled up by the line of cars and fluttering police tape.

The pack was already there. A dozen of them, clustered around a woman. They were hunched up in their coats, some sheltering beneath umbrellas, all taking notes. A few Dan recognised. Reporters from local papers, news agencies, websites and radio stations, photographers too.

Everyone knew. Everyone had been tipped off. Everyone except him.

Dan swore to himself, pulled on a coat and jogged over. Rain splashed up his trousers and into his shoes.

The woman was short, squat, wearing a long mac which almost reached the ground. All the hacks were listening to her intently.

'... so, we're searching the lay-by now, then we'll start going through everyone who might have had reason to want him harmed.'

'That's a hell of a list,' an older man grunted, prompting some nods of agreement.

'Maybe, but it's what we've got to do. We'll hold a press briefing when we've got more to tell you.'

'Can we name him yet?' a younger woman asked.

'We're not doing so officially, but that's up to you, of course. His family – what there is of it – is being told now.'

'And is any of this on the record?'

The woman folded her arms, and there was some muted laughter from the pack.

'Guess that's a no then,' one of the photographers said. 'So when do we get some snaps and quotes?'

'When Chief Inspector Breen gets here. He won't be long.'

Dan just had time to glimpse some of the other reporters' notebooks. The pages were filled with writing. He had managed only a title, "Lay-by murder."

That was hardly going to make a story. He looked around, to see if he knew any of the other hacks. One woman looked vaguely familiar.

'Hello,' Dan said, above the noise of the rain. 'It's, err, Kate, from the Daily Press isn't it?'

'Karen, from the Weekly News.'

'Sorry, yes, of course. So, what did she say? The detective?'

'Sorry, I haven't got time to talk at the mo. Got to file some copy. They'll be doing another briefing later.'

Dan looked around for someone else to ask, but the pack had dispersed, returning to their cars to shelter from the rain. He swore again and jogged back to his own car.

The dashboard clock said it was coming up to nine. The late news was on air at half past ten. It was a fifteen-minute drive back to the studios and it would take at least twenty minutes to cut a report, if they really shifted. So he had to leave here by ten, at the very latest. He had an hour and he possessed no facts and an equal number of pictures.

Thunder rumbled around the sky.

It was not proving to be one of the better days in the life of Daniel Groves.

A thumping on the window startled him. The flattened distortion of a chubby, beaming face pressed up against the glass. The door opened and the soaking figure tumbled untidily in to the passenger seat. Such were the dramatic entrances of Ellis Hughes, the paparazzo known simply as Dirty El, a nickname he had worked hard to win and richly deserved. El's deviousness in pursuit of a lucrative picture was legendary.

'Evening, Dan mate. Surprised to see you here. Is there some angle about the local wildlife being frightened off by the shooting then?'

Dan explained that he was now a former environment correspondent, but a serving crime reporter.

'Yip, yip, yahoo!' El reached out a dripping hand and shook Dan's. 'Welcome to the foul world of filth. You'll love it. Looks like we'll be working together plenty now then.'

They'd long been drinking buddies, El living just half a mile down the road from Dan, right in the city centre, but they seldom met on stories. The photographer wasn't interested in the cute and fluffy animal and countryside tales which were Dan's staple. The snaps that sold were the shockers, so where there was scandal, there was El.

Which could now be very useful indeed.

'What do you know about what's happened then?' Dan asked.

El looked puzzled. 'Didn't you get that briefing?'

'No. I got here too late.'

'Didn't you get a tip-off?'

'No,' said Dan patiently.

'So you don't know nothing?'

This time Dan didn't bother replying. El grabbed one of Dan's scarves from the back seat and started drying himself off. 'You got to get up to speed mate,' he chuckled. 'You're so way behind you're not even off the starting blocks. You're trying to race Formula One in a Robin Reliant.'

Dan freed the scarf from El's grip. It was his favourite. 'So, what's happened?'

'It's Bray, Dan mate. Big bad Edward Bray, the bastard businessman. He's got his comeuppance. Someone's potted him. Boom, boom, bye bye Bray! It's a corker of a story. Everyone's gonna want the piccies. El's bread's in the oven and it's baking beautifully! Gotta go, think I see the big boss cops coming.'

El was out of the car door and lumbering inelegantly back towards the cordon. Dan groaned, briefly closed his eyes, then followed.

Nigel had arrived and was getting the camera out of the boot. He spotted Dan heading for the cordon and followed.

'What's going on?' the cameraman asked. 'I just got this call saying scramble and that you'd meet me here. Someone said you were doing crime now.'

'*We're* doing crime.'

'Are we?'

'Yep.'

'So what's going on? What happened?'

Dan wasn't surprised to find he didn't want to talk about it. 'I'll explain later. For now, we've got an hour and a bit to get something sensible together. Let's get on with it.'

The pack had gathered again and Nigel pushed his way through, Dan beside him, holding the microphone. Positioning was all in a media scrum. The closer you were to the front, the better your shot and the clearer the sound.

There was a little resistance from the other journalists, but not much. This briefing felt different from earlier. No longer a gaggle, now the hacks stood orderly and arranged, like a class of children facing a feared teacher.

They'd formed a neat semi-circle, and had left a respectful distance between themselves and the focus of their attention; a tall and lean man, with dark hair and a swarthy complexion. He wasn't wearing a coat, sheltered from the unrelenting rain by an umbrella the woman detective was holding above him. Despite the weather, he was dressed in a fine dark suit, clearly bespoke and expensive, and his shoes had somehow managed to evade the sticking mud and remain impeccable, even shining in the lights of the TV cameras.

El raised his camera and loosed off a series of snaps. The man's eyes flicked to him, narrowing, and El dropped the camera and mumbled an apology.

'Who is he?' Dan whispered.

'Adam Breen. Greater Wessex's top detective. He does all the big cases. You know it's a singer and dancer of a story when he's about.'

The man finished scanning the hacks, nodded to himself, and spoke. His voice was strong, effortlessly dominating the noise of the downpour.

'Ladies and gentlemen, thank you for coming here this evening. You'll appreciate enquiries are at an early stage, and so there's only a limited amount I can tell you. But what I can say is this. We were called here at six o'clock this evening, when we found a man's body. Paramedics confirmed he was dead. He had been shot at close range. I am assembling a team of detectives, and a major inquiry is getting underway. I would appeal to anyone who might have been passing here earlier, or thinks they know anything about what happened to get in touch. Thank you.'

A pause as the hacks finished their notes, and then came the questions.

'Is it Edward Bray?'

'I know some of you believe you are already aware who the victim is, but we are not confirming his or her name at the moment.'

'What was the murder weapon?'

'I can tell you it was a shotgun.'

'Have you got any suspects?'

Adam Breen flicked at a piece of fluff which had attached itself to his sleeve. 'Aside from the entirety of the human race, it's too early at the moment to have any suspects.'

'Was the victim killed here?'

'We believe so.'

'And he died instantaneously?'

'Yes, we think so. Now, are there any more questions?'

Dan was writing fast, taking down the details. It was some story. He thought fast, wondered if he had all the information he needed. He was now a crime correspondent, however unwitting and unwilling, and it was a matter of pride for a good hack to pose a smart, thoughtful and perceptive question at a news conference. Sometimes it was simply to get an answer, often just to show you were there and that you had the guts and nous to do it.

Maybe it was time to make his mark, to let the other hacks know a new boy was in town.

'Err, Mr Breen?' Dan heard himself saying.

'Yes?'

He had the man's attention. The camera whirred as Nigel zoomed in the shot for the close-up. The microphone was poised.

All was ready. It was time for the first question of his new job.

Better make it a good one. Sharp and slick. Professional and cool. Penetrating and evocative.

A question all the other journalists would envy.

The trumpet fanfare to herald the coming of a new age.

'Do you think this was a ...' Dan hesitated, wondered just what it was he was going to ask. But all eyes were on him. There was no stopping now.

'... was this a – umm – a professional hit?'

There was an odd silence. The detective studied him, folded his arms. 'A "professional hit"?'

'Err, yes.'

A couple of chuckles rose from the pack. A radio reporter whispered something about the rebirth of Chicago in the 1930s. All the hacks, all the photographers were staring at Dan.

And all were grinning.

It may not have been quite the mark he intended to make.

'No,' Adam Breen said finally, and his voice sounded wry. 'I do not think this was a "professional hit", as you so eloquently put it. In my experience, practiced assassins rarely lurk in forsaken lay-bys on rainy nights in the hope of finding their prey, nor do they use shotguns as their weapon of choice.'

The official television rule book says a reporter does his own little address to the eagerly watching world – a piece to camera – when a story suffers a scarcity of pictures and he has important information to impart. Or, sometimes, when he needs to look the viewer in the eye because he's analysing or assessing a situation to give his expert summary, or perhaps simply when he needs to show he's there, at the very centre of events.

The unofficial addendum says it's simply about vanity. And it was surely the moment to announce the arrival of *Wessex Tonight*'s new Crime Correspondent.

If he was going to have to stand out in the rain to get a story he might as well reap some glory for it.

When Adam Breen had retreated from the pack, Dan told Nigel to keep recording and did his spiel. He waited for his friend to film the lay-by, the constables on sentry duty and the forensics officers coming and going then took the camera tape and drove back to the studios.

Jenny was on the late shift and waiting. 'Two rush edits in the space of a few hours,' she noted. 'You spoil me. And congratulations on the new job. I did warn you to watch out.'

It was a simple edit and they were finished by a quarter past ten. Dan started the report with pictures of the scene, talked about the discovery of a man's body and the police beginning a murder investigation. The only tricky editorial issue was whether to suggest the victim was Edward Bray, but as the police couldn't yet say whether his relatives had been told Dan had no trouble in deciding against it.

It had been drilled into Dan from the very start that one of the strongest rules of television, of all media in fact, is that bereaved people should never learn of their loss from a broadcast, newspaper or website report. If there is no good way to break bad news then there is a least worst method. That requires the input of sensitive humanity and certainly not the efforts of a hack.

Instead, Dan hinted at it, reported the victim was thought to be a well-known local businessman. He used a clip of Adam Breen, saying the man had been shot at close range and that a major investigation was getting underway. The story concluded with Dan's piece to camera, telling the viewers the police wanted any witnesses to come forward.

As they checked the report back, Dan found himself wondering which of Edward Bray's many enemies had been hiding in the rain and darkness of a lay-by, waiting with a shotgun, finally resolved on a course of action and ready to end a life. The slight pressure of a finger on a trigger, an echoing blast, a flare of fire and the shock of sudden death in one short second.

It reeked of hate and loathing, a septic grudge long nurtured and an irresistible lust for revenge. It was the stuff of books.

Dan wandered slowly downstairs to his car. It took a while to notice the rain had stopped. He aimed a grateful nod at the sky and drove the half mile home.

When he got back to the flat, he let Rutherford out and watched the dog scrabble around the corner to the garden. Dan stood in the doorway and gazed up at a clearing of stars in the

24

night sky. He didn't once think of the tablets in the bathroom cupboard, or the whisky in the kitchen, both of which he had feared would be needed to help him through the dark hours of the coming night.

He was too busy wondering what tomorrow would bring, as the hunt for the person who killed Edward Bray began.

He had an idea too. One which, if he could pull it off, would prove immensely helpful and even more fascinating.

Chapter Three

THERE ARE DAYS IN the darkest pits of December and January, the dreaded nadir of the sullen English winter, when it never truly gets light. The best you can hope is for the night to reluctantly give way to an opaque greyness at somewhere approaching nine o'clock in the morning, and for that dour, slatey state to persist until about three in the afternoon, when it simply gets dark again.

This was one of those days. But Dan hardly noticed.

He woke early, soon after six, feeling awake and refreshed, and took Rutherford for a run before getting in to the office well before eight. He didn't go into the newsroom, that would be to invite all kinds of incredulous comments, and, more importantly, distractions. Instead Dan made straight for the corner of the building that was the News Library, unheralded repository of almost fifty years of the wisdom of the Southwest. Since the inception of *Wessex Tonight* no important event had unfolded in the region that wasn't recorded in pictures, interviews and commentary here.

Here too was Edward Bray, a living memory, and Dan wanted to get a better sense of the man.

He checked the computer's index, rifled through the lines of shelves of video tapes, found the ten or so which contained stories on Bray, sat at one of the players and began to watch. Dan could vaguely recall some of the reports about him, most, as El had so memorably put it last night, on the theme of Bray the Bastard, at least in subtext. But what he discovered was both a surprise and a puzzle.

The first stories fitted the stereotype. There were a couple, dating back several years. Bray was a property man who owned scores of houses and flats in Plymouth, and a change in the law had prompted him to remove a swathe of tenants before they accrued powerful new rights over how long they could stay in their homes, and what they could demand of the landlord.

Some of the people had tried to fight, so many in fact that

two days had been set aside for the dozens of hearings at Plymouth County Court.

The report started with a group of people standing outside court, chanting "Save our homes, save our families." Some were waving placards, all bearing the words "Bray the Homebreaker". There were men, women and children too, even a couple of babes in arms, wailing along with the cacophony.

The reporter explained the protest was to draw attention to their cause, forty families facing eviction from Bray's properties. As the day went on, family after family emerged from court, almost all in tears, all saying they had lost and would be evicted within a month. By the end of the day, even the judge had expressed sympathy with the people brought before her, but had also made it very clear that the law was quite straightforward. If the landlord wanted the families out, then out they had to go.

The most powerful interview was with a man called Andrew Hicks. His wife stood beside him, her face hidden behind her hands, her muffled sobbing audible. He hugged her close and told the reporter, "We've lived in that house for nine years. We moved there to care for my mum, who's been getting more and more frail. She's just over the road. We've got friends all along the street. We love it. We were going to start our own family there, when the time was right. And now he's thrown us out for no better reason than that he's worried we might make him splash out a few hundred quid on some decorating." Hicks's voice broke, before he rallied and finished with a choking, "The man's got no heart. Bray's a bastard, pure and simple."

The next story came from the following night. There were more protests at court, but this time the banners had changed. Andrew Hicks' emotive motif had found resonance. All read. "Bray the Bastard". But the outcome of the day remained a familiar one. Another twenty families facing eviction.

There was no interview with Bray in either report. He'd refused to speak to any of the media. The best *Wessex Tonight* had managed was a snatched shot of him disappearing into a taxi. But even in that, Bray managed to convey his feelings. Behind his back, he flicked a V sign at the camera.

Dan tapped the desk in mock applause. The man was a pantomime villain. All he needed was a black cape, a fiendish cackle and a damsel in distress to tie to a railway line and the image was complete.

There was another report, dating from a few months later, when Bray evicted yet another swath of tenants from more of his houses. This time an MP got involved, pleading with the government for a change in the law. But the wheels of democracy never grind fast, if ever they grind at all, and the plea was briefly pontificated upon before being entirely ignored.

A year later came another story, and this time it was edged with new fury. Bray suffered days of protests outside his offices before the issue quietened. Some of the demonstrators were positively frothing and near-apoplectic. It was, Dan thought, the businessman's own daft miscalculation. This time, Bray had picked not on mere expendable humans, but instead, defenceless animals, and, even worse, that bastion of English society, most treasured and untouchable of pets, the domestic feline.

The Wessex Home for Unwanted Cats was in financial trouble and in desperate need of a saviour. A fine Georgian building, just outside the city centre, it could hardly have been more attractive to a property developer. Word went round that Bray was in talks about its future. But this rumour had a most unexpected twist; that on this occasion the secretive businessman was motivated not by money but emotion. He was, it was said, a cat man himself; he had a couple of much favoured felines of his own.

The future was purring happily.

But as so often with rumours, they were on the hopelessly wrong side of utterly misguided.

Bray bought the home, gave the staff and their beloved felines notice to quit, and with that brought down upon himself all the vitriol and venom of this cat-loving nation. It was only a quadrupling of the three-month period of notice which finally eased the protests at his doors.

Dan got up and wandered down to the canteen to get himself

a coffee. He noticed he was starting to like Edward Bray. If not personally pleasant, then the man was a journalist's dream. He had as much regard for public opinion as a merchant banker, sailing away from a grinding recession on his luxury yacht, heading for sunnier climes and sipping idly at an expensive gin and tonic funded by the vast pension he had never worked at all hard to deserve in any way.

The fast beat of stilettos in the car park outside brought Dan back to the canteen. Lizzie: wearing stalactite heels early in the day. A danger sign if ever there was one. He quickly wrapped himself in a handy curtain and waited for her to pass.

The first stage of his great plan required that he had to sell her the idea. But, before that, he needed to weigh the odds in his favour, and that meant finding out more about Edward Bray. Dan peered furtively out of the door. There was no sign of his insane editor. He walked quickly back up to the library and closed the door.

Now came the surprise.

Dan had a few more Bray reports to work through and was ready to find further tales of evictions and protests. But instead he uncovered a hitherto unsuspected heart.

The man had saved a hospice.

St Jude's was in trouble. Tempestuous economic times meant donations had dried up, and the institution was in danger of going under. *Wessex Tonight* carried a couple of stories warning the end was, if not exactly nigh, then perhaps only months away. Some of the interviews with patients were powerfully moving, one old man talking about how he would have died alone in his cold flat were it not for St Jude's. A young woman spoke about the wonderful care it gave her mother, and the precious gift of dignity it bestowed in the woman's dying days.

The hospice had a proud history of more than a hundred and twenty years of such work, thousands of grateful supporters, and the finest of reputations.

Imagine then, the shock when Edward Bray was spotted meeting its trustees at a local hotel.

St Jude's was another place over which any property developer would salivate. It was a detached and elegant Victorian building, in beautiful grounds on the cliffs overlooking the great natural harbour of Plymouth Sound and the east Cornwall coast. The views were stunning, which surely gave real comfort to the patients. But they would also give delight to the potential owners of the scores of flats into which the grand old building could be converted, and help to persuade them to part with impressively large sums of money.

The story had been covered in all the local media. Dan clicked at his computer, checking the online archives. The newspaper headlines made the simple point. "The Bastard Poised to do for the Hospice" read one, 'Angel of Death for the Hospice" said another.

There were interviews aplenty with fearful residents and their relatives, some even pleading with Bray not to close the place they had come to so depend upon.

'Fat chance,' Dan muttered to himself. 'The milkman of human kindness has hardly been a regular caller at his door.'

But then came the surprise. Or perhaps shock might have been a better word. To put it mildly.

Edward Bray had saved St Jude's.

Even the tone of the *Wessex Tonight* report was incredulous. The hospice had released a statement saying that a "very sizeable" donation from Bray meant its future was secured for many long years to come. There were no ifs and buts, no caveats, no provisos or conditions. It was a simple gift, an act of pure generosity and humanity.

Dan choked and nearly spat out his coffee. He had to rewind the tape to check what he'd just seen.

By request of Mr Bray, no one from the hospice would be giving interviews, and nor would the man himself. And there the story more or less rested. Many had made attempts to find out what was behind the donation, but with little success. The nearest any of the journalists came was an unsubstantiated suspicion that Bray's mother had been a patient at St Jude's before her death eight years ago.

Dan scribbled a couple of notes on his pad, sat back and

stared at the screen, the fleeting image of Bray getting into a taxi captured on it. A chunky man, with short, fair hair and a ruddy complexion. In his early thirties in that image, he would have been pushing forty when he was killed by a shotgun blast in a dark and lonely lay-by.

'Who the hell are you then?' Dan muttered. 'Come on, make up your mind. Is it philanthropist, or just a bastard businessman? And who, of that very respectable list of enemies you managed to make, wanted you dead so badly as to go ahead and do it?'

He picked up his satchel and headed for the newsroom.

It was time for the next phase of the plan to get underway.

Lizzie was sitting at her desk, a whimsical smile on her face. She was one of those rare people whom smiling just didn't suit. Her lips were too thin for the expression to work, made it look more like a warrior's satisfaction at the death of a bitter foe than any form of human pleasure. It was as effective as painting a little grinning face on a hand grenade.

A Lizzie smile could also indicate trouble in exactly the same way as did the height of her shoes.

Dan approached with due caution.

'Ah,' she said, spotting him instantly. 'Just the person I was looking for. Our new crime correspondent. And with a corker of a maiden story to launch his new career. Good to see that you're in early to work on it.'

'Extra early in fact.'

'Oh?'

Dan explained about his hour in the library and what he had found. Before she could interject, he added, 'I think we have to get into the case in depth. We need to find out who Bray really was and why he did the things he did.'

'And how do you propose to do that? We haven't managed to crack it before. And he's not exactly likely to talk now, is he?'

Dan put on a good-natured smile for his editor's idea of wit. 'No, but the police are going to have to go into his life in detail to try to find out who it was that killed him.'

'Granted. And?'

'And getting into all the minutiae of their investigation is what we need to make stories for us.'

She looked more interested. 'So how do you plan to go about that?'

'You sit on those police liaison meetings, don't you? You're friendly with the senior officers.'

'Yeah, dull but necessary. Come on, get to the point. What're you thinking?'

'How about getting me in to shadow the Bray investigation? It could be good for us and the cops. They get to put out a positive message about the progress they're making. I get the inside track on the inquiry, and more importantly I get a crash course in detective work. I'm going to need it for the new job.'

She nodded thoughtfully. 'Not a bad idea. There's something else we could use too.'

'What?'

'There's an election due soon and we've got some key marginal seats in the region. The Home Office would love a bit of good news on the law and order front. If I have a word with a couple of local MPs too they could help pave the way. Right, I'll do it later. But first ...'

There was always a but with Lizzie, and usually more than one. Her mind was a fruitful breeding ground for caveats.

'Yes?' Dan said, trying not to sound wary.

'One of the researchers knows Bray's dad. He wants to speak out about his son being killed. Get to it. I want a report for the lunchtime news. I want poignancy and emotion. I want – "He may have been a bastard, but he didn't deserve to die." I want a live broadcast too. I want the works and I want it good. Go on then, what are you waiting for?'

Dan wasn't waiting. He was heading for the door. As he was about to leave, she called, 'Do I get the feeling you're starting to get into this new job?'

'I'm reserving judgement,' he replied.

Chapter Four

IT'S KNOWN IN THE trade as the Death Knock and is widely dreaded. A journalist calling to talk to a bereaved relative about the loss of a loved one. Of all the range of possible outcomes, one thing alone was certain. You never left feeling better about life.

The most common reaction was anger and abuse and a straightforward and often creatively obscene request that you should leave. In a way, that was the easiest to take. You could accept it, understand the hurt and upset and know you were merely a target for the venting of emotion. It was fair enough.

Surprisingly often though, the mother or father, sister or brother, son or daughter or husband or wife would be happy to talk, perhaps even keen to do so. They wanted to pay tribute to the wonderful person they had lost, needed the world to know what a fine and special individual had been taken, and explain the cold void which would be left behind in so many lives.

They were the hardest of all. They were unfailingly tearful, upsetting and moving, and lived long in the memory.

Dan had done them before, in his days as a general news reporter, years ago before he became the environment correspondent, largely insulated from such distress. And each he could recall and in exact detail, the soft, crumpled faces, blurred with misery, and the endless tears.

Well, he'd better start getting used to them once more. The demons of his new job demanded it.

Nigel drove them, north, out of the city and into the great natural wilderness of Dartmoor. The rain of last night had at least blown through, to be replaced by a grey and glowering sky. The last time Dan had been on the moor was the week before, covering a story about the endless intrusion of bracken into the sacred landscape and the increasingly desperate efforts to stop it.

His previous life. Safe from shotgun murders and death knocks.

Dan noticed he'd begun thinking about the plastic bottle of tablets hidden in the bathroom cabinet again.

'You OK?' Nigel asked. 'You've gone quiet.'

'Just thinking.'

'About the interview?'

'Yeah.'

'Know what you mean. I dread them too. They're like having your soul slowly put through a mangle.'

The cameraman found a CD of 70's music, all chirpy disco beats. Dan managed to tolerate almost a whole song before he reached out and turned down the volume. Nigel didn't protest. It was hardly a fitting symphony for what they were about to go through.

Arthur Bray lived in Yelverton, a village on the edge of Dartmoor, only twenty minutes drive from Plymouth city centre. It was popular with commuters, had a shop, a couple of pubs, even a petrol station and a butcher's. His house was on the fringes of the village, detached and large, a long gravel drive leading to the door.

Nigel parked beside a black jeep and turned to Dan. 'How do we play it?'

'What?' he replied, distractedly.

'Come on, get with it. You'll need to be sharp for this. I said – how do we play it?'

'Good question. Well, you set up the kit and I'll try to get him talking, do my best to break the ice.'

They got out of the car. Dan suffered a vision of himself at the north pole, kneeling down and trying to chip away at the polar cap with a small hammer. Such was the task of breaking the ice in a death knock.

He hesitated, then rang the bell.

Arthur Bray clearly hadn't read the script.

He was supposed to move slowly, laboured with the burden of grief in all that he did. His eyes should have been red, inflamed with the countless tears, his posture hunched with the weight of sorrow and his words stumbling and stuttered as he tried to force them to form through his suffering.

To none of this did he conform.

He opened the door briskly, shook their hands with a firm grip and ushered them into a large and light living room. He was a small man, with thinning white hair, wearing a navy cardigan and open-necked shirt, but he had a certain strength, as though the years were yet to do their insidious work.

'Best we get on with this, eh?'

'I'm sorry?' Dan replied, taken aback.

'I'm sure we've all got better things to do. I want to get some shopping in this morning, then perhaps play a round of golf later, if the bloody weather permits. No doubt you want to make it all into some sort of broadcast, like you people do.'

'Err, Mr Bray ...'

'Arthur, please.'

'Arthur, we are talking about your son here. Edward. And ...' Dan struggled to find the words, before ending lamely, 'what happened to him.'

'Yes. Dreadful business. But hardly unexpected, eh?'

Dan realised he was floundering badly. He'd been caught so far off balance it was a wonder he didn't fall over. Arthur Bray's reaction felt as surreal as going to a funeral service, when a stripper suddenly arrives and begins her act.

'Hardly unexpected? Your son being murdered?'

'It was bound to happen sooner or later, given the way he conducted himself. I tell you what, I'll make some tea, then I'll explain.'

Arthur Bray disappeared into the kitchen. Dan looked at Nigel, who just shrugged.

'Well, we're going to get quite a story,' the cameraman said. 'But I don't think it's exactly the one we were expecting.'

They sat on the sofa in silence and accepted the mugs Bray handed them.

'I've got all the fine tea-set stuff,' he said. 'But I only get it out when the vicar comes round. You strike me as more the mug type.'

'I think that might just about sum up my life,' Dan replied, with feeling.

Arthur offered them sugar, which they both refused. He sat

back, crossing his legs.

'Look, I think I'd better make one thing clear here. I'm doing this interview because the police asked me to. They think it might help bring some witnesses forward. I'm not doing it for Edward, or anything like that. My son and I no longer have – had, sorry – a relationship. We effectively agreed on a divorce several years ago, and since then have had nothing to do with each other.'

Dan set down his mug, couldn't keep the disbelief from his voice. 'A divorce?'

'I can think of no other way to describe it. We reached a financial settlement, and said we would not contact each other again. We both preferred it that way. Look, perhaps it's easier if I tell you the story. Then we can do this interview thing, and we can all get on with our lives.'

Arthur Bray fumbled in his pocket, lit up a large cigar, puffed out a cloud of blue-grey smoke, and began.

He was a self-made man, who had built up the business from a standing start. Going back thirty years or more he had been left a substantial legacy by a relative, which he'd invested in property. It was just before prices started their breathless rise. The company's income grew, more houses and flats were purchased, and soon Arthur Bray was very well-off, bordering on simply rich.

'I was a good businessman though,' he told them, through puffs on the cigar. 'Not like this modern lot who just take the money and run. I looked after my tenants. I made sure their homes were smart and comfortable. I never ripped them off. And I helped with social housing too, and community projects. I'd done well, and I thought it was right that others should share my fortune.'

Time rolled on, Edward had grown up and decided to follow his dad into the family business.

'I was delighted,' Bray explained. 'I was planning to take early retirement. I could hand it all on to Edward. He would be looked after, as would my tenants, and the business could continue to flourish and carry out its charitable work. It all seemed ideal. But it didn't quite work out that way.'

Now, for the first time, his voice changed. It grew quieter, more reflective and rueful. Bray got up from his chair and pointed to a picture of a woman on the windowsill. She was standing by a river, smiling, a little self-conscious in the way many have when faced with a camera, but nonetheless she looked kind and attractive.

'My wife, Elizabeth. This is my favourite picture of her. It's from just after we were married. I won't go into the details, but she developed lung cancer. It was quick, mercifully. After her death, the relationship between Edward and me ... well, it – changed.'

In that one word was a world of repressed emotion. It was buried deep, long hidden, but so obviously still there, in the tone of the man's voice, the way he winced as he spoke.

'We stopped getting on. Well, that's an understatement, in fact. He was very close to his mother, and seemed to take her death out on me. As if losing her wasn't enough.'

The man's voice faltered again, and he sat back in his chair.

'Edward didn't just take it out on me. He wanted vengeance against anything to do with me. He started persecuting the company's tenants, pushing up their rents, evicting them when they couldn't pay. He stopped all the charitable work. He retreated into himself, just cut the world off. All he was interested in was making money. I tried to talk to him, but we only ended up having dreadful rows.'

Another hesitation, longer this time, then, 'In one ... well, I think we both said some things we shouldn't have. That was where it ended. He'd already taken over the business by that point. I still had a minority holding, but it wasn't enough to stop him. He paid me off and we agreed we wouldn't speak again. It was as simple as that. And then he just got worse and worse. You've probably seen some of the stories. Evicting tenants, just because they'd have rights to ask for their homes to be redecorated. It's sad to say, but from then on I felt rather glad I didn't have to speak to him again. He did nothing but ill for the world.'

Dan sipped at his tea, then said quietly, 'Apart from the

hospice.'

Arthur looked at him sharply and drew his cardigan around his chest. 'I'd rather not talk about that, if you don't mind,' he replied. 'Now, is it time for this interview?'

Nigel took the hint and began setting up the camera. Dan tapped a pen on his notepad, thought through what he'd just heard. Arthur's story had answered some of his questions, but raised many more.

Nigel's phone rang, and he walked outside to answer it. 'Lizzie,' he explained, when he returned. 'She's lined up an interview with the police for the lunchtime news. At the lay-by. She wants you to do it as part of your live report.'

The grandmother clock in the corner said it was just past eleven. The lunchtime bulletin was on air at half past one. Time to get a move on. All the questions spinning in Dan's mind would have to wait. All except one.

'Arthur, what you had to tell us was interesting background, don't get me wrong, but when it comes to the interview ...'

'I understand,' he said. 'I know the media drill. You don't need all that family strife nonsense. It just complicates things. You want a nice, emotional soundbite. I think I can manage that.'

After the interview they declined the offer of more tea, pleading the pressing deadline. As they walked back along the corridor to the front door and said their goodbyes, Dan couldn't help but notice the large shotgun cabinet, and the shiny, well-tended array of weapons arranged within it.

The daylight made the lay-by no more attractive. But Dan found himself studying it with an unexpected interest.

It was effectively just a slip road off the dual carriageway, a widening of the tarmac where cars and lorries could pull up. But the parking area was hidden from the main road by a mound of grass, covered with a thicket of trees.

The police cordon was gone, the forensic investigations completed. Dan took a few paces towards where Bray would have been shot, kicked thoughtfully at the ground and turned towards the main road.

'Interesting,' he said.

'What?' Nigel asked. 'And don't you think we should be getting on with the story? It's almost noon.'

'Yep, in a sec. I was just thinking. Where I'm standing I can't be seen from the main road at all.'

'And?'

'And it's very noisy here, with all the traffic zipping past.'

'So?'

'So, if there are no other cars or lorries here, as there doubtless wouldn't be on a very wet night, and if for example, I chose to shoot you ...' Dan shaped his fingers like a gun, pointed them at his friend, 'No one would see, and no one would hear.'

'You're talking about how Bray was killed.'

'Yep. Lure him here on a pretext, say some kind of secret meeting, be waiting when he arrives, and bang! That's it. A perfect place for a murder. No witnesses, and an easy get away, straight onto the dual carriageway. It was a well planned killing.'

Nigel gave him a look. 'You're not getting into this new job a little too much, are you?'

'No, no, just thinking. But – what are the odds we've just met a prime suspect for the murder?'

Nigel looked puzzled, quickly followed by appalled. 'His dad?'

'Yep. He told you about their estrangement – or divorce, as he put it. What if it wasn't as clear-cut as he says? And he's got a cabinet full of shotguns.'

Nigel shook his head. 'Maybe you should be thinking about cutting this report?'

'I'm just about to get on with it. But there is one question I would like the answer to, before we finish with this story.'

'Which is?'

'Why did it change?'

'The relationship between father and son?'

'Exactly. The way he said it. It made me shiver.'

'I know what you mean. Families normally pull together after a death. We certainly did.'

Dan patted his friend's shoulder. Nigel had lost his wife, Jayne, to breast cancer, and was bringing up his two young sons James and Andrew on his own. It wasn't easy with the hours the cameraman had to keep, and the boys approaching the difficult adolescent years too. His family had rallied around, helping out as much as they could, and they managed. But knowing Nigel as well as he now did, Dan could sometimes feel the void in his friend's life.

'I know you did,' Dan said. 'I've seen how it brought your family together. But in the case of the Brays, it led to a bitter split. And I can't help but wonder why.'

The Outside Broadcast van was parked a little further up the lay-by, "Loud" Jim Stone, the engineer was asleep in the cab with his feet up on the dashboard.

Dan took a malicious pleasure in hammering on the window. Loud opened one eye, curled his lip, picked some unidentified foodstuff from between his teeth, stretched, and finally opened the door.

'Good of you to turn up,' he grunted, his thicket of a beard twitching.

'Our pleasure,' Dan replied smoothly. 'We've got an edit and a live to do.'

'A canyon of the deepest and widest joy.'

Loud started spooling through the tape. His nickname came from his taste in shirts. Today's was a kind of red, white and blue paisley print that only a drunken, possibly drugged, and quite likely deranged designer might come up with. It was a commonly raised query in the newsroom how such a committed misanthrope could delight in so colourful a wardrobe.

No one had dared venture the question, let alone come close to finding an answer.

The edit was straightforward. It usually was with the best stories. They tended to tell themselves.

Dan started the report with some of last night's pictures of the lay-by and explained how Edward Bray had been found there, killed with a shotgun. Then it was into a long clip of Arthur. He had been as good as his word, told the camera that his son may have been disliked by many people, often even hated, but that he didn't deserve such a fate, to be blasted to death in a savage attack. Anyone who could do such a thing could not be allowed to roam free, must be brought to justice. His words were controlled, but powerful for that.

The edit was finished by just after one, giving Dan plenty of time to prepare for the live broadcast. Lizzie had demanded a doughnut. Newcomers to the newsroom were always puzzled by the term, a piece of pure TV jargon. In normal English, it meant the newsreader would introduce the story, Dan would come in with a live setting of the scene, his report would play, then he would sum up, or in this case, do an interview to end the sequence.

He was scribbling a couple of notes on what to say when a hammering at the door of the van stopped him. It was the kind of beat produced by someone practiced in official knocking. Peremptory and demanding of instant attention.

Outside stood the tall man and squat woman detectives of last night.

'Good afternoon,' Dan said, warmly.

'Is it?' Adam Breen replied, with a voice from the tundra. 'From what I can tell, to go with the demands of my new and very high profile murder case, I'm in receipt of a whole set of additional troubles which have somehow been foisted upon me.'

'Really? What?'

The detective gave him a cool stare. 'You.'

'Me?'

'Yes. You.'

'Ah.'

'Ah indeed.'

'So, I'm coming to join you then?'

'So it would appear. I'm always asking for more staff, particularly on a big case like this, but I have to say you weren't exactly what I had in mind.'

They held a look. Dan reached out a hand. Adam Breen eyed it warily, then shook it with a firm grip. The woman did the same. Her grip was, if anything, even stronger.

41

'I don't think I know your name,' Dan said.

'Suzanne Stewart. Detective Sergeant Stewart to you,' she added meaningfully.

Another pause as they all stared at each other. Nigel coughed pointedly. 'We're on air in fifteen minutes,' he said.

Dan nodded. 'Let's sort out your interview, Mr Breen, then we can talk about the other stuff later.'

They walked over to where Nigel had set up the camera, looking back on the lay-by, and Dan explained what would happen in the broadcast. Most interviewees, when faced with being live on television, showed, at the least, a hint of nerves. It would often be a continual twisting of the foot, an interlacing of the fingers, perhaps the jingling of keys or money in a pocket. Not Adam Breen. He stood calmly, arms folded, waiting.

He was wearing a fine coat, which Dan suspected was cashmere, but wasn't knowledgeable enough in the ways of fashion to tell for sure. It was a subject he'd never really got the hang of. Today's suit was different from last night's, a charcoal grey, but equally bespoke and expensive. The only slight hitch in the detective's impeccable appearance was the shading of a shadow of beard, dark and pronounced, despite it being only halfway through the working day.

Dan popped into his ear the moulded plastic which linked him to the outside broadcast van and studio, via a radio receiver clipped to his belt. He heard Loud muttering to himself about being late for lunch because of inconvenient news stories, followed by Emma, the director's voice.

'Can you hear us OK, Dan?'

He gave a thumbs up to the camera.

'Right, we're a few minutes to air. You're top story. The next time we talk to you it'll be for real.'

Dan mentally rehearsed his lines, felt the adrenaline starting to tingle its way through his system. There were few highs to beat live broadcasting. He suspected he would be doing plenty more of it in future. When he'd been covering the environment, he presented the odd outside broadcast, but they were more common on the most serious stories.

His new world.

The title music of *Wessex Tonight* played in his ear, then Craig, the newsreader came in.

'An emotional appeal this lunchtime for public help in finding the killer of the notorious local businessman Edward Bray,' he intoned. '*Wessex Tonight* has been speaking to his father, about his shock at the killing. Our Crime Correspondent Dan Groves is at the lay-by where Edward Bray was murdered.'

'Cue Dan,' Emma prompted.

'Yes, Craig, it was here, last night, that police found Mr Bray's body.' He gestured along the tarmac. 'They believe he was killed just about where I stand, the attacker using a shotgun. A murder investigation is now underway.'

Dan's report played. When it ended, he said, 'Joining me now is the detective leading the hunt for the killer, Chief Inspector Adam Breen. So, how is the inquiry going?'

'It's moving quickly,' he answered smoothly, still no hint of nerves. 'We're working through Mr Bray's movements yesterday, who he saw, where he went. We're also talking to anyone who might have met him in the last few days, and going through his current business dealings too. Effectively, we're building up a picture of his life.'

'To find a motive for the killing?'

'That is one of my priorities.'

'It's a difficult investigation?'

'Mr Bray knew many people, and had dealings with even more. His business interests were extensive. I expect it to be a sizeable and lengthy inquiry.'

'But you're confident you will find the killer?'

'Yes, I am. I'll tell you this now. It may take a while, given the size of inquiry we're dealing with, but rest assured. I will find him.'

Dan thanked the detective and handed back to the studio. He pulled out his earpiece, let loose a long breath. The maiden live broadcast of his new life had been successfully navigated. The milestones were coming fast.

'Right,' Adam Breen said, 'if you'll excuse me, I'm going back to Charles Cross to get on with the inquiry. There's lots to do, to say the least.'

'What do I do?'

'You're going to come and join me. Report to the police station for nine o'clock prompt tomorrow morning, when your induction as a bizarre trainee detective will begin.' He paused, then added wryly, 'I can hardly wait.'

Suzanne Stewart was shaking her head, her lips pursed and face set. But Adam Breen looked almost amused. Dan tried to keep the excitement from his voice, instead to make it as calm and commanding as the detective's.

'Fine,' he said. 'That's good for me. I'll see you then.'

Nigel drove them back to the studios, and they grabbed some of the last remnants of what had been lunch from the canteen. Shepherd's pie.

'Made with real shepherds from the taste of it,' the cameraman observed, but quietly enough not to offend the chef.

Dan picked at his food but didn't feel hungry. He left half of it, Loud pouncing eagerly on the bonus meal. Instead he walked upstairs, found Jenny and they started work on the report for the evening news. They kept it much as lunchtime's, starting with the dramatic, night-time pictures, then hearing from Arthur Bray. It was classical television, the strongest images and interviews first.

Then they added a clip of Adam Breen, talking about how the investigation was going, before Dan summed up by saying the inquiry might take time, but the police were confident of finding the killer. Lizzie checked the report, approved it in her usual less than wholehearted way, and, after pleading a late finish last night Dan was free to go home, naturally with the proviso he would return to work within seconds if there were any developments.

Back at the flat, he took Rutherford for a run around Hartley Park, then made an almost passable supper of pasta with a tomato sauce. It was remarkable how the tang of a bit of fried bacon could cover up bland and banal cooking. Dan ate as he watched his report on *Wessex Tonight*. Rutherford, as ever, looked back and forth between the television and his master, the puzzlement clear on his face. He'd never come to terms with

Dan's magical ability to be in two places at once. Walks, food and the occasional bit of fuss were all he needed for happiness.

Dan wondered what to do with the rest of the evening. The adrenaline of earlier had long since ebbed. He kept thinking about tomorrow, noticed he was finding it hard to settle again. He wondered what kind of reception he would get. Suzanne Stewart and Adam Breen hadn't exactly sounded delighted that he would be joining them.

Dan wandered around the flat, picking up books and putting them down, shifting a couple of ornaments, then putting them back where they were. It was a beautiful flat, mid Victorian, high ceilings with ornate plasterwork, but it could sometimes feel large and hollow with just the two of them here, particularly during the dense, dark nights of the winter.

He paced slowly into the bathroom, opened the cabinet, gazed at the plastic container, reached out and tapped it, then pushed it back into its hiding place and walked into the lounge.

Dan logged in to the internet, looked up police procedures in murder cases and read for half an hour or so. But he could sense the information wasn't settling in his mind. An advert for computer dating flashed up at the side of the screen. Apparently love, excitement and ecstasy were all only a few seconds away. That was quite a claim, but nonetheless alluring – he could do with some. He clicked on it, and was taken to a matchmaking site.

They were offering a free month long trial, so, purely out of journalistic curiousity, Dan entered his details and searched for women in Plymouth. He thought he'd better dispense with anyone under thirty. Tempting though the prospect might be, they were likely to be overly demanding. Well into his thirties now and with the fire of the teenage libido quenched, bed was a place largely dedicated to sleep in Dan's pragmatic eyes.

It was remarkable how many local women there were, all avowedly in search of love. When he'd ruled out those who went on at length about their star sign, others who described themselves as cuddly, and the impressively large number who were interested in "a good time", he came down to Kerry. A professional, she said, also in her mid 30s, slim and attractive.

She liked to keep fit, particularly walking the moors, but also going out, in particular enjoying eating and drinking.

Dan typed a brief reply:

> I liked your ad. Snap! to all your description, bar the attractive – will reasonably decent looking in a rugged, weatherbeaten kind of way do?! This fellow Plymouth professional would like to know more.

He found some music to listen to and a book which was mostly entertaining, spent an hour reading, then decided to go to bed. An early night was a good idea. Tomorrow promised to be an interesting day.

Dan still wasn't quite sure whether to be excited or daunted.

He was about to shut down the computer when it pinged with a message. Kerry:

> Weatherbeaten sounds good, rugged even better! Where's this hunk been hiding then?! Whereabouts in the city are you?

He typed a reply, got one straight back. They exchanged a few emails, Dan talking about having a busy job and limited opportunities to meet people, her sharing the lament. They did favourite foods, places to go out and preferred haunts before Dan finally realised her messages were filling with hints.

> So – *when* do you go to your *favourite places*, and *who* with? And ***when might you be going there next?***

It was only the bold text and italics which switched on the light of understanding. Otherwise, Dan thought ruefully, he could have been emailing her all night and still not getting it. No wonder he'd been single all these months.

> I was wondering whether you fancied meeting up?

he typed, and sat back nervously, waiting for the response.

Sometimes short seconds could stretch so long.

An advert for a sailing holiday flickered across the top of the screen.

Dan tapped a finger on the keyboard, ruffled Rutherford's fur.

She was good enough not to keep him waiting, and even better to resist the lure of sarcasm, however justified:

Well, that would be lovely. When?

Tomorrow?

Another jittery wait, but another mercifully quick reply:

Done. Look forward to it.

They exchanged mobile numbers, agreed to call, or being thoroughly modern professionals to text, said goodnight, and Dan shut down the computer and headed for bed.

Tomorrow promised to be an interesting day indeed.

Chapter Five

HOW AGONISINGLY ELUSIVE CAN be the promised land of sleep. Dan twitched and fidgeted, rolled and itched, and finally managed to get some rest in the small hours. Even then, his dreams were interrupted as his mind fixated on ridiculously petty worries about what to wear and exactly what time to turn up at Charles Cross Police Station.

Adam Breen had said to be prompt. So he would have to be early. But not so early as to look hopelessly keen.

And as for clothes – that was even worse. His wardrobe was entirely tuned to his days covering the environment, all hardy walking boots, chinos and rugged shirts. With some luck, urgent ironing, and a bit of rummaging at the back of the cupboard, Dan thought he could just about put together a suitable outfit, but it would only endure for a couple of days at best.

And then there was the thought of the evening. It was ages since he'd last been out on a date. He'd have to remember not to talk too much, and, if they decided to have some dinner, keep his mouth closed as he ate.

Living on your own could be fatal for your manners.

To shift some of his morning lethargy Dan took Rutherford for a run around Hartley Park. The weather was overcast and chilly, but at least it was dry. Dawn broke as they jogged, the ink of the night slowly diluting to the dull light of the day. There were a couple of other dogs out with their owners, but Dan let the Alsatian off his lead, content in the knowledge he'd never shown the slightest interest in fellows of his species.

The roads around the park were quieter than usual, probably some people had already stopped work for Christmas, the children too had broken up from school. Dan wondered what he would do with his time off. Most likely the usual; make a reasonable effort at some passable cooking for once, get Rutherford a turkey, see Nigel and play surrogate uncle to James and Andrew, go out for a few beers with El. It was how it had been for years aplenty now.

Dan increased his pace for a final fast lap of the park. Rutherford ran effortlessly alongside, occasionally darting away to sniff at a tree or bush. They stopped by a bench, Dan catching his breath and stretching out his muscles before putting the dog back on his lead and walking over to the flat.

As he got dressed into his unfamiliar attire, Dan noticed he felt as jittery as on his first days at work when he was a young trainee journalist.

He got to Charles Cross at twenty to nine, way too early for any appearance of nonchalance. Dan drove around the corner, found a shop, bought a paper and sat in the car outside trying to read it. He didn't take in a single story.

A quarter to nine. The base of his back was sweating unpleasantly. The shirt Dan had chosen was formal and well starched, good and smart, and all the more uncomfortable for it. The dusty black brogues pinched at his feet too. As for the unaccustomed tie, it was like a ligature.

He felt oddly as though he was dressed for a job interview.

Ten to nine. Dan turned on the radio and found a news channel. Each report seemed to be about a crime and the police's efforts to solve it. The top story was still the Edward Bray murder; a presenter was talking about the apparent lack of progress in the investigation so far. Dan turned the radio off.

Five to nine. He started the engine, put the car into gear, drove to the back of the police station and pressed the call button by the heavy metal gates.

'Hello?'

'Hello, it's Dan Groves, from *Wessex Tonight*. I'm here to see Mr Breen.'

The speaker crackled with laughter, several different voices in the rising chorus, and all finding something remarkably amusing.

In the background, Dan thought he heard someone shout, 'The glam new boy's here everyone. Ready for a giggle?'

'Do please grace us, and come in,' said another voice with exaggerated politeness, and the gate began to swing back.

He parked the car in one of the visitor spaces and got out to find Adam Breen striding towards him.

'Morning, probationer Detective Constable,' he said. 'Follow me, and I'll get you a security pass and take you up to the MIR.'

'The MIR?'

'Major Incident Room. It's called an acronym. Come on, we haven't got time to hang about.'

He turned and made for the rear doors. Dan followed. Of the four floors of windows of the police station, at least half were filled with faces. All were grinning, and there was plenty of pointing going on too.

Dan ignored it and kept his eyes set on the doors.

An insistent tapping from a lower window made him turn. Pressed hard up against the glass was a naked backside with a policeman's helmet on the top. The window was closed, but despite that, Dan could still hear near riotous laughter roaring from within.

Adam Breen was undeterred, kept striding towards the doors. Dan checked he still wasn't looking, lifted a middle finger and waved it at the window.

'That's enough of that,' came the detective's sharp voice over his shoulder.

'Err, what?'

'Just let them have their fun is my best advice to you. The novelty will soon wear off.'

'How did – how did you know?'

Adam stopped and turned. 'Reflections are a detective's friend,' he said, pointing to the plate glass of the police station's back doors. 'Don't think you can get away with anything. You're being carefully watched, so remember that. Now let's get you signed in, and I can take you through the case. We've got some interesting, and, in fact, utterly bizarre information already.'

The MIR was at the top of the police station, up four flights of stairs. Adam ignored the lift and took them effortlessly, Dan struggling a little way behind. He was tempted to loosen his tie, but as the detective was as impeccably turned out as ever he decided against it. A couple of cops passed them on the way, sly grins and smirks on their faces, but Dan ignored them.

Already, and again in his dealings with Adam Breen, the impression he'd made wasn't exactly the one he'd planned.

The MIR was deserted, apart from Suzanne Stewart, who was working away at a computer. She immediately stood up when Adam walked in, like a puppet summoned by a master's string. Such was the respect in the gesture that Dan wouldn't have been surprised if she'd saluted.

'Everyone's already out on inquiries,' Adam explained. 'That's the way I like it. You don't solve crimes on the phone, or at a terminal. You have to get out there and do it.'

The MIR was the size of a large classroom, one wall facing out on to Plymouth city centre and the shell of Charles Church, largely destroyed in the Blitz, now standing as a memorial to those eternal wartime sacrifices. A line of felt boards stood opposite, a picture of Edward Bray in the middle.

Adam noticed Dan staring. 'I know what you're thinking,' he said. 'Aren't they a bit outdated in these days of computers doing everything? Well, two points. First I like the team to have a picture of the crime they're trying to solve in front of them, and that means looking the victim in the eye. It keeps everyone focused. Secondly, those boards will set out the web of connections between all the people involved in the case. And seeing those can often give you the key to the crime.'

Already there were pieces of card with names printed on clustered around the photo. Dan took a step forwards and squinted to look, but Adam coughed pointedly.

'Let me give you a little warning,' he said.

'Yes?'

'All *Wessex Tonight* broadcasts are now being recorded and monitored. Every word you say, and exactly how you say it will be scrutinised. Each vowel, and every consonant. One hint of anything being aired which I haven't approved, one step out of line and ...'

Adam didn't need to finish the sentence. But, helpfully, Suzanne decided she did.

'We didn't want you, let me make that very clear. We were told by our senior officers you were joining us. We didn't have a say and we're not exactly happy about it. You're here on trust, apparently. Which is ironic, given that you're a journalist.'

'Hey, come on,' Dan protested. 'Give a guy a chance.'

'We have. Otherwise you wouldn't be here at all.'

'I could be useful you know,' Dan bridled. 'I'm not daft. I could help with handling the media, offer a different perspective on the investigation.'

The resulting silence was loaded with so much disbelief that a snow plough would have struggled to shift it.

'Well, thanks for making me feel so welcome,' Dan said finally.

'My pleasure,' Suzanne replied.

Adam held up his hands. 'OK, now we all know where we stand, let's get on with the job. So,' he said to Dan, 'To start off with, do you want to hear the voice of the killer?'

They stood either side of Suzanne while she clicked open a file on her computer. A waveform began dancing on the screen.

From the speakers came, 'Hello, emergency operator, which service do you require?'

There was a pause, the hiss of the phone line, then a male voice, heavily muffled. 'Man's body. Lay-by. Three miles east of Plymouth.'

There was another second's crackling of static, then the whine of the disconnection tone.

'So, what do you make of that?' Adam asked.

'Me?' Dan replied.

'Yes, you. Come on. You're here to learn about police work. Start thinking like a detective.'

'Well – what time was the call made?'

'5.58. Just a couple of minutes after Bray got to the lay-by, we think.'

'So only seconds after he was shot?'

'Yep.'

'Which means it could be the killer.'

'Yes.'

'Or an accomplice.'

Adam nodded. 'Yes. Good.'

'So the key question is ...'

'Yes?'

Dan took a second to think. 'If he, or she, or they have just killed Bray, why bother to phone it in?'

'Indeed. And the answer is?'

Dan scratched at his back. The shirt was itching unpleasantly. 'An attack of conscience?'

Suzanne let out a contemptuous snort. 'What, a few seconds after murdering him? In the hope of an ambulance and a miracle resurrection?'

'OK, maybe not. To put the police off the track?'

'As far as I can tell, it put us on the track,' she replied heavily. 'Straight to the lay-by, to find the body.'

Dan felt his cheeks colouring. He looked to Adam for help, but the detective said nothing, just stood with his arms folded, perhaps a hint of amusement on his face.

'Well, I don't know then,' he said. 'What?'

'Maybe to give us a time of death, nice and exactly,' Adam replied. 'So we can be sure, more or less to the minute when Bray was killed. And how would that help our murderer?'

'It would help ... if – it would help ... I don't know,' Dan replied, trying not to sound tetchy. This was worse than his long forgotten school days, being picked on by a detested teacher in a disliked class for an answer he had no hope of being able to give.

'An alibi,' Suzanne said, patronisingly. 'It would help our killer if they'd set up an alibi somewhere else, and needed us to be sure of the time Bray was killed to make it work.'

Dan nodded. 'OK. I can see that. But ...'

'But?' Adam said.

'But – it might not be the killer at all.'

'Go on.'

'It might just be an innocent person who happened to be in the lay-by at the time of the killing. Someone who witnessed it.'

Another snort from Suzanne. 'And yet this witness disguised his voice, and hung up as soon as he'd told us about the body?'

'Sure,' Dan said, trying to keep calm and thinking fast. 'Maybe he didn't want to get involved. That happens.'

'And why would he report the crime if he didn't want to get involved?' Suzanne asked sarcastically.

'Maybe he was up to something he didn't want found out. Like some meeting place for sex or something.'

Suzanne was shaking her head, but Adam looked thoughtful. 'All interesting ideas, and all possible,' he said. 'At this stage, we rule nothing in or out. The phone our mystery witness – or our killer – used to call us is a pay as you go mobile, so it can't be traced to an owner. The labs tell us that apart from knowing the voice is that of a male, it's too muffled to match against any suspects we might find. The man was probably talking through a blanket, or something like that. So, on that score, all we have at the moment are theories. Right, that was the interesting information I told you about earlier. Now, do you want to hear the bizarre bit?'

There was no surprise in the labs' headline conclusion about the murder. Edward Bray had been killed with a shotgun. The relatively concentrated pattern of the wound in his chest indicated it was not sawn off, and none of the pellets were rifled in any way that could be matched with the barrel. In short, there was nothing distinctive that could reveal which gun was used.

Also, in a rural region like the South-west, so full of farmers and country landowners, there were hundreds of shotguns in circulation. Getting hold of such a weapon would present few difficulties.

Both these facts, Adam explained, would not help them find the murderer. But there were, however, two peculiarities to the killing, which might.

Firstly, Edward Bray was shot in the heart.

'It's not exactly fair to test your detective potential on this,' Adam said to Dan, 'so I'll just tell you. That our killer went for the heart is unusual. Most will aim for the head, as that's more likely to guarantee a kill. It suggests this was no professional job. The choice of weapon backs that up. Professionals use pistols, not shotguns.'

Dan tapped a finger on the table.

'Yes,' Adam asked, sharply. 'What are you thinking?'

'You don't miss much, do you?'

'I try not to miss anything. So?'

'I was just wondering ...'

Dan told Adam about his research in the news library, the impressive number of passionate enemies Edward Bray had accrued over the years.

'So, I was wondering,' he continued, 'whether shooting him in the heart was symbolic in any way. Whether it might indicate an attack motivated by sheer hate.'

'A bit crime fiction, isn't it? More the stuff of books than real detective work.'

'But possible.'

Adam nodded thoughtfully. 'Yes, possible, I'll allow you that. Particularly when I add the bizarre piece of evidence the labs have given us.'

'Which is?'

Adam took a couple of paces towards the felt boards and tapped the picture of Edward Bray.

'As part of the attack, the lost although apparently unlamented Mr Bray was kicked in the face. But get this ...'

He paused like a veteran actor, ready to deliver the denouement of a play, wanting to be certain he had the audience's complete attention.

And he did.

'Yes, get this,' Adam continued finally. 'Edward Bray was kicked in the face – but only after he'd been shot dead.'

Adam allowed a long pause for the image to settle on the MIR. When the detective was sure the drama of his point had been made and it was time to leave the stage, he gestured to Dan and headed for the door. But there was one thing the apprentice investigator had to know first, however overawing might be these first moments of his initiation into a criminal inquiry.

'Mr Breen, may I just ask a question?'

The sharpness of the look suggested not.

Dan swallowed. 'It is a very quick one,' he persisted. 'I

promise.'

'Go on then.'

'What's that about, then?'

Dan pointed to the wall of the MIR, by the door. Hung there, in a plain black frame and set behind a sheet of glass, was a piece of paper, A4 sized.

On it was printed simply;

992 619U

Adam hesitated. 'Ah, that,' he said, quietly. 'That's the final question of one of the biggest cases we've ever investigated – and one we still haven't been able to solve, even all these years on. Do you remember the story of Mitchell Bonham?'

Chapter Six

IT TOOK AN EFFORT to concentrate on the road. Dan's head was full of that hour in the MIR, the revelations he'd already heard, and what they would do next.

The first interview with a witness.

Or, as Adam Breen had put it, 'Initially a witness, anyway.'

'Meaning?' Dan asked, as they walked down the stairs from the MIR.

'It's remarkable how quickly a witness can become a suspect in this business.'

All it needed was a musical sting to emphasise the drama of the detective's words. Dan was beginning to suspect his new colleague was something of a frustrated actor. He certainly enjoyed a little theatre.

Which thought Dan deposited safely in his mental bank. It might just be useful, when it came to the need for a story.

Teasing his mind too was the case of Mitchell Bonham. It went back fifteen years, to well before Dan's time at *Wessex Tonight*, but the story had such notoriety he knew it anyway. Some of the older hacks still talked about it, using the whispered tones that, in generations long past, might have been reserved for huddles around the camp fire and the scariest of stories.

Bonham was a nobody and a nothing, a thin, balding, middle-aged clerk in a solicitors, a man who finally found meaning in his life by taking life. He killed once, then again and again, murdering for no better reason than curiosity, to find out what it felt like. To end the lives of his fellows, and yet still be able to walk amongst the milling throng, the mass of people passing by unaware of the invisible mark he carried so proudly.

He killed five people, mostly younger and homeless, without being caught and began to grow arrogant with it. Bonham taunted the police with a series of letters, boasting that he was too clever and would never be captured. The story became one of the biggest in Britain at the time.

Eventually he was arrested, as is so often the case, by a combination of luck and good policing. Dozens of extra officers were patrolling the streets. He was seen by a beat constable, talking to a beggar in a subway on the outskirts of Plymouth city centre. Bonham panicked and ran when he was questioned, but, after a chase, he was captured. Under interrogation, and with DNA evidence from previous crime scenes against him, Bonham admitted he had been planning to kill the man to add to the tally of his victims.

He was put on trial, convicted and sentenced to life in prison. It was one of the rare cases where life would actually mean life. And there was one particularly important reason for that.

Bonham showed no remorse. Indeed he appeared to struggle to understand what was wrong with what he had done. But there was a lingering suspicion he may have had more victims than the five murders of which he was convicted.

Hundreds of people go missing in Devon every year, and many are never traced. It's difficult to be accurate, but statisticians estimate that in the whole of the country perhaps two hundred thousand people disappear annually.

Bonham was by no means forthcoming or helpful during his interrogations, and an obvious question was raised about his sanity. But he did sometimes burble names. Jim and Jack were the two most common males ones, Maria, Emma and Linda his three favourite females.

Records were checked and investigations carried out. Bonham's lifestyle and movements were analysed, but no evidence was found, nothing was proved.

At his trial, when Bonham was convicted, the judge addressed him in the dock. He told the man he might hold out some hope of being released from prison – albeit in many long years time – if he told the police whether he had indeed killed others, and now confessed who they were and where their bodies had been hidden.

Bonham stood in silence, staring straight ahead, then quietly asked for a piece of paper. The packed courtroom, lawyers, police, journalists and public all watched as, behind the plate glass of the secure dock he scribbled hard. It was the purest of dramas. The wait for what the killer would write. His last secret finally revealed.

The sheet was then passed back to the judge.

On it was scrawled;

992 619U

They were driving north, out of the city centre, towards Crownhill, part of the conurbation that is modern-day Plymouth, a mix of housing estates and offices. It was where Bray's company was based, and, Dan reminded himself, where Kerry lived.

He wondered where they would go for their date. A restaurant would be the classical choice, but he wasn't at all keen on dining like that, preferring the informality of pubs to uncomfortably high backed chairs and customers spending much of their time watching each other. Maybe a gastro pub would be a good compromise, except that the city hardly boasted much of a choice.

He sighed. Romance was such trouble. It was odd that whenever he was in a relationship he tended to want to be out, and whenever out, then to be in. Perhaps that was just human nature.

Dan slowed the car for a pedestrian crossing, a couple of older ladies were bumbling along carrying a myriad of multicoloured shopping bags. Both wore thick coats, hats and scarves, despite the day being mild on the winter's scale.

He'd ended up driving. 'If I'm stuck with you, I might at least make use of it,' Adam had said charmingly, then lapsed into a silence as he studied some of the notes contained in a folder Suzanne had given him.

Dan's happy flare of excitement at the prospect had quickly been extinguished. He'd hoped for a police car, the enjoyment of watching other motorists slow subserviently, glancing over nervously as he passed. All he got was a battered old Vauxhall, which smelt of rotting sandwiches and stale cigarettes.

His disillusionment must have been apparent. 'We like to blend in with the crowd,' noted the annoyingly observant

Adam. 'That's another lesson for you. No marked cars for the CID.'

Before they'd left Charles Cross, Dan told Adam about his interview with Arthur Bray, the man's estrangement from his son, and also his shotguns. Without a word of appreciation or thanks Suzanne noted it down for further investigation that morning. They had been about to leave when one final irritant was inflicted on Dan.

A young man walked into the office, eyed him with interest, and said, 'I've lost then. Damn.'

'What was that about?' Dan asked Adam as they'd walked across the car park.

'You don't want to know.'

'It's about me, isn't it?'

'Well spotted.'

'What is it?'

'Are you sure you want to know?'

'I think I'd rather know than not.'

'OK then. There's a sweepstake running. On how long you'll last.'

'Is there?'

'Yep. And Jim there, he drew the shortest time. An hour, I think it was.'

'Oh. Well, I'm dreadfully sorry for him.'

'Don't worry. His loss will be someone else's gain.'

'You really know how to make a man feel welcome, don't you?'

Adam stopped, and Dan wondered what he was going to say, whether whoever had got the next time slot in the sweepstake was about to scoop the pool.

'Listen,' the detective said, but his voice wasn't hostile. 'Let's get one thing straight. It's absolutely true we didn't want you. There's no space for passengers on a big case, particularly a high-profile one like this. But as you're here, I'm prepared to give you a chance. I suggest you keep your head down, keep quiet and learn what you've come to learn. The police haven't come anywhere near to this modern world of politeness and political correctness, pretend though we sometimes may. We still like our goading and teasing. The best you can do is to try to rise above it. OK?'

'It does get a little wearing.'

'Then wear it. OK?'

Dan nodded. 'OK.'

And off they had driven. To see their first witness, or, potentially, their first suspect. Edward Bray's long-serving secretary, Penelope Ramsden, a woman with a surprising story to tell.

Bray's office was an undistinguished, functional 1970s building of concrete and dark glass, which had been left as far behind by the advances of fashion as flares and platform soles. Dan recognised the complex from the story he'd seen, when it was besieged by protesters. He parked just outside the main doors.

Adam got out of the car, made to walk in, then stopped and asked, 'What are you waiting for?'

'Well, I didn't know whether you'd want me in on this.'

'Why not?'

'It feels – I don't know, sensitive I suppose. This is the real thing, isn't it? The heart of what you do. Interview people and try to work out whether they might be a murderer.'

Adam rolled his eyes. 'Come on in. You're here to learn about police work, and this is an important part of it. Just remember, you're here on trust, so keep quiet, observe, and later you can tell me what you make of her.'

They walked along a corridor, all tiles and brick, punctuated by the odd door, water fountain and poster advertising fitness classes and diet plans. All in preparation for the heavy guilt which inevitably followed the excesses of Christmas. There was no sign of any festive decorations.

An automatic door swung aside, and they were in a large, open-plan office containing rows of desks with people bent over them. No one looked across at the visitors. It was strangely quiet and felt clinical and sterile. In front of them was a larger desk, behind which a woman was sitting.

'Ms Ramsden?' Adam asked.

She looked up. She had dark hair, overlarge glasses, and a

figure which polite people would call full. Her chubby face was puffy and her eyes small and tinged with red, the colour magnified by the thick lenses of her glasses.

'Yes?' she said quietly. Adam introduced them, then asked, 'I know this is a difficult time. How are you?'

She stared at him, gulped, and suddenly sprang up from her chair and lumbered towards the door. It swung open and she disappeared down the corridor and into a toilet. Adam let out a groan and followed.

Dan stood one side of the door, Adam the other. From inside they could hear the sound of sobbing.

'Is it, err – is it always like this?' Dan asked.

'No. This is one of the more straightforward interviews,' Adam replied heavily. He knocked on the door, called to her, but received only more crying as a response.

'What do we do?'

'We wait.'

Several minutes passed. Dan sat himself on the floor. Adam paced back and forth for a little longer, then did the same.

From the toilet came a low wail, followed by more sobbing.

'I'm no expert, but I'd say she was upset,' Dan ventured.

'Well spotted. You really are going to be a valuable addition to the investigation.'

Adam rubbed at a dot of dust on his polished brogue, reached over and knocked again at the door. There was no response, save perhaps a small diminution in the crying.

They waited on. To fill the time, Dan asked, 'Do you live in Plymouth?'

'Why?'

Dan sighed. 'It's for *Wessex Tonight*. I want to do an exposé. Senior detective in living in a house in city where he works shocker. It should make a great splash. Or I might just have been making conversation while we wait for the storm of grief to blow itself out.'

'OK, no need for sarcasm. Yes, I live in Plymouth.'

'Where?'

'Peverell. Down by Central Park.'

'Not far from me. I'm up in Hartley. You got any family?'

In the half light of the corridor, Dan couldn't quite be sure, but he thought Adam flinched. The detective ran a finger over the thick gold band of his wedding ring and said quickly, 'We'll have to get her out in a minute. We can't hang around here all day.'

He got up and knocked on the door again, harder this time. From inside the toilet came slow footsteps, and Penelope Ramsden emerged. She was clutching a handful of tissues, her face lined with misery.

'He's dead,' she said, so quietly they had to strain to hear. 'And I never told him. He never knew.'

'Knew what?' Adam prompted.

'That I loved him. All these years I've worked for him. All these years and he never knew.'

The tears were starting to fall again. Adam led her to a side office and sat her down on a chair.

'I can see you're very upset, Ms Ramsden. We won't bother you for long. But there are a couple of things I need to check. First of all ...'

'He was a good man!' she interrupted, her voice a yelp. 'All those things people said about him, they weren't true. He was always kind to me. I know I'm not thin and pretty, like those young secretaries. But he gave me a chance and he always looked after me. He was a good man!'

'No one's saying he wasn't ...'

'I loved him,' she sobbed. 'And he never knew. And now he'll never know. Poor, poor Mr Bray.'

It took Adam another half hour of gentle coaxing and questioning before he found out all he wanted to know from Penelope Ramsden. The time was punctuated by continual bursts of tears, and much wiping of eyes. On two occasions Dan was dispatched to fetch more tissues.

He thought about pleading the environment and the future of the planet in an attempt to stem the flow, but decided against it. Long and sometimes embarrassing experience had taught Dan that his humour, like a holiday in a desert, could be too dry for many, and it hadn't exactly worked well so far.

During the second errand, his mobile rang. It was Lizzie, and she was in an unusually jovial mood.

'How's the crash course in police work going?'

Dan looked through the glass, at the senior detective with the pained expression comforting the lachrymose woman.

'It's not quite what I was expecting, but it's certainly interesting.'

'Good. But don't forget the deal. I don't just want you disappearing for days. The Bray murder is a big story. I want updates on it. I want exclusives. I want reports.'

'Well, you know we agreed we could only report what the police let us.'

'Then get negotiating. It's a quiet news day. You don't have to produce anything for the lunchtime bulletin, but I want a story for tonight.'

She hung up before he could argue. Not that there was any point. In Lizzie's personal dictionary, under D there was a long entry for dictatorship, but the ones for debate and discussion were missing, presumed lost.

Adam thanked Penelope Ramsden, told her it was likely they'd need to speak to her again and headed for the doors. The pace of his walk indicated considerable relief at the prospect of escape.

It had been a difficult interview, but also a productive one. In the weeks leading up to the murder, Edward Bray was involved in his usual series of negotiations with various people about the possibility of buying more land and property. None had appeared particularly acrimonious, but Adam had a list of the people concerned who would now be interviewed, and their whereabouts on Monday evening checked.

He also had a list of Bray's business dealings and associates going back for a year, including a couple of people who had become bitter and angry or made threats. They were underlined on the sheet, and would be seen quickly.

Adam had subtly asked Penelope where she was when her boss had been shot. If she realised the point of the question, she showed no sign of it. She had been at work, she said, here in the office, filling in some accounts which had to be ready for the next day. Everyone else had gone home, so no, no one could verify that.

Adam nodded thoughtfully, but said nothing.

The person Edward Bray was meeting at the lay-by was recorded as a Mr Smith.

'Surprise, surprise,' Adam whispered, as Penelope took another toilet break. 'Like adulterers, killers aren't terribly imaginative when it comes to their cover names.'

The murderous Mr Smith had said he owned some land near the A38, which he was interested in selling. The lay-by was chosen as a meeting point because, even in the dark, you could get a good idea of exactly what area was on offer, its geography and potential, its access to roads and services. In essence, all a property developer would need to quickly assess a rough value and begin negotiations.

Such meetings were, according to Ramsden, commonplace. And the reticence of Mr Smith to give more details about himself in his phone calls was also standard. Some deals could be shady and confidentiality was key. The less someone thought you knew, the happier they tended to be.

She could recall nothing distinctive or unusual about the man's voice. She had spoken to him on several occasions and there had been nothing to raise any suspicions. She had taken the details of what he was offering and discussed the matter with Mr Bray, who had asked her to set up a meeting.

And thus she had, unwittingly, helped to arrange the death of the man she professed to love. Which thought, naturally, prompted another flood of tears that would have been sufficient to see Noah heading hurriedly for the ark.

'You mentioned you'd spoken to this Smith on several occasions,' Adam said, when the latest torrent had abated. 'What else did you discuss?'

'Nothing, apart from what he had to offer and the meetings.'

'Meetings? Meetings plural?'

As she spoke, Adam listened carefully, and tightened his already pristine tie. The first meeting had been set for exactly a week before, also at six o'clock in the evening, but Mr Smith had rung to postpone it.

'When did he ring?' Adam asked.

'Lunchtime or so. I can't remember exactly.'

'What did he say?'

'Just that he'd have to call it off, but would ring to rearrange later in the week.'

'Did he say why?'

'Just that something else had come up.'

'And how did he sound?'

'Perfectly normal.'

'When did he rearrange for this Monday?'

'On Friday. In the afternoon.'

It was several seconds before Adam asked another question, and even when he did, Dan suspected the detective was still thinking about what Penelope had just said. It was almost as if one of those old-fashioned light bulbs had appeared above his head, the kind they use in comics to indicate a character having an idea. It could scarcely have been clearer that he thought he'd found an important clue.

Back in the car, Dan waited while Adam scribbled some notes. The day had remained persistently grey, but had now also developed a little drizzle. He watched the droplets form and grow on the windscreen and wondered again where to take Kerry that night, and how to provide Lizzie with a story.

In just a few hours that morning he'd learned enough to put together a corking exclusive which would make even his insatiable news editor content, if not actually happy. But Dan was determined he wouldn't be making some cop's day by winning them a pretty pile of money in the sweepstake which was riding upon his back.

The experience of shadowing a murder investigation was far too fascinating to throw away so cheaply.

'Right,' Adam said, looking up. 'What do we make of what the heartbroken Penelope had to tell us?'

'Err – me?'

'There doesn't appear to be anyone else in the car.'

'Sorry, it just surprises me when you want my opinion.'

'It's all part of the training. So, what did you reckon?'

Dan thought his way through the interview. 'She seemed

genuinely upset. Distraught in fact.'

'No chance she was putting it on?'

'I don't think so, no. Do you?'

'No, I don't think so either, but I've seen stranger things.'

'And why would she put on an act of being so heartbroken anyway?'

Adam shrugged. 'What about if she had in fact told him she loved him? Plucked up her courage, finally said so, and how about if he laughed in her face? Spurned her? Told her she was far too dull and ugly for a man like him. It might have sent her into a rage and made her decide to kill him. She could have fabricated this Mr Smith and his meetings to get her boss to the lay-by, waited for him, and boom!'

'Blimey.'

'Blimey what?'

'Well, you accused me of being a bit crime fiction earlier. That sounds way off the radar. I thought she was genuinely upset.'

Adam nodded. 'OK, for what it's worth, that was my feeling too. But this is an illustration for you, and another important lesson. Get used to being lied to. Believe no one. Suspect everything and everyone. It's a cop's way.'

'Nice. How lovely and cheery.'

'You wanted to know about police work. That's the way it goes. It's a world of deceit.'

The door of the offices opened and a couple of young men walked out, lighting up cigarettes.

'Right,' Adam said. 'So, in a word, what was the main point to come out of that interview?'

'The meeting.'

'That's two words, but yes, spot on. The cancelled meeting. If what Penelope told us is true – and we'll check the incoming calls to the company, but I bet we get another untraceable pay as you go mobile – then whoever killed Edward Bray planned to do it the week before, but called it off. And so – why might he, or she, do that?'

Dan tapped a finger on the steering wheel. 'He got cold feet? Something else came up which meant he couldn't make it?

Maybe an illness, something like that. Or perhaps the gun didn't arrive in time. Any one of a load of possible reasons.'

'Exactly. But find that reason and ...'

'You've got your murderer.'

'Absolutely. So, we have an important clue. Now let's go talk to some of the other possible suspects, see what they were doing the Monday before Bray was killed and whether they might have had reason to cancel any appointments.'

Dan started the car and was about to put it into gear when Adam's radio burbled.

'Emergency! Back up required! Emergency!'

It was a call to all available officers to head for Millbay. The man who was attacking prostitutes had struck again, but this time he'd been spotted as he tried to escape. Police officers were giving chase, and needed help to corner him.

'What are you waiting for?' Adam snapped. 'Go!'

Chapter Seven

DAN CRUNCHED THE GEARS and squealed the car out onto the road, accelerating hard. It was like being a boy racer again. He looked over at Adam, expecting a reproach, but received only an approving nod. The detective had his radio clamped to his ear, monitoring the chase.

'Keep going, don't hang around,' he said. 'We don't want to miss the fun.'

He relayed the story of what had happened. There were few prostitutes on the streets now after the attacks and the man had gone to a massage parlour. The women, already jittery enough, were suspicious. They'd shut the door in his face, but he'd been quick and strong, jammed it open with a foot and slashed at one woman with a knife. She'd suffered a couple of defensive wounds on her hand and arm, but wasn't seriously injured.

Upstairs, another of the women called 999 and a passing patrol was scrambled. They'd spotted the man running away, chased him along a couple of streets and alleys, but then lost him. The cops were sure he was still in the area and wanted back up to help flush him out.

Dan took the turn into Millbay and found a patrol car barring his way. He pulled up. Adam hopped out, had a quick word with the officer who was on sentry duty and beckoned to Dan.

'They reckon he's down here somewhere. We've got him boxed in. Come on, let's go hunting.'

Dan hesitated. 'Come on,' Adam snapped. 'There's no time to waste.'

The description of the man they were hunting danced before Dan's eyes. About six feet two, powerfully built and carrying a long and vicious knife, which he wasn't afraid to use.

Around them, police vans were pulling up and cops were assembling. All were wearing body armour and stab vests, some protective helmets too.

Dan and Adam were wearing suits. Standard, soft cotton suits.

'Err,' Dan began. 'Are you sure about this?'

'You not feeling up to a little sport?'

'Well ... I am a hack, not a cop.'

'You wanted to see police work in action. This is it. The real thing. Either follow me now, or get the other side of that cordon.'

Dan's throat felt very dry. 'OK,' he managed, and jogged after Adam.

Drizzle was drifting from the sky, clammy and cold. They were in one of the older areas of the city. The terraced houses backed onto cobbled alleys. The place was thick with passages, gardens, lock-up garages and sheds. A thousand places to hide.

Dan found himself thinking – you could walk past the man without ever knowing he was there. The first you'd realise was the white hot pain of the knife between your shoulder blades. And then the darkness of enveloping death.

He started shivering.

Adam was a few paces ahead, scanning back and forth. He was half crouched, moving slowly, stealthily. A couple of large green wheelie bins were pushed back against the wall. The detective edged towards them, then sprung forwards.

Nothing.

'All clear here,' he said, cheerily.

Dan didn't move.

'You can walk on now,' Adam added, pointedly. 'It's safe. Come on.'

A couple of cops jogged along the alley. Adam held a brief conversation, directed them up a passage to the left.

'I'll go straight on,' he said. 'Dan, you take the passage on the right.'

The words felt like an assault.

'Me?'

'Yes, you.'

'Up there?'

'Yes.'

'That little passage?'

'Yes.'

'Alone?'

'Yes,' Adam replied, patiently. 'Just scream if you see anything.'

'I will,' Dan replied, with feeling. 'Don't you worry about that.'

The passage was narrow, just wide enough for two people walking side by side. Every few yards there were wooden gates, leading into back gardens. The stone paving was full of moss and slippery with the drizzle.

Dan took a step forwards, trying to tread as gently as he possibly could. The area sounded unnaturally quiet. The police must have sealed it off, stopping all the traffic.

In this few hundred square metres was a posse of police officers, in full protective gear, with batons, CS gas, taser stun guns, firearms and a desperate knifeman.

Not to mention Dan Groves, TV reporter, a man who had never faced a violent confrontation in his life, who was armed only with a notebook and pen, and protected solely by a cheap suit.

He couldn't have felt more out of his depth if he'd been treading water in the mid Pacific.

In the distance, a siren squealed. Dan spun around, screwed up his eyes. There was nothing behind him.

Ahead was a couple of piles of rubbish, some cardboard, some wood, a line of bins. And all these gates. Behind any of which could be …

He stopped the thought before it grew.

His heart was thumping hard.

Dan's mobile rang. He jumped at the sudden sound, fumbled for it. Lizzie.

'Have you got me a story yet?' she barked.

'I was just about to call you,' he lied.

'Why are you whispering?'

'I'm with the cops. They reckon they've got the guy who's attacking prostitutes cornered. In Millbay. Can you get Nigel down here, and fast?'

She hung up without answering. Dan suspected he could take that as a yes. He switched his phone to silent and checked around. There was no sign of anyone.

He took a pace forwards, then another. Ahead, on the left, was the first gate. It was brown, chipped and covered with mildew. Tentatively, Dan reached out, then pushed at the handle.

It was securely locked.

He almost smiled.

The brick walls on either side were too high to climb, and many were topped by barbed wire, or inset with shards of glass. If the man was here, he must have gone through one of the gates, or be hiding behind the rubbish or bins.

Dan stepped gingerly on.

Another gate, also firmly locked. And another.

Overhead, a seagull screamed, making him flinch.

Another gate, blue this time, a white number nine painted neatly on it. He tested the handle.

The gate swung slowly open.

Dan gulped, then carefully poked his head into the garden. A children's slide. A rockery. A tiny lawn. No crazed knifeman.

Quietly, he closed the gate again. Feet thudded along the end of the alley. Dan spun around. It was a couple of cops, jogging past.

It was an effort to stop himself running after them.

Ahead was the pile of rubbish and bins. He took a pace forwards, then another, then hesitated. On the ground was a lump of wood. Dan picked it up and brandished it in front of him.

The drizzle chose that moment to develop into a light rain.

Dan poked at the rubbish with his makeshift club. Some soggy and faded carpet. A pile of hardcore. An old television. A few bottles.

Now a movement. Behind the bins. A blur of colour. Shifting fast. Dan raised the club, readied himself to strike.

Tried to aim at the knife he knew would be flashing towards his heart.

The sharp steel which would pierce skin and muscle and bone in an instant.

A cat scuttled out, ran off down the alley.

Dan slumped back against the wall and tried to force himself to breathe evenly.

'Hey!'

The shout shocked him. The club was in the air again, ready.

It was Adam, peering around the corner of the alley, accompanied by a couple of cops in full riot gear. All three were grinning broadly.

'You didn't really think I'd let you go hunting a knifeman on your own, did you?' Adam said. 'This area's been searched. I just wanted to see if you were up to it. Come on, we reckon we know where he is now.'

Dan heard himself growl.

It was an alley very similar to the one they'd just checked. A couple of cars, some piles of rubbish, a line of garages, a few gates. At each end were lines of police officers.

The rain was coming in harder now, cold and forceful in their faces, beating on the street and the vans. Dan pulled his jacket closer around his chest. At the far end of the alley he could see Nigel, filming from behind the police cordon.

'Anything to do with you, that, by any chance?' Adam asked. 'Or just a happy coincidence?'

'You can't expect to mount a sizeable operation like this in the middle of a city without someone noticing,' Dan replied, as neutrally as he could. 'Besides, catch the attacker and it's great publicity for the police. A safer city, a good job well done.'

Adam looked thoughtful, but didn't reply. The cops were moving up the alley, one line from each end, converging slowly. They were taking it easy, checking the gates, poking at the rubbish.

A distant clock struck noon. If they caught the man soon, they could still get the story on the lunchtime news.

'Of course, if you do arrest the guy, we'll need an interview,' Dan added. 'From a senior officer, preferably a smart and an articulate one. Someone to be the face of success, who can tell us how important it is that this man has been caught.'

Adam just nodded, but Dan noticed he adjusted his tie and kept checking his reflection in the window of a police van.

One of the cops opened a gate and stood back while four more piled untidily into the garden. Seconds ticked by. The odd echoing creak or grating sound emerged as they shifted objects in their search. Eyes watched, people waited.

Ready for the moment of capture. The end of the hunt.

The team returned, calling, 'Clear.'

A crowd of onlookers had gathered at each end of the cordon. There were even a couple of children there, perhaps brought by their parents to relieve the tedium of the long Christmas holidays. It was remarkable what passed for entertainment for some.

One line of police officers had reached a white van, parked halfway along the alley. A cop tested the back doors, pulled one open.

A scream echoed through the air. There was a burst of movement, a flailing arm, and a flying figure appeared. Dan saw a quick glint of honed metal in the air before the man disappeared under a crowd of black-clad officers. There was a brief struggle and he was led to a police van and pushed into the back.

The onlookers burst into applause.

Adam nodded. 'Good result,' he said. 'Come on, let's get back to Charles Cross to dry out, then we can get on with the Bray case.'

One of Lizzie's favoured sayings is that there's no rest for the wicked. In fairness, it may be entirely appropriate when dealing with journalists, but Dan noticed she used it most often in relation to him, although he tried not to wonder exactly what that indicated.

For now, it meant there was no chance of a return to Charles Cross. Nigel took him straight back to the newsroom, so they could get the story of the arrest of the man suspected of carrying out the series of attacks on prostitutes on the lunchtime bulletin. By the time Dan started editing it was almost one o'clock, but it was a straightforward report and simple to cut.

The easiest, and most common way of telling a TV story is chronologically, and sometimes, as with a developing drama, it's the only way. So Dan began the report with Nigel's pictures of the cops milling about, then forming lines at either end of the alley. He wrote about the police launching a major operation after the man had attempted to attack another prostitute and the area of their search converging on one street in Millbay.

Next came the key part of the story, the one the viewers would remember. It was pure news, the moment of change. It had to be handled thoughtfully.

One of the most powerful techniques in television, Dan thought, is also one which requires courage. Put simply, it's the art of knowing when to shut up. In real life, many struggle to get the hang of it, and plenty never do. So for a profession as garrulous as the media it is particularly difficult. But, for a reporter, it is a very worthwhile art to master.

As Jenny laid down the shots of the police officers moving towards the van, Dan simply wrote, 'Finally, there remained only one possible hiding place for the attacker,' and then let the pictures tell the story. The blur of action of the man leaping from the back of the van, the shouts and the officers grappling with him told the tale far more strikingly than any words ever could.

To round off the report, it was time for a clip of interview with the police. Adam had made a particularly poor show of reluctance, before agreeing that yes, he was the most senior officer at the scene, and yes, the public probably should hear from him about the importance of the arrest.

He had checked his appearance one final time in the mirror of a police van, soothed his wet hair into a presentable pattern, and had given a strong, clear and effective soundbite, just as Dan expected.

'This was a difficult and dangerous operation,' he said, 'in which police officers put their own lives at risk to catch a man who has proved a grave menace to the public. I'm proud of my officers for their work and delighted we have made the city a much safer place by what we did here today.'

Dan signed off the report by saying the man was currently being questioned and was expected to be charged later.

He made a point of sitting beside Lizzie in the newsroom as

the bulletin was broadcast. The report was the lead story, and tagged as an exclusive.

When it had finished, she didn't comment, so Dan started humming the Dambusters theme to himself, the tune growing progressively louder and increasingly self satisfied.

'All right, all right,' she said at last. 'Decent exclusive, acceptable report. I'm glad your attachment to the cops is working out. It was a good idea of mine to get you in with them.'

'Of yours? Yours?!'

'Yes, mine. Now, what are you doing sitting around here? Hadn't you better be getting back to it?'

Dan picked up his satchel and headed downstairs. He stopped off in the changing rooms, drying himself as best he could, then found Nigel, who was kind enough to have offered him a lift back to Charles Cross.

This afternoon, Adam had said, they were going to interview some suspects.

'You mean witnesses?' Dan asked.

'No,' the detective replied meaningfully. 'This time, I mean suspects.'

Chapter Eight

IT WASN'T YET TWO o'clock, but already the shades of grey in the sky were darkening in preparation for the coming night. The month had crept ever onwards, and they were almost upon the shortest day. All the cars they passed on the way back to Charles Cross had their headlights on, raindrops dancing in the sweeping beams, the hurrying people dressed in long coats and thick hats and carrying umbrellas to resist the pervasive downpour as best they could. Puddles of standing water lurked along the roadsides, rivulets and streams gushing to the greedy drains.

Nigel dropped Dan off at the back of Charles Cross and he dashed through the rain to his car. He always kept some spare clothes in there, in case of being sent away overnight, along with a wash kit and shaver, and he was fed up with feeling damp. As he manoeuvred inelegantly in the tight space of the driver's seat and wrestled on the dry shirt, his mobile warbled with a text alert.

It was from Kerry. "Hello there! Hope your day's OK, and the rain hasn't put you off meeting tonight!! Any ideas where and when yet? x"

Ah, the agony of the etiquette of replying to a text from a potential suitor. Too quick and you looked overly keen, too slow and you were uninterested. Too brief and you were terse, maybe even rude, too extensive and you were insincere, perhaps even mocking. There was none of the authentic human communication in a text, no smiles, winks and warmth in the tone of a voice, no expressions and inflexions.

Dan had resigned himself to being one of that large number of people who would never get the hang of successful flirtatious texting. A couple of years ago he managed to end one relationship before it started by trying to make a joke, the lady in question taking instant offence and sending a very direct reply. Sometimes the old ways of meeting people and establishing interest could seem so easy and attractive, he thought. Get introduced by some friends. Have a boring old chat.

All now rendered at best quaint, and more likely obsolete.

Well, one question was easy to answer. He would have to reply now. The entire afternoon was already accounted for, even if it had only just begun. He would spend a few hours with Adam interviewing suspects, then it'd be back to the newsroom to update his report on the arrest of the man who had attacked the prostitutes.

Simple and straightforward, that was how it must be. Dan typed, "No, of course not put off, looking forward to it. Still working on where, will text later with ideas, but say about 8? x"

He briefly debated whether to add the litter of exclamation marks that so many women seemed to favour when writing texts or emails, but decided against it. Kerry might find it evidence of a burgeoning rapport, but perhaps just sarcastic. It wasn't worth the risk.

He'd have to work out soon where they could go. All the bars in the city would be busy with Christmas drinkers, the restaurants likewise. A first date demanded somewhere quieter, where they could grab a little corner table and have a relaxed chat, not shout at each other amidst a boisterous throng and pumping disco beats.

Dan smiled at himself. He could sound like a very old-fashioned man, sometimes. Perhaps he should hire a cloak to lay down for Kerry when she faced a puddle.

The clock in the car said it was two, the time Adam had told him to be back. He'd better get up to the MIR, he could work on the venue later.

Dan was about to make a run for the police station's back doors when he saw it. While he'd been engrossed with texting, someone had sneaked up and added a faux blue light to the top of the car. It was made of paper and cardboard, bound together with sticky tape, and had "The TV Detective" written around the base in thick black marker pen.

Dan shook his head and jogged for the doors, ignoring the lines of grinning faces in the windows.

*   *   *

The MIR was boasting a new addition, and one which was immediately worrying. At the far end was a large television, with built in recorder. The picture was frozen on the end credits of *Wessex Tonight*'s lunchtime news.

Adam was standing by the screen, a remote control in his hand, Suzanne sitting at a desk, typing at a computer.

Neither of them spoke.

'Well, I'm back,' Dan said, trying not to sound nervous.

'Yes, we'd noticed,' Suzanne replied. 'Being detectives and all that. We spotted your presence almost straight away.'

Another silence.

'Is everything OK?' Dan asked.

Adam folded his arms.

'I mean … have you been watching my report?' Dan added.

Suzanne looked away, continued typing. Adam picked up a file of papers.

'Yes,' he said. 'Yes, we did watch it.'

He flicked through some of the sheets. A strip light hummed in the ceiling.

'And?' Dan prompted. 'Was it – err, was it OK?'

No reply.

'I mean, well – I thought it was a pretty good piece. I thought I did a decent job of it.'

More silence.

'Well, it made a good splash, didn't it? The lead story and all that.'

Suzanne and Adam exchanged a look.

'What?' Dan asked. 'What's going on? What's the matter?'

Adam sat down on a desk and swung a leg. 'I don't know whether I should tell you this.'

He ran a hand over his stubble, pronounced and already dark once more.

'What?' Dan urged. 'Tell me what? What's going on? Are you kicking me off the inquiry? What's happening?'

The door opened, a uniformed sergeant walked in and put down a pile of papers in a tray. Suzanne thanked him, and the man left again.

Adam waited for the door to close.

'Well, what is it?' Dan repeated. 'Look, if you're throwing me off the case, I'd rather you just told me instead of playing these games.'

Adam got up and turned off the television. 'A few minutes ago, I got a call from the Deputy Chief Constable. He'd been watching your lunchtime news. He likes to keep up with the media, as you know.'

'Ah,' said Dan.

'Ah indeed.'

'Well – what did he say? What?!'

Adam picked up his coat, slipped it over his shoulders and reached for a couple of files.

'He said ... he said it was a good idea of mine to get the cameras along on the operation to catch the attacker, and to go on the TV to talk about the arrest. He said it was great for public reassurance, and looked very positive for the force. He commended me on my fine work.'

There was another silence.

'Did he now?' Dan said, trying to keep the relief from his voice.

'He did. Right, come on. We've got some suspects to see.'

He headed for the door. Dan followed.

'I told you I might actually be useful,' he said quietly.

This time, he thought, just maybe the resulting silence wasn't perhaps filled with quite so very much disbelief.

They headed for Plymouth Hoe, the great natural harbour and iconic heart of the city.

Dan was driving again, Adam studying his notes.

'Jon Stead and Andrew Hicks are who we're going to see,' he said. 'In this case, I say suspects because Hicks is one of those named by Penelope Ramsden as threatening Bray. He came into the office quite a few times apparently, shouting abuse. They had to call the police on a couple of occasions. He detested Bray with a passion.'

The name was familiar, and Dan chased it through the passages of his mind. 'Yes,' he said. 'I saw him on a report in our News Library. He was chucked out of his home by Bray.

We interviewed him at court. He was the one who coined the infamous epithet "Bray the Bastard".'

'Well, his pal Stead was also chucked out of his house by Bray,' Adam replied. 'So he too has a reason to hate the man. It should be an interesting chat.'

The men were spending the afternoon fishing from a jetty by the Waterside pub. Dan parked the car and they walked over to find the two figures, who were so wrapped up in waterproofs that they resembled postal packages.

The wind and rain were spraying patterns across the waters of the sound, obscuring the green and orange floats which bobbed forlornly in the sea. To Dan, lover of cosy pubs and crackling firesides, it didn't feel remotely like a pleasant way of spending an afternoon. He had though come to appreciate the zeal which accompanied many a hobby, be it fishing, trainspotting, or whichever passion seized the great spectrum of human imagination.

Years ago, as a cub reporter, he had been sent to cover a story about a family whose weekends were dedicated to collecting the identification numbers of electricity pylons. Initially, he had thought it a spoof, but with some research found it was a genuine hobby. The marching across boggy fields, sometimes at considerable personal risk, to discover a unique identification plate, was indeed considered a worthwhile way of spending your leisure time by some. Many pages on the internet were dedicated to it, one even titled, without a hint of irony, "Pylon of the Month."

Hicks and Stead reeled in their lines and they all shook hands. Adam suggested they sheltered by the side of the pub while they talked, for which mercy Dan was grateful. He could sense the rain seeping in to his new and previously pleasantly dry shirt.

Hicks was a big man, some six feet or so tall and well built, Stead thin and wiry. He hardly said a word in the whole conversation, preferring instead to gaze out to sea, as if ruing the passing fish he might be missing as they talked.

Adam explained why they were here, and Hicks began to

smile.

'Is something amusing you, sir?' the detective asked.

'Oh yes.'

'Which is?'

'Bray getting himself murdered.'

'You find that funny, do you?'

'Very much so. The man was a bastard. He deserved it.'

'He deserved to be blasted through the chest with a shotgun?'

'I'd say so. The only problem I'd have with what happened was that it was a bit quick. I'd have preferred it if he'd suffered more.'

Adam's voice was marked with a warning. 'Are you sure this is the sort of thing you should be saying to a police officer?'

Hicks shrugged. 'Why not? You haven't pulled my name out of a hat, have you? You know damn well what he did to me. After he chucked us out of the house, me and Linda split up. A year later, my mum died, and I wasn't there when she went. I would have been if I was still in my house. Anytime I'm passing his office I like to pop in and have a go at him. He was a bastard and he deserves what he got.'

'So – you killed him?'

Hicks laughed loudly. 'No, mate. I'm sorry to disappoint you, but I didn't kill him. But when you find out who did, let me know and I'll shake his hand.'

'Then where were you on Monday evening at about six o'clock?'

'I dunno for sure. I think we were out fishing, weren't we Jon?'

The man beside him nodded, but didn't speak.

'What, in the rain we had on Monday?' Adam asked.

'It don't make no difference to the fish,' Hicks replied. 'They get wet whatever the weather. I might have been out fishing, but I might have been home too.'

'Can anyone confirm that?'

'Jon can.'

'Anyone else?'

'I think we picked up a couple of bits of shopping on the way home. You can ask the old lady in the shop by the river. Otherwise no.'

Adam turned to Jon Stead. 'And you, you'd back this up?'

'Yes,' he replied in a quiet voice.

'Did you hate Edward Bray too?'

Stead nodded. 'Course he did,' Hicks added. 'He threw Jon out of his home as well. In fact, that's how we met. At the court. When Bray was doing his mass evictions thing. The man was a category one, gold plated, top notch bastard.'

This time, Adam didn't thank the men, just told them he would need to speak to them again and turned to go. But before they could walk away, Stead put a hand on Dan's shoulder and said, 'You're that man off the TV, aren't you?'

Dan suppressed a groan at the dreaded words. They would invariably be followed by an ear bending about the ridiculousness of the plot of some soap opera, the lamentable state of an actor's dress sense, or the lack of decent programmes on the box nowadays, none of which he had any influence over whatsoever.

'Yes,' he said resignedly. 'I am the man on the telly.'

'You used to do environment stuff, didn't you?'

'Yes,' Dan said once more, thinking how far off his previous life now seemed.

Stead reached out and shook his hand again, this time with enthusiasm. 'I liked your reports. You always stuck up for us fishermen. When Greater Wessex Water polluted the Sound here with sewage they never told us, just let us carry on fishing in it. But you found out and gave them a good going over. You should go back to covering environment. You were really good at it.'

Dan found he was afflicted by a rare phenomenon. He didn't know what to say.

Next on the menu of suspects came Gordon Clarke, a businessman like Bray, but now with one distinct commercial advantage over his former rival. He was still alive.

Adam read the briefing as Dan drove them to Ermington, a

village some ten miles to the east of Plymouth in the pure Devon countryside of the South Hams. Clarke had rented a shop from Bray, had a couple of difficulties with paying the rent, and was quickly evicted. He'd taken the matter to court, but had lost. Clarke was notable as he too had made threats against Bray at the time, and gone on to start up a website for people to leave their thoughts about the businessman.

It was, in principle at least, dedicated to the discussion of entirely legal ways in which Bray's business ambitions could be thwarted. But it had quickly become a forum for ranting, and sometimes even dark fantasies about the kind of things certain people would like to do to Edward Bray. Many were highly creative, and even more were painful and messy.

The site had been shut down, and Gordon Clarke warned to desist by both the police and Bray's solicitors.

Dan turned the car off the A38 and followed a narrow road south towards Ermington. They were surrounded by the kind of scenery that, in the sunshine, would make a director of commercials for butter smile. In the current rain it just looked forlorn. Trees drooped under the weight of the falling water and the countryside was fogged with a dank mistiness.

Clarke's latest office was in a small business park, on the outskirts of the village. It was a computer supply company, the latest in a long line of ventures. From his CV, his way of working was clear. He would set up an operation, keep it going for a year or two, then close it down again when profits were looking thin and immediately start up a new company.

There were allegations and hints – none proved – that suppliers and customers had been left out of pocket by the sudden moves.

'A resourceful man then,' Adam mused, 'with plenty of drive, possibly no great respect for the law, and another who very much hated Edward Bray. In short, a decent suspect.'

The grandly titled business park turned out to be a small set of factory units. 'But then,' as Clarke explained, as he ushered them into his office, 'when you're selling online, it doesn't matter what your base is like. It's the website, the product and the service you offer that are important.'

He was a tall man, well built, his dark hair subtly highlighted in a way that reminded Dan of lower league footballers. It seemed an advertisement for untrustworthiness. He was wearing a suit which was modern and did its best to appear expensive, but couldn't quite master the illusion. The material was a little too shiny, the stitching a hint too obvious.

'Before you ask, I didn't kill him,' Clarke said.

Adam gave the businessman a lofty look. It was certainly an interesting opening gambit.

'I didn't ask, sir,' he replied. 'But since you come to mention it, what were your feelings towards Edward Bray?'

Clarke smiled, but without any warmth. 'Now come on, officer, you know my feelings. They're precisely why you're here. I'm not ashamed to tell you I hated the man. But I was hardly alone in that. If I'm a suspect, I must be one among scores.'

'You are indeed,' Adam replied emphatically.

'Well, it wasn't me. I haven't seen Bray for months. I've been trying to leave him behind and move on in my life. I've been doing a little meditating, attempting to improve myself. Hatred can be so very destructive. It blinds a man, you know.'

They talked a little about Clarke's dealings with Bray, and his current business, a new way of designing and building computers bespoke to a company's needs, a subject of which Dan possessed little understanding, and even less interest.

It was growing dull, being a passenger in these interviews. Life would be far more interesting if he could be allowed to pitch in with the odd question, but Adam had warned him to adopt the Victorian child model. Dan could be seen, begrudgingly, but certainly not heard.

He found his mind wandering once more to that night, and where to take Kerry, then realised the answer had been presented to him just an hour beforehand. The Waterside Inn was boasting a new menu and it was far enough away from the city centre not to be too crowded. If the weather cleared, he could probably just about get away with it seeming a well-considered setting for a tentative foray in the vague direction of romance.

Adam was getting up from his seat, thanking Gordon Clarke for his time. 'There is just one more thing sir,' he added. 'It would help to eliminate you from our inquiries if you could tell us your whereabouts on Monday evening at about six o'clock.'

Clarke opened a diary on his desk. 'Bristol,' he said. 'Well, on the way back by then in fact, but if you need a more exact location, I'd guess somewhere on the main rail line between Exeter and Plymouth.'

He smiled ingratiatingly, the look having exactly the opposite effect to that which was intended.

'And can anyone confirm that, sir?' Adam asked.

'Plenty of other passengers. Ellie, my secretary. I'd been in Bristol all afternoon, having a look around. I'm thinking of opening an office there, and wanted to get an idea of the potential market and competition.'

Clarke showed them out. In the rear view mirror, as they drove away, Dan watched him. There was still mist in the air and spray from the car's wheels too, but he was almost sure the businessman breathed out a heavy sigh of relief before turning and walking back into his office.

Chapter Nine

DEADLINES, SOMETIMES HIS LIFE could feel full of deadlines.

After an absorbing hour at Charles Cross, going through the case with Adam, Dan had only just managed to get back to the newsroom in time to cut a new version of the story about the arrest of the prostitute attacker. If truth was told – which it very much wasn't, because it was not the kind of truth Lizzie should hear – Dan had almost forgotten his day job, so immersed had he become in the excitement of the Bray case.

And now another deadline loomed. Kerry was picking him up at eight, it was ten minutes to, and he still hadn't decided what to wear.

It's a common myth about a woman's indecision in the wardrobe, Dan reflected. The uncommon truth, never admitted outside of the brotherhood of course, is that men are just as badly afflicted and often even more so.

It was as problematic as trying to work out the right form of text to send her. Too smart an outfit and he might seem desperate or staid, too sloppy and he could come across as louche, or uninterested.

Together, Dan and Rutherford stood in the spare bedroom and eyed the rack of clothes.

'What do you reckon, dog?' Dan asked, holding up one shirt, light blue with red climbing roses. 'Too flamboyant? Makes me look untrustworthy? Like I'm trying to be too young? Or some kind of gigolo?' He tucked in his stomach. 'Unflattering on my figure?'

Rutherford sniffed at the shirt and flinched. 'Yes, see what you mean, it could do with a wash,' Dan noted. 'OK, how about this one?'

It was plainer, black with thin vertical orange and green stripes. As he examined it, Dan wondered what kind of a mood he had been in when he made the purchase, or more significantly, perhaps, the state of the lighting conditions in the store.

Rutherford blinked, lay down and rested his head on his paws.

'Ah, you're hard to please, but then you may have a point. Come on, we're running out of time. This one?'

Now Dan proffered a white shirt, with blue paisley swirls. Rutherford yawned, got up and trotted back towards the lounge.

'Thanks for all your help,' Dan called after him. He put the shirt back on the rack and chose his default option, a midnight blue model. It was always a home banker, fitted him snugly and went well with his colouring.

Five to eight. Just time for another quick run through of the day. Dan sat on the great blue sofa, listened for Kerry's taxi, and let his mind run.

After the lunchtime news all the media had picked up on the story of the arrest, although none had the pictures. When Dan and Adam got back to Charles Cross after seeing Gordon Clarke, although it wasn't his case, Adam had been good enough to check on how the questioning of the attacker was going.

A few more issues to tie up had been the answer, but they were almost at the stage where he would be charged. The man had admitted the attacks, and was amidst a long and ranting justification. The detective leading the inquiry, a middle-aged and affable inspector, had promised Adam he would call when the suspect was formally charged, so Dan could break the news. It was a fair deal, Adam said, given the positive publicity he'd generated for the police.

It was just before five o'clock, darkness now firmly ensconced on the city. They walked back up to the MIR to find it deserted.

In the large and silent hollowness of the space, as if it was an irresistible magnet, Dan's eyes were once again drawn to the framed piece of paper on the wall.

992 619U

He wondered what it could mean, whether murder, or perhaps murders, could really be hidden in those six numbers and that letter. Again though, he came up with no ideas. When he had a rare moment, safe from covering stories and learning about criminal investigations, Dan told himself he would sit down and have a proper think about it.

A note from Suzanne said she'd gone out to check on a couple of issues and would go home afterwards, but would see Adam first thing tomorrow morning. She also left a comprehensive summary of how inquiries were going.

'That's very Suzanne,' he said. 'Hard-working, thorough, and methodical. She's a fine officer, and it's about time she moved on from being a sergeant. Right, while we wait for news of the charges, let's have a recap and a think. Tell me what you make of what we've heard this afternoon?'

This time Dan didn't hesitate to venture his opinion. 'Clearly a trio of people who hated Bray. So Hicks, Stead and Clarke all had obvious motives. I guess they could have found the means, given that shotguns are relatively easy to get hold of. I suppose then it comes down to opportunity, and whether they might have had the guts to do it.'

'And?'

Dan thought his way back through the interviews. 'I'd say yes to Hicks and Clarke, no to Stead. He struck me as too much of a mouse.'

'Mice can cause a lot of damage too, you know.'

'Yes, but if you're asking for a hunch, that's it.'

Adam nodded. 'Hunches, feelings, they're an important part of police work, as you've realised. But whatever you might have seen on the TV, facts are the cornerstone of the job. Tomorrow, I'll get the teams checking all their alibis. We'll talk to Clarke's secretary, this woman in the shop that Hicks and Stead say they saw, and I'll have a mobile cell analysis done too.'

'A what?'

'Locating where their mobile phones were. It can give you a minute by minute picture of a person's movements, and is often accurate to within a few feet. It's a powerful tool. We might as well check where Penelope Ramsden was too, while we're at it.'

'You still fancy her as a suspect?'

Adam considered the question. 'I don't think she's as strong a suspect as those others, but she can't be ruled out.'

'And Arthur Bray?'

'We'll do him too.'

'Have we got anyone else to see?'

Adam checked through the notes Suzanne had left. 'The teams are working on all the usual areas, everyone Bray knew, had dealings with, who might have wanted him harmed, etc. It's quite a field of candidates, but no firm leads so far.'

'So, what do we do next?'

'What do you think we need to do? What strikes you as missing in all this so far?'

'Are you testing me, by any chance?'

Dan thought it couldn't have been more obvious if Adam had sat him at a desk in a hall, waited for the clock to strike, then told him to turn over his paper and begin. But all the detective would say in reply was, 'Just consider it that I'm checking to see if you're paying attention.'

Dan walked over to the window and pulled himself up on the sill. The city was alive with the lights of the night, cars filled with people making their way home, shop windows, restaurants, bars and clubs trying to lure in customers. The ruined church stood watch over it all, shining in the wash of its attendant floodlights.

'Edward Bray,' he said, finally. 'I'd still like to know more about him. I'm not sure we've got a proper sense of the man. What was behind the estrangement with his dad, for example? Why did he have such a zeal for the hospice?'

'OK, but is any of that relevant to the case?'

'We don't know is the simple answer. It could be. So we'd better find out, hadn't we?'

Adam gave him a look that Dan couldn't read. 'Indeed we had. Tomorrow morning we'll go and see Eleanor Paget, the Chief Exec of the hospice. Of all the people we have to talk to, she probably knew Bray best. They worked together a lot, and apparently it wasn't an easy relationship. Right, before we finish for the day, let's do one more thing – this time part fact and part feeling. A timeline for the killing, and how it was done.'

He walked over to the felt boards, found a piece of paper and began writing.

???? One week before killing – cancelled appointment – original murder plan??

Actual killing – Monday.

5.40.Bray leaves city centre business reception for meeting at lay-by.

5.55 (approx) Arrives at lay-by.

5.59 999 call reporting body.

6.08 First police on the scene.

'So,' Adam said, 'we don't have anything in the way of forensic evidence from the lay-by. There are no tyre tracks, no footprints. The rain washed them all away. And the Scenes of Crime team didn't find any fibres or hairs our killer might have kindly discarded either, to make our lives easier. He was too careful for that. So we'll have to do this the old-fashioned way, think through it all without that evidence. Right, first the murder itself. When was Bray killed?'

'Clearly in those four minutes between him arriving at the lay-by and the 999 call.'

'Correct. Right then, those are the facts as we know them. But that's the easy bit. Now give me the fantasy. How was it done?'

Dan closed his eyes. He could see Bray arriving at the lay-by, pulling up in that big jeep of his. It was dark and the rain was pouring down. He would have squinted through the gloom, made out another car, probably the only one there, parked somewhere close to it.

So, what next? Bray was always on time and wasn't a patient man, they knew that. He was renowned for continually using the old business cliché, "Time is money". He wouldn't have sat waiting, would only perhaps have paused to pull on a coat, then got out of his jeep and walked towards the car.

It's noisy, with cars rushing past on the dual carriageway, their wheels slicing through the wet making it even louder. And it's very dark. It's mid winter, the rain's coming in hard, and there are no lights in the lay-by.

His eyes won't have adjusted to the blackness. He'll be stepping carefully towards the car, ready to meet Mr Smith, preparing to talk commerce, do business.

He won't be suspicious. Why should he be? Meetings like this are commonplace. And he can sense the aroma of money to be made.

But it's all a trap. The myth of Mr Smith has lured him to the lay-by. He too knows Bray is always on time, usually a few minutes early in fact. He's been waiting there. He's even earlier, and he's ready. He sees the jeep pulling in. It's instantly recognisable as Bray's. He sees the familiar figure behind the wheel. He knows he's got his man.

And there are just seconds left to run of Edward Bray's life.

Our attacker is crouched down by the side of the car. The shotgun is in his hands.

The jeep parks, the door quickly opens, just as he knew it would. Bray doesn't waste time. And now he can see the man walking towards him, slowly and carefully in the darkness.

The man he hates, loathes, detests and abhors. So much so that he's made his plan and is ready to murder.

The plan which is finally at its culmination.

All it takes is that last second of courage. To stand up. To aim the gun. To pull the trigger.

Bray's close now, just a few feet away. He can make out the shape of a man. Maybe he says, 'Hello? Mr Smith?'

And perhaps that's the last thing he ever says. The double barrels swing. They're pointing right at his heart. The final moment's resolution. The overwhelming power of pure hatred. The finger squeezes the trigger. The plug of hot shot flies. It cuts its fatal path through the air. And Bray falls.

He's dead as his body hits the wet tarmac.

Mr Smith calmly puts the shotgun back in the boot, calls the police and drives off, safe in the black encompassing anonymity of the night.

Dan opened his eyes to find Adam staring at him. The detective was tapping the edge of a desk in mock appreciation.

'Oh,' Dan said, quietly. 'Was I doing all that out loud?'

'You were. It was a bit flowery at times, but not a bad

effort.'

Adam added a row to the timeline.

5.57 Bray shot.

'So, that's how it happened. But there are still some big questions we have to answer,' he said. 'Key questions, in fact.'

'Why call the police right after the killing, and why the cancelled appointment the week before?'

'Precisely. So tomorrow, when the teams go through our suspects' alibis, those are the most important areas they'll be looking at. Whether anyone relies on us knowing exactly what time Bray was killed to exonerate him, and what was going on in his life that Monday of the week before which might have forced him to change his plans.'

They were interrupted by a knock on the door. It was the other detective, to tell them the man had been charged.

'Hell!' Dan gasped. 'It's half past five. We're on air in an hour. I need to get back to recut my report.'

They agreed what he could say, Dan jogged down the stairs to his car and drove back to the studios. To save time, instead of starting from scratch they took the lunchtime news version and changed only the end.

'Tonight, a man has been charged with attempted murder,' he added. 'Detectives haven't formally named him and say their inquiries are continuing, but they believe he was motivated by a desire for revenge, after contracting an incurable sexually transmitted disease from a prostitute.'

It was another little exclusive titbit, Dan's reward for providing such good publicity for the police. After the programme, Lizzie had said, 'Not bad,' as a verdict on his efforts, impressive praise for her.

Outside, Dan heard a taxi rumbling to a stop.

Yes, it had been a good day. And now he wondered what the coming night would bring.

Their first meeting came as if the director of a low budget romantic comedy had shouted "Cue".

Dan swung open the door just as she was about to ring the bell. She stood, frozen, her finger poised over the button. He lurked, static in the doorway. In the second he saw her standing there, Dan realised he'd been so wrapped up in thoughts of the Bray case that he hadn't in any way prepared for what to say or do.

'Err, hello,' was his magnificent opening line, followed by the almost as inspired, 'it's Kerry, I presume?'

At least she had the decency to refrain from sarcasm, however justified it might be.

'Yes.'

She smiled and leaned forwards for Dan to kiss her cheek, just as he reached out to shake her hand. To try to compensate, he took her hand and kissed that instead, then saw what an idiot he must look and kissed her cheek too.

'It's OK, I won't work my way anywhere else for now,' said the World's Funniest Man.

Her smile didn't falter, and Dan hoped she was one of those wonderful and highly sought after women who took pity on men's bumbling inadequacies, and perhaps even found them entertaining rather than just emetic. The laws of supply and demand meant they were always rare finds; naturally being in heavy demand and short supply.

'It's – err – nice to meet you,' added the professional journalist, demonstrating his great mastery of words.

'It's good to meet you too.'

Dan tried to take a surreptitious look at his date. He'd already registered that she was tall, as he hadn't had to stoop to kiss her. She was wearing jeans and a tight black top, which still bore a couple of creases from the packaging and hinted that it was bought newly for the occasion. But Kerry's most striking feature was a scarce and mesmeric combination. She had blonde, shoulder length hair, with looked natural, but brown eyes.

His brain seemed to be registering that she was, in summary, very attractive.

This impression built as quickly in Dan's mind as a sculptor forming a figure from a mighty block of stone. And just as subtly, apparently.

'Are you OK?' she asked, her head tilted to one side.

'Oh, yes, sorry. Just thinking.'

'Well, shall we go? It's cold out here.'

'Yes, yes, sorry.'

She stepped back to the taxi, while Dan locked up the flat. By no means for the first time in his life, he chastised himself on his talents with women and used the seconds to try to regain some composure.

In the taxi, Dan realised he only had a few pounds in his wallet. Trying to borrow some from Kerry would hardly be ideal, so he asked the driver to stop at the cashpoints on Mutley Plain. An acknowledging grunt, the universal language of taxi drivers, indicated assent.

The cab pulled up in the bus stop, right next to the sign saying, "Strictly no Waiting, Taxis Included". Dan hopped out, and walked straight into Adam.

'Oh, hello,' he said.

'Hello.'

'What are you doing here?'

Adam sounded tetchy. 'Getting some cash, surprisingly.'

'Sorry, stupid question.'

'Yes, it was.'

This was a very different Adam from the smart and cool professional of the daytime. He'd taken off his tie, but was still wearing his suit, and the stubble around his face was thick and dark, the effect being to make him look like an unemployed banker. Despite the chill of the evening, and the ever present hint of rain, he wore no coat.

'You off for something to eat?' Dan asked lightly.

'Yeah.'

'On your own?'

'Apparently.'

'See you tomorrow then?'

'I expect so.'

Adam was away, walking rapidly into the night. Dan watched him go. The detective's shoulders were hunched, and he was stalking along with a slouch. Around him, groups of people smiled and laughed, but his expression was dour. He was clutching a newspaper, and disappeared into a bar.

Behind Dan, the taxi's horn hooted. He turned and walked back to the cab.

The date, if such it could be titled, was starting to improve. Dan had a pint of beer in his hand, the Waterside was busy, but without it being overwhelming, just sufficient to create a contented rumble of chatter, and they'd been given a good table, right at the back, overlooking the Sound.

Dan wasn't surprised. He'd used one of his favourite tricks to make sure they were well looked after. When he'd phoned the restaurant to book the table, he asked for the manager to call him back later, ostensibly to discuss the wine list. When the call came he switched it to his answer machine.

"Hello, this is Dan Groves of *Wessex Tonight*. Sorry I can't take your call at the moment, but please leave a message and I'll get back to you."

It was guaranteed to make tradesmen, or car mechanics, or any form of business wary of trying to con him, and instead provide the best service they could.

He'd also rediscovered the briefly missing art of conversation. Kerry asked about his hobbies and he'd talked of Rutherford, going out walking, and his search for the Ted Hughes Memorial.

'I know it's on Dartmoor somewhere,' Dan said. 'It's just a question of finding it. And as there are 368 square miles to work through it's proving quite a challenge.'

She laughed. 'You must have managed to narrow it down a bit?'

'Yes, that's true. I got hold of a copy of Ted's will. It asked that a memorial to him be placed on the moor, between the sources of the rivers Taw, Dart, East Okement and Teign. He loved the area. So I found the sources, and plotted the mid point between them, but it isn't there.'

'How come?'

'I think because Ted gave his friends discretion about where to put the memorial, so they chose somewhere that would be most appropriate for him.'

'And what does it look like?'

Dan sipped at his pint. 'That's part of the trouble. All I know it that it's a granite stone, carved with his name. And, as you can imagine, there are more than a few bits of granite on the moor.'

Their meals arrived and they started eating. They'd both gone for steak, Kerry asking for hers to be cooked rare, prompting Dan to nod in approval. His was blue, and after the usual argument with the manager, and her pleading of food safety regulations, he'd finally got his way by promising not to sue them if he should die.

While they ate, Kerry told him some more about herself. She was a local lass, had moved away from Plymouth only to go to university in Leeds, now worked as a manager at the regional electricity company. She was in charge of customer service, which meant much biting of the tongue and faked and forced diplomacy.

Dan kept her talking, which had two advantages. One, he was hungry, his steak was proving good, and he didn't want his mouth distracted from the business of eating it. Two, a lesson he'd learnt early in life was that commonly, to make someone think they were having a good time, the best method was to get them chatting about their favourite subject. Which in the case of most people, was themselves.

Dan noticed he was finding Kerry's eyes increasingly attractive, but they were also stirring a dangerous memory. The hazel shade was the same as Thomasin's, the woman he'd met in his final week at university. He'd known straight away about the strength of his feelings for her and tried to build a relationship. But the merciless clock had worked against them. They'd left for new places, many miles distant, her to study to become a solicitor, Dan a journalist, and they'd slipped inevitably apart.

It had never stopped feeling like unfinished business, one of the most dangerous sensations of life. And since then, all those years ago, he still managed to compare every woman to her.

No wonder his relationships never lasted.

Well, tonight he would not be doing so. He was resolute

about that. Absolutely determined.

But Kerry's eyes were so very like Thomasin's.

Dan forced his mind back to tonight and ordered them some more drinks. She liked white wine, crisp and dry, sipped it demurely, left just a hint of lipstick pattern around the glass, picked out by the background lights.

'Tell me about the online dating thing,' he said. 'I just thought I'd give it a go and was lucky enough to meet you. Have you tried it before?'

She put down her fork, smiled. 'Once or twice.'

'And?'

'I've been on a couple of dates.'

'How did they go?'

'One bloke was …'

'Yes?'

'Well, exactly the sort you fear. He slurped his drinks, dripped food on his jacket, kept chewing his nails all night, and talking about his hobby.'

Dan reminded himself once more to watch his table manners.

'And his hobby was?'

'Building scale models of cruise liners.'

'How fascinating.'

'Quite.'

'So no second date?'

'Very perceptive.'

'And the other guy?'

'He was much nicer. A guy who works at the Further Education College. But he'd only been divorced for a few months and he was a bit intense.'

'Do you think it works, computer dating?'

'I think it gives you better odds than stumbling around bars, meeting people at random. At least this way you know you've got something in common before you decide to get together.'

She excused herself and went to the ladies. It was fortunate timing. As Dan was staring out of the window a large rat walked nonchalantly along the harbour wall. He put down his fork and gazed thoughtfully at the food.

When she came back, they talked about their careers, friends, families and aspirations. She enjoyed holidays abroad, didn't know whether she wanted to have children, would like to write a book and get an allotment so she could grow her own vegetables. Dan talked a little about some of the bizarre stories he'd covered, and was surprised when the barman called time.

'I've had a lovely evening,' she said, as they hailed a cab.

'Me too. I'm sorry if I disappointed you by not making models of cruise liners, but a man has to accept he can't be everything.'

'Maybe you can work on the cruise liners for next time? I'm not due to be working at the weekend.'

Dan didn't hesitate. 'Then let's get together. I'll come up with a plan and text you.'

The taxi rumbled them home. Sitting together, in the back, their legs brushed a couple of times and neither hurried themselves to escape the contact. The city was alive, people rushing between pubs and clubs, making the most of the dying hours of the living night.

At the flat, Dan pecked her on the cheek and went to get out of the cab.

'Try again,' she said, and this time he kissed her lips.

He hesitated, wondered what to do, but she said, 'Now you can go,' pushed him playfully out and closed the door, but wound down the window. 'See you at the weekend.'

'I look forward to it.'

Dan let Rutherford out into the garden, had a wash, then sat up for a while, listening to some music. He lay on the great blue sofa, thought back over the day, and had an idea.

For the past three or four years, he'd resolved annually to keep a diary. Dan was never quite sure why. Perhaps it was a sense of the passing years, a need to record something of his life, or maybe just pomposity, but he'd been determined to do it. Every year he'd gone out to buy himself the requisite journal, and every year duly failed to fill it in. All the books were in his bedside cabinet, gathering not memories but dust.

He fished out the volume for the year that was coming to a close, crossed out the date and instead inscribed carefully on the front, "Diary of my new life."

Inside, he wrote a title. "Case one – Edward Bray," beneath which he added a brief outline of how the businessman was killed, and then, "I'm SURE Gordon Clarke is hiding something. And for that matter, so is Adam Breen."

Chapter Ten

AS IF FOR AN early Christmas present to the long-suffering land, a weak winter sun had risen in the sky. It was hardly warming and rejuvenating, more skulking than dominating, but at least it was a break from the greyness and the rain of the last few days and very welcome.

It was dark when Dan woke, and cold, the clearing of cloud over the nighttime hours allowing what little precious heat the city had accumulated to seep away. He wrapped himself in the duvet until the central heating grumbled into life, then took Rutherford for a run around Hartley Park.

It was one of those rare mornings he witnessed the precise moment dawn breaks, the first slice of the red sun edging into the new sky over the hills to the east. Dan stopped and watched, clouds of his drifting breath growing in the clear morning air. Rutherford sat beside him and watched too.

Some spectacles can still all before them.

Dan was due at Charles Cross at ten. He briefly debated whether to pop into the newsroom first, but that would be to invite an attack from the strange editor beast that lived there, so instead he used the spare hour to do some much-needed shopping.

The city was quiet, the assistants he met puzzled that someone could need to begin their purchasing so early. But in a men's store Dan found a kind, older chap who eyed him with some expertise and perhaps a little well-disguised pity. He suggested a range of shirts, jackets and ties which might suit Dan, and duly relieved him of several hundred pounds.

It was only when he was loading the clothes into the car that Dan realised, had he waited a couple of weeks, until the sales, he would have saved himself a considerable sum. Still, at least he would have a wardrobe to, if not compete, then at least keep pace with Adam, albeit very much as a straggler in the fashion race.

The detective was waiting in the MIR when Dan arrived, at five to ten exactly. A couple of other officers, sitting at the back of the room, held a brief whispered conversation, before one rolled a piece of paper into a ball and threw it theatrically into the bin. Dan sensed another loser in his sweepstake.

Adam had his back turned and arms folded and was studying the felt boards. Today's suit was navy blue with a faint, almost imperceptible chalk stripe and the shirt was crisp and pure white.

Even from this range, it easily eclipsed the new ensemble in Dan's boot.

'Morning, probationer detective,' Adam said, without looking round.

Dan wasn't surprised, but he was nonetheless interested. 'How did you know this time?'

'That it was you? Your footstep. It's a little trepid, like someone who isn't quite sure they should be here. It's very different from the other officers. Right, let's go.'

He handed Dan the car keys. 'To the hospice. This should be interesting. From what we're hearing the relationship between Edward Bray and Eleanor Paget could be a stormy one.'

As was his habit, Adam hardly spoke in the car. He leafed through his papers, made the odd noise of interest and scribbled down a couple of notes.

Last night's encounter on Mutley Plain was not mentioned. Dan briefly debated whether to raise it, but decided against it. It felt like a classic non-event, something which could not be discussed. This morning, the detective was back to his smart, efficient and decisive self, and that was the end of it. There was no other Adam Breen, only this model.

It was a fine morning to visit the hospice. The sun had risen higher in the sky, turning the Sound into a silver sheet. Several people were out walking in the grounds, a couple being pushed in their wheelchairs, blankets wrapped around them.

They waited in a long and echoing tiled corridor before a creaking of the old wooden staircase announced the arrival of Eleanor Paget. They shook hands. Her grip was firm, but with just a hint of perspiration, despite the cool of the day. Dan sensed the nervousness in her, and knew from Adam's thoughtful look that he did too.

Paget asked a passing nurse to get them some cups of tea, the tone of her voice making it clear it was one of those polite requests which is actually a command. The man looked alarmed to be stopped, then relieved to hear the mundanity of the issue. He didn't demur in the slightest and sped to do her bidding.

Paget led them to a small office, just a desk and a couple of chairs and apologised for its size.

'I like it to be modest,' she explained. 'All the room we have here should be devoted to the guests. I think a grand office in a charity gives off entirely the wrong signals.'

She was a tall woman, in her late thirties, perhaps early forties. Her hair was dark and the cut layered and obviously expensive, her clothes fashionable, smart and equally stylish. On the surface at least, she was a model of modern femininity: calm, self-assured and precise.

Dan immediately found himself thinking she had to be a long shot for a murderer, given her chosen profession of caring, then chastised himself for jumping to conclusions.

'Anyone can be a killer,' Adam had said yesterday, in one of the little speeches Dan had quickly come to understand he was fond of giving. 'Doctors and nurses have killed, brothers and sisters, husbands and wives, children and parents. Murderers can be old and young, black and white, religious and atheist. That's all a matter of history. If something snaps in the mind, be it a fast process or slow, anyone can kill.'

Dan was tempted to ask if he could write that down, but feared being seen as facetious.

'How was your relationship with Mr Bray?' Adam asked, after a brief preamble about how the hospice was faring.

Paget stared into space, then said, 'I hope you appreciate, this is going to be difficult for me. He was extraordinarily generous to us. In fact, without his help, we would not be here now. It's as simple as that. So I don't in any way want to denigrate his memory.'

'But?'

'But, naturally I don't want to mislead you either. And Edward Bray was not an easy man to work with.'

'Go on.'

She hesitated. 'I think he found the difference between running a business and a service hard to comprehend.'

'In what way?'

Her lips thinned. 'Well, firstly, he seemed to think that because of his generosity, he had a right to influence how the place was run. It was made clear to him from the outset, even before he'd given us all that money, that he didn't, but I don't think he heard. Or perhaps he didn't want to hear.' She paused again. 'So he would try … to bring his weight to bear.'

'Is that an understatement, by any chance?' Adam asked quietly.

She nodded. 'Yes.'

'He tried to tell you what to do?'

'Yes.'

'Persistently?'

'Almost unceasingly in fact.'

'And you resisted?'

'Yes.'

'You had rows?'

'Yes.'

'Often?'

Another hesitation. 'I wouldn't say often.'

'But they weren't uncommon?'

'No. They weren't.'

There was a silence. Outside, an electronic bell warbled. Fast footsteps echoed up the corridor. There was a hesitant knock on the door and the tea arrived, the nurse parking the cups on the desk and making a hasty retreat, as if this sanctum was a place to be feared and avoided. The way the man behaved reminded Dan of the feelings *Wessex Tonight* staff experienced when summoned to Lizzie's office. It was never a call to be told how jolly well you were doing, and how wonderfully delighted with your work the editor was.

'So, was there anything specific you disagreed about?' Adam prompted, after they'd each picked up their cups.

Paget managed a brief, humourless smile. 'Mr Bray could disagree with just about anyone on almost anything.'

'But anything in particular?'

'Well – I suppose the development of this place. For years, we've had vague plans for renovation. Nothing spectacular, just a bit of modernisation. But he had a real passion for changing it. He walked round with a clipboard, assessing how we worked, then he presented me with a report recommending changes.'

'Significant changes?'

'Fundamental ones. His analysis said we could accommodate a third more customers – we try to use the word guests, or occasionally perhaps patients, but he would always say customers – if we changed the dimensions of people's rooms.'

'Made them smaller?'

'Yes.'

'And you said?'

'I said no, of course. It would mean a great deal of disruption to people who are nearing the end of their lives. You can't treat them like that. They come here to die in peaceful surroundings, not in the middle of a building site. The trouble with Mr Bray was ...'

'Yes?'

'Well, if you want me to be absolutely honest, he saw everything as a business. How to cut costs, how to be more efficient, how to produce more television sets, or cans of beans, or whatever. And you just can't treat dying people like commodities.'

Adam jotted down a couple of notes. As ever, the detective's questioning had been sharp and precise, cutting to the core of what he wanted to know. But there was something missing. To Dan, it felt as though the obvious target had been peppered with hits, but there was something just behind it, more subtle yet still important that they hadn't touched, the image behind the mirror's glass.

Adam raised a couple more points, about the people who worked at the hospice, the guests and their families, anyone who might have had a particular disagreement with, or reason to dislike Bray, before he came to an issue which he introduced as his final one.

'Please don't take this the wrong way, but what were you doing on Monday evening at about six o'clock?'

Paget answered quickly, and Dan could see she had been prepared. 'I was out running. I often go for a jog about that time of day.'

'Whereabouts?'

'Around the grounds. And a bit of the cliffs too, if I'm feeling like it.'

'Even in the rain?'

She nodded. 'Yes. I go whatever the weather. I find it helps to give me thinking time.'

'And did anyone see you when you were out?'

'No, I don't think so. Not surprisingly, there weren't many others about that night.' She thought for a second, then said, 'Actually, I think Sally saw me.'

'Sally?'

'She's one of our guests. She likes a walk around the grounds too and goes out in most weather.'

Adam thanked her and got up from his chair. Dan rose too. There remained a ghost in the interview, he could feel its presence, but they still hadn't mentioned it. He wanted to ask, but he was here on trust and had been told very straightforwardly to keep quiet. He could feel the sweepstake running, almost as if a commentator was describing its progress in the background.

And he very much didn't want it to end yet.

Adam opened the office door and stepped out into the corridor. Dan shook Paget's hand, made to follow, then paused. On the wall hung a photograph, a group of patients in the summertime, all smiling at the camera, a couple even waving.

Sweet opportunity beckoned.

'Do you take photos of all your – err, guests?' he asked.

'Those who are happy to, yes. It's all part of their memory.'

Adam was standing in the corridor, looking back, arms folded across his chest, one polished shoe tapping on the tiles.

The commentator's voice grew louder.

'It's a nice idea,' Dan said.

'We think so.'

'Almost like school or college photos.'

'Almost.'

From the dense presence of the detective in the corridor came a cough sufficiently pointed to be used as a spear.

Dan wondered if they were on the sweepstake's home straight. But he'd prepared the ground and he'd gone through the build-up. He knew he had to ask.

'Was Edward Bray's mother a guest here?'

Adam took a step forwards, back into the doorway of the office. Paget glanced at him. The look was fast, nervous.

'Is that relevant to your investigation? I mean, when Mr Bray made his contribution to us we did agree on confidentiality. He wanted us to say only that the hospice would survive, thanks to his generosity, and nothing more. I appreciate now that he's dead the agreement no longer applies and I want to help you, but ...'

Her voice tailed off. Dan let his eyes slide to Adam. The detective's face was impassive. Seconds ticked past. Finally, he gave a small, very slight nod.

'In that case, I can tell you – yes,' Paget said. 'Mrs Bray was a guest here. Now, can I help you any further, or may I get on with my work?'

Adam's eyes slowly edged to Dan.

'There is just one more thing,' he said, trying to keep the tremble from his voice. 'Do you know what was the cause of the friction between Edward Bray and his father?'

Paget let out a slow sigh. 'Yes, I do. But in this case I'm sure it's not relevant to your inquiry ...'

'It was to do with Mrs Bray though, wasn't it?' Dan interrupted. 'It was something about the mother's death that caused the estrangement between father and son.'

She hesitated, went to speak, stopped herself. Finally, she said quietly, 'Look, I understand your interest, but I think if you really must find out about that you should take up the matter with Arthur Bray, not me.'

*　　　　*　　　　*

It felt a very long walk back to the car. Adam was silent the whole way.

Dan opened the door, got in and sat waiting for instructions. None came.

A couple of birds landed in one of the bushes bordering the hospice, hopped and chattered to each other.

Adam took out his papers and wrote a note. Dan shifted awkwardly in his seat, squinted against the morning sun.

He thought he could hear the commentator, announcing the winner of the sweepstake. Some cop would be going home considerably richer tonight.

Still, at least he'd learned a fair amount about detective work, and how major investigations were carried out.

It was just a shame he wouldn't be around to find out more.

A great shame.

Still, it had been interesting while it lasted. Enthralling in fact.

Ah, time to get it over with.

Dan hoped he wouldn't have to face a dressing down as well as being kicked off the investigation. He'd never got the hang of being quietly contrite. His temper wasn't designed for it.

Nor, if he was honest, his arrogance.

He went to speak, but found his voice wouldn't quite come.

Adam looked up, and this time Dan managed a throaty, 'Well?'

'Well what?'

'You know what.'

'If I knew what I wouldn't be asking.'

It sounded bizarrely like an argument Dan had had with his last girlfriend, prior to her announcing that she would prefer it if not only did they never speak again, she would like them never to meet again, and was considering emigrating in an attempt to ensure that was the case.

It hadn't been a great relationship.

'OK then,' Dan said petulantly. 'I mean me, breaking my silly little vows and not staying silent, like a good boy. I mean asking a question, daring to think I might have something useful to contribute. And actually finding something out too. Sure, we don't know whether it's relevant, important or whatever, but it must be better to know so we can work out whether we need to find out. It's an important point, isn't it? What caused the split between Edward Bray and his dad? I thought it was a decent question, and one that should be asked. And if you think …'

With rare self-awareness, Dan realised he was ranting and forced himself to shut up.

'Well then?' he added, setting his chin in the air.

Adam tapped his pen on the files. 'You are here on trust,' he said calmly. 'I would indeed prefer it if you kept quiet. And if there's something you really think you need to contribute, then it would be better if you asked me first. But …'

'But?'

'But, as that was a reasonable question and might indeed be relevant, on this occasion we can put it down to beginner's enthusiasm and overlook it.'

Adam went back to his notes, and even had the audacity to begin humming a gentle tune to himself.

A feeling rose in Dan which would grow very familiar over the years to come. He could imagine his hands reaching out to throttle Adam Breen.

He took a couple of breaths to calm himself, then asked, 'Right, where next?'

'Back to Charles Cross. I need some time to go through what we've heard from all our witnesses – or suspects – and work out where to take the inquiry next. I doubt it's something you'll find interesting, or useful. You can have the afternoon off, from detective work at least.'

Dan flinched. 'You are chucking me off the case after all. I knew you would. You're just doing it nicely.'

Adam gave him a look. 'I can assure you I'm not. When I chuck you off the case, you'll know about it. It won't be at all nicely.'

The fickle princess of luck had favoured him with a kiss.

And, Dan thought, if it hadn't turned him into a handsome prince, it had at least made him feel as though life was running his way.

It was early evening and he was walking down to Mutley Plain to meet El for a drink. In his invitations the photographer always said, "Fancy a beer?', only ever the singular, never plural, but it was inevitably more misleading than a government minister's parliamentary statement. El had never drunk a single beer in his life, and nor had anyone who dared to venture out with him.

A night with El was invariably accompanied by a morning with a sore head.

Dan had got back to the newsroom just before lunchtime to find a prevailing state of excitement. The lack of a manic phone call from Lizzie, demanding a story, had suggested something was going on, and now he found out what. The government had announced a major order for some new destroyers, and in a region with historic naval connections like the South-west that meant jobs galore and for years to come.

Wessex Tonight would be dominated by the announcement, with a series of reports and live interviews, and for those not involved, that meant the opportunity to quietly disappear, if so minded.

Dan had found himself so minded, and duly planned to disappear quietly.

He had lunch in the canteen, an ill-defined pie, filled out a few expenses claims, checked on the progress of a couple of court cases and generally took it easy. By three, he was ready to slip away, and then, with the timing that only those in league with the Devil can master, El rang. He was babbling about a story, a highly lucrative one, which he badly needed Dan's help with. Could they meet tonight to discuss it? Over a beer, funded entirely by him, naturally.

They could. An El in need of help was a generous friend, it had been a busy and productive week, and a beer or two was clearly justified.

Before he left the newsroom, just to reassure himself, Dan called Charles Cross and was put through to the MIR. He'd asked for Adam's mobile number earlier in the week and was answered only with a raised eyebrow. He didn't bother pursuing the question.

A young woman answered, and after the clamping of a hand over the mouthpiece and some ritual background chuckling the detective's masterful voice graced the line.

'I just wanted to check with you about tomorrow,' Dan said, trying his best not to sound nervous. 'To see what we're going to be doing.'

'I'm not sure yet. But at the very least we can start working through what the teams have found out about our various suspects and their alibis – or lack of them. Can you come to Charles Cross for ten and we'll take it from there?'

'Sure.'

So, he was still on the inquiry, he'd asked his first question in a police investigation and it had been judged by Adam to be a good one. He had a date for the weekend, some beers in prospect for tonight and it would soon be Christmas. The Swamp was at bay, the tablets still hidden in the bathroom cabinet, unused and unrequired. Even the fine weather of the day was holding.

Sometimes life could be almost worth living. Dan allowed himself a brief grin as he walked.

El was waiting in the Old Bank pub, sitting right in the far corner. He was seldom happy unless he sat with his back to a wall. The explanation, he said, was twofold. Firstly, he always liked to see if there was anything happening which might be worth a photograph. Secondly, in all his years snapping various criminals and hoodlums he'd managed to accrue a considerable number of enemies, and wanted as much advance warning as possible if any were bearing down upon him.

El had already got a couple of pints in, so Dan sat down and had a sip. The photographer looked at him expectantly, rocking back and forth on his seat. He resembled a schoolchild who knew a birthday treat awaited when lessons were finally over for the day, and was within minutes of the sacred bell.

Dan realised he wasn't to be afforded any time to enjoy his drink. 'OK, what is it?'

'Need your help, badly, badly, badly. Snappy snap a piccie for lots of lovely loot.'

Dan blinked hard. At times of excitement El had a tendency

to adopt a language all of his own. Dan was practiced in translation, but even he was left baffled by some of his friend's more impenetrable babble.

'Meaning?' he asked, patiently.

El explained, in roughly comprehensible English. He'd been tipped off that a local scoutmaster had been arrested on suspicion of paedophilia. It was potentially a big case, the allegations going back twenty years or more. He was a well-known man, prominent in business and the community, a tireless fundraiser for charity and a greatly respected figure of impeccable reputation.

'They always are,' Dan observed sadly.

In a quiet police operation he had been arrested and taken to Charles Cross for questioning. There he was being held, and was expected to remain in custody for several days.

Then came the problem, the crease in El's contentment. There were plenty of pictures in the various newspaper and TV archives of the man, but none dated from within the last 18 months.

'So ...' El said, grinning.

'So, a current snap would be worth thousands to you.'

'Yep.'

'And probably even more if it could be taken at the police station, to emphasise his fall from grace.'

'Yeppy yep.'

'But he's safely in the cells and you haven't got a hope of getting one.'

'Bingo! The man on the TV holes in one.' El leaned forward, whispered slyly, 'And the word is that you're in with the cops.'

Dan sat back on his seat. 'Well, I'm shadowing the Bray case. But there's a big difference between that and getting them to parade a suspected paedophile so you can get a snap of him.'

El pulled a face. 'There'll be a big night out for you if you can help poor old El. Call it his Christmas present.'

Dan promised he would have a think and perhaps a word in the right places, to see what he could do. But, as often with El, it felt like he was asking the impossible.

They chatted about the various stories El was working on, the usual round of snaps of villains and victims, when Dan's mobile rang.

He jogged outside and answered. It was a withheld number, which usually meant work. But not this time, at least not his official work.

'Dan, it's Chief Inspector Breen.'

'How did you get my number?'

'Never mind that. Are you at a pub?'

'Well, outside one. How did you know?'

'I can hear the guilt in your voice. How many have you had?'

'Only a couple.'

'Well, don't have any more. We've got an important lead, but it means a long trip and an early start tomorrow. Can you come into Charles Cross for seven?'

Dan didn't hesitate. 'Sure.'

They chatted a little more about the details of what they would be doing, Dan hung up, went back inside, finished his pint and made his apologies. It would be the quietest night he had ever known with El, but from what Adam had just said he suspected it would be well worth it.

Chapter Eleven

THE FINE WEATHER PERSISTED, but its blessing of yesterday had today turned to a curse.

They were driving east, directly into the rising sun. Dan flicked back and forth at the visor and in twenty minutes of irritable experimentation and adjustment managed to prove a rule of motoring. No matter what angle he found for the flap it was never quite right, either allowing the blaze of the sun to dazzle his eyes, or block out so much of the road that he might as well have been driving in Braille.

Adam had reclined in the passenger seat, his eyes closed, and his hands folded contentedly over his stomach. Dan glanced enviously, and a little tetchily across.

'No, I'm not asleep,' the detective and mind reader said, without opening an eye. 'I'm just thinking. And yes, I will share the driving with you. In a while, anyway.'

'Well, thank you so very much,' Dan replied, trying to keep the sarcasm from his voice.

They were heading for Brighton, a long trek, maybe three-quarters of the girth of southern England, across five counties and busy roads. Adam calculated that if they left Plymouth at seven, they would suffer only a quiet rush hour in sleepy Dorset and maximise the chances of an easy trip. Now, for the first time, they were going to meet a man who Adam described as a "strong suspect".

They passed Exeter and turned off towards Dorset. Now, as if suffering a famine of funding, the roads became thinner, a mix of single and dual carriageway, designed to help the driver where possible, but in fact having the effect of making the area a magnet for accidents. The sun gradually shifted into the southern sky and Dan stopped squinting. He turned on the radio, was rewarded with a irritable grunt from the still reclining detective to his left, and turned it off again.

A couple of colleagues in the newsroom had asked about the glamour of shadowing the police. Dan dutifully built up the excitement of being part of a major inquiry, the initiation into esoteric knowledge and the feeling of the power of justice guiding your actions.

Oddly enough, he'd overlooked to mention he spent much of his time as a chauffeur.

A motorbike roared by. It must have been doing well over a hundred, despite a looming bend. It was followed by another one. Adam opened an eye then closed it again.

'Take it easy,' Dan muttered to himself. 'Don't burn yourself out.'

'I won't,' came the easy reply.

They reached Dorchester and passed Poundbury, Prince Charles vision of a modern community. It marked the edge of *Wessex Tonight*'s broadcast area, and, as if on cue, Dan started to feel twitchy about what he was doing. He'd agreed instinctively to come to Brighton without properly thinking it through and without discussing it with Lizzie.

In principle his job was self scheduling. He told the newsroom where he should be going and what stories he should handle. But with a boss like Lizzie that was never going to be the sweet reality.

Dan thought he could probably justify the trip. It was certainly part of his education in the mystic ways of the detectives, and it might be an important breakthrough. But then again, it could well come to nothing and he would be a long way from home if the newsroom started demanding a story.

To distract himself, Dan thought about El's request. But it was a tough ask and he couldn't see any obvious way to help the photographer get the snap he needed. Instead, he worked through the weekend and thought about where he might take Kerry. They could visit another pub or restaurant, but it would surely be better to inject a little creativity.

The car rumbled as they crossed a bridge over a glittering river and with it came the inspiration. If the weather held, Dan had the perfect idea for their next date. It was original and romantic, would make Rutherford happy, and be useful too in a long-running quest which had grown to an inch from an obsession.

'What are you smiling about?' Adam inquired, this time having the decency to sit up in his seat.

'I, err ...'

Dan debated whether to say, then realised his history of trying to deceive the detective was hardly impressive. But before he could speak, Adam added, 'Ah, it's a woman thing I think.'

'Yes.'

'A new woman?'

'Yes.'

'You going on a date?'

'Yes.'

'Where?'

Dan told him. 'Cute,' came the verdict. 'Nice idea. It'll make for a good day out.'

'I hope so. What are you up to at the weekend?'

Adam's expression changed in an instant. A portcullis had come slamming down.

'Not a lot.'

He settled back into the seat, closing his eyes again. Dan drove on.

Just before they reached the motorway at Southampton, they swapped seats and Adam took the wheel. He drove like a police officer who has people in the car he doesn't quite trust. Every slight manoeuvre was announced with an indicator, and their speed was a constant 70 miles per hour.

Apart from a slight hold up caused by a badly parked delivery lorry near Worthing they made good time. It was only when they reached the outskirts of Brighton that Adam deigned to impart the full briefing on who they were going to see, and why.

His name was Alex Spearing. He was a property developer, and a man who had a sizeable grudge against Edward Bray.

The story went back a couple of years. A hotel on Brighton seafront was closing, the Victorian block on offer for redevelopment. The property market was simmering nicely and there was much interest in turning the building into flats, many boasting balconies and fine sea views. The word was that the contract could be worth millions.

A building firm, which had a history of working with Bray, was interested and got together with the businessman to put in a bid. He would provide the cash, they would do the work on the conversions, the profits would be split.

Such was the interest the sale went to an auction. Bray and Spearing were the final bidders. Both were very well resourced and even more determined.

'It's not clear from the briefing what happened at the sale,' Adam said. 'But from what came later, it looks to me like the men got involved in a macho bidding war. I think they offered to pay much more than the building was worth as they tried to outdo each other. Put simply, it came down to pride. And that can be very dangerous. I've seen pride lie behind many a murder.'

Spearing won. At the time, the analysts said he had paid a great deal of money, but, if his plans worked out, and if the property market held up, he could still make a decent profit.

It was one it too many.

The housing market faltered and failed. Prices started to fall, first a couple of per cent, then more, finally gaining momentum to savage losses. Flats were hit even worse. There was a flood of supply and a desert of demand.

Spearing just about managed to keep his business afloat, but he had to sell a large proportion of his properties. He went from being a very rich man to the owner of just another struggling business. It was touch and go whether it would survive.

And, naturally, Spearing could never accept he might just have written the script for his own tragedy. As people do in times of adversity, he looked around for someone else to blame.

And there was Edward Bray.

He had sent threatening letters, and on the occasion of a business trip to Plymouth made a point of going to Bray's offices to make his feelings clear.

On the basis of all that alone Spearing would have been someone the police, in their euphemistic language, would quickly have spoken to "in order to eliminate him from our inquiries". He would have been phoned, an appointment made, detectives from Brighton sent, not the officer in charge of the case, all the way from Plymouth, and with no warning.

But two other factors came into play. Firstly, Spearing had what Adam contentedly referred to as "form". And not just any form. As a horse in a steeplechase must enjoy fences and ditches, and an athlete in a marathon must be au fait with endurance, so a potential killer must have a taste for violence.

And Spearing did. He had been convicted of two counts of assault against his tenants, one leaving a woman with minor injuries, the other, a young man, with a broken nose.

He had served six months in prison, and came out a reformed man.

Or so he said.

Because then came the second factor.

Alex Spearing lived in Brighton. The great majority of his business was in and around Brighton. His friends were in Brighton.

But on the afternoon and evening of Monday, December 14th, Alex Spearing was in Plymouth.

They made a brief stop in the city centre, then drove to Spearing's office. Where once he'd had an impressive building at the heart of the commercial quarter, now the company had moved to a few rooms in a run-down terrace. There were plenty of parking spaces available along the street, always a sure sign of an absence of affluence.

'Right,' Adam said, as he got out of the car. 'Just another friendly word. This could easily become a nasty confrontation, but, whatever, it's a key interview, probably the most important so far, so if you could keep quiet I'd be grateful.'

Dan noticed his throat was feeling dry and his back had begun to sweat. Memories of the hunt for the man who attacked the prostitutes flitted through his mind, the knowledge that at any second he could be facing someone armed and desperate to escape.

'OK,' was all he managed to say.

Adam checked his reflection in the car's window and strode

into the office. A young woman was squatting down, filing some papers. Beyond her was another door, a little ajar. Adam pushed past and into the room at the back.

'Morning,' he said, cheerily.

'Oh fuck,' replied the man sitting behind the desk.

Spearing turned out to be surprisingly affable, ostensibly at least. When Adam had explained what he wanted, the businessman visibly relaxed.

'I thought you were the bailiffs,' he said. 'Come to take what little I've got left. The bastards.'

He spat the words with a sting of bile. It could hardly have been clearer his business was on the cliff edge, and the land beneath eroding rapidly.

Adam went through a string of questions about Spearing's dealings with Edward Bray. Dan noticed the technique was exactly the same as his own when interviewing. First, the gentle warm up questions to establish a relationship, get the person talking, then hit them with what you really wanted to ask.

There was the hint of an odd smell in the room, which Dan couldn't place, but which he knew he'd met before somewhere. He sniffed hard, but couldn't bring the memory home. Under the desk, out of sight of Spearing, Adam's foot tapped against Dan's ankle. He took the hint, sat still and breathed easily.

The room was tatty, and apart from a board covered in letters and memos, many of them ringed with red borders, no attempt had been made to make it look more businesslike. Dan wondered how much fight Spearing had left to keep his company going. Everyone, however tough, has their threshold of surrender.

He was a tubby man who looked pasty, tired, and drawn. His appearance was nigh the opposite of the photograph Adam had in his file. In that, Spearing was much thinner, dressed in a well-cut suit, had a tan and looked strong and healthy. Now the man's hair was too long and straggled over his ears, and there were a couple of stains on his jacket.

'I should have asked,' he said. 'Do you want a cup of tea?'

Adam declined the offer. 'Then do you mind if I pop to the

loo?' Spearing asked.

The detective nodded and Spearing got up, walked out of the door and down a corridor, towards the back of the building. A door crashed open and through the window they could see Spearing lumbering fast towards a gate in the back garden.

It had surprised Dan that, in contrast to the police dramas he'd seen so often on the television, his experience of the investigation so far had revealed very little swearing. But now, for the first time in their acquaintance, Adam found a profanity.

'Arsehole,' he said, but didn't get up from his chair.

Spearing was wrestling with the gate, tugging at it, but it refused to give. He glanced over his shoulder, stood back and gave it a mighty kick, then another.

Still Adam didn't move.

'Do you think we should do something?' Dan asked mildly.

'We have done something,' Adam replied. 'Remember the little stop in town?'

'Oh yes. Sorry. In all the anticipation and excitement, I forgot.'

Still the gate wouldn't move. Spearing took another run up, slammed himself into it, then yanked hard at the handle. This time it flew open.

He pulled himself up and lurched towards the opening, straight into the arms of the two waiting police officers.

'Right then, let's try again,' Adam said, when Spearing had been escorted back to his seat. 'And this time, if you could bear in mind that you're a suspect for murder and that I've had a little rummage through your desk.'

The man's mouth fell open, although it wasn't clear which of the points Adam had raised was bothering him the most. It was cold in the room, but despite that Spearing was sweating.

While he was outside, Adam had opened a couple of drawers in the desk and found a clear packet containing a white powder. He dipped in a fingertip, tasted it and nodded to himself.

'Cocaine?' Dan asked. 'I think I recognised the smell from the toilets of the odd shady nightclub I've visited.'

'Yep. You did your best to give us away by gulping at the

air like a dying fish, but it'll be a useful bit of leverage.'

'Sorry. I'm doing my best, but I don't think I've quite got the hang of police work yet.'

Adam didn't reply, just waited for Spearing to return.

'Right then, about the murder of Edward Bray.'

'I didn't kill him.'

'You didn't like him.'

'I bloody hated him.'

'I'm sorry, I stand corrected. You hated him and you were in Plymouth on Monday evening when he was killed.'

Spearing visibly recoiled. 'I wasn't.'

Adam sighed and folded his arms. 'I don't know why we have to go through these routines. You people always leg it when we come calling, so we always put cops round the back. We get some important information, you deny it. It's like a bad comedy. So, as I was saying, you were in Plymouth on Monday evening.'

'I wasn't.'

'Right, if I could just remind you about the little packet of special recreational powder in your desk drawer.'

The businessman looked away. Finally, he said, 'It's only a little bit. And just for me. Times have been difficult lately. It helps me get by.'

'And it's not particularly what I'm interested in. Now, about Plymouth on Monday?'

'Yeah, all right, I was there.'

'Why?'

'Business.'

'What business?'

'The usual. Looking at places. I wondered if there might be some bargains to be had in the housing. Property going cheap. I'm stuffed here. It's all too expensive. No one wants to know me. I was hoping there might be something to help me get back on my feet.'

'Who did you meet?'

'No one. I just went to look around.'

The disbelief was as subtle as a drunken proposition. 'You just went to look around?'

'Yeah.'

'You drove all that way, hundreds of miles, to look around?'

'Yeah.'

'You didn't meet anyone who can confirm what you were doing and when?'

'No.'

'So you just walked around all day, looking at properties?'

'Yeah.'

'In the pouring rain?'

'Yeah.'

Adam sat back on his chair. 'This is going to come as a terrible shock to you, Mr Spearing, but I'm afraid I don't believe you.'

The businessman looked entirely unsurprised. 'No.'

'OK then, let's try this one more time. Either you start telling me the truth, or you're under arrest on suspicion of murder and for possessing Class A drugs.'

Spearing laid his head down on his hands. 'Shit,' he moaned.

'Which I would say just about sums up your position,' Adam replied. 'Now then, last chance. What were you doing in Plymouth on Monday?'

Spearing raised his head. 'If I tell you the truth, it doesn't go any further, OK?'

'I don't think you're in any position to barter. Just tell me what you were doing and we'll take it from there.'

And, slowly, Alex Spearing did.

Chapter Twelve

THEY LEFT SPEARING IN the tender care of the two large Sussex Police constables while they went to get some lunch.

'We can't do anything for an hour or two, while Suzanne checks out his story, so we might as well,' Adam said. 'Plus, it'll give him time to stew, and might make him more inclined to talk.'

They walked for a few minutes to the Lanes, a maze of shops, restaurants, arcades and boutiques, just outside the main shopping centre.

The sun was high in the sky now, and the day almost warm for an English winter. A few people sat outside the cafes, the insulation of coats and scarves well tucked around them. All the shop windows were full of tinsel and glitter, and suggestions for last minute Christmas presents. They passed a baker's, the air rich with the smell of mince pies. Seagulls wheeled, screeching in the air, circling a row of rubbish bins, looking for their cuisine of choice.

'It's just like being back in Plymouth,' Dan mused.

He stopped at a second-hand jeweller's and scanned the gold and silver in the display. They had a fine selection of watches, particularly Rolex. "Best prices in town", read a sign.

'My last watch packed up a few weeks ago,' Dan said. 'I've always wanted to get myself a decent one.'

'How about a decent lunch first?' Adam replied.

There were so many restaurants it was difficult to choose. All were boasting special offers, fixed price menus, the familiar two-for-one deals. They looked at the menu of a Chinese buffet, a quaint Italian place, then a French bistro.

Adam's phone rang, he picked it out of his pocket, went to answer and then stopped when he saw the name on the display. Something in his face changed. With a policeman's way, he held up a peremptory hand to Dan, as if to say wait, and stalked around the corner.

Dan used the time to ring the newsroom. He'd turned his

phone to silent for the interview with Spearing and hadn't been in the least surprised to find four missed calls, but just a single message. That could mean only one thing. It was the tempest known as Lizzie, and as surprising as the sun rising, or rain in the summertime, she wanted a story.

'You're where?' came the incredulous reaction, her voice hitting a note of which an irascible toddler would have been proud.

'Brighton.'

'I'm sure this is my omission, but I don't remember Brighton being in our patch.'

'Technically, it isn't. But there's a hot lead here, the possibility of a big story for us, so I thought I'd better come.'

'The possibility?'

'There might be an arrest – the first one – of a prime suspect for the Bray murder.'

'Might be? Might be doesn't make stories. Might be doesn't fill the programme! Might be doesn't fascinate the viewers.'

Dan sensed the rocket was on the launch pad, and the countdown was nearing its climax. He held the phone a little way from his ear. Lizzie in full flow could be painfully loud.

'I want news! I want reports! I want developments! I want them now! Get back to me when you've got a story happening, not when something "might be".'

Dan pulled a face at the phone and returned to studying the menu. French food had never been his favourite. Too fiddly, and rarely coming in sufficient quantities for the demands of his rapacious stomach.

Adam skulked back around the corner. His face was like a storm cloud over the hills.

'I can't do lunch,' he snapped. 'I'm going to have to nip off. Meet me back at Spearing's place in an hour.'

'Are you OK? Is it work?'

'No, it's not work and yes, I'm fine.'

His hand was gripping his mobile so hard the skin had turned white. Seldom could someone have sounded less fine. Adam turned and walked quickly away.

*   *   *

Dan bought himself a newspaper, walked back to the Italian and enjoyed an excellent lunch of fresh pasta in a tomato and bacon sauce. Like a good parent, he slipped out of the restaurant for a few moments and rang his downstairs neighbour who reassured him that Rutherford was fine, had been taken out for a walk and was currently chewing happily at his own lunch.

Dan tried not to be disappointed about not eating with Adam, but mostly failed. He wanted to talk through the case, particularly what the detective thought of Spearing. The businessman had eventually, and with great reluctance, volunteered the information about what he was doing in Plymouth. It involved a woman, he said, someone with whom he had been having an on-off affair for quite a while. She was married, so he had booked a hotel and they had spent much of the evening together before she returned home.

When Adam asked, with genuine sensitivity Dan thought, if it wasn't a long way to go for a tryst, Spearing said, 'You probably won't believe this, but I didn't see it as just a night's fun. She's very special to me. I hardly even noticed the drive. Things are bad for me at the moment. I was feeling low. I just needed to see her and hold her.'

Adam nodded, but insisted on taking the woman's contact details, reassuring Spearing that she would be spoken to discreetly. His story would also be checked with the hotel.

It had felt like a turning point in the interview. Whereas before Adam was pointed and probing, even occasionally hostile, now he became more sympathetic.

Dan wondered if he might be beginning to understand the boundary lines between the personal and professional Adam Breen.

Suzanne and another detective were checking Spearing's story. They would have an answer as to whether he could have been the killer of Edward Bray within a couple of hours.

Dan paid the bill, and with a nod to the season left a generous tip. Sitting in the restaurant, on his own, he'd begun to feel lonely. He was a long way from home and Christmas was coming. Just as it had been for as long as Dan cared to remember he'd be spending much of it in the flat, with

Rutherford, opening the presents he'd bought the dog, then the ones he'd bought for himself.

The Swamp sucked hard at the edge of his mind.

In a fatal instant of reflection the eternal foe was back.

It was there, lurking in the dark shadows at the gates of his mind. The enemy he carried everywhere and which would never quite leave him, no matter for how long he ran or how hard he battled.

It was the perfect prison. The jail inside yourself.

The Swamp of the depression that had stalked Dan for all his days.

With its darkness and dankness. Its cloying, sticky, fetid and apathetic air. Its unconquerable mountains. Its greyness and its vastness, and the unshakeable certainty that it could never be escaped.

Dan tried to cheer himself, thinking of the coming weekend and his plans for a day out with Kerry. It was time to tell her his idea. He sent a text and got one back as quickly as a top tennis player returning a serve.

"That'd be lovely! What a great idea! Look forward to it! x"

She was certainly a woman who liked her exclamation marks. Only the kiss had survived the scattergun of punctuation. But the message revived his spirits and he smiled.

Dan ignored the warning voice at the back of his mind, telling him of the danger of mood swings. They had always been an omen of the Swamp gathering its strength.

Well, it could naff off, for now at least. Dan had promised himself the tablets would stay in the bathroom cupboard, and he was holding to that. He wasn't resorting to them again.

The problem was in his head. As must be the solution.

The false hope of the little bottle of pills could stay hidden. Let them gather dust. He could carry the fight himself. And he would .

Dan was going to cheer himself up further. It was time to not so much splash, but more deluge, out on some naughty Christmas shopping, all entirely for him.

The shop was an anachronism, with its oil lamps, fob watches, chandeliers and grandfather clocks. The man behind the counter even wore a waistcoat.

He spotted Dan eyeing the window display and turned on the showman's patter.

'I see you're bare on the wrist there, good sir. Well, you've come to the right place. We've got the best watches and the best prices in town, and as it's Christmas I might even be able to go a little further and offer you a seasonal knockdown deal.'

Dan was shown a selection of watches, some picked out in gold, others silver, and more than a couple with glittering jewels sparkling from their beautiful faces.

It felt like slipping under a hypnotist's spell.

'I need something good and robust,' he said.

The shopkeeper looked him up and down. 'And fit for some adventuring, I'd say, judging by sir's fine physique.'

'Well, perhaps the odd bit of walking and some running.'

'And from sir's clothes – no doubt the need to appear smart, stylish and successful.'

'Oh yes.'

'But without being flash.'

Dan wasn't sure how to take that. He was wearing one of his new jackets and a new shirt too, and flash was exactly what he'd thought when he bought them.

'Not too flash, no.'

'Perhaps a little bit flash? A small flare of flashiness? For the benefit of the ladies?'

'A little flash would be fine.'

The man's practiced hand darted to a silver watch at the edge of the display.

'Et voilà!' he proclaimed. 'The Rolex Submariner. Ideal for all the gentleman's requirements. Robust, yet a little flash, the perfect watch for the adventurer.'

The price tag looked like the culmination of a long maths lesson, but Dan was already reaching for his wallet.

It's an unfortunate fact of life, Dan reflected, that what we want people to notice, be it a new haircut, or a pair of shoes, they rarely do. However, that which we would much rather they

127

missed, like a blossoming spot or a stain on a jacket, can almost always be guaranteed to catch the eye.

Such was the way with Dan's new watch.

Despite it being winter, he felt the need to take off his jacket at every conceivable opportunity and roll up his sleeves at the slightest chance. He kept looking at the watch, monitoring each passing minute in the hope of catching a wandering eye.

And no one noticed.

Adam's mood had not improved. They met back at Spearing's office to find the businessman talking to some prospective tenants. The two Sussex constables had the diplomatic decency to wait outside, but close enough to catch the man should he make another run for it.

He didn't, and Dan suspected that told Adam all he needed to know, even before Suzanne's call came through.

Spearing's alibi checked out. The woman he met, after being guaranteed confidentiality, had verified it, the hotel receptionist had verified it, and on the unlikely assumption they were in league and both lying, the diligent Suzanne had viewed the hotel's CCTV and that verified it too. Spearing was checking in at the very moment Edward Bray was checking out, for the final time.

They got back into the car at just before four o'clock, according to the new watch, which still hadn't attracted any of the attention it so patently deserved. Dan assumed he was driving and he was right. Adam didn't say a word, just climbed wearily into the passenger seat. This time he didn't recline, instead he sat staring morosely out of the windscreen.

Dan made a couple of attempts at conversation, which were rebuffed with monosyllabic grunts, as effective as mere waves against mighty cliffs. Instead he turned on the radio, found a news channel and concentrated on that.

Lizzie had called earlier, and Dan broke the bad news to her that there would be no story.

'A day wasted!'

'It wasn't wasted. It was a good idea to come, just in case. And I learnt some more about police work.'

'The viewers didn't learn anything about the police

investigation into Bray's death though, and that's the point of you shadowing the cops. I want a story, I want it on Monday, and I want it without fail. You hear that? Without fail!'

At least it was Friday and he had two days break from his manic editor and her relentless demands. And he had a new watch, proud on his wrist for all the world to see.

Except the world still hadn't had the decency to so much as notice.

It was a good hour into the drive before Adam spoke. 'Well, it came to nothing, but we had to go.'

'Yeah, you're right. What did you do about his little cocaine stash?'

'I left it to the Sussex boys to decide about that. They might just turn a blind eye. It's a lot of paperwork for not much of a crime, and the guy was on his knees as it was. The Sussex cops do though reckon Spearing might have been up to some tax fraud as well, which is probably why he ran, but they can sort all that out. Now, what time do you reckon we'll get back to Plymouth?'

'Depending on the traffic, by about eight. You in a rush?'

'No,' Adam replied heavily. 'Not in the least.'

They chatted a little more about what would happen in the inquiry over the weekend. Unless there was a particularly urgent development there was no need to pay for hours of overtime, so the investigation would tick over with just a few junior staff working. And, as Adam put it, 'Bray will still be dead on Monday,' so he planned to have most of the weekend off.

'Good,' Dan replied. 'That means I can too. I could do with it. It's been quite a week.'

They lapsed back into silence. Despite it being the Friday evening before Christmas they were lucky and didn't hit any hold-ups. It was only when they were on the outskirts of Plymouth, at just before eight, that Adam sprang his surprise.

'Have you got any plans for tonight?' he asked.

'No. I was just going to go home. You?'

'No. None. Do you fancy a bite to eat and a beer?'

Dan would have turned around to check no one else was in

the car, if he hadn't had the benefit of a four-hour drive to assure him of that point.

'Yeah,' he said slowly. 'That'd be, err – good.'

Dan parked the car at Charles Cross, and they headed into town.

All the bars were filled with people, full of the spirit of the season, and ably assisted by the alcohol they were so eagerly consuming. Women wore tinsel in their hair, men Santa Claus hats and beards. This time next week it would be Christmas.

The sky had stayed clear and the air had grown cold and sharp with it. Groups of committed smokers huddled in beer gardens and outside doorways, taxis rushed back and forth, loading and unloading their shouting and staggering cargoes. The city echoed to the pump of music and the shouts and screams of the weekend revellers. It was no place for the sober.

Adam and Dan walked past a couple of pubs, the music too loud, the crowd too boisterous for it to be worthwhile trying to find a table. On the edge of the waterfront of the Barbican they found a bar which was a little less packed and had a decent menu.

'It does beer,' said Dan, squinting through the misty glass at the promise of the pumps.

'And food,' Adam replied. 'Come on, I need to unwind.'

They found a table for two at the back. A waiter slid over, favoured them with a soppy smile and made a show of lighting the fine red candle that stood between them.

'I can't help but suspect,' Dan said, 'that our waiter believes we're a couple.'

Adam took off his jacket. 'Don't. I've got enough problems on that front as it is.'

Dan kept quiet, waited, held the detective's look, but Adam quickly grabbed a menu and began studying the lines of dishes.

'Looks OK,' he said hurriedly.

'Yes. Looks OK.'

And for the next few minutes they discussed the menu. In fairness, it looked better than OK. The bar had just taken on a Thai chef and was offering a tempting array of dishes. The waiter, who was still smiling, brought them a couple of pints of beer, and it was fresh and tasty. Dan made a note to come back here soon. Real ale and Thai food, a heady combination.

Most of the drinkers had congregated around the bar, and where they sat it was quiet enough to talk without being forced to shout.

'So, if nothing much is happening over the weekend, what do we do on Monday?' Dan asked.

'Go through what the teams have found out about our various suspects' movements and alibis around the time Bray was killed. Then, by a process of elimination, try to narrow down who the murderer might have been.'

'Do you think you'll get him?'

'We'll get him. It may take a while, but we'll get him. Our murderer has left us one big clue, which I think will give him away.'

Adam looked at Dan expectantly, and he sensed another test. 'The cancelled appointment. From exactly a week before Bray was killed.'

'Spot on. That's the key to the case.'

Their starters arrived, a couple of fish soups. Clouds of delicious scent wafted from the bowls.

'Mmm, excellent,' was Adam's verdict. 'So, how're you finding police work?'

'In a word, fascinating. More to the point, how am I doing at it?'

'In a couple of words, pretty well.'

'It hasn't been easy. I didn't exactly feel welcome to start with.'

'You weren't, to say the least. But you're doing better now.'

Dan lay down his spoon. 'Am I?'

'Yep. With your coverage of our knifeman, you made a few people realise you could be useful. You've kept quiet, listened and learned, not risen to the taunts, and you've also made me some money.'

'Have I? How?'

'The sweepstake. As I had the power to chuck you off the case, I didn't enter it – in case, by some bizarre coincidence, you were thrown out at the very moment I'd picked and I was accused of fixing it. But I did put in my money and took the final option, the one that no one else would want.'

'Which was?'

'That you wouldn't get thrown off at all this week – and you haven't. So I've won. For which I will buy you a beer.' Adam lifted his glass. 'Cheers!'

The waiter brought them some more drinks followed by their main courses, a couple of green curries. They were also delicious. A party of young men walked into the bar, looked around and quickly left again.

'Not enough women here,' Adam observed. 'I was the same myself at that age.'

Dan studied the detective, wondered whether he wanted to talk, but kept quiet. So far, every effort he'd made to find out more about Adam and his life had ricocheted straight off the armour plating of his defences.

The fire of the curry had prompted their glasses to empty once more, and the waiter brought replenishments. Adam took off his tie, curled it up carefully and slipped it into his jacket pocket. Dan noticed he was feeling light headed, probably a combination of the efforts of the week, a long drive today, and the beer. He would sleep well that night.

He checked his watch, held it up high and made a point of studying it at length, but still no one noticed, still less produced the requisite admiring comment. The magnificent chronometer said it was just after ten, but oddly the clock on the wall was registering ten past. The clock must be wrong, could in no way be any form of competition for the global apex of the watchmaker's art of which Dan was the proud new owner.

They talked a little more about the inquiry, the various people they had met over the last few days and finished their drinks.

'Time to get the bill, I think,' Adam said, and took out his wallet. Dan glimpsed a picture of a young boy, perhaps six or seven years old, smiling from a photograph.

'My son, Tom,' Adam explained. 'A little terror sometimes, but a great lad.'

Dan studied the picture. 'Aren't they all terrors at that age? He looks like you.'

'Yes, so people say. I'll probably take him to the football at the weekend.'

'Plymouth Argyle?'

'Yep. We usually re-enact the match afterwards. I have to go in goal, of course.'

'Of course. Well, that sounds fair enough to me. It's a father's duty to be peppered with shots.'

'Yes.'

'Are you planning anything much else at the weekend?'

'Not much,' Adam said quietly. 'Not a lot, no.'

They paid the bill, thanked the smiling waiter and left him a good tip. He deserved it, he'd had plenty of exercise at their behest. It was early enough to make getting a taxi straightforward, most people were still in the bars, not yet heading for clubs or home. They hailed a black cab, piled in and settled into the seats.

'Mutley Plain please,' Adam told the driver.

'I thought you lived in Peverell?' Dan queried.

Adam stared out of the window. They passed a couple of police officers trying to break up a fight, and a group of women clustered around a young girl who was being violently sick against a wall.

'Yeah, I sometimes live in Peverell,' Adam said finally. 'What I mean is …'

His voice tailed off. The cab stopped at some traffic lights, then rumbled forwards again.

'Well, what happened is this,' Adam continued. 'Annie, that's Tom's mum, and I, well we …'

They reached Mutley Plain, the strip of bars and clubs buzzing with a procession of people.

'Anywhere along here guv?' the driver asked.

'Yeah, just here'll be fine,' Adam replied.

The taxi stopped and the detective climbed out. 'Look, I'll tell you another time,' he said. 'See you Monday.'

He patted Dan's shoulder, turned and walked off into the night, disappearing up a side street. Thoughtfully, Dan watched him go. He was almost sure that as Adam got out of the cab his eyes had looked red and tearful.

Chapter Thirteen

DAN HAD PREPARED AS best he could for the date, making sure to shave well, brush his teeth comprehensively, shape up his hair, even apply a little manly fragrance, and remind himself to be attentive and amusing, but primarily interested in her. It was an intimidating list, but he thought he might just about be able to carry it off.

Rutherford however had made no such vows. The moment he met Kerry for the first time he jumped up and planted a couple of muddy paws on her jacket.

'Yuk!' she gasped. 'Thanks very much!'

Yet again in his life, Dan found himself apologising for his dog. They'd only just picked her up and already made a less than outstanding impression. When Rutherford had been calmed, Dan and Kerry exchanged a brief kiss, got into the car and set off. From the back seat the dog kept up a low whining for almost the whole of the hour's drive.

'He does that when he's excited,' Dan explained. 'And the prospect of having a new friend and being out on Dartmoor for hours is more than enough to set him off.'

'That's fine by me. I love dogs.'

In fairness she sounded as though she meant it, and at the mention of the word Kerry was rewarded by the thrusting of a wet nose into her neck.

It was another fine day, the sun again dominant in a clear sky. They drove out of the city and onto the moor, passing Yelverton and the turn to Arthur Bray's house. Dan found himself thinking about the old man's shotguns, wondering whether the father could have killed the son, or if the murderer was one of the others they had met last week.

'Are you OK?' Kerry asked.

'Yes, fine thanks. Why?'

'I just thought you were muttering to yourself.'

'Err, no. Just, err – humming. A little tune. As it's such a fine day.'

She smiled in that way people do when they meet someone who they think to be unbalanced and want to distract the said suspect from the fact that they're trying to edge away.

How well the date was going. Not fifteen minutes in, Rutherford had already carried out a muddy assault and slimed her with his nose, and his master had started talking to himself about a murder investigation.

It just had to get better from here, or it would be yet another Christmas in his familiar single state.

'So, how's your week been?' Dan asked.

'Oh, fine. Lots on, as ever, but nothing special. I had my hair cut yesterday.'

So she had. Dan muttered an apology and tried to retake the lost ground with some lavish compliments, but he feared that after initially missing the new style his tongue would be seen more as lead than silver.

'I had some pain-in-the-backside customers,' she went on, 'but that's pretty standard for the human race. How was your week?'

Dan told her a little about the Bray investigation and the trip to Brighton. He made a point of rolling up his sleeve.

'I did some Christmas shopping while I was there,' he said meaningfully, turning his wrist back and forth so the Rolex caught the sunlight.

She smiled, and this time it was genuine. 'Oh, that's cute of you. I did wonder what to do being as we've only just met, but that means I can confess I've bought you a little something too.'

Dan smiled too, hoped it didn't look pained, rolled his sleeve back down and made a mental note to get a present for Kerry.

Much of the rest of Devon appeared to be Christmas shopping too. The road heading into Plymouth was busy with cars, the way out onto the moor far quieter. They reached Tavistock, took the back way through the town, past the cattle market where Dan had covered many a story on the annual Dartmoor pony auctions. The road broke out onto the open moor, a great green valley and a running stream to their side.

'This is beautiful,' she said. 'It's a lovely idea of yours to come for a walk. Thank you.'

'It's my pleasure. I thought it'd be fun to do something different.'

Another half an hour's patient driving through the moor's 40 miles per hour speed limit and they were in the village of Belstone. Dan parked the car on the green, by the old stocks, opened the door and the explosion of Rutherford detonated. He ran back and forth, sniffing at benches, cars and bushes, before returning. Dan slipped the lead over his neck and they set off, south, following the River Taw.

'So, where exactly are we going?' she asked, as they walked along a narrow road, towards a five-barred gate.

'Good question. I hope to a place where the memorial might be. You remember I told you Ted Hughes asked for this block of granite inscribed with his name to be placed between the sources of four rivers?'

'Yes.'

'Well, we're going to that area. I've walked a lot of it already, looking for the thing. We're going to try another part, right up by the source of the Taw. It'd be great to find the memorial, but if we don't it's a lovely walk anyway.'

She almost managed to hide her qualm. 'How far is it?'

'Just a few miles.'

'And what kind of ground?'

'There'll be a bit of scrambling over the odd boulder, a little climbing and some bog to look out for, but otherwise fairly straightforward.'

To her credit, Kerry didn't look deterred. She did take a glance at her fingernails, manicured and impeccable, and Dan wondered if this was really the kind of date she would choose. Her walking boots also looked suspiciously new. Her hair had been down, no doubt to make sure he wouldn't miss the new style, as he duly had, but now as the breeze gathered strength she tied it up.

Dan remembered his mental checklist and opened the gate for her, making sure to close it behind them. They walked through some trees and emerged into a shock of view, a great natural amphitheatre, a mile or more of plain bounded by rising tors.

'Wow,' Kerry said.

'I'd say wow about sums it up. This is Taw Marsh.'

The wind puffed and ruffled, playing with their clothes as they stood and stared. The sun had risen into the southern sky, pouring its yellow winter light down onto the land and casting a silhouette of a distant hill. Dan pointed towards it. 'That's Steeperton Tor. The blocks on the top are military huts. It's where we're heading.'

They walked on, Rutherford leaving them to sniff along the course of the river. A couple of sheep watched warily, but the dog showed no interest. The track started to fade into the moorland, a marker of where most Sunday walks ended. The ground was hard and cold underfoot.

The Taw too began to thin, to become no more than a brook, its rushing waters cascading north towards the Bristol Channel.

'I always find it remarkable,' Dan said, 'how it can be so tiny here, near its source, but only around 30 miles away at Barnstaple it's such a mighty river.'

A pack of Dartmoor ponies was grazing at the grass, a mix of greys, chestnuts and browns. One lifted its head, let out a low whinny and tossed its mane. The ground was pitted with the crescent imprints of their hooves.

The path started to unwind against them, the gradient growing. Soon, they were both panting with the effort. Rutherford ran circles around them, showing no signs of any breathlessness. They stopped for a rest, looking back on the Marsh, the thin ribbon of the mercury river winding through the green baize.

Dan found Kerry's hand in his. 'It's stunning,' she whispered.

'I think we might make a walker of you yet,' he replied. 'This is what it's all about. The wonderful tranquility.'

As if on cue, a plane droned overhead, cutting through the peace of the moor. They walked on, forded the river, hopping from rock to stone and followed a military track as it climbed up the side of a tor.

'Where are we heading for?' she panted.

'The source of the Taw. We won't get that far, but it's about the only place left I haven't looked. And from the odd hint I've been getting from Ted Hughes' friends, I'm sure the memorial is in that area.'

'They give you clues?'

'Yes, and I think they enjoy it. They know I'm looking and I think they want the memorial found now. It's been quite a few years since Ted died and it was placed here, and they want people to be able to visit it. Occasionally a letter, or sometimes a little note, will arrive at the studios with a clue in.'

'You should write about it. It's a lovely story.'

'If I find the thing I just might do that.'

Further down the track the inevitable happened. For Dan, it was only a surprise that it had taken so long. Rutherford plunged into the river, was paddling madly against the current, thrashing the water into a froth, but making no headway whatsoever. He turned and let it wash him downstream, his mouth hanging open in his smiling face.

The dog swam with the flow for fifty yards, then spotted a gap in the bank, clambered out and sprinted towards them.

'Run!' Dan yelled, but Kerry, inexpert in the ways of mad hounds, was far too slow. Rutherford leapt up, then shook himself into a blur, a rainbow spray of riverwater covering her.

'Oh, lovely,' she gasped, trying to brush off some of the droplets. 'Thanks dog.'

Dan was choking, tried to hide his laughter. 'Occupational hazard,' he gasped, through the mirth.

The banks of the river grew steeper, granite blocks clinging to the sheer slopes. They weaved and clambered their way through, Dan quickly checking around each boulder for any hidden inscriptions. There were none. He looked at his watch. It was just after one o'clock. He scanned around, found a rock with a flat top and stopped.

'Time for some lunch,' he said, producing a couple of sandwiches and a bottle of water from his pocket and placing them on the improvised picnic table. They shared the food, throwing the odd titbit to Rutherford, and following them with a couple of dog biscuits. A pair of crows swooped from the clear sky and were rewarded with a crust.

Kerry bent down, tied up a shoelace. 'How much further are we going?'

'Not much. We want to get back well before it gets dark. Can you manage another half an hour or so?'

Dan noticed he was still finding the combination of the blonde of her hair and the brown of her eyes enticing, particularly in the flattering sunlight. They tidied up the debris of their snack and walked on. There were fewer boulders now, but Dan still made a point of walking around each to check it. If the memorial was anywhere, it would most probably be here.

'It could be any of them?' Kerry asked.

'It could be, but from the hints I've been getting it's one boulder on its own, in a place which would have appealed to Ted.'

'And where would that be?'

Dan shrugged. 'That is the question. He loved the moor, and he was a keen fisherman. So, I'd say anywhere with a good view, preferably close to a river or stream.'

'So around here would be ideal?'

'That's what I'm thinking. But I've got my hopes up before and not found it. Three years I've been looking for the thing. Three years! It's about the longest running story I've ever tackled and I still haven't put it to bed.'

The river was little more than a trickle now, mostly hidden by the clumps and tumps of wiry moorgrass. The land opened up, the tors slipping away, and the ground grew boggy and uneven, filled with pits and holes. They trod carefully, the mud sucking at their shoes. There were few boulders here, just the occasional one rising from the green plain and mostly camouflaged with lichens and moss.

'It won't be one of those,' Dan said. 'The hints are that the memorial was brought here from another part of the moor after it had been inscribed. Those have been here far too long.'

'So what do we do now?'

'Call it a day, I suspect. We're right up by the source of the Taw now. Another area hunted and no success. Ah well, it was a lovely walk, but I think it's time to turn back.'

Kerry's face was flushed and she couldn't hide the relief in her voice. 'If you insist.'

They stood together and slowly turned, taking in the entire panorama. A couple of layers of cloud had formed in the sky, softening the sunlight. Shadows were starting to form on the land, shading patches of the moor with grey and black.

Rutherford wandered off towards the river, sniffed his way along it, then disappeared behind a small hillock covered with grass. Dan squinted through the sunshine. On the top he thought he could just make out a block of stone.

'Hey!' he said. 'Hey!'

'What?'

'A little hill with great views, overlooking the source of the Taw. Come on!'

He was away, moving as quickly as he could over the ridged ground, the excitement spurring him on. Sticky bog pulled at his feet, but he kept going.

Dan tried to calm himself, prepare for the inevitable disappointment. This was by no means the first time he thought he'd found the memorial. And time and again he'd been wrong.

Rutherford loped up, following his path, Kerry a little behind them. The boulder looked just the right size, around six feet or so in length.

He felt his excitement growing. Dan was sure he could see writing on its face.

Or perhaps it was just the projection of his hope.

He half stumbled, righted himself, kept striding. Kerry was calling something about being careful, but he hardly heard.

The sun was lower in the sky, casting its flames over the moor, making him screw up his eyes against the glare, but he was almost at the hillock. Dan began striding over its side, clambering at the grass, pulling himself up.

His feet slipped and he tumbled back, found his grip and lunged forwards again, onto the top of the mound.

He stopped, stared.

It was only when he found the strength to take another couple of steps forwards, run his hand over the stone, feel the physical truth of its existence that Dan finally believed it.

There, in front of him, was a grey granite boulder. On it was inscribed the name of Ted Hughes, OM – for the Order of Merit he was awarded – and 1930–1998, the dates that marked the sweep of his extraordinary life.

The three-year quest was over.

A day may develop its own momentum. A bad one can get worse, deteriorate markedly, and then proceed rapidly downhill, a good one can just keep on improving.

Happily for Dan, Saturday December 19th fell into the category of the latter. And how.

He hardly noticed the walk back to Belstone, the growing chill and the gathering darkness, nor did he have even a sense of Kerry and Rutherford's weariness, still less his own. He drove them back to Plymouth in a daze.

He had finally found the Ted Hughes memorial.

When they got to Kerry's little end-terrace house in Crownhill, it was only her question, 'What are you doing now then?' that prompted Dan to realise he had thought nothing of the evening, or how to end their date. He wasn't even sure how it had gone. In truth, he could remember little apart from finally finding the stone. His inspired response of, 'Don't know,' led her to reach across, turn off the car's engine and lead him and Rutherford to her front door and usher them inside.

In the kitchen, Dan sat and sipped at a mug of hot tea. Rutherford chomped hungrily at some biscuits, then lay down beside the radiator and closed his eyes.

The dog was right. It had been quite a day.

Kerry fussed around, occasionally stopping to softly slip a lingering kiss onto Dan's neck. She made the odd comment about feeling chilly, being covered in mud, and how she could very much do with having a good long soak in a hot bath to warm up, added a couple more kisses, then emitted what sounded like a frustrated sigh and disappeared.

Dan wondered what was wrong. Upstairs, he thought he heard the sound of a bath running.

He sat down beside Rutherford, ran a hand over the dog's head and was rewarded with an appreciative whine. Perhaps it was time to get off home. He'd probably said something stupid, or offended Kerry in some way. It wouldn't be the first time a relationship had ended in such circumstances. Tact and diplomacy could be foreign lands to him.

It was a shame. Dan suspected he was growing quite fond of her. Nice place too. He vaguely appreciated it was a cosy house, small and modern, but impeccably kept and comfortable. Outside was a little garden, also trim and neat. He could happily have spent some time here.

Dan tried to distract himself by thinking about that piece of paper on the wall of the MIR. His initial idea was the string of numbers, 992 619, could be a grid reference. But to that suggestion Adam had rolled his eyes theatrically.

'The thought had occurred to us,' he said, heavily. 'No go. It's a quarry in the East Midlands, which of course got us all excited. We thought it would be the ideal place to dump some bodies. So we sent a mob of searchers up there. They spent days but didn't find a thing, not a hint of anything at all.'

Dan nodded. 'Yeah, I thought a grid reference might be too literal. Bonham wasn't daft, was he? And he liked to taunt you. It has to be something more subtle, more cryptic.'

Adam had agreed, but then added, 'Like what?' And to that, Dan had no answer.

He tried to think more about what the solution to the puzzle could be, but little was really registering with Dan, apart from one resonant point. He let his mind run back over the day and whispered it quietly to Rutherford, lest for fear he might scare the sacred fact away.

Finally, after all that time and searching, he had found the Ted Hughes memorial.

'Come on then dog,' he said, standing up and heading for the door. 'It's time we were getting home. I'll shout goodbye as we leave.'

It was only when Kerry returned, dressed just in a towel, holding out her hand to lead him upstairs and talking about the bath being hot, ready, and filled with bubbles that The Great Romantic understood that yet again he had missed a whole barrage of hints.

Chapter Fourteen

IT WAS THE WEEK of Christmas, for some the start of the slow wind-down to the holiday; for many others the break had already begun. The roads were noticeably quieter, no bored children staring from bus windows, and fewer commuters, faces resigned in misty car windscreens. Even the weather was playing along with the seasonal upturn in spirits, a high-pressure system, beloved of the *Wessex Tonight* weatherman, lingering over the country and bringing its attendant blue skies and sunny, chilly, days.

Christmas was on the Friday, meaning an extended run of time off for many. The expressions of the people Dan passed as he drove to Charles Cross seemed softer, perhaps with the anticipation of release from the routines of work, and the chance for some justified over-indulgence. This was no ordinary Monday morning, grimmest of the week's grind.

It was coming up to nine o'clock and Dan had parked at the back of the police station. His arrival prompted less mirth than before, just a couple of half hearted jibes. Perhaps even the Christmas spirit had infected the police, or maybe the novelty of the TV detective was wearing off.

Dan checked his reflection, made sure his hair was orderly and tie straight and was about to head for the door when his mobile rang. It was Lizzie, and the festive feeling had clearly evaded her so easily it might have been travelling at speed on a custom built bypass.

'Right, today I want a story. After that jolly awayday gadding about in Brighton last week I want a story, I want it exclusive, I want it good and I want it now. You got that? It's quiet on the news front, with all these selfish people having time off for Christmas. No one's even committing any crimes! So I want a story. Well, what are you hanging on the phone for then? Go find me one!'

Dan sighed, made some reassuring noises and hung up. There was always the discovery of the Ted Hughes memorial to offer, but he'd decided to keep that quiet for now. The Bray case was too fascinating for any distractions. Plus, in the week before Christmas he wasn't ready to hike back up onto the moor with Nigel, laden down with camera and tripod, to film the stone. They could broadcast the story in the new year, when the weather started to improve and people were looking for new walks to try.

Just as Dan was about to put the phone away it warbled with a text. Kerry.

"Morning! Hope you have a good week and those nasty people don't work you too hard! It's Christmas! I'm off all week!! If you want your little present, pop round anytime! xx"

Even more exclamation marks than before, Dan noted, and also added kisses. No doubt to mark the development of their relationship. He'd made no attempt whatever to resist joining her in the bath on Saturday, and even less the short journey from the bathroom to her bed. But, come Sunday morning, Dan had felt the familiar fear building.

Overnight, the two wardrobes in her bedroom had transformed into the pair of ogres so dreaded by the mainstay of the male species; expectation and commitment. Dan hurriedly got up, pleaded the need to look after Rutherford, and left.

There had been no communications on Sunday. Despite Dan suffering a series of bouts of wrestling with his conscience and his decency and gallantry, the fear of moving at speed towards the hazardous land of coupledom had triumphed, and he hadn't sent her a message. He was planning to do so today – honestly, Dan told himself, he was – but she had got there first.

Which meant he now had to come up with a reply. And a Christmas present. And some form of decision about whether he wanted to spend any part of the festive holidays with her.

Not to mention finding a story for his insatiable editor.

The sunshine of the morning's mood dimmed.

It was almost nine o'clock. Adam had said he wanted to start work on the Bray case again at nine, and that meant the hour itself, not a few minutes past. Dan headed for the police station doors.

*   *   *

Adam held up his arm and stared pointedly at his watch. 'It's ten past nine,' he said.

The clock on the wall concurred. Dan checked his new Rolex. There must be some mistake. It said the time was just on the hour. Surely such a superlative, stylish and elegant, not to mention expensive, timepiece could never be wrong. But, from the look on Adam's face he sensed now wasn't the moment to argue, so he sat on the edge of a table and muttered an apology.

'Time isn't money in this business,' the detective added tetchily. 'It's more important than that. Time is justice. The longer a case runs the more difficult it gets to solve. So let's get on with it.'

The daytime Adam was back, committed investigator, orator and leader, not to mention something of a grouch. It was such a contrast to the more subdued and emotional model of Friday night. There was another oddity about the man today, too. For once, he hadn't shaved well, the shadow of his beard was patchy, he looked tired, and his shirt was – remarkably – not impeccably ironed.

Adam pointed to a couple of new boards which had been added to the MIR. They were filled with the names of the suspects.

'Study them,' he said. 'Take it all in. Then we'll have a chat about what you think we should do next. I'm going to get a coffee. You've got ten minutes.' He tapped his watch. 'That's ten minutes *exactly*.'

The first name on the boards was that of Arthur Bray. He had no mobile phone, so there was no opportunity to trace his movements a week ago, when his son was murdered. He claimed to have been at home at the time of the killing, but there was no one to verify that. He had the means to kill Edward, with his cabinet of shotguns, and possibly the motive, with their festering disagreement, the "divorce", as he had described it.

So, Arthur Bray remained a suspect.

Eleanor Paget's claim to be out jogging at the time of the shooting had been verified, but only to an extent. Dan's experience of interviewing eyewitnesses had taught him early that five different people who all saw the same event could give five very different accounts of what had happened. Thus it was with police work.

Sally, the guest at the hospice who Paget said saw her jogging had been spoken to, and thought she could remember it. But she was an older lady, almost eighty, and taking some powerful painkillers, which made her recollection hazy. No, she couldn't be certain it was Eleanor Paget she saw. The rain was heavy and visibility poor. And as for timings, she thought it was sometime before six o'clock, but couldn't be sure.

It was only a fifteen-minute drive from the hospice to the lay-by. Paget could have made it, carried out the killing and got back without anyone noticing. She had the motive, those rows with Bray, and possibly the means if she had got hold of a shotgun. But she would have needed an accomplice, if that call telling the police about Bray's body had indeed been made by someone involved in the murder.

A footnote, in Adam's handwriting, added that this was thought probable, but by no means certain. It could, as Dan had said, have been made by a man who witnessed what happened, but didn't want to get involved, for whatever shady reason.

Paget did own a mobile phone, but analysis indicated it had been at the hospice at the time of Bray's murder. That though meant nothing. She could have left it in her office as she jogged, or as she went to carry out the killing.

The summary of all the information about Eleanor Paget ended with the conclusion that she had by no means been eliminated from the inquiry.

Adam had added another interesting note, saying "I'm sure I know her from somewhere, not certain where, maybe some connection with a case ages ago – must check this."

Next came Hicks and Stead, grouped together as their alibis depended upon each other. Both had clear motives, and could have obtained a shotgun without great difficulty. They claimed to have been in the shop by the river around the time Bray was killed, and the lady who ran it had been interviewed.

There were no CCTV cameras in the store. They had been tried, years ago, but proved too expensive and too fiddly, she said, but she did recall the men coming in, and for two reasons. They were heavily wrapped up in their waterproofs, a colourful yellow, and one – probably Hicks from the description she gave – had broken a bottle of milk. He'd been a gentleman about it she said, so rare these days, and insisted on paying for it and helping to clean up the mess.

As for the all important issue of timing, she couldn't be quite sure, although she thought it was sometime after half past five. But the shop was on the embankment, only five minutes or so drive from the lay-by, so that didn't help rule out Hicks and Stead.

Both had mobiles and they had duly been traced. The records showed the phones at the river until just after half past five, then moving to the shop, finally travelling to the men's respective homes, just a couple of hundred yards from each other. Crucially, both phones were on the move, and almost at the houses, at the time Bray was killed.

Another note warned that the movement of a phone did not, of course, guarantee it was with its owner. It also said the lady in the shop was at the rump end of middle age, her eyesight was far from sharp, and her description of the two men was poor, relying mostly on their build. But the conclusion at the end of the details of the inquiries into Hicks and Stead was that, on balance, they had become considerably less prominent as suspects for the killing.

It was the classic police cliché of "keeping an open mind", although by no means expressed as concisely.

Gordon Clarke's alibi had also been thoroughly checked. His mobile phone trace led to Bristol, just as he had said, and it was on the train on the way home when Bray was killed. Clarke's bank card had been used to withdraw some money in Bristol city centre. His secretary. Ellie, had been interviewed, and said she had received several texts from him during the day about ongoing business matters.

That was perfectly normal. Text was often his preferred method of communication she said, particularly when travelling on a train as he preferred to sit in the quiet carriage, where mobile conversations were banned. Ellie had deleted the messages, but was absolutely certain they came from Clarke as they contained details about current business matters which only he could know.

The bottom of Clarke's entry on the board read, "She could be lying to cover for her boss, but there's no apparent motive, and no suggestion that's the case. From this, despite him having a clear and powerful motive and the potential to obtain a shotgun, we have to conclude Gordon Clarke has also become less prominent as a suspect."

Finally came the details of the inquiries into Penelope Ramsden. She described herself as an old-fashioned woman who had no mobile phone, and her claim to have been at the office when Bray was killed could not be verified by anyone. The last couple of members of staff had left the building at half past five sharp and she was still there then, but the drive to the lay-by was only ten to fifteen minutes. She could have made it in time to kill Bray. There was no obvious motive, but, as Adam had said, they didn't know what might have happened between her and Bray which could have led to her wanting to kill him, perhaps in a jealous rage.

She remained a suspect.

With all the possible killers, inquiries had revealed no reason for any to be forced to cancel an appointment on the Monday before Bray was killed. It was a fine day, and Arthur Bray had been playing golf, verified by a couple of friends and the club itself. Eleanor Paget was at work, as normal, also confirmed by several staff. Hicks and Stead were fishing and seen by several other anglers who had also turned out on the river to take advantage of the good weather. Gordon Clarke was in a series of business meetings and had a range of impeccable witnesses to prove that. Penelope Ramsden had been at work, for much of the day with her late boss, verified by dozens of other staff.

The vital clue as to why the murder was apparently deferred for a week was still eluding them, and proving all the more teasing for it.

'That, I would reckon, remains the key to the case,' Adam said, as he walked back into the MIR. 'And before you ask, I could see you staring at it on the boards, and thinking about what it means.'

He handed Dan a plastic cup filled with a poor impersonation of tea. Even the smell made him grimace.

'So,' the detective continued, 'what do we do next?'

'Err ...'

'Err indeed,' came the rapid response. 'Thank you, but not the greatest of insights. I was hoping for something a little better.'

Dan bridled. 'Well, it's still a hatred, or revenge killing. Because Bray was shot in the heart, and there was that kick in the face after he was dead. Nothing's changed there.'

'Yep.'

'And we've still got our little list of suspects, some of whom are now looking more likely bets than others.'

'Yep.'

'But we've still got no evidence.'

'Yep. All true, but none helpful. Come on, tell me something I don't know.'

'So we ... we – '

Adam folded his arms, waited expectantly, and indeed annoyingly. Finally, Dan said, 'Look, are you in a rough mood today? Had a bad weekend or something?'

Instant anger flashed in the detective's eyes. 'My weekends are my business.'

'Sure, but ...'

'You got that? My business and mine alone.'

Dan held up his hands. 'OK, OK. It just ... I don't know, feels like I've done something wrong and I don't know what it is.'

'I'm only doing what you wanted. Trying to get you to think like a cop.'

'Well, give me a clue then.'

'Your clue is that we're trying to find a clue.'

Adam sipped at his coffee. Dan was about to try his tea, but the acrid smell made him think better of it. The door opened and Suzanne walked in. Her lips, always as thin as a parched river evaporated almost entirely when she saw him. She sat down on a desk on the opposite side of the MIR. Dan felt he was caught in a classic pincer movement.

'I give up then,' he said, tetchily. 'I don't know.'

Adam nodded condescendingly. 'Well done. That's an important lesson of investigations, one you needed to learn. Sometimes we don't know either. So far, there's been plenty of action, buzzing around, seeing suspects. But it's not all glamour. It's common to hit a hiatus. A real life inquiry isn't like you see on the TV. We don't sit in the pub for half the time, suddenly have a brainwave and go out and arrest the killer. It's hard graft. Isn't it Suzanne?'

She nodded emphatically, but clearly didn't feel sufficiently moved to make the effort to speak. Dan tried giving her a half smile, but it wasn't reciprocated.

Adam went on to outline what would happen next. It sounded far from exciting. Research would continue on Bray's life. More checks would be carried out on the suspects, their backgrounds and associations. The detectives would be looking for any links between them which might suggest a conspiracy of ideas or actions. They would all be re-interviewed and put under a little pressure to see if their stories matched the accounts they had given initially. Any discrepancies, any evasions, would be noted and worried away at.

Dan saw his hopes for a story fading fast.

'And that's it?' he said, trying not to sound disappointed.

'That's it,' Adam replied. 'That's the reality of police work. Hard, mundane toil.'

'Well, maybe I could help.'

Suzanne at least had the decency to turn her splutter of disbelief into a cough, but it made little headway in disguising the vast and snow-capped mountain range of her scepticism.

'How could you help?' Adam asked.

'What about if I did a story? Appealing for witnesses.' Dan concentrated hard, so he wouldn't sound sly. 'If you let me put out a little titbit about the inquiry, like saying that Bray was kicked in the face after he was killed, that'd get plenty of attention. I could interview you, and you could ask for witnesses to come forward. It might work.'

Adam shook his head. 'No, I want to keep those details to

ourselves for now. It's better if we just quietly carry on with the inquiry.'

'But I could really get you some interest.'

'No. I'll let you know if I need any more coverage.'

'But I ...'

'I said no. That's it. Decision made.'

The words were as brutal as a door slamming. Adam turned away, walked over to the boards and studied the lines of writing there. Suzanne joined him and they began a whispered conversation. Dan swung a leg back and forth and wondered what to do. Sitting in the MIR, watching nothing much happening hardly felt appealing. And he kept hearing Lizzie's words in his head and her demands for a story.

The clock on the wall said it was half past nine. Dan thought his way through the case, looked for some insight that would give them a lead, or some compelling reason to produce a report, but came nowhere close to approaching either. He found his mind wandering to what present to buy for Kerry. Perhaps some jewellery, that was always a safe bet.

His mobile rang. A withheld number. That meant the newsroom, and more manic insistence for a story. Dan switched the call to his answer machine. It would buy him a few minutes, but not much more.

'So, err, is there anything I can do?' he asked.

Neither of the two detectives bothered to turn around. 'No,' Adam said, over his shoulder. 'Just keep quiet and watch.'

'Watch what? You two having a chat?'

'Yes,' Suzanne said coldly.

'Are you sure we shouldn't be putting out some kind of story?'

'Absolutely.'

A quarter to ten. Dan knew he'd have to ring Lizzie soon. If he didn't have a story to offer he'd probably get called in to cover something ridiculous, just to help fill the programme. There was always a shortage of staff at Christmas as people took leave to be with their kids. That meant he could end up reporting the dreaded staples of yuletide, Santa Claus visits to hospitals, choirs full of discordant children, or festive treats for the cats at the local animal home.

He dropped his pen on the floor, bent down to pick it up and hit his head on the desk. Dan swore and groaned. Fickle Lady Luck had not just deserted him today, but was making a point of waving two fingers in his direction.

But then, as it so often can, life changed in an instant. The door of the MIR swung open.

A woman leaned into the room and said simply to Suzanne, 'I'm off out to speak to some neighbours of Hicks and Stead.'

'OK, thanks Claire.'

Dan glanced over. He must, he estimated later, have seen the woman for about a second and a half before the door closed again. But it was sufficient.

She was entirely and utterly, totally and comprehensively, and fully and wholly his type. Claire's hair was dark, and cut into a bob, his favourite style. Even this fleeting sight made it obvious she had a fine and elegant figure.

Her voice was clear, feminine and strong, her face an artwork which a master sculptor would have spent many weeks labour upon and delighted in the outcome. The few words Dan had ever heard this woman speak now skipped around his ears, as an entrancing melody.

And she must have been about 30 years old. Which, the computer of his brain instantly told him, was just the ideal age for his partner.

Dan gazed and gawped and stood and stared, until the trance was broken by a look like a right hook from Suzanne.

On his notepad, Dan wrote the word "Claire", inked it into bold type, and underlined it.

But at least he managed to resist the teenage temptation to draw a heart around it.

The door began to open again. Dan hastily checked his tie, smoothed his hair and looked up, armed with his best smile.

Which faded fast.

A uniformed inspector strode in and said to Adam, 'I don't suppose you've got any spare detectives I can borrow?'

'Why?'

'You won't believe this, but some bastards have had a go at the war memorial, the huge one on the Hoe. They've stolen some of the bronze plaques. There'll be hell to pay. I need as many cops as I can get hold of to try to catch the thugs and get the plaques back.'

'Sorry, Paul, all my detectives are out on inquiries.'

'Come on, you must have someone? I need to get this one sorted.'

'No one at all. The pressure's on to solve this case and I need all the staff I can get. Sorry.'

The man shook his head and quickly left the room. Adam and Suzanne returned to their discussion.

Dan stared in disbelief. He coughed loudly, but got no reaction. He tried again, yet still with no response. From their determined lack of interest Dan thought he could have a seizure, perhaps even undergo spontaneous human combustion and it would probably pass unnoticed.

'Can I say something?' he ventured, finally.

'If you must,' Suzanne replied.

'That thing about the war memorial and its plaques. That's a disgrace.'

'Yep,' said Adam.

'Well, don't you think you should be doing something about it?'

'It's not one for CID. Uniform can handle it. We've got a murder to solve.'

'Well, you're not exactly solving it at the moment, are you?'

Adam turned slowly around. 'What?' he said, dangerously.

'All I'm saying is that if you're not making any progress on the case at the moment, maybe you should pitch in to try to find the plaques? It's a dreadful crime. The people remembered on them died for us, you know.'

'I'm well aware of that. But uniform can handle it.'

'Surely the more ...'

'I said,' Adam interrupted sharply, 'uniform – can – handle – it.'

The two men stared at each other. 'OK then,' Dan replied, trying to keep his voice calm, 'how about some media coverage? I could get the story out, and ask people to look out for the plaques.'

Adam's voice was ominously quiet. 'I'll say this one more time then. Uniform can handle it. And you're here on trust. No stories without my say so. Now, go back to what you should be doing. Sit quietly, and watch.'

Sometimes, someone can only take so much. And now the dam of resentment, which had been building nicely, could no longer take the pounds of piling pressure.

It breached and burst. And with some style.

'Ah, bollocks to you,' Dan heard himself saying.

'What?'

'I said – bollocks. That's boll-ocks. Don't give me your pompous bloody lectures. With something like this I can really help and I damn well should. I can get everyone looking out for the plaques. I'm going to find that Inspector and offer to do a story. And I bet he bites my arm off.'

Adam took a slow pace towards Dan. He swallowed hard, but held his ground.

'If you do that,' the detective said quietly, 'you know exactly what it'll mean.'

'Oh whoopee fucking do,' Dan replied, and turned and made for the door.

Chapter Fifteen

ON THE BUTTRESSES OF the war memorial on Plymouth Hoe are brass plaques which bear the names of seven thousand sailors who died in the First World War. Dan had once stood here with Nigel and his two young sons, and to attempt the impossible task of giving them an imaginable idea of the number of people who were killed in the Great War he'd asked James and Andrew to begin reading out the names.

They'd got as far as a couple of hundred before realising the extent of the task. And, as Dan had then said, remember that's just one single memorial, for one solitary city, for one branch of the armed forces only. Multiply it by many thousands and you start to get some idea of the actual number of people who died.

The boys had gone quiet.

It was here the attack had been carried out. In the far corner of the garden, beneath a statue of a watching Royal Marine, instead of a line of five plaques there were five rectangles of discoloured stone.

'I don't believe it,' Nigel whispered. 'Of all the shocking stories we've covered, this, well …'

His words tailed off. Dan nodded, as did Inspector Paul Getliffe, the tall and balding man Dan had inelegantly chased down the stairs of Charles Cross police station, and to whom he had offered the power of television to help catch the thieves. The gift was duly not just accepted, but hugged and squeezed. The story would be broken on the lunchtime news. The outside broadcast truck was on the way and Lizzie had demanded a report, with a live introduction and summary.

'Not bad,' had been her verdict on the story. 'It sounds like it is actually almost just about possibly worth letting you go off with the cops.'

Dan took that as a compliment, but didn't raise the question of for how much longer he would be doing so.

Nigel got down onto his knees to film some low shots of the missing plaques, while Dan took the details of the story from the Inspector. The plaques had been stolen sometime overnight. They were held on to the wall by bolts, which had been sheared off. The suspicion was that the plaques would have suffered serious damage, but until they could be recovered it was unclear what state they were in.

The most damning part of the story was that the plaques had probably been stolen for their scrap value. The price of bronze had risen steeply of late. The police estimated the five plaques might fetch a few hundred pounds from a scrap dealer.

The names of around seven hundred men were inscribed on them.

Dan's rough mental calculation put that at about fifty pence a man.

It was a point he would be making strongly in the script.

And all this at Christmas time, too.

From Adam Breen, Dan had heard nothing. He'd half expected a phone call, formally throwing him off the inquiry, and perhaps a few pointed remarks to go with it, but there had been only silence. He tentatively asked Inspector Getliffe about Adam, but the man had been discreet and said, in an understanding voice, 'Don't be too hard on him. He's got a lot on his plate at the moment, and he's having a difficult time.'

It was half past eleven, the sun high in the winter sky. Nigel shifted the camera around to film the great tower of the memorial, silhouetted against the passing clouds.

The sound of fast footsteps and a low moan made them turn around. A middle-aged woman was staring at the wall where the plaques had stood.

'No,' she wailed. 'My grandfather's name was on that one.'

She walked slowly down the steps and ran a hand over the grey and black smears, the only reminder now of the stolen plaque. Dan stepped back and pulled the Inspector with him so Nigel could film. In one shot her reaction summed up the story.

They waited a couple of minutes for her to regain her composure, then Dan introduced himself and asked if she would be prepared to say a few words about the theft.

'Damn right I would,' came the forthright reply. 'But you'd better have a bleep machine for cutting out swearing ready.'

From the studio, Craig read his cue with just the right note of appalled disbelief.

"Thieves have stolen some of the bronze plaques which commemorate sailors lost in the Second World War from the memorial on Plymouth Hoe. The attack has caused widespread outrage. Our crime correspondent Dan Groves is at the memorial now."

Dan was standing with the tower behind him, said, "Yes, the memorial here is a poignant reminder of the sailors who died fighting for our freedom, but who have no grave except the sea.'

He began walking, Nigel panning the camera around to follow.

'More than twenty thousand sailors are remembered here,' Dan continued, gesturing to some of the bronze plaques he was passing, their faces flashing in the sunlight. 'But in this corner, thieves have taken five plaques. Now the police are asking for urgent public help in getting them back.'

His report played. The viewers had already seen the wall where the plaques once stood, so Dan started the story with Rachel Parker, her wailing at the sight and her interview. It required a couple of takes before her words were acceptable for a daytime TV audience, and to Dan's surprise, she hadn't cried, but what she had to say was powerful nonetheless.

'To do this – it's a disgrace. It's the lowest form of thuggery. It's despicable. My grandfather and others like him gave their lives for the freedom of people today and to have some of them steal these plaques for a few pounds – well, they're scum, that's the only word I can use. Just foul, horrible scum."

Then came some close ups of the wall and the marks left behind, and a clip of the interview with Inspector Getliffe. He too said what a dreadful crime this was and appealed to the public for help in getting the plaques back.

For his live summary, Dan reiterated that message, asking anyone who might know who was responsible, or had any idea what had become of the plaques, to get in touch with the police.

He gave out the *Crimestoppers* number too.

'Thanks for all this,' the Inspector said, after the broadcast. 'Do you think it'll get much reaction?'

'Oh yes,' Dan replied emphatically.

Sometimes in life, all you can do is wait. As a journalist it was a fate which often befell Dan. Whether it was waiting for a jury to return a verdict, a police officer to emerge from a crime scene to grace the media with a comment, or perhaps even just sitting in the outside broadcast van, waiting for half past six to come around so he could present a live report.

But despite all his experience of it, Dan didn't do waiting well.

Following the lunchtime news, the police had been inundated with phone calls. Inspector Getliffe said he had never known a more vociferous public response. Hundreds rang in, many just to voice their outrage, but some to say people they knew, or were aware of, or maybe even just thought were odd had been behaving suspiciously. Almost every scrap dealer in the area was reported as having a potential involvement.

Officers were sifting through the deluge of information, looking for the real leads in the barrage of anger. The Inspector thought the answer to solving the case would be in the information, but it would take time to follow it up and to carry out the necessary inquiries.

In the meantime, Dan waited. Lizzie had pronounced the story "pretty good", praise indeed from her notoriously mealy mouth, but naturally she had immediately followed the words with a series of demands for *Wessex Tonight*. Another outside broadcast, another cut story, and preferably one that this time revealed the plaques had been found and the evil criminals apprehended. It would be best of all if a baying mob could be filmed outside the police station as the foul gang was brought in to face the vengeful might of richly deserved justice.

It was a shame, she added, that the fine old punishments of being hung, drawn and quartered, tarred and feathered, publicly stoned, or simply just hanged, were no longer considered acceptable.

She concluded by saying it was a good job she wasn't a judge, or the Home Secretary, to which Dan felt able to add his most heartfelt agreement.

It was coming up for two o'clock, the day still fine, but the sun now already making its way back down towards the horizon, adding an extra slice of chill to the air.

Dan sent Nigel and Loud back to the studios to get some lunch. For now, there was nothing else they could do. Inspector Getliffe had promised he would call as soon as there were any developments. There was no point trying to film anything else, or edit a new version of the story for later. They would have to see what the afternoon brought. So, for now, all they could do was wait.

Dan headed into town to get himself a sandwich and do some shopping. It was busy, just as he had expected, and he knew he still had no idea what to buy for Kerry. He sent her a text saying it would be lovely to meet at Christmas time, but deliberately avoided specifying when, then bought a pasty and a coffee from a takeaway shop and sat on a bench in the yellow sunshine, watching the hordes of shoppers charging by, and trying to think.

It wasn't easy. Dan noticed his mind kept slipping to Adam, and wondering how the detective would throw him off the Bray case. He hoped it wouldn't be an attempt at a public dressing down. His temper had never got the hang of such humiliations, tended to turn them into shouting matches. A quick phone call would be preferable, but so far he'd heard nothing. He wondered if all that would happen would be him turning up at Charles Cross tomorrow, having his pass taken away and being told dismissively to leave.

No doubt accompanied by gawping, grinning faces in each and every window.

Dan got up and started walking slowly past the shop windows, slipping through the human stampede and hoping for inspiration. He stopped at a lingerie shop, the dummies, judging from their expressions, delighted to be wearing a selection of red and black underwear. All that lace and frilly adornment looked itchy and hopelessly uncomfortable to him, but as there was such a mass of it, clearly it had to be ultra fashionable, irresistibly sexy, and all that a woman could ever possibly want.

Dan gazed at the window and let his eyes run over the models. The prices were remarkably steep for garments made of so little material. The profit margins must be huge. It took him a few seconds to realise a couple of older women were watching him.

'You're that guy off the telly,' one of them cackled.

'Yes,' he said resignedly at the dreaded words.

'Hoping to get lucky?' the other asked.

As he had apparently met the ageing female version of Morecambe and Wise, Dan thought he would respond in kind.

'No, it's a present for my mum,' he replied.

When they didn't laugh he added a smile to emphasise the jolly jape. They grinned too, one exposing far more teeth than it should ever be possible to fit in a human mouth, but Dan noticed they had begun edging awkwardly away.

'It's all a myth we like that stuff,' the toothy one said over her shoulder. 'If I were you I'd get your mum something else.'

Dan walked on, along the high street. He did have a vague memory that gifts of lingerie might not be as welcome amongst women as men thought. He would buy Kerry something else, something more creative and guaranteed to be enjoyed. But despite another half hour's searching, inspiration continued to prove annoyingly elusive.

He was on the edge of abandoning the thankless quest and starting to trudge back towards the Hoe, when another shop window display gave him an idea. Dan popped in, and after a few minutes chat with a very helpful sales assistant, the perfect present was duly purchased.

Loud was already back by the war memorial and engaged in a delightful operation to clean his grimy fingernails with a small screwdriver. He didn't even have the decency to stop when Dan climbed into the van.

A small posse of media surrounded the memorial, TV crews filming, photographers snapping, reporters waiting, hoping to catch a visiting relative for a comment. It was just as Dan had expected. The story was already running on the national news. A government minister had expressed shock, a philanthropist had pledged as much money as it took to either find the plaques, or have new ones forged.

The story was building momentum nicely.

Dirty El bounced up to the van and poured out some burbled appreciation. Dan had called him earlier to tip the photographer off about the story. His pictures had been bought by all the national papers, earning El a pretty pile. It had lifted his mood to a level sufficient to prompt one of the dreadful rhymes El tended to produce at times when he thought life was favouring him.

'This crime it's a dreadful, scandalous horror,
To see the plaques, some chavs come borrow,
We've gotta help get 'em back,
Let justice attack,
But meanwhile, El cashes in with a lorra ...'

He waited for a couple of seconds, before adding the missing 'loot!'

Even the notoriously insensitive Loud looked pained. 'Yuk,' pronounced Dan, who could think of no better judgement.

El took a mock bow. 'Christmas night out on me,' he babbled. 'To mark my gratitude. And while we've got a mo and El's luck's running hot hot hot, any news on getting a snap of the pervy scoutmaster?'

'No,' Dan replied quietly. 'And I don't think I will have. I suspect my attachment to the police may be coming to an abrupt end.'

It was almost four o'clock. The sky was darkening fast. Time to get on with the edit. Dan made one final call to Inspector Getliffe. Officers were still out on a series of inquiries, some of which were looking promising, but so far there was no definite news about where the plaques might be and who could have taken them.

That meant tonight's story would look much the same as the lunchtime version. They'd have to put up a couple of lights, so the viewers could see what had happened to the memorial, but the outside broadcast van carried a generator for just such occasions so that wouldn't be a problem.

Dan again began the story with Rachel Parker, as she was the most powerful of the interviews, then added a clip of the Inspector, but also put in a snippet of interview with a veteran's group and a local MP. Everyone wanted to voice their outrage on this story.

It was a simple edit and they were done by a quarter to five. Nigel offered to get them a round of coffees from a nearby café while they waited to do the live broadcast, a gift that was gratefully received. The sky was still clear and the evening was rapidly growing colder.

And then, with the work mostly done, the story changed. It was as though fate was in a whimsical mood, and merely awaiting her moment.

Dan's mobile rang. Inspector Getliffe.

'We've got the plaques.'

'All of them?'

'Yep.'

'What state are they in?'

'Three OK, two damaged.'

'Where?'

'A scrapyard just outside Plymouth.'

It was ten to five. Dan took some directions and did a couple of quick mental calculations. It would be tight, but just about feasible.

'Meet us at the yard?' he said.

'Now?'

'Yep. We'll do five minutes of filming of the plaques, a quick interview with you, then we'll get it on *Wessex Tonight*.'

They were lucky. The traffic was light, the hour just before the onslaught of the rush and there were fewer cars on the road with the Christmas holiday. They got to the scrapyard just after five.

It was a sprawling place, thick with the smell of oil, filled with teetering piles of rusting cars and muddy and rutted ground. There were a couple of emaciated and rabid snarling dogs, both fortunately tethered with thick chains, and a welcoming sign which said, "Trespassers will be shot".

The plaques were laid out on a blanket in the boot of a police car. Three had suffered scratches, but two were twisted, bent and buckled, as if someone had tried to break them into pieces. Nigel concentrated his shots on those. The scores and marks cut through the columns of the names of the dead men.

It didn't take much to imagine the viewers' reaction.

Dan took a quick briefing from the Inspector, they did an interview, then jumped back in the car and headed for the Hoe. But now luck had turned against them. Every road they took faced them with more lines of static cars, rows of red tail lights stretching into the distance.

To save precious time Dan worked on the revised script as Nigel drove. One of the most important principles of news states that the freshest pictures should come first in a report, particularly when they're as striking as the damaged plaques. But that would mean re-writing and re-editing the whole story, and that would endanger the cardinal rule.

Get it on air. In whatever form, forget the artistry, just beat the deadline.

Dan glanced at the clock. It was coming up to half past five, an hour until *Wessex Tonight* went out, and they were still sitting in sticky traffic. Time was acutely against them.

There was another way, and it would have to be tonight's weapon of choice. Known in the news trade as the "Delayed Drop", it was effectively a tease, the presenter telling the viewers there had been some major development, but without letting them see it until late in the story.

Nigel swore quietly to himself, turned down a back lane and started working his way through the rat runs. The car swung from side to side with his manoeuvres, the sodium streetlights highlighting the concentration on his face. They were making better progress now. Dan called Lizzie and outlined his idea.

'Done,' came the instant response. 'If that's what it takes. Just make it happen. Now stop wasting time talking to me and get on with it.'

It was twenty to six when they got back to the Hoe. Loud grabbed the tape, quickly spooled through the shots. Dan explained the plan, and the engineer nodded.

'Bloody good idea. It'll save me poor heart.'

They would present the broadcast just as they had before, except this time Craig would read a revised cue, talking about the plaques being found. Dan would come in with his live link and show the viewers the memorial and the marks on the wall where the plaques had been. His report would feature all the outraged reaction they already had, but after the clip of the MP's interview they would use some of the new shots of the damaged plaques.

In his commentary Dan explained how, within the last hour, they had been found at a scrapyard following a tip-off. Then it was a clip of the Inspector, thanking the public for their help and saying how delighted he was the plaques had been recovered. It was the quickest way of working and guaranteed to get the story on air.

TV purists might not have liked it, but the structure did work well. Dan could feel the viewers' ire building, then their relief at the plaques being found, then another flare of anger as they saw how badly damaged two of them were.

To finish the broadcast, in his live summary Dan told the camera that three men had been arrested on suspicion of theft and criminal damage and were now being questioned. He was thanked, and the programme moved on to its next story, an analysis of how the Christmas shopping season was going and what it meant for the economies of the region's biggest towns and cities.

Dan thanked Nigel and Loud for their efforts and was about to drive home when he remembered to turn his mobile back on. He always kept it off during outside broadcasts, as his friends would commonly see him on the television and think it a fitting time to sends texts filled with jibes about his attire, just to see if they could distract him.

The phone beeped its little message alert. There was indeed a text waiting, but it was from a number Dan didn't recognise.

Puzzled, he pressed the read button.

"Can you come to Charles Cross after your broadcast please. We need to have a chat. Adam."

He stared at the words and sighed. Not even the call from

Lizzie, offering an unconditional, and thus highly unexpected, "Well done" lifted his mood. Following the unpardonable slight, the festering of the animosity and the build up of the tension, it was, as they said in those wonderful old Westerns, showdown time.

Dan climbed resignedly into his car and headed for the police station.

Chapter Sixteen

BY THE TIME HE was trooping up the stairs towards the MIR, Dan had prepared himself for the ordeal.

He was tempted to return the coming broadside. Perhaps to start, he'd point out that Adam was behaving like a control freak or just a child, maybe even add another colourful opinion or two about the way he had been treated while with the Bray investigation.

Then he could go on to conclude that what he did about broadcasting the plaques being stolen had proved to be right. They had been recovered, according to Inspector Getliffe, because of a tip off from a woman who had been watching *Wessex Tonight*'s coverage.

But, as always, there was a but. Dan would doubtless have to work with Adam again, and probably the next time there was a big and newsworthy case. He'd quickly learned the Chief Inspector was generally regarded as one of Greater Wessex Police's finest, both amongst his colleagues and the media. He handled most of the major inquiries.

Dan couldn't afford to be frozen out and have Adam Breen refusing to speak to him.

So, when he'd climbed this next flight of stairs and reached the MIR, he knew how he would handle the dressing-down. He would listen to what Adam had to say, politely and quietly. Dan would tell the detective he understood but couldn't agree, and gently emphasise that the plaques had been recovered. He would conclude by saying he would, of course, leave the police station and the Bray inquiry if Adam wished it, but hoped they could work together again professionally in the future.

As he reached the last few steps, Dan noticed his pace was slowing.

It was such a great shame. Shadowing the inquiry had been fascinating. No matter how he tried, he couldn't pretend to himself he wouldn't miss it.

And there was even the thought, just the remote possibility, that on the couple of occasions they'd had a more relaxed chat, Dan had begun to wonder whether he and the enigmatic Chief Inspector might even have been on the long path to becoming friends.

He almost walked into a cleaner who was busily sweeping the floor, apologised, straightened his tie and began taking the last few steps towards the MIR.

Dan wasn't surprised to find his thoughts drifting to home, a restorative cuddle with Rutherford, and the little plastic bottle of pills in the bathroom cupboard.

A dark and cold Monday night, just four days before another solitary Christmas, was a brutally effective wrecking ball for the fragility of your mood.

The Swamp was sucking hard.

Dan hesitated outside the door, rolled his neck, clenched his fists, tried to adopt a calm and confident expression, and walked into the MIR for what he entirely expected to be the last time.

In his life, Dan had come to notice that a fair few of his plans worked and another, probably roughly equal number, didn't. But a much greater proportion than the combination of the two didn't have a chance to make any impact whatsoever on the world.

No matter how much time and effort he put into formulating a strategy, instinct or sometimes just emotion would often take over.

Thus it was that evening.

Adam was sitting on a table, staring broodingly at the line of felt boards, as if willing them to give up the secret of who had murdered Edward Bray. He looked tired, his tie was low on his collar and his skin shining with a gathering sweat.

He turned as the door opened and was about to speak, but Dan got there first.

'I'm going,' he said. 'Don't worry about that. I just came to say I got your message, I know what it means and I'm off. You don't have to go on at me, give me a rollocking or a little lecture, or any of that crap. I'm off. I won't bother you again. I just came to say that.'

168

Dan nodded hard to emphasise his words.

'But I have to say, I think it's a real shame. Well, worse than that in fact. I think it's stupid. Petty, really, if you want to know the truth. I thought we were working together well. I thought I'd showed you how I could be useful to you. Look at the publicity I brought when you caught that nutter who was attacking the prostitutes. That really did you good. We could have done more like that. I could even have helped you get some witnesses to come forward in the Bray case.'

Adam was shifting on his chair, his mouth opening to say something, but Dan had sped into his flow and wasn't about to stop.

'I don't know if you noticed, but we got the plaques back. That was a real disgrace, a dreadful thing to do, nicking them. I don't care what you're going to say, about me disobeying your orders, or being here on trust, or a crime like that not being a matter for CID – of course it was one for CID! What's the point of your job if you don't tackle the crimes which bother the public the most? And that one did. You should have seen the reaction we got when we broadcast the story. And the tip off about where the plaques were – that came from someone who saw the reports I did. Did you know that? Did you even bother watching them? I'm not saying that I single-handedly got the plaques back, of course I'm not, but I certainly played a big role in helping.'

Adam was getting up from the desk now, raising a hand, but Dan had by no means finished.

'And if you really want my opinion, and I probably shouldn't say this, but I'm going to anyway, then I think you're being daft. Well, worse than that – ridiculous in fact. I reckon you did want me off the inquiry after all, no matter what you said about giving me a chance, and this is your golden excuse to do it. I've done everything I can to help. I've done background research in our library for you. I've driven you around. I've offered to make the media work for you. I even asked a couple of questions, and you yourself admitted that they were good ones, that they might have been important to the case.'

Adam now had both palms in the air in a gesture that oddly

didn't look angry, not even reproachful, instead just calming. But Dan was riding on the swings of his temper and gaining momentum all the time.

'And do you know what? I shouldn't say this either, because it'll probably give you even more satisfaction now that you're kicking me out, but I've really enjoyed shadowing the inquiry and working with you. I was all nervous and intimidated when I got moved on to doing crime. But you've taught me masses, and I really appreciated that. And you know, I even got to enjoy it. And I was stupid enough to hope you might be coming to value having me around, and that you were starting to see that I could really help.'

And now Dan had to pause. He had no choice. He'd run out of breath.

When he'd gulped in one more quick lungful of air, he added, 'Right, so that's it then. I'm off. I'm going. Just say what you've got to say, get your pathetic little lecture out of the way, and I'll be gone.'

He folded his arms and stared defiantly at Adam. There was a silence, then the detective said, 'I only wanted to apologise.'

Dan blinked hard. 'What?'

'I wanted to apologise. For how I behaved earlier. Oh, and to thank you as well. For helping us get the plaques back.'

A bizarre memory flitted through Dan's mind. It was from his childhood days, many years gone. He had a skateboard and had found a backstreet which ran straight and true down a lovely long hill. He'd walked to the top, gathered his courage, stepped onto the board and kicked himself underway.

Quickly he'd begun to build up speed until he was careering downhill at an exhilarating rate. Lampposts and bins and doors and gates were flashing past, but he rode on, eyes wide with the excitement, concentrating hard on keeping his balance.

The thrill of the descent was dizzying. On and on he'd hurtled, delighting in the freedom and adventure, his heart racing, his chest breathless.

Then a car had backed out of a drive, right into his path, and he'd smashed into the bonnet.

Fortunately, Dan was blessed with the pliable body of many

young boys, and so was only bruised and winded. But the sudden and shocking halt to a seemingly irresistible momentum was exactly what came to his mind with Adam's words.

'Oh,' said Dan.

It was several seconds before he could find a follow up to his inspirational response, one which contained the same number of letters, but was not really any more communicative.

'Ah.'

A little more time elapsed before Dan added, 'You wanted to ... apologise?'

'Yes.'

'And – thank me?'

'Yes.'

'Really?'

'Yes.'

'Oh.'

Adam took off his tie, carefully rolled it up and placed it into his jacket pocket.

'Well, there was one more thing,' he said.

'Yes?' Dan replied, warily.

'To ask you if you fancied a beer.'

'Now?'

'Yes.'

'Tonight?'

'Still yes.'

Dan found that he did indeed very much fancy a beer.

Before they left the MIR, Dan rang his downstairs neighbour, went through his usual round of apologies about the unpredictable beast that was his work and asked ask him to look after Rutherford. Walking into the city they found it was that rarest of Monday nights, a busy and boisterous one, so they avoided the centre and instead found a run of bars in a backstreet off the Barbican.

Dan was about to push at the double doors of the first of the welcoming line when Adam stopped him.

'What?' Dan asked.

'Which door were you going to try? Of the two?'

'The left-hand one.'

'I reckon it's locked.'

'Why?'

'Try it.'

Dan did. The left-hand door was indeed firmly locked. Adam pointed to the handle of the door on the right. It was shiny with wear.

'Just another little example of police work,' he said. 'If you're still interested.'

Smug is a wonderful word. It's short, sharp and often unbeatably appropriate.

They walked into the bar, and this time Dan stopped.

'What?' Adam asked.

'The shoes.'

The place was mainly filled with men, and most were wearing white trainers. All of which were far too bright to ever have seen any sporting activity, except perhaps for running from the forces of the law.

'A little example that I'm still interested in police work, and even hope that I might have some talent for it,' Dan added. 'White trainers equals lager drinkers, equals no good ales, equals not our kind of place, wouldn't you say?'

They walked further down the street, found a bar which was quieter and filled with people wearing normal shoes. Dan was going to get the drinks in, but Adam said it was his round, part of the apology for his behaviour earlier, and made for the bar.

There were a few free tables, so Dan picked one at the back of the room. The chair was padded and unusually pleasant for a pub, unlike those places that seem to think comfortable chairs beguiled customers into relaxing, drinking more slowly and so spending less money.

Adam brought the drinks over. The beer was good as well.

'I think I like this place,' Dan said. 'We must make a note of it.' He checked the menu. 'The food looks tasty too.'

They sipped at their drinks. Adam leaned back on his chair and said, 'Right, shall I bring you up to date on the Bray investigation?'

'Please do.'

'It won't take long.'

That was an impressive understatement. It took just a sentence. There was no update. Despite the team of detectives looking at the background and associations of all the suspects, they had found nothing new to suggest an undiscovered burning motive or obvious opportunity for murdering Edward Bray. All remained as had been earlier. They had a list of suspects, some of whom appeared better bets than others for the killer, but no clear indication who had carried out the murder.

'Right then,' Adam said. 'Let's make the leap from facts to feelings. But first, I'd better warn you – this can be dangerous. It's important not to get fixated on a suspect for no better reason than that you've got a feeling he might be the killer. On the other hand, instincts are an important part of police work. So, let's go through our list. Do you have any real sense who the murderer might be?'

Dan swirled his drink.

'No,' he said. 'No strong feeling. I did get the impression Gordon Clarke was hiding something. He didn't seem comfortable with being interviewed and I reckon he looked more than a little relieved when we left. But that could be because of any old business fiddle.'

'It could. Plenty of people get uncomfortable with the law around. And he's got a good alibi.'

'Yes. As have Hicks and Stead, but ...'

'But what?'

'I don't know. I just felt – it's difficult to put into words, and it's about Hicks rather than Stead, but it was a kind of feeling that he would be able to kill Bray. I could sense the loathing in him. Maybe it's because of those stories we did that he featured in, but I felt he could be a killer.'

'Both Hicks and Stead have got decent alibis too. Not perfect, but decent enough.'

'Yeah, I suppose so. Is there such a thing as a perfect alibi?'

Adam smiled. 'Not often. With some diligent work I can normally knock a hole in most of them.'

The main part of their pints had already disappeared. It was often the way with the first drink of the evening. Dan went to

173

the bar and brought back some replenishments. The bar staff were efficient and friendly. This place truly was a find.

'What about the others then?' Adam asked. 'Penelope Ramsden?'

'I still think she's an outside bet, even though she's got no alibi. I thought she was genuinely upset at her boss's death.'

'OK. Eleanor Paget?'

'More of a possibility. She's got that steel about her which might give her enough resolve to kill. The hospice staff are scared of her, that was obvious. And just look at the way she stood up to Bray – that can't have been easy, given what we know he was like, and the fact that he donated all that money to the hospice. She could have hated him enough to kill him, maybe even to stop the changes he was trying to make to the hospice. Although she was charming, I wouldn't like to get on the wrong side of her. I bet she can be ruthless, but I suppose that goes for anyone who gets to a senior position in a company or organisation.'

'She was nervous though, to see us.'

'Yes, but as you yourself said, most people are when the police come calling. However innocent they might be, it's only natural.'

'True enough. I'm glad to see you're listening. I had her checked out anyway, and there's nothing on the computer about her. Paget's got no criminal record of any sort, not even points for speeding. As far as the law's concerned she's completely clean.' Adam looked thoughtful and added, 'I'm sure I know her from somewhere though. Well, it'll come to me. Right, finally on our little list, Arthur Bray?'

Dan considered the question. 'I don't want to think it, it's almost too horrible to consider, but yes, I'd have to say he's a strong suspect. He's got the shotguns, he's got no alibi and by his own admission he's got a motive. I certainly think we need to find out what caused the estrangement between him and his son. What do you think?'

'I think you're right. Not just about Arthur Bray, but all of our suspects. None stands out to me as being the obvious one we should focus on.'

'So what happens next?'

'We carry on with the dull bit, which as I told you is the real truth of investigations. We keep working on the case, keep looking at the suspects and the crime, keep hoping for a break.'

More people were filling the bar. It was growing warm, the windows misting. Dan took off his jacket.

'It still comes down to that vital clue, doesn't it?' he said. 'Why the murder was put off for a week.'

Adam nodded. 'I think so. But none of our inquiries have thrown up a reason why any of the suspects would have to cancel something they were planning on the Monday the week before Bray was killed.'

'And is there anything I can do to help? Any more reports I can put out which might be useful?'

'You mean you need a story?'

'Well, I'm never averse to them.'

'I noticed. No, I genuinely don't think there's anything else you can do at the moment. I reckon we just keep working the case quietly and see what our inquiries throw up. Look, let's leave the work thing aside for now, I could do with a break. Tell me a bit about yourself. Have you always lived in Devon?'

Adam got them some more drinks, then Dan went through his history. As he recounted his story, he noticed it felt oddly like a date, a getting to know you session remarkably similar to what he'd gone though with Kerry.

Like many journalists, Dan had lived an itinerant lifestyle in his younger years. Your first job tended to last only a few months as you were ambitious, ever on the lookout for a bigger newspaper, radio or TV station, or, today, a website. Moving town or city tended to be an annual occurrence, if not even more frequent.

Dan related how he had started in the broadcasting industry as a DJ, on the radio and in nightclubs. It was something he'd begun at university. Bored with his degree in natural sciences, he'd taken it up as a hobby because of a love of music, a fondness for the sound of his own voice, and a belief that the glamour of the job attracted girls. He'd started to get bored with the limited challenges of playing records and talking about them, had crossed over into the radio newsroom, then been spotted by a TV station as having potential and offered a trainee role. For a man with an impressive store of vanity, the lure of having his face in thousands of living rooms, night after night, had proved much too tempting to resist.

He'd got some experience, learnt the TV trade and then taken a job in London. It was the first time Dan had worked in the capital and he'd found it not to his taste. Everything was hustle, be it for a seat on a bus, a drink at a bar, somewhere to live, even, occasionally in the polluted metropolis, for a lungful of air. A job as a reporter with *Wessex Tonight* had come up, an old friend had recommended a more sedentary, but quirky life in the South-west, Dan had applied and been appointed.

He'd expected to spend perhaps a couple of years in Devon. But, as happens to so many in a region renowned as a graveyard of ambition, the good life had beguiled him and in Devon he had stayed.

'Any regrets?' Adam asked, with one of his usual perceptive questions.

'Perhaps one. I expected to travel a bit more as a reporter, right across the world even. I wonder what would have happened if I'd stuck it out in London. Maybe I'd have been covering the biggest stories the planet gets to see. But on the whole, no, no regrets. So, what about you? What's your history?'

Adam didn't reply. His finger went to his wedding band and pushed it back and forth. He looked about to speak, but then sipped at his drink, excused himself and headed for the toilets. Thoughtfully, Dan watched him go, then sat back and looked around the pub. There were so many smiling faces. It was remarkable what a drink and the prospect of some time off could do for people's mood.

'You OK?' he asked, when Adam returned.

'Yeah, fine. Just feeling tired, and a bit frustrated. It's been a week since Bray was killed. I was hoping we'd have made more progress by now. We could do with a break.'

'It's just that?' Dan asked quietly.

'Just what?'

'Just the case that's bothering you?'

Adam leaned back on his chair, rolled his neck. Finally he said, 'Yeah, more or less – maybe.' He hesitated, then added quickly, 'So, you wanted to know about my background?'

Adam picked up his pint and recounted his story. He was a local lad, born and schooled in Plymouth. He stayed on at school to take A levels, but had little idea what career to choose. An uncle was a detective inspector in London, so the young Adam had asked what the life was like and received a sufficiently encouraging response to apply. He had been taken on as a probationer by Greater Wessex Police, and spent several years on the beat.

'A lot of cops will tell you this is nonsense,' he said, 'but they were great days. I had my own patch to patrol, I got to know all the people and I really enjoyed it. There were some nasty bits, of course, like this.'

Adam wobbled the crook of his nose. 'Broken by some drunken idiot on a Union Street Saturday night,' he said. 'But it goes with the job. For every thug there are a thousand good people out there, and that's something cops don't remember enough. We get used to being lied to and abused, but the vast majority of people are very decent and they're on our side.'

PC Breen, as he then was, had done his time in uniform, was spotted as one of the brighter of the young intake of new constables, and told that perhaps he might consider working in CID. But he decided against it, said he was enjoying his work on the beat and thought that he was making a real difference to the community he served.

Then had come the moment his life changed.

Adam's sister was raped.

'She's younger than me,' he said. 'Sarah's her name. She's very clever, very pretty, tall, with long blonde hair. She'd just finished her A levels and was deciding which university to go to. She had her pick, could have done whatever she wanted and gone on to whichever career she chose. The whole of her life was there, just waiting in front of her.'

And now his voice fell. 'She was attacked on her way home from a night out. Beaten and raped. Put in hospital. She survived, but after that she was a different person. She became quiet and withdrawn. She tried going to college, to see if that helped, but she couldn't stick at her course. She dropped out and got a flat and a job in a factory in Hull. She chose it because she'd never been there before. She wanted somewhere new, away from everything that had happened. I hardly speak to her now, just a brief call at Christmas and that's about it. She doesn't seem to want to know about anything or anyone that might remind her of the past.'

Adam slowly shook his head. 'The bloke who did it was never caught. And you can guess how that feels.'

An attachment had come up to CID, and PC Breen had duly become DC Breen. Talented and now very driven, a couple of years later he was a Detective Sergeant, five more after that and he was a Chief Inspector.

'And that is as far as I go,' he said emphatically. 'I have to deal with enough admin, budgets and management stuff as it is. Any higher up the chain and I'll be unlikely to ever see a criminal again. As a DCI you get to run the biggest cases and actually be a part of the investigation too.'

Over in the corner of the bar, a man had begun playing a guitar. He looked unfocused and well the worse for wear. The music was so far off the notes he was probably aiming for that the tune was almost unidentifiable, but it was a measure of the Christmas spirit infusing the bar that plenty of people dropped coins into his guitar case anyway.

'So, the job's good,' said Dan, laying heavy stress on the word "job".

'Yeah.'

'What about the rest of life?'

Adam took a deep draw at his pint, then said, 'You don't give up, do you?'

'No. I don't. But then, nor do you.'

'That's true.'

A barman came to collect their empty glasses. Adam thanked him, ran a hand over his stubble and yawned. 'Oh, I know what I meant to ask you,' he said.

Dan raised a theatrical eyebrow, to make sure the detective

was well aware he hadn't missed the U-turn in the conversation. 'Yes?'

'Had a good weekend, did you?'

'In what way?'

'In the woman way.'

'Ah.'

'Ah indeed.'

Dan tapped a hand on the table. 'How did you know?'

'It would have been harder to miss. You practically swaggered into the MIR this morning.'

'Did I?'

'You did.'

Dan explained what had happened on Saturday, but, being a gentleman for once, he left out the unexpected events at Kerry's house. His swagger of earlier probably said more about that than mere words could.

Adam nodded and smiled, but it was a tired look. Dan hesitated, then said quietly, 'So, what about you? Is there a woman in your life?'

The smile disappeared. Adam's finger went again to his wedding band. He finished his pint, then said, 'Another?' and disappeared to the bar before Dan had time to answer.

The man with the guitar had completed his improvised set, which prompted more people to donate money than had been the case while he was playing. The place was a little emptier now. It was one of those feeder pubs, where people meet to start the evening, for a chat and to begin the lubrication process, before moving on to bigger and noisier bars.

Dan noticed he was feeling relaxed. The beer was doing its fine work, accompanied by the reassurance he wasn't being kicked off the Bray case. He could have sworn Lizzie issued some unqualified praise earlier for his work on the war memorial story, but perhaps that was just the hallucinatory effect of the alcohol.

It was a common enough syndrome. After a few beers, Dan could feel handsome, charismatic, and sexually magnetic, but usually had the benefit of the solid anchor of self-awareness to understand it was only a passing dream.

Adam brought over two more pints and sat down. He stared into the amber liquid, then lifted his head and watched the headlights of the passing cars.

Dan waited quietly.

'All right, all right,' Adam said, finally. 'Her name's Annie. And that's the problem. I don't know how much in my life she is.'

Even from the small, passport photograph, she was evidently a beautiful woman. Long dark hair swept over her shoulders, and her eyes were an enticing shade of brown. Adam's hand trembled as he held out the wallet containing her picture.

'And you've seen Tom, my son,' the detective added quietly, shifting the pictures around.

It could have been a picture of the young Adam. Tom had his father's dark and tussled hair and was smiling in the not quite convincing way that many people have when unused to adopting the expression.

Dan made the usual noises about Annie's looks and Tom's handsomeness. He let the silence run awhile, then said, 'So, what's the problem?'

Adam took a long drink of his beer and rubbed at his eyes. 'It's my fault,' he said. 'My fault entirely.'

It was the old story, but with a twist. Annie was a nurse, and they'd met at a bar which was having an "Emergency Services Night", back when Adam was a Detective Constable.

'I tried to impress her with talking about how important CID was, how busy, how exciting, all the big and dangerous cases I worked on. Standard man stuff, you know how it is. We were in the corner of the bar, having to shout above the music. And she said to me – "What big case are you on at the moment then?"'

Adam's face slipped into a wistful smile. 'I had to admit I was on the trail of a couple of people who were nicking diesel from farmers' supply tanks. Well, I was only a probationer at the time really. She laughed, I laughed, and that was it. We were together from there.'

They'd seen each other for a few more months before moving in to a rented flat just outside the city centre. All was going beautifully and Adam had proposed. Being the old fashioned type, he'd asked Annie's father for permission first and it had been happily granted. But he'd managed to keep it as a surprise and waited until he and the unknowing bride were taking a summer evening's walk on the Cornwall coast.

'It was like Hollywood,' he said mistily. 'The sun was setting away to the west. The sea was lapping gently below us. Birds were wheeling in the air. I took her hand, stopped her, said there was something I had to ask and popped the question. She said yes straight away. It was beautiful.'

Adam didn't mention whether he or Annie had cried with the moment, but Dan didn't need to ask.

They bought a house together in Peverell, a three bedroom, semi detached Georgian place. It was a little run-down, and as often with newlyweds they were short of money, but they worked hard together to renovate it.

The perfect love story just got better. Annie became pregnant. They refused to be told whether the child was a boy or girl, wanted to wait for the surprise. And on the 4th July – ironically, Independence Day, as Adam pointed out – Thomas Clive Arthur Breen was born. The boy's middle names were taken from Annie and Adam's fathers.

Even Dan, a pessimist by birth, a cynic by experience and a sceptic by training, found a lump forming in his throat at the story. It must be the beer, he thought.

All continued as if scripted by a poet. Annie went back to work, but shifted her role, took a job as a research nurse to make her hours more predictable and suited to the demands of a young family. Adam was promoted to become a Detective Sergeant.

And now the first whispers of trouble rose.

'You know how it is with a career,' he said. 'When you're on the upwards path and keen and ambitious you stay all hours. I was starting to get involved in my first big cases and they don't run on a nine to five basis. I was away from home a lot, but Annie was understanding – mostly.'

As a sergeant, Adam had just about balanced the needs of his work and family. As an Inspector, he'd "got away with it" as he put it. But when the next promotion came, and he was leading the biggest inquiries, the cracks in the relationship turned to fracture.

'We started arguing a lot,' Adam said. 'I suppose it was fair enough. Looking back, I was hardly at home, but you don't see it at the time, do you? I kept missing important dates. Not like birthdays or our anniversary, I always managed to make time for those, but things like parents' evenings and football matches Tom was playing in. I kept promising I'd make more time, but you know what it's like. It's always tomorrow. And then it doesn't happen.'

The clock on the wall said it was well after ten. The night was moving on quickly.

Adam paused and took another long drink of his beer.

'Then came the crunch,' he said slowly. 'Annie's patience snapped after I missed a – well, this is going to sound ridiculous. You'll think it's something like Tom's school play, or a prize giving ceremony, but it was much more stupid than that.'

He hesitated and rubbed at his forehead. 'Tom had to go to the dentist for some fillings. I know no one likes the dentist, but Tom absolutely detests it. He's scared stiff, gets all worked up for days beforehand. It goes back to when he was five or six and fell over in the street. He bashed out a couple of teeth and had to have some emergency work done. It was really painful and he's never forgotten it. Anyway, so he's got this appointment, and he's pretty frantic about it. I promised I'd go with him, but we had an armed robbery which I got called out to. Annie had to go instead, despite her having an important meeting that day. And that was it. I came home to a quiet house. It was much worse than the tears and shouting I expected. Annie just said she thought it was time I moved out for a while.'

Adam tipped back the remains of his pint and added quietly, 'I didn't believe her. But she was absolutely insistent. And then we had a row, and it was ...' His voice tailed off. 'Anyway, it was more than apparent she wanted me to go. So I did.'

Adam was living in a flat off Mutley Plain. It was small,

cold, noisy and unpleasant, and less than half a mile from the comfort of his family home, the short distance a constant reminder.

'And this is what's really been rankling me,' Adam said. 'I was looking forwards to Christmas. I assumed I'd be spending most of it at home, even if it was only for Tom's sake. But Annie's saying she's not sure how much time we should spend together. Whether it might be better for Tom not to get used to having me around again. And that's why ...'

Adam swallowed hard. 'That's why I've been a bit up and down lately,' he said, with a masterstroke of understatement. 'I'm not normally like this. I think I've been taking it out on you, which I shouldn't have. Maybe it's why I flew at you this morning. Because you looked so contented, and I could see it was down to a woman. So – sorry for all that.'

He raised his empty glass, and Dan clinked it. The detective's eyes were shining in the dim light of the pub.

'I'll get us another beer,' he said, and quickly got up and headed for the bar. It was Dan's round, but he thought it best not to mention that. Sometimes a man needed an escape route.

They had another beer, then hailed a cab. As it stopped on Mutley Plain, Adam held out a hand and Dan shook it.

'You know what,' the detective said, his voice a little hazy. 'It's actually rather pleasant having you around. You bring a different perspective and that's refreshing. You have this knack of making people talk to you too, and that's more than useful in this job. Getliffe said so earlier, when I had a chat with him. You put people at ease and make them open up.' He nodded and added, 'Hell, I can hardly believe it, but you even managed it with me. Night.'

Adam was away, walking fast but a little unsteadily along the road. Dan got back to the flat, collected Rutherford from downstairs and took him out for a quick walk, partly to apologise for neglecting his friend and partly to clear his head.

When he got back, there was an answer machine message on his phone. It was from Adam.

"Thanks for a good night. I feel better for it. Don't bother calling me back, I'm going to get some sleep, but can you come to the MIR for nine tomorrow morning please? It looks like it might be an interesting day. I've been up to a little trick I hadn't told you about and I've just got word of a possible breakthrough in the case. It's about time we got to use the interview room."

Chapter Seventeen

THE TITLE "INTERVIEW ROOM" might perhaps sound passably pleasant, but the reality was an anachronism which wouldn't have looked out of place in a 1950s east European state.

It was below street level, the only natural light coming from a tiny rectangle of a window at the far end. And even then, the brave few beams had to be both keen and determined to make it inside. The window was covered with thick metal bars and grimy, opaque glass. The room was bare-bricked, adorned only with a thin and unwelcoming whitewash and small and cold. In the coming years Dan would discover that the temperature was remarkably consistent, no matter what was the weather outside, be it snowstorm or heatwave.

As for interview, it was more usually an interrogation which took place here.

It was Dan's first visit to the room, but Adam greeted it like an old friend, patting a fond hand on the grey metal door, and saying, 'Many a case I've cracked in here.'

And that was clearly well known in the station. As they walked into the custody block, the sergeant behind the desk grinned and said, 'Your usual, Mr Breen? I've reserved it specially for you.'

Interview Room number two, the smallest of the pair, the coldest, and by far the most oppressive.

'And that,' Adam said contentedly, 'equals the most likely to make your suspect feel like talking, so they can escape ASAP. It's exactly how an interview room should be. None of these soft furnishings and pastel colours of your modern politically correct nonsense.'

The furniture, if as such it could be so described, consisted of a table and three chairs. The table was so basic it would have pleased a puritan. A wooden board held up by metal legs might be a better description. On the side nearest the door were two plastic chairs, opposite them another. Adam seated himself in one, Dan tried the other, but then got up again and went to stand by the door.

'I've seen those TV shows too,' Adam said, over his shoulder. 'The ones where the nasty cop stands and the nice one sits. They're not really true to life, but if you want to stand over there, go ahead. Now, give me a moment so I can work out how to come at this interview.'

Dan leaned back against the wall. Its coolness was welcome. He was feeling warm, despite the temperature of the room, but whether it was the legacy of this morning's run with Rutherford, or the anticipation of what was to come, he wasn't sure.

He'd woken early, taken the dog for a few laps of Hartley Park, then driven down to the police station. Adam had been waiting, and instead of ascending the stairs to the MIR as Dan had expected they headed down, to the custody suite. As they walked, the detective explained about the potential breakthrough.

He'd had all the suspects put under surveillance.

'You didn't tell me,' Dan objected sulkily.

'I didn't trust you then,' came the straightforward response. 'But I'm telling you now.'

Surveillance is expensive and intensive in terms of staff, Adam said, but sometimes, often in fact, there was no choice. He'd grown frustrated with making indiscernible headway, Greater Wessex Police's most senior officers, the High Honchos as they were known, were agitating for progress, so they'd authorised a couple of nights of observations.

The first revealed nothing of any interest. The second, last night, had looked to be going the same way.

Arthur Bray was at home and watching the television. He'd walked around the house a couple of times and stopped to look at his shotguns, even run a hand over one, but whether or not the gesture might be interpreted as suspicious the watchers couldn't say. It could just be a man who was proud of his collection of guns.

Adam clicked his tongue as he related that part of the story, but it wasn't apparent whether he thought the information was important.

Penelope Ramsden was also at home, and painting, not in the DIY sense, but on a canvas. Inquires had discovered she was an amateur artist of some renown, particularly in demand for portraits. The officers watching her house couldn't tell for certain, but they thought her current project was a large picture of the late Edward Bray.

'And of that too, I'm not quite sure what to make,' Adam observed. 'It reinforces her story that she loved him, but also helps the theory that if he had spurned her she could easily have killed him out of jealousy.'

Eleanor Paget was working late at the hospice. At one stage she went for a walk around the grounds and seemed to be talking to herself, occasionally in an agitated manner, but the surveillance team couldn't get close enough to hear her words.

Regarding that nugget of observation, Adam had let out a sigh and said, 'It could be a tormented soul, lamenting the murder she'd committed, of course. But equally it might just be her practicing some speech to a group of fundraisers.'

Andrew Hicks had been at home, as had Jon Stead. Both were doing nothing more suspicious than watching the television. The night looked doomed to be another for the sizeable scrapyard of good ideas.

But then came the change. Hicks left the house, called for Stead and they went together to the local pub.

And as for Gordon Clarke, he too had been at home, that was until a taxi arrived to pick him up. It took him to the Red Lion, the same pub in which Hicks and Stead were sitting. And when Clarke arrived, they all shook hands and embraced warmly.

The three men clearly knew each other well.

And yet, said Adam, even that wasn't the most interesting part. The men had been kept under surveillance, but hadn't said or done anything which might be of interest to the police. They'd just sat, chatted, and drunk beer.

Then though, when they had left, the two watching detectives made some inquiries in the pub. With some heavy leaning on the reluctant landlord, they found that Hicks, Stead and Clarke were regulars there. And on several occasions in the past few months they had been overheard all talking together about ways to kill Edward Bray.

Gordon Clarke had been called first thing that morning and invited to the police station for a chat.

'Suzanne put it in exactly those terms,' Adam explained. 'She didn't say why, of course. He was suspicious, naturally, but she said it was just routine. Then he asked what would happen if he didn't come. She was happy to reassure him that would mean a couple of detectives having to come to his office and arrest him, then bring him in. So, he said he'll be here in a minute.'

It hadn't taken Dan long to learn there was much psychology to detective work. Adam wanted Clarke here to play the next stage of the investigation game on his territory, in this cold and intimidating room. The man would be off balance, wouldn't know what to expect, would probably think that if the police had strong evidence against him then he would already have been arrested.

Suzanne would see Hicks and Stead at the same time that Clarke was in the police station. But it was his which was the most important interview. If the three had plotted together to murder Edward Bray, then the resourceful and motivated Clarke was probably the ringleader. So, it was the decapitation strategy. Take him out first, and if he could be cracked, all else would follow.

'If you could keep quiet on this one, I'd be grateful,' Adam said airily. 'It might well be a vital interview. Depending on what I hear, I could even arrest him on suspicion of murder so I can hold him while inquiries continue. Just keep quiet and watch, if you'd be so kind.'

Dan breathed out hard. It was better drama than those police TV serials he'd begun watching, the very ones where he had indeed got the idea he should stand by the door during an interrogation, just like the hero always did.

It was Tuesday morning, just three days before Christmas. Perhaps it would be the day the Edward Bray murder case was solved.

Clarke was brought in to the interview room by the custody sergeant. He was led to the chair and asked to sit down. His hair had been cut and newly highlighted, but he wore the same shiny suit as before.

Adam didn't look up. He was scribbling some notes on a piece of paper. Clarke stared at him, then leaned forwards on his chair. He coughed pointedly, but Adam kept writing.

Clarke sat back, crossed his legs, then uncrossed them again and cleared his throat.

Still no reaction from Adam.

'Nice place you have here,' the businessman said.

'Thanks,' Adam replied, but still didn't look up from his notes.

Clarke shifted awkwardly on his seat and looked around the room.

'It's cold in here,' he observed, pulling his jacket tighter around his body.

Adam didn't reply.

Now Gordon Clarke began itching at his cheek. 'Look, what is all this about?' he said finally.

Adam glanced up. 'I think you know,' he said quietly.

'I can assure you I don't.'

'I think you do.'

There was a silence. Outside, in the muffled distance, a lorry rumbled past.

'It's about Edward Bray,' Adam said. 'The murder of Edward Bray.'

Clarke's face was shining with a gathering sweat now, despite the chill of the room.

'And what's that got to do with me?'

Adam didn't reply, just looked the man in the eyes.

Clarke broke off the stare and shifted again on his chair. 'Look, what is going on?'

His voice sounded thin, tense. He picked again at his cheek.

'What the hell is going on?' he barked.

'Edward Bray. The murder of Edward Bray,' Adam repeated. 'Killing Edward Bray …' he paused, and then added, 'just as you were heard discussing in the Red Lion – on several occasions – prior to the murder.'

Clarke squinted at Adam, then closed his eyes briefly. When he spoke, he sounded strangely relieved. 'Oh, that.'

'Yes – that.'

'I can explain.'

'I've heard that before,' came the menacing reply. 'But I hope, for your sake, you can.'

The businessman sat up in his chair. Dan took a subtle step forwards and studied him. He was sure Clarke looked more relaxed now.

'Some of the local gossips been talking to you about our game, have they?' he said.

'Go on.'

'It's hardly a secret.'

'Go on.'

'In fact, it's our favourite drinking pastime. Fantasising about how to kill Bray.'

Gordon Clarke told his story easily, and without even a hint of embarrassment.

He had first met Hicks and Stead at the county court, on one of the days given over to Edward Bray's litigation against his tenants. They sat waiting for their cases to be called, chatted, found common ground in their hatred of Bray, swapped mobile numbers and became friends. They often went out for a few beers together, and on one of those drunken nights a bizarre new entertainment was born.

The Kill Edward Bray game.

The rules were a little hazy, but the point seemed to be to murder the man in the most painful and entertaining manner possible – but all entirely in the imagination, Clarke insisted. His own personal best solution, as it were, was to run over him with a steamroller. The vehicle would be moving very slowly, inch by inch in fact, and, to prolong the agony, starting at Bray's feet, naturally.

Adam shook his head, but kept listening.

Hicks' favourite idea had a historical theme. He wanted to

re-enact a gladiatorial contest, to see how Bray would fare against a pride of hungry lions. Clarke said he pointed out that this might be over a little too quickly to make a winning suggestion, but Hicks was confident Bray would give a good account of himself. Nonetheless, however long it took, he thought it would provide a wonderful spectacle.

Stead, as befitted the quietest of the trio, had to be pushed to an idea, but eventually said he would be happy to see Bray publicly stoned to death. The other two thought the concept unimaginative, but had to concede it had the advantage of allowing all Bray's many enemies the opportunity of casting a gleeful rock or two.

Whatever, for each method of punishment, the public would be invited along, to witness the humiliation and dispatch.

'And which of your lovely imaginings actually won the game?' Adam asked, in a voice that was a hammer of sarcasm.

'I'm not sure any did,' Clarke replied easily. 'I don't think that was the point. We were all a bit the worse for drink and just enjoying ourselves.'

He was definitely more relaxed now, sitting back on the chair, his legs crossed.

'It's all bloody ridiculous this, isn't it?' Adam snapped. 'Not to mention gross. Grown men, fantasising about how to murder someone.'

Clarke shrugged. 'You didn't know Edward Bray. You didn't suffer at his hands.'

'Did you kill Edward Bray?'

'No. I didn't. I freely admit to thinking about it, even talking about it, but it was all just a game. I didn't murder him. As I've told you, and as you've no doubt checked and found out, I was in Bristol when he was killed.'

Adam tapped a hand on the table. 'Well, I have to say, this all gives me sufficient grounds to hold you here pending further inquiries,' he said.

There was a knock at the door. The custody sergeant opened it and began to speak but was pushed aside by a sizeable and severe-looking woman.

'Just what the hell is going on here?' she barked at Adam.

There was a second's silence. The strip light in the ceiling buzzed loud.

Adam said heavily, 'Ah, Ms Francis. I should have known.'

'Chief Inspector Breen,' came the icy reply. 'It really is me who should have known.'

It was apparent the two knew each other well, but even more obvious was the mutual dislike. It had turned the still air sour. She had short blonde hair, greying over her ears, and pale, watery blue eyes which rarely blinked. Her features were sharp and severe and her face prematurely lined. But what distinguished her most was her complete lack of adornments. She wore no jewellery, no make-up, and her suit was black and plain, her shirt a strict and simple white.

The woman was a walking definition of austere.

'I take it by your arrival here you're acting for Mr Clarke?' Adam asked.

'You are as perceptive as ever, Chief Inspector. And I take it by the fact that you're investigating the case he will certainly have need of my services.'

Another silence. The pair stared at each other. The already chilly interview room felt like it was now playing host to the dawning of a new ice age. Only Gordon Clarke was enjoying the moment. He'd started smiling.

'Mr Clarke asked me to come here as soon as I could,' Francis continued. 'I was a little delayed by a small matter in court, for which I apologise – to my client, Chief Inspector, not to you, naturally. Now, if I may have a few minutes with Mr Clarke, as the law states I must unquestionably be allowed.'

She glanced towards the door, folded her arms and waited expectantly. Gordon Clarke's smile widened. Adam didn't say anything, just walked out of the room and closed the door heavily behind him. In the corridor, the sergeant started to apologise for letting her in, but Adam reassured the man he had little choice. The law was on her side, as she was well aware. Anyway, it was apparently renowned in police circles that arguing with Julia Francis was akin to attempting to stand in the way of a fully laden, runaway, articulated lorry, heading down a steep hill.

'She's the local criminals' favourite solicitor,' Adam explained quietly as he stood with Dan in the corridor. 'Very much in demand by the worst undesirables. Many a nasty crim she's got off on some wheedling technicality or dirty dodge. She's not exactly popular around here. I've had more than a few run-ins with her myself.'

'Funnily enough,' Dan said, 'I guessed that.'

They waited in the corridor. Adam made a quick call to Suzanne and listened to what she'd found out from questioning Hicks and Stead. The expression on the detective's face said her inquiries were faring no better. Ten minutes passed. A couple of police officers wandered by and said good morning to Adam, but he just nodded in return.

'Francis being here is going to make life a whole lot more difficult,' he said. 'I'm willing to bet she'll come out demanding Clarke be released immediately. If I so much as raise an objection, she'll be threatening court writs, complaints to the High Honchos and the local MP. I wouldn't be surprised one day to hear her threatening to petition the Prime Minister, the American President and the Pope.'

As if on cue, the interview room door opened. 'Mr Clarke will see you now,' Francis said, managing to make it sound as if they were the lowest of door-to-door salesmen lurking seedily at the rear entrance of a manor house.

Adam walked back in, Dan following. Gordon Clarke was sitting at the table. If anything, his smile was broader even than before. The third division footballer had scored a hat trick.

'This is how it goes, Chief Inspector,' Francis said. 'Is my client under arrest?'

'No.'

'Do you intend to arrest him?'

'I'm not sure yet.'

'I'll take that as no then, knowing you as I do. What evidence do you believe you have against him?'

'He hated Edward Bray.'

'Along with hundreds of others. What specifically?'

'He was heard discussing killing Mr Bray.'

'As part of a game, which he now admits to be juvenile and

193

ill-judged, but nonetheless, merely a game, just a fantasy, however distasteful. Do you have anything else you would wish to raise?'

It was a ruthless, quick-fire dissection of whatever case there may have been against Gordon Clarke, an assassination by machine gun.

Francis waited, but Adam didn't reply. 'And, of course, my client has an alibi, has he not?' she said, with a tone of finality. 'One which I can see by your face you have checked, and found impossible to undermine, despite no doubt expending your best efforts. So, Chief Inspector, unless you have anything else to put to Mr Clarke, he and I will be leaving now.'

Dan and Adam walked back up the stairs. 'Bloody woman,' Adam grumbled. 'I suspected the moment she walked in the game was up. We don't really have a thing on Clarke and she knows it.'

Suzanne was waiting in the MIR. She favoured Dan with a brief, frosty glare, then told Adam all she had learnt from Hicks and Stead.

Hicks had been seen first and happily admitted the game, even delighted in it. His version of the men's favoured methods to "Kill Edward Bray" tallied precisely with those given by Gordon Clarke.

'He was even happy to add a few more,' Suzanne said. 'He started going on about the relative merits of a public hanging, but I'd had enough by then and stopped him. Stead was more reticent and at least had the decency to look a little ashamed, but when I pushed him he admitted it all too.'

'What's your view of that then?' Adam asked.

She shrugged. 'It's certainly interesting they know each other. The connection is there that could point to a plot between them. We've seen it before often enough, people brought together by a shared purpose, which then turns into a conspiracy. But ...'

'But what?'

Suzanne considered for a moment. 'Well, Clarke's not daft, nor is Hicks, and Stead may be a bit quiet, but he's not stupid either. So if one, or two, or all of them had killed Bray, I can't believe they'd meet up for a few beers only a week or so after. And certainly not somewhere as obvious as a pub, and particularly not one where they'd been talking about killing Bray before. They'd want to lie low, surely.'

Dan cleared his throat, was about to speak, then saw Suzanne's look and stopped.

'No, go on,' the ever-observant Adam prompted. 'What did you want to say?'

'Well, just that it could work both ways, that argument, couldn't it? As you say, they're smart. If they were responsible for killing Bray, they could have come out like that, all meeting up for a nice drink, to double-bluff us. They'd probably guess the story of them knowing each other and the "Kill Edward Bray" game would emerge at some point. We'd conclude they'd never have done all that and then got together for a beer if they genuinely had been plotting to carry out the murder, and then actually gone and done it.'

Suzanne let out an unattractive snort. 'That sounds so farfetched as to be over the horizon and out of sight,' she said. 'If you have to venture an opinion at all – only if you really have to, that is – maybe you could keep it a bit more plausible.'

'I reckon it's possible,' Dan retorted, huffily.

'So are lots of things. The sun not coming up in the morning. The High Honchos giving us unlimited resources for a case. Julia Francis applying to become a Special Constable. Me meeting a trustworthy journalist. But it doesn't mean they're very likely.'

'Now look ...'

Adam held up his hands. 'OK, let's not fight amongst ourselves. We've got enough on as it is. For what it's worth, I'm still suspicious of Hicks, Stead and Clarke. Let's do some more work on them. Suzanne, I know it's a big job, but get the team going through the CCTV of Plymouth and Bristol train stations for last Monday, to see if we can spot Clarke and pin down the timings. Let's see if Hicks and Stead had access to a car which might have got them from the river to the lay-by in time to be waiting to kill Bray. Work with traffic and use the

Automatic Number Plate Recognition system. See if that throws up any suspicious movements of any of our potential killers.'

She nodded, walked to the end of the MIR and picked up a phone. Adam stood, staring out of the window.

'Right,' he said, when he turned around. 'Time's against us. I got a call from the Deputy Chief Constable this morning. For reasons of finance and public relations, but most importantly the force's crime statistics and the compiling of the annual report, he made it very plain he wanted this case cleared up by Christmas. It's a high profile one, and I think he can see a glossy page dedicated to it and how very efficiently we cracked it. That only gives us another couple of days. So let's get solving some mysteries. First, let's find out what happened between Arthur Bray and his son to lead to this so-called "divorce", and whether it could have any bearing on Edward's murder.'

Adam paused and gave Dan a thoughtful look, then added, 'And because I think Arthur Bray could well react better to you than me, it might just be time for you to carry out your first investigative interview.'

Chapter Eighteen

THEY CAUGHT UP WITH Arthur Bray on the golf course, the seventh hole in fact. As they were walking out to the green, Dan mused how this must be one of the odder venues for an interview in a criminal investigation.

'Not really,' Adam replied. 'I've known much stranger. I've caught a killer on a rowing boat in the mouth of an estuary, and even one on a waltzer at a funfair.'

Dan's imagination fired and he asked for details, but Adam wouldn't be distracted. The detective had an air of resolution about him this morning. He was striding fast and purposefully and more than once had ventured the forceful opinion that it was about time this case was cracked. They had their suspects, now it was just a case of pushing and probing until the killer gave himself away, or they found the vital piece of evidence which would expose him.

It was coming up to noon. Dan found his mind wandering to the mysterious Claire, the dark haired detective he'd seen briefly in the MIR. He chided himself and instead forced his thoughts to Kerry, and when they would get together to exchange presents. She'd already dropped a couple of hints about how she was spending Christmas Day at her mum's, on the eastern outskirts of Plymouth, and there was plenty of spare food and drink for guests. If he went, it would be the first Christmas he hadn't been largely alone for longer than he could remember, but ...

But, why was there was always a but in life? Spending a day like Christmas together reeked of commitment, and Dan was by no means sure he was ready for that.

The sky was a uniform grey, but the day was dry, if not warm. That wasn't a problem, as the speed Adam was walking was quite sufficient to keep any chill at bay. It was like a route march. The golf course was busy, pockets of people in their brightly coloured jumpers clustering together to inflict injury on the small, white balls, or to discuss the merits of various shots.

197

The still air was punctured with the odd zing of a stroke and the thud of a ball hitting a fairway, or just as commonly, crash-landing in the undergrowth.

It was mercifully quiet on the news front, and Dan suspected he would be free to work on the investigation today. He'd called Nigel earlier to see what was going on and had been reminded it was the day of *Wessex Tonight*'s Christmas Special. That meant choirs of children, carols, and minimal news. The cameraman was currently trying to corral a pack of six-year-olds into a passable rendition of Hark the Herald Angels Sing. From the discordant noise in the background, it sounded quite a challenge.

So long as no big stories broke, Dan should be safe from the tyranny of Lizzie. He decided not to call in. It could be asking for trouble. She would ring if he were required. As with sleeping dogs, it was by far the best policy to let manic editors lie.

Adam had asked what Dan thought of Gordon Clarke, and his reaction to the questioning of earlier.

'It was odd. He was definitely nervous at first. I was sure he had something to hide, something he was clearly worried about being found out. But when you raised the "Kill Edward Bray" game he seemed to relax.'

'What do you make of that?'

'I suppose that he's up to something, but it might not be connected to Bray's death. Maybe it's a business thing, perhaps a fraud, something like that.'

Adam nodded thoughtfully, but didn't reply.

The golf course was on the edge of Dartmoor, only a few miles from Arthur Bray's house. They had knocked earlier, found no one at home, and Adam had then called at all the houses around until they found a lead on where their victim may be. As Bray had no mobile phone, this visit would be a surprise.

At the club house, a wizened middle-aged man, who introduced himself as one of the board and who smelt of whisky, despite the early hour, confirmed Arthur Bray's presence. He estimated his party would be at the sixth or seventh hole. They'd checked the sixth, just missed him, and were now heading towards a familiar stocky figure.

Am I still taking the lead in this one?' Dan asked, trying not to sound nervous.

'So long as you don't make a mess of it.'

'Thanks for making me feel so relaxed.'

'My pleasure.'

'What do I ask him?'

'I'll do the preliminaries, there are a couple of little things I want to check. Then you can come in. It's not so much a fact interview as a feely one. We know what he was doing when his son was killed – or claims to have been doing – and all that stuff. I want to know more about his character, and particularly what was the reason for his so-called divorce with Edward. Use that charm of yours and get him talking. He'll feel less threatened by you than me.'

A couple of rabbits were nibbling at the grass at the edge of the fairway and stopped to watch them walk by. There was even a hedgehog too, scurrying busily for a clump of undergrowth, perhaps awoken by the mildness of the recent weather. They crossed a small, timber bridge over a shallow stream and picked their way through a patch of gorse. Dan spotted a gleam of white in the thicket, bent down and picked up a ball.

'It's a sign,' he said. 'That it's my lucky day, and that today we'll crack the Bray case.'

'It'll take more than a lost and found golf ball to make me believe that,' came the deflating reply.

They reached the green. Arthur Bray was bent over a putter, taking a couple of practice swings. Dan stopped, but Adam walked on, his footfall thudding on the firm turf. Bray ignored him and took the shot. The ball missed the hole by a good three feet.

He looked up irritably. 'Thanks. I was on for a birdie there.'

'I'm sorry to interrupt you, Mr Bray,' said the detective, who sounded anything but. 'However I'm afraid we need to have another chat.'

'Can't it wait until I've finished my round?'

Adam's look was reply enough. Bray sighed and walked

over to his partner, a slightly younger man, who nodded and began rummaging in his golf bag, eventually producing a shooting stick and a silver hip flask from which he had a good sip. Bray took one too, then returned to where Adam was standing.

'How can I help you this time?' he asked patiently.

Adam explained that inquiries were still ongoing and he needed to check on a couple of points. He asked Bray if he knew anyone else on the list of suspects. He'd met Eleanor Paget once or twice he thought, and even spoken to her on a couple of occasions, although only passing good mornings and comments about the weather.

Dan nodded to himself. His theory was holding together and his plan about how to approach the man was looking sound. Bray also knew Penelope Ramsden by sight, although he hadn't really spoken to her.

'I was well out of the business by the time she was there,' he said. 'As you know.'

He leaned on his club and waited for the next question. Dan felt Adam tap at his foot.

'Thanks for that, err – Arthur,' he began, taking his cue. 'So, how's the golf going?'

'The golf?'

'Err – yes.'

'It was going well.'

Of the approximately two seconds duration of the sentence, the word "was" took up about a second and a half.

Manfully, Dan tried again.

'Right. And how are you – err – coping?'

'With the golf course?'

'No, with the – well, you know …'

'The death of my son?'

'Yes.'

'Fine, thank you. Just as I'd already told you.'

Dan suffered another tap on his shoe from the impatient detective.

'And – err – any plans for Christmas?'

'Yes. Some peace and quiet.'

If he was being honest, Dan thought, his first interview in an investigation wasn't going terribly well. His attempts to prepare the ground for a smooth conversation had resulted in the terrain remaining entirely overgrown, pitted with pot holes, and perhaps even sown with the odd land mine for good measure.

'Now, if you've finished inquiring about my welfare, may I get on with my round?' Bray asked.

'There is only one other thing I think we need to know.'

'Yes?'

'Well, it's ...'

'Yes?'

Adam was nodding a less than gentle encouragement, Bray just standing, waiting. Dan took a breath. Some subjects resisted skirting. Some atmospheres couldn't be eased. Sometimes a dive into the dark waters was the only way.

He hesitated, then said, 'We really need to get to the bottom of why you and Edward – well, had that falling out.'

Bray folded his arms. 'It was a little more than a falling out, as I believe I made very clear.'

'Well, yes, but ...'

'And as I've said, it's very personal and I don't think it's relevant to your inquiries.'

'I appreciate that, but it can be odd how little things turn out to be important ...'

'I don't think this is.'

The old man's voice was firm and his face was set. Dan glanced to Adam, but no help was forthcoming. It felt like another challenge, but perhaps more important than any that had gone before.

His mettle was being well tested.

'Now, was there anything else?' Bray asked. 'Or may I finally get on with my round?'

From a distant tree across the fairway, a crow cackled. A breath of wind tickled some of the gorse and teased at the man's thinning white hair. He began to turn, as if to walk away.

'She died in the hospice, didn't she?' Dan said quickly.

Bray stopped. 'What?'

'That's how you know Eleanor Paget. Your wife, Edward's

mother, she died in the hospice.'

'I … I don't see what that has to do with any of this.'

For the first time, his voice was less certain. Bray fumbled in his pocket, took out a packet of cigars and some matches. He was about to light up when he stopped, stared at the cigar and slowly placed it back in the packet.

It was that look. There was something in the look.

'I don't really want to go back over what happened with Elizabeth, if you don't mind,' Bray said, but his voice was thin, lacking in any strength, almost a mumble. 'I'd just … I'd like to be getting on with my round now.'

'It was cancer, wasn't it?' Dan asked.

'What?'

'Cancer killed your wife. I'd say – lung cancer, in fact.'

'What? How did you …'

'But she didn't smoke, did she?'

'How did you …'

'She didn't smoke, and you did. And she contracted lung cancer. And Edward blamed you for it.'

The defiance was gone, banished in an instant of truth. Arthur Bray closed his eyes and hung his head.

It wasn't quite as simple as Dan had suspected, but then – as he said to Adam later, trying not to sound smug but mostly failing – life very rarely was.

Arthur Bray stood, head bowed for a good couple of minutes. Finally he looked up, stared out across the golf course, to the distant grey tors of Dartmoor and said quietly, 'I still don't think it's relevant to the investigation, but if you insist, and you will then give me peace, I will tell you.'

And so he did.

Elizabeth Bray had indeed died of lung cancer in St Jude's Hospice. She had lived with Arthur for more than thirty years, during which time he had always been a smoker. Such are the sufferances of love. Yet with one of those quirks which fate so enjoys, Arthur had suffered no ill-effects, but she had contracted the disease.

The doctors' opinion was that, of course, they could not say that Arthur's smoking caused the cancer, but equally they couldn't say it hadn't.

Edward Bray was devoted to his mother. In a childhood where his dad was often away, or working long hours, she was the focus of his emotions as he grew up. The news that her illness was terminal sent him into a spin of remorse and rage. And, as people often do at times of great strain in their lives, he looked for someone upon whom to vent his anger.

That person was his father.

'It wasn't all due to Elizabeth's death,' Bray explained. 'That wouldn't be fair. Edward and I had been getting along badly for quite a while. He was taking over the business, but running it in a very different way to me. He was far harder. I prided myself on looking after my tenants. I used to give them much more of a chance if they were having problems paying their rent. But he was ruthless. He would evict them more or less straight away. I thought he was heartless, he thought I was a sentimental old fool whose time had passed. Perhaps it was a generational thing, but we never saw eye to eye.'

The relationship may not have been good, but it had at least continued. That was, until Mrs Bray's diagnosis.

'He was at the hospice with her nearly all the time,' Arthur said. 'For her sake, we tried to keep the disagreements between us a secret, but it was by no means easy. I fear she must have sensed it. And when she died, that was when it all ended with my son too. He rounded on me with a dreadful fury, we rowed and eventually we agreed we would have nothing more to do with each other. That was the divorce thing I told you about.'

If Dan had been carrying out this interview as a reporter, he would have gone on to ask the dreaded, "How did you feel?" question. But Arthur Bray's posture, bowed over and leaning hard on his golf club, and the haunted look on his face, answered that more powerfully than words ever could. The man was of a generation brought up to restrain their feelings, but some emotions can escape even a lifetime of conditioning.

'It wasn't just me he took it out on,' Bray continued. 'It was the world. He was really tough on his staff, and his business associates. And as for his tenants ... well, I hardly need tell you about that. You've seen all the stories about the people he evicted. Perhaps persecuted might even have been a better word. He became a very bitter man.'

He had taken another long sip from the flask offered by his friend, and asked if that was all they needed to know. Adam had nodded, Dan said yes, and Arthur Bray had slowly walked off across the green and on towards the next hole.

Against the great backdrop of the grey Dartmoor sky, he looked a small man in a very big world.

'Well,' Dan said, as he drove them back to Plymouth, 'that's one set of mysteries solved then. What happened to the relationship between Bray and his father, why he was so very ruthless, and then why, despite that, he saved St Jude's. And what a dreadfully sad story it is.'

'Yes indeed,' Adam replied, but then went on to rather spoil the poignancy of the mood by adding, 'But does any of that help us find who killed Edward Bray?'

And to that question, Dan had no answer.

They were almost back at Charles Cross when Adam's mobile rang. He listened for a few seconds, then said, 'Really? But she won't say on the phone? OK, I'll get there now,' and hung up.

Dan didn't have a chance to ask what the call was about. 'Eleanor Paget's rung in,' Adam said, before he could raise a word. 'She's got something she needs to see me about – urgently and in person, she says. This might be our break. To the hospice please, and fast.'

It should have been only five minutes drive, but it took another fifteen in the Christmas traffic. The city was thronging, full of shoppers weighed down with handfuls of bulging bags. Families and groups of friends disappeared into pubs and restaurants, seeking a few minutes respite from the retail storm. The rituals of the season were nearing their chaotic climax.

Adam kept checking his watch, wishing cars and buses out of their way. Such was his agitation Dan wouldn't have been surprised if he'd started asking, 'Are we there yet? Are we there yet?' He was like a child on Christmas Eve, waiting for the clock to turn to the sacred midnight hour.

A couple more crawling roundabouts and they reached the hospice's drive. Adam was out of the car the second it stopped moving. Dan parked and hurried after him.

Paget was waiting in her office. She shook their hands again, then said, 'I'm not sure if this is important to your investigation, or even if it's relevant, but I thought I had to tell you. I'm sorry to ask you to come here, but it didn't seem right to do it over the phone. In fact, I was in two minds whether I should say anything at all.'

Adam leaned forwards. 'Carry on please,' he urged.

'It may be nothing, but ...'

'Please, let us be the judge of that,' he interrupted impatiently. 'What do you want to tell us?'

'Just that – well, that I know one of your suspects for the murder of Mr Bray. Perhaps your prime suspect, even. And I have to say, I think he's a very odd man.'

Adam's eyes widened. 'Which one? And how do you know he's a suspect?'

'I know because he sent a text to tell me, just a little earlier. And as to who – it's Gordon Clarke.'

Dan had to stop himself letting out a low whistle. Adam took out his pad and began writing careful notes.

Clarke was, so he claimed, in love with Eleanor Paget. The two had met at a business reception a few months ago.

'With hindsight, I should have seen it,' she said. 'He latched on to me straight away, and he wouldn't let go. We exchanged business cards, as you do at these things, and he's hardly left me alone since.'

She gestured to a fine bunch of flowers sitting on her windowsill. 'Those are from him. They're not the first to arrive here either.'

Her tone was hardly one of a flattered and charmed woman. 'I've been trying to let him down gently, but with no luck. I think I'm just going to have to tell him straight out that I'm not interested and ask him to leave me alone.'

Just after the reception Clarke had sent a text, saying what a pleasure it was to meet her. He'd followed it up with some flowers, and then an invitation to share an evening drink.

'I went because I suppose I felt I should,' she said. 'He seemed a nice enough guy, if not really my type. I only meant to go out for an hour, but he insisted on buying me dinner. It was impossible to say no. Since then, he's always sending text messages and emails. That's how I know he's a suspect. He sent me a message earlier to tell me that he'd been questioned. I expect he thought I'd be impressed. That's when I called you.'

'Why do you think we should be concerned?' Adam asked. 'Has he said something to make you suspicious he might have killed Edward Bray?'

She poured a glass of water from a plastic bottle and took a drink. 'I called you for two reasons. Firstly because I know the police look for links between people in murder cases – I've read enough books to be aware of that. But also, and far more importantly, I ...'

Her voice faltered. 'Go on,' Adam prompted.

'Well, this is where it gets difficult.'

The detective tried a sympathetic smile, but it was as effective as a veteran hangman eyeing his victim.

'Please, go on anyway. We're more than used to hearing difficult things.'

'But it feels like I'm trying to get him into trouble.'

'Not at all. You're just doing your duty as a good citizen.'

Dan winced. That line was doubtless well-practised and even better intentioned, the product of a hundred investigations and more. But nonetheless it felt like the said hangman reassuring his victim that what was about to happen was all for the best.

Paget hesitated, then said, 'Well, he did go on about Mr Bray quite a lot. It was clear he really hated the man. I mean – detested him, with an absolute passion.'

Adam sounded disappointed. 'Is that all?'

She, in turn, sounded surprised. 'Isn't it enough? I mean, I'm not a detective, but it sounds like it could be a motive for murder, doesn't it?'

'Perhaps. But a lot of people didn't like Edward Bray.'

Adam had stopped writing notes. Whatever revelation he was hoping for had clearly failed to materialise. The play had stopped short. The scene had been acted out, but the eagerly anticipated dramatic denouement had gone absent without leave. He clicked his tongue a couple of times, thanked Paget and got up to leave.

She escorted them to the main doors. 'I hope I haven't wasted your time, Chief Inspector,' she asked tentatively. 'I just thought you ought to know.'

Adam was back on his gentlemanly, diplomatic form. 'Not at all, of course not. What you've told us might well be important. Thanks for doing so.'

She smiled. 'Good. I have to confess, I was worried about telling you. And I must admit, I was a bit naughty about Gordon's feelings towards Mr Bray too.'

Adam was almost at the car, but Dan paused, asked, 'In what way?'

'Well, I have to confess, I used them rather.'

'How?'

'I told Gordon that I was having more than my share of troubles with Mr Bray too, particularly with his endless plans for the hospice. I used him as a bit of an excuse, as to why I couldn't see Gordon again. I said I had far too much on dealing with Mr Bray for any distractions, however pleasant they might be.'

Adam turned sharply. 'What did you say again?' he asked.

Adam didn't speak for the whole of the drive back to Charles Cross, but it was clear from his expression he was lost in the case, thinking it all through. And his attentions were focused on Gordon Clarke.

If the man always had one very obvious motive for murder, with his long and well exhibited hatred of Edward Bray, then now the tally had doubled. His fascination with Eleanor Paget, and the possibility of him believing the removal of Bray would leave the way clear for the relationship to develop was a rich addition to the potential case against him.

The man had surged ahead of the field. He'd gone from being a clear suspect, to a strong suspect, and now the prime suspect.

Adam bounded up the stairs to the MIR to find Suzanne, and

demanded an instant de-brief on the results of this morning's investigations. Dan sensed the moment to be small and silent. He slunk to the back of the room and leant against the windowsill. It felt akin to being a child eavesdropping on the esoteric conversation of adults.

Today, Christmas Special or no, angelic children and carols notwithstanding, *Wessex Tonight* could have a scoop on the first arrest in the Edward Bray murder case.

It had been a busy morning in the inquiry, the detectives working through all the tasks Adam had set them earlier. Dislike her as he might, Dan had to admit Suzanne's briefing was impressively thorough and comprehensive.

The first issue was transport, and the potential for all the suspects to make it to the lay-by in time to be waiting for Bray to arrive. No cars or vans had been hired anywhere in the Plymouth area by any of the six. There had been the usual spate of thefts of various sorts of automobiles, but all had been investigated and resolved and none appeared connected with the case.

That left the suspects' own vehicles. All had cars, apart from Andrew Hicks. Gordon Clarke's was in his garage at home all day, so he said, but that couldn't be verified. He'd walked to the station to catch his train to Bristol, it being only a matter of ten minutes. When asked why he didn't get a taxi, given the wet weather, Clarke said he had considered doing so, but the rain eased just before he needed to leave. Besides, he had added, reluctantly, business wasn't booming at the moment and money was a little tight.

Jon Stead had a car, but it was being used by his wife Vicky, a fact confirmed by both her, her sister and the company she worked for. The couple had a year-old baby son, Joseph, who her sister was looking after while Vicky returned to work on a part-time basis.

Arthur Bray said his car was at home, Penelope Ramsden that hers was at the office and Eleanor Paget said hers was at the hospice. None of this could be independently confirmed or denied.

The Automatic Number Plate Recognition System had been

checked. It uses a comprehensive network of cameras and stores records of vehicle movements for a month. None of the plates of the cars owned by the suspects showed up as travelling anywhere near the lay-by around the time that Edward Bray was murdered.

'That doesn't mean anything though,' Adam observed. 'Criminals have got to know about the system now, just like they're aware we can trace their mobile phones. False number plates are easy enough to get hold of. Just slip them over the real plate, or replace it for a while, and that's the system foxed.'

Next in Suzanne's account came the CCTV pictures of Plymouth and Bristol railway stations. She clicked on a computer and brought up the images. Adam stared, then let out a long groan.

Despite civil liberties campaigners citing the prevalence of CCTV as evidence of Britain's surveillance state, the truth, as Dan had quickly come to learn, is rather more mundane: many CCTV cameras don't actually work at all, and are only installed as deterrents. And of those that do work, the pictures are frequently little more than useless. The camera is either pointing in the wrong direction, or the quality of the images are so dark and dull, grainy and blurred as to make them hopeless in aiding any form of detective work, let alone coming close to being reliable enough for use as evidence in court.

These images were typical. The picture was fuzzy and gloomy, the shot was wide, so lacking any detail, and the rain and darkness of the day weren't helping. The images from Plymouth showed a man walking quickly in to the train station, the shot lasting no longer than seven or eight seconds. The Bristol pictures were a little better, but not much. They captured the same man walking out of the station entrance and climbing into a taxi.

In both sets, the man was wearing a long raincoat and sheltering under an umbrella, which obscured his features.

'It looks like Clarke,' Suzanne said. 'It's his build. For another little check, I sent a detective to his office. It was ostensibly to check on his movements over Christmas, just in case we needed to speak to him again, but in reality to see if he's got a coat like that. And there it was, hanging up just inside the door, and that umbrella beside it too. From what I, and the detective who saw them can tell from the pictures, they look to be exactly the same ones.'

Adam turned away from the computer and swore.

'In other words,' he added, 'there's no evidence to help us at all.'

'No sir,' Suzanne replied.

'Is it worth getting Clarke back in? Arresting him this time? Trying to put some heat on him?'

'On what basis? That he's taken a fancy to someone else who's got a connection with the case, and might hope getting Edward Bray out of the way would give him more of a chance with her? I can imagine what that solicitor of his would say about that.'

Adam nodded. 'Yeah,' he said sulkily. 'But you'd agree he remains our prime suspect?'

'I would sir. But I don't think we've got anything like enough evidence even to arrest him. And I don't think we should rule the others out either.'

Adam sat down heavily on a desk. The clock on the wall said it was just after one.

'Let's have some lunch then, and see if that brings any inspiration. If we're going to get this case cracked by Christmas, and make our beloved High Honchos happy, then we're running out of time.'

As perhaps befitted the festive season, the children and their carols went undisturbed by the spectre of breaking news. There were no developments in the Bray case that afternoon.

For Dan, it was an important, if tedious lesson. So far, he'd greatly enjoyed the twists and turns of the investigation. It felt dynamic and fast moving, continually full of surprises. In fairness, Adam had warned it wasn't always thus, that long and sometimes frustrating periods of hard work, with little happening, were more the reality of detective work.

This afternoon, Dan very much felt that for himself.

He sat in the MIR and watched Adam and Suzanne go

through piles of paperwork, witness statements and records of the movements of their suspects. They raised the odd point, even occasionally ventured a theory, none of which led to anything approaching progress.

Dan did his best to distract himself by working on the puzzle on the wall. Bonham's string of characters danced on the edge of his eye line, felt like it was calling, waving and taunting.

992 619U

Dan had always prided himself on enjoying a good riddle. When some rare and precious spare time allowed, he would often attempt – and commonly come somewhere close to completing – a cryptic crossword in one of the newsroom broadsheets.

He'd tried looking up the letters and number on the internet at home, but found only reams of financial data and some references to a far distant galaxy. Both of which dated from long after Bonham's conviction, and neither of which offered any help.

The "U" had kept tickling his mind and prompted a strange thought that perhaps it could refer to a German U-boat of Second World War vintage. But some more research sunk that line of inquiry as effectively as a barrage of depth charges.

Dan did his best to come up with a lightning strike of inspiration, but his sullen brain was proving immune to prompting. Eventually he gave up and returned his attentions to Adam and Suzanne.

But still nothing of note was happening in the inquiry. And by five o'clock, hate to admit it though he did, Dan was very bored.

It was a relief when Adam called a halt to the day. He told Suzanne and the other detectives in the MIR to go home, rest, and they would start afresh tomorrow.

Dan waited for everyone else to depart, before asking, 'What shall I do? There doesn't seem much point me coming back tomorrow and just sitting here, waiting for something to happen.'

'That's fair enough. It's not exactly interesting. Why don't you go back to your newsroom tomorrow. I can always call you if there is some development. Are you off home now then?'

The question was oddly tentative. 'Not necessarily,' Dan replied. 'What did you have in mind?'

'Do you fancy a beer? And maybe something to eat?'

'Yeah, I'd like that. But can I sort out my domestic life first?'

'Oh yes? Have you got that woman waiting for you?'

Dan smiled. 'Not exactly.'

He explained about Rutherford, how he had been neglecting the dog lately, and the guilt that brought.

'If I can get home, take him out for a run, shower and change, I can meet you on Mutley Plain in a couple of hours.'

'Done.'

The Old Bank pub was the honoured venue, lacking in atmosphere, but rich in ales, a contrast unlikely to deter Dan.

As he walked down the hill towards Mutley Plain, Dan realised with surprise that, for the first time during his meetings with Adam Breen, he didn't feel nervous.

Around him, the Christmas procession continued. Even some of the passing cars were bedecked with tinsel and plastic Santas. It was only early evening, but plenty of the people were already by far the worse for wear.

The night was still dry, but had turned suspiciously warm. Long experience of the mercurial moods of the weather in the South-west made Dan think it indicated that rain was on the agenda. The *Wessex Tonight* forecaster had prophesised it too, but that counted for little. Dan had been amused to read an article carried in all the papers which reported that scientists had concluded the best way to predict tomorrow's weather was simply to say it would be the same as today's.

Which, in one study, more or less reduced a whole profession to being largely a waste of time, in his humble opinion.

Dan stopped at the cashpoint. He had to queue and was a couple of minutes late, so he wasn't surprised to find Adam already waiting. He'd also had the decency to get a couple of pints. It was interesting that the detective too preferred a table with his back to the wall and a good view of the pub, and probably for similar reasons to El.

Police and photographers, professions of paranoia. To which pairing Dan suspected he could probably add journalists too. None was ever going to win a popularity contest.

They shared some pleasantries about the clemency and busyness of the evening, before Adam sprang his surprise.

'We've had a – well, I don't know what to call it. It could be something, it could be nothing. To say it's a development is putting it too strongly. It might be, it might not. Let's say, we've had an – occurrence. It came after you'd gone home. I didn't bother calling you because I'm not quite sure what to make of it.'

It had been dawning on Dan that alongside the detective's fondness for theatre and his obsession with his wardrobe, he was also a fan of the irritating art of delayed gratification. And there it was, encapsulated in just a single statement. It was more like a crossword clue than a straightforward method of delivering information.

Adam was waiting, an expectant look on his face. When you stripped away the defences and began to get to know him, for an experienced senior detective in his early forties the man could behave remarkably like a child.

'Go on,' Dan said patiently.

'Penelope Ramsden.'

'What about her?'

'She had an accident.'

'What sort of accident?' Dan asked, in a strained voice.

'A car accident. A crash.'

'It happens.'

'It does. But not like this.'

Adam sat back and nodded, his face full of a knowing look.

Dan sighed. 'Wouldn't it be easier if you just told me?'

After a sip of his beer, perhaps more to aid another little build-up of the suspense rather than quench his thirst, Adam did. Ramsden had pulled out of the drive of Bray's offices too fast, hadn't checked what other traffic was coming and her car had been hit by a lorry. She was in the local Tamarside hospital, unconscious, her condition assessed as serious but stable.

'Right,' Dan said. 'Sad, but it happens. I wish her a speedy recovery, but I don't quite see how it has any bearing on the inquiry.'

Adam smiled. 'Maybe. But you might think differently when I tell you what happened in the minutes before the crash.'

The police had been called to Bray's offices. It was the end of the working day. Several of the staff rang in at once. Penelope Ramsden, they said, had gone mad. She jumped up from her desk, let out a piercing scream, picked up a chair, smashed it into her own computer, then several others. She broke a couple of windows, a television and a photocopier, screaming all the while, before running outside and into her car, driving off and being hit by the lorry.

Dan sat silently, digesting the news. 'OK,' he said slowly. 'So, it's either just anguish at the death of the man she claims to love, plus maybe fear for her future now he's gone and the future of the business is uncertain, or it's …'

'Quite,' Adam replied. 'Maybe it's the fact that she can't live with having killed him.'

'So what do you do now?'

'We,' the detective said quietly.

It took Dan a minute to comprehend all that tiny word meant. In the mundane surroundings of a high street pub, a seminal moment had passed.

'Sorry, we.'

'We question her. We find out just what that little outburst was about. But we can't do it yet. The doctors say she'll be in no fit state to answer any questions for a few days.'

'Well, that's certainly an interesting – occurrence.'

'Indeed.'

The two men sat in thought as they watched the evening flow around them. Parties of men and women stood at the bar and eyed each other in that way the lubricated think of as subtle, but all others see as simply lecherous.

Then Adam sprang surprise number two of the evening. He cleared his throat and congratulated Dan on his handling of the interview with Arthur Bray.

'I suspected you might get on better with him. And you found out what we needed to know. Well done on that. I doubt he would have told me.'

'Really? I thought I struggled.'

'You did at first, but you kept going and you got there. People respond well to you. I think they like talking to you. Plus, well, there's something else too.'

'Like what?'

'It's like – you can see inside people. You understand what makes them tick. You did it with Arthur, sensing the reason for the breakdown of his relationship with Edward. I've never been good at that psychology bit. I prefer facts.'

Dan felt his face flushing, and his spirits rising with it. 'Well, err – thanks,' he muttered.

They sipped at their drinks in silence, then Adam leaned forwards and said, 'Who did it? Come on, who do you really think killed Edward Bray?'

It was a question which had been with Dan all afternoon in the MIR, and had followed him home that night. Even running around the park with Rutherford, he couldn't shake loose its hold. For the incurably curious, a mystery could easily become an addiction.

'I think it's hard to bet against Gordon Clarke,' Dan said. 'What do you think?'

'I agree. He's got motive aplenty. Being the suspicious sort I am, I had Paget's story checked, just to see if she might be spinning us a line to try to distract attention from herself as a suspect. But it's all true. A couple of other people at that business reception say she and Clarke spent ages talking, almost to the exclusion of anyone else. Staff at the hospice confirm that flowers from him arrive more or less weekly. So he could be motivated by thinking that removing Bray would give him a real chance with Paget. Love can be the most powerful motive for action.'

'But,' said Dan. 'Although that's all true, where's the evidence? Apart from suspicion and circumstance, we've got nothing.'

'Agreed. And do you know what? I'm coming to doubt whether we're going to get any actual hard evidence. We haven't by now, after all, and we're a week and a day on from the murder. This killing has clearly been carefully planned. I reckon the only way we're going to get a conviction is if we can push someone to incriminate themselves.'

'How? Surveillance hasn't worked. Nor has any of the interviewing.'

Adam picked up his beer, took a long drink. 'Yeah,' he said. 'What we really need is a break. And so far we haven't had one. Nowhere close.'

'You know what I keep thinking about?'

'What?'

'That cancelled appointment. The one the week before Bray was killed. It must indicate something happened for the killer to put the murder off.'

'Yeah, but we've been through all that. It was a dead end. None of our suspects had anything come up unexpectedly which might force them to delay their plans.'

'I've been thinking about other possibilities too,' Dan said. 'What if there was a conspiracy, say between two or more of our suspects? That voice, the person who reported Bray's body at the lay-by, that was a man. So if a woman killed him, it would have to be a conspiracy. Maybe the fact that it's proving a difficult case indicates several people were involved, all painstakingly planning it out.'

Adam held up his hands. 'Hold on. We can't even find the evidence to point to one person yet, let alone several. As you said yourself, the person who reported Bray's body could just have been a passer-by who didn't want to get involved. It happens. Let's just keep working at it without dashing off after wild possibilities.'

A couple slipped through the crowd and sat down at the next table. Adam watched them settle, then said, 'Well, I reckon the High Honchos are going to be out of luck with their lust for a result by Christmas. Ah well, let's forget it for now. There are other things in life apart from work.'

The change in his voice was marked, from winter to spring

in a second.

'Oh yes?' Dan said. 'Anything you care to share?'

'I spoke to Annie earlier. She said she was missing me, as was Tom.' The detective's face broke into a smile, perhaps the first truly genuine one Dan had seen. 'We are going to be spending Christmas together. It doesn't mean we're back together of course, there's still a long way to go, but ...'

He didn't need to finish the sentence. Dan reached out a hand and Adam shook it. 'I'm delighted to hear it,' Dan said, with real feeling. 'This calls for a celebration.'

He headed to the bar to get them some more drinks. A woman thrust a piece of mistletoe at him, followed by her very full and red lips and yelled, 'Give me a kiss, Mr TV man!'

It was a measure of Dan's mood that he did, with no attempt to demur or dodge.

The evening passed by easily in a haze of conversation, so much so that they almost forgot to eat. Dan scrambled to the bar and just managed to get them a couple of cheap curries before last food orders were called.

When he got back to the table, Dan felt relaxed enough to ask Adam about the scoutmaster and the charges against him. It wasn't the detective's inquiry, but as a police officer and a father he knew plenty about it. There was no doubt about the man's guilt, and it was thought unlikely the case would go to trial as the evidence was so strong.

The scoutmaster had taken photos of himself abusing children, which had been found stored on his computer.

'Hundreds of photos,' Adam said quietly. 'Bloody hundreds.'

'He deserves to be exposed then,' Dan added.

'I'd say what he deserves is a fair bit more than that.'

It was time for a change of subject, before the unpleasantness of the conversation soured the evening irreparably. Dan told Adam about his plans for the holiday, his dilemma about whether to see Kerry on Christmas Day, and, after much agonising about the present he had bought for her.

The detective did not produce the required reaction. He started chuckling.

'What?' asked a piqued Dan. 'Don't you think it's a good idea?'

'It's certainly practical,' was all Adam would say in reply.

By the end of the evening it was an unsteady path they wended from the pub, picking their way through the last remnants of the drinking detritus that swirled or staggered in the currents of the night. Adam promised he would call Dan in the morning if there were any significant developments and they set off for their respective flats.

'A break,' was the last thing Adam said, before he staggered off down the street. 'We just need a break.'

And, as if fate had heard the plea, felt the benevolence of the season and decided to change her fickle favour towards the investigation into the murder of Edward Bray, tomorrow the break would finally come.

Chapter Nineteen

THE CALL CAME IN at seven minutes past nine. And as so often with luck, one piece of fortune gave rise to another. If it were not the case, the break could so easily have been missed.

The detective who answered the phone in the MIR had a whole and unprecedented ten days off for Christmas, starting from tomorrow, the eve of the big day itself, and a four-year-old son who was filled with infectious festive joy. She had slept well, there were no traffic jams on the way into Charles Cross, only that rarest of wonders, a smooth and easy commute, and DC Cathy Tingle had also just heard that she was soon to become a DS. Those sergeant's exams she had worked so hard for, despite the demands of her young son, she had passed, and passed well.

It was going to be a great Christmas. And that was before even came the call.

DC Tingle had only been in the MIR for ten minutes. She'd got in to Charles Cross well before nine, had time to forage a coffee from the canteen and share the news of her impending promotion with a couple of colleagues, before settling in the MIR to continue her work: more inquiries into the background of Edward Bray, just in case there might be a hidden motive for murder lurking there.

And then the phone rang.

The operator had taken a couple of minutes to discern what the man wanted before patching him through. He was nowhere approaching either coherent or eloquent.

And if DC Tingle had been a more impatient woman, and in less of a warm mood, she might not have teased out what it was the man had to tell.

He was speaking in a thick Devon burr, and his syntax made his sentences an oral version of a maze. He was also one of those people who know they have a point to make, but instead of getting to it continually circle around.

'What I want to tell 'ee, well, I's sorry if I be bothering 'ee, but I sees the news yer see, so I knows about the murder, that killing thing of the bloke that no one liked, the guy who got killed, just up the road from 'ere it was …'

DC Tingle waited for a brief pause in the passing shower of words and prompted, 'You mean the Edward Bray murder?'

'That it be! That be it! That's the one, m'luvver.'

'What do you want to tell us about it?'

'Well, see, it be Christmas, and there ain't a lot going on, not on the farm, not at the moment like, so I don't like being idle, not me, me dad said that always made work for the Devil see, idle hands and all that, so I's thought I'd do some ditching like.'

'Ditching?'

'Aye, bit of ditching like.'

'Digging a ditch?'

The burr took on a surprised tone. 'Digging? No me lover, no digging, we's got plenty o' ditches. Hundreds of the buggers we's got. Clearing! Clearing 'em oot. Them gets blocked up see, specially in all this rain and mud like. Ain't yous never 'ad to clear a ditch?'

DC Tingle couldn't say she had. 'So, what was it you wanted to tell us about the ditch?' she persisted.

'Well, that's it see. I's was clearing me ditch from first thing, the one runs down bottom of long meadow, down by the road see, and that's when I saws it. I's found it, I did. I's didn't know what ter do at first, I's just looked, then I thought about it and remembered all that fuss with the police and on the telly and all that, so I thought I's best be calling yer like.'

DC Tingle waited for another rare gap in the rustic monologue, then prompted, 'Saw what? Found what?'

There was a pause on the end of the line. The answer, when it came, was simple, but not helpful.

'It. That's when I's found it.'

One more try, Cathy told herself, and then she would get on with some real work.

'What did you find, sir?'

And then, amongst the great heap of ice shone the hidden diamond.

'The gun. That's when I's found the shotgun.'

Dan had been sitting in the news library, attempting to avoid Lizzie, but well aware it was a hopeless task. It was like trying to dodge your destiny.

He'd arrived at work, plodded up the stairs to the newsroom and heard her berating the early producer for the lack of decent stories in the breakfast bulletins before he'd even reached halfway up the flight. He rapidly turned around again and made for the canteen. Dan just had time to get a coffee before the fast thud of stilettos warned of the prowling editor beast's imminent arrival, so he slipped out of the back doors and headed for the library.

It was only a temporary respite, but better than nothing. Sometimes it took a while to start the day, and the onslaught of Lizzie could set back progress by several hours.

Dan had already rung Adam, who hadn't been surprised to hear from him. 'No, there are no developments yet,' the detective said patiently. 'Yes, I will call the moment something happens. Yes, I know you need a story but I can't just create them, however much I might like to.'

So, he would face Lizzie without a sacrifice to offer. Still, at least he'd resolved one issue this morning. Another text had arrived from Kerry, asking again about plans for Christmas, and Dan had steeled himself and given her a call. He would love to see her, of course he would, but he had a lonely, vulnerable and sensitive friend who he'd promised to look after on the day itself and he couldn't break that pledge. How about they get together on Christmas Eve, to exchange presents and celebrate the season?

There had been disappointment in her voice, but she'd taken it well enough. Best not to tell her the lonely and sensitive friend was Dirty El, as vulnerable as a fortress and surely one of the most scurrilous and insensitive people to shame the planet.

El had called earlier too, not to ask about Christmas but instead whether there was any possibility of getting a snap of the scoutmaster. He was still being held in the cells at Charles Cross and the papers were howling for it.

Not yet, Dan said, but perhaps. While in the police station

canteen yesterday, he'd overheard a conversation between a couple of officers which might give them a chance. It would require working a little trick and some waiting for the moment and opportunity, but should be possible.

The clock ticked round to a quarter past nine. Time for the newsroom morning meeting: the forum for ideas for tonight's programme. The facing of Lizzie could be postponed no more.

And then came the call.

The gun had been found in an overgrown ditch on the edge of a field by the road to Ermington. It was no more than a couple of miles from Gordon Clarke's office.

Dan thought he knew Adam well enough now to see what the detective was thinking. Clarke would have driven this way most days. If he was planning a killing, he would need somewhere to get rid of the shotgun. He wouldn't want to risk driving far with it in the boot of his car. The ditch was only a few miles from the lay-by, perhaps five or ten minutes drive at the most. And Clarke would know it was in a remote spot where no one was likely to walk, deep, very overgrown, and filled with water. If the gun were ever found at all, it would be likely to take a long time.

But they'd been lucky. They'd got their break. Courtesy of a bored farmer and his Christmas ditch clearing.

Dan had run into the newsroom, stopping the morning meeting in a second.

'What?' Lizzie snapped, arms folded, lips thin and heel grinding the carpet; a true triple whammy, three danger signs at once. My, she was in a bad mood today.

'Bray case, cops, they've found the shotgun that killed him.'

'Can we film it?'

'Yes,' Dan panted, without hesitation.

'Interview the cops?'

'Yes.'

'Splash it on the lunchtime bulletin?'

'Yes.'

'As an exclusive?'

Now Dan paused. He hadn't asked Adam about any of this.

But the climb down from the self-inflicted summit was far too vertiginous to contemplate.

'Yes,' he heard himself say.

'Go on then, get moving. What are you waiting for?'

Dan had grabbed Nigel and together they'd driven to find Adam standing at the edge of the field. The area had been cordoned off, a bored constable patrolling back and forth, more to keep warm than for any purpose of maintaining the security of the site. A couple of Scenes of Crime officers, all clad in their white overalls, were on their hands and knees, leaning into the ditch. The sky was grey with a fine and drifting rain and a wakening wind blew at a line of trees.

Nigel hooked the camera onto the tripod and started filming. Adam took off his overcoat to reveal a smart black suit, drew himself up to his full height and adjusted his tie to make sure it was impeccably straight. He looked on at the SOCOs in magnificent, studied silence, with the air of a vengeful Angel of Justice whose moment had finally come.

Such was the act, Dan was tempted to shout "cut" when they'd finished filming.

Nigel took a couple more shots of the area, to provide some context, then Dan sidled up and whispered to Adam, 'What's the plan?'

'Get the thing out and get it analysed. It'd normally take days, but with the less than subtle help of the High Honchos' clout it's going to be done straight away.'

'And in terms of the media?'

'By which you mean you?'

'Yes.'

Adam pulled Dan away from the site. 'Look,' he said, 'We've got to be a little careful. I can't even say for sure it is the gun that killed Bray.'

'I know that, but realistically? In a field this close to the murder scene? And so near to the office of the prime suspect?'

'What do you want to do?'

'Film the SOCOs doing their bit, then the gun when it's brought out and put in on the lunchtime news.'

'I don't know. It may be a bit premature ...'

'It'll be great for public reassurance. It'll show you're making progress with the case. And I can put an appeal for witnesses into the story, in case someone saw the gun being dumped.' Dan paused, then added, 'We'll have to interview you, of course. And once we've put it out – as a little exclusive, naturally – everyone else will pick it up and the story will be splashed everywhere. Along with your picture and quotes.'

Adam began nodding. 'Well, if you put it like that then, I suppose it's OK.'

Dan thought it was one of the poorer shows of reluctance that he'd seen.

In many detective dramas Scenes of Crime Officers are lauded as modern-day miracle workers, blessed with a nigh supernatural ability to find the elusive piece of killer evidence that solves a case. That may well be true, Dan thought, but there is a drawback to SOCs that the writers don't feature. They work slowly and, like bus drivers, council workmen, or civil servants, they cannot be rushed.

Dan chafed. It was half past eleven, he was wet through, very cold, and still the shotgun hadn't been removed from the ditch. There were only two hours until the lunchtime news was on air, he'd already suffered half a dozen calls from Lizzie, demanding progress reports, and he still didn't have the golden shot, the one that told the story in a second.

It would be the headline which would run around the country, a white overalled officer carefully lifting the murder weapon from its watery hiding place.

Adam had explained the need for patience. The SOCOs had to work their way around the gun, to make sure they found any evidence that may have been left. And when it came to the weapon itself they had to proceed painstakingly slowly, so as not to lose any fibres, hairs or flecks of skin, that vital evidence which might give away the identity of the person who last handled it.

The person who, in all probability, murdered Edward Bray.

They were closing in on their killer.

But it was taking time.

The stoic Nigel stood beside his camera, hood pulled tight over his head, ready for the moment the gun would appear. El was beside him, camera tight to his eye. Dan had pointed out to Adam that for maximum coverage all the newspapers and websites would need a high quality photograph as soon as possible, and he had a simple way to ensure one was available.

Adam chewed briefly at his lip, then nodded his assent and Dan had duly summoned the paparazzo. The promised reward was a bottle of the finest malt whisky to help their Christmas Day pass jovially.

The bonus prize was the look on Adam's face as the chubby bumbling man with the bodywarmer and wild hair panted his way up to the scene, and launched one of his dreadful assaults on the world of verse.

"As a way to get the boot,
It's surely no great hoot,
Certainly not much fun,
Being shot with a gun,
But to El it means lots and lots of loot!"

No one could find any words to reply. Dan noticed that for the remainder of the time the photographer lurked around the scene Adam kept a watchful eye upon, and wary distance from, him.

It was probably a fifteen-minute drive back to the studios from here, maybe twenty, depending on the traffic. It would take at least half an hour to edit the report, perhaps a little more. So that meant, realistically, they had until half past twelve. Adam had been interviewed and said all the right things, although it had taken him a couple of efforts to get the words precise enough for his exacting standards.

All they needed now was the shot of the gun. And the two SOCOs were still on their hands and knees, bending over the ditch.

The weather was closing around them, a shroud of grey, the rain coming in harder, a gentle beat on the surrounding leaves. The odd car swished past, but the road was pleasantly quiet.

One of the white overalled figures stood up. Nigel and El both leaned forwards.

The man stretched his arms, rolled his neck, then knelt back down again. Dan swore, prompting a reproachful look from Nigel. The SOCOs resumed their work.

A distant clock rang noon. Dan checked his beautiful new watch, which he'd now given up trying to get other people to notice. Still no one had. It said ten to twelve.

'What time do you make it?' he asked Nigel and El. Both had modern digital watches, plastic and cheap, but the kind that boast an accuracy of within a second a year. Both said noon.

Dan gave his flashy and expensive chronometer a thoughtful stare.

A couple of crows landed in the field and pecked at the furrows of mud. It looked a halfhearted gesture. Even the moods of nature can be shaped by the might of the weather.

The SOCO was standing up again, but this time slowly. And now he was bending over, reaching out. From down in the ditch his colleague's hand rose, and it was gripping a plastic bag. Slowly, very carefully, almost reverentially, the man took it, held it for a few seconds, as if to be absolutely sure it was real, then turned and walked directly towards the cameras.

Just as Adam had asked him to.

The picture was pure drama.

With each step the SOCO took, the contents of the clear plastic bag became ever more apparent.

It was dripping with water, wrapped with tendrils of weed and plant, coated with patches of dark and slimy mud and the odd long-dead and decomposing leaf.

But it was unmistakably a double-barrelled shotgun.

The report was a pleasure to write. It had natural suspense, and was just a case of letting the pictures tell the story, but adding a few words of embroidery to make clear what was going on.

First, a little build-up to heighten the tension.

'The police were called to the corner of a field, near to the lay-by where Edward Bray was murdered, after a tip-off,' Dan wrote, while Jenny lay down pictures of the SOCOs working at the ditch.

'Specialist Scenes of Crime officers carried out an extensive and careful search. Their objective – to preserve any evidence that may have been left here by the killer. For several hours, they worked through the ditch.'

Jenny added the shot of Adam looking on, the concentration intent in his eyes.

Now it was time to deliver the punchline.

'Then, just after noon on the day before Christmas Eve, and ten days since the murder – the police hunting for the killer of Edward Bray had their breakthrough.'

And now Dan again used that most powerful of weapons in a TV reporter's armoury – silence. Jenny laid down the picture of the SOCOs fiddling around, and then walking towards the camera with the gun.

Some sights needed no explanation.

Next it was a clip of Adam, being upbeat and positive, but still lacing his words with a warning.

'This is certainly a very significant development and could well be our breakthrough. It might just give us the vital clue that leads us to whoever carried out the murder. But first, we've got lots of forensics work to do, to see what the gun can tell us.'

To end the story, Dan did a piece to camera. He asked anyone who may have seen anything suspicious in the area where the gun was found on the evening that Bray was killed to get in touch with the police. It was a long shot, but worth a try. The report might just prompt a dusty memory.

The story was the lead on the lunchtime news, tagged as an exclusive. *Another* exclusive, Dan was tempted to add, as Lizzie was sitting within earshot. When the bulletin had finished, she pronounced the scoop "pretty reasonable", but set off for the canteen wearing a rare smile. When she'd left the newsroom, a couple of other journalists voiced their relief and even thanked Dan for making their lives more comfortable by taming the ogre with the rich fare of an exclusive. Lizzie had been in a venomous mood all morning.

Adam rang just after the broadcast. The police had been deluged with calls from other journalists, checking the details of the story. It would soon be running everywhere. The labs were working on the shotgun now and promised to have some

227

preliminary results by later this afternoon.

It is part of a scientist's training to be loath to draw any conclusions until an experiment had been performed and re-performed and re-re-performed to the extremes of repetition. But in this case, the technicians were already confident the gun had been found in time to give the police some highly significant clues as to who had killed Edward Bray.

Chapter Twenty

THE ARREST WAS PRECISELY timed.

Dan sat in the back of the CID car, behind Adam and Suzanne and kept quiet. It wasn't easy. There were so many questions he wanted to ask, and he wasn't even sure he should be here.

'This feels – I don't know, a bit odd,' he'd said to Adam as they were about to leave Charles Cross.

'In what way?'

'Well, this is the real thing, isn't it? This is about as serious as it gets. An arrest on suspicion of murder. The first one in the case. And I'm only a hack, and ...'

'You wanted to know about police work,' the detective interrupted. 'This is it, the real thing, as you so eloquently put it. You're part of the investigation, so you can see it through. We're almost there now.'

And Dan, despite himself, couldn't help shivering.

Adam had called just after four o'clock. The results from the labs were through. And they were damning. He explained what the scientists had found, and what it meant.

In around an hour's time, the police would be making an arrest. This was not for filming, or broadcast, Adam made that very clear, but if Dan wanted to come along ...

Dan gulped hard and managed to find the breath to say yes.

He went to find Lizzie and tried to be as nonchalant as possible, but those laser eyes had a penetrating power. There were, he lied, no developments in the story yet, so he hoped a similar version of the lunchtime report would suffice for tonight. If that were the case, he'd like to go to meet some of the detectives just to check nothing else was happening.

Dan laced his request with vague hopes of finding a follow up story for tomorrow, another exclusive, naturally. Lizzie's mood had remained favourable, so the regal permission was loftily granted.

Dan left hastily, before she could start asking questions.

He had to concentrate hard on the drive down to the police station. The case was spinning in his mind. What the scientists had found, even if it wasn't conclusive, pointed clearly to the guilt of one particular suspect. But how could that be, given the person's alibi?

A pedestrian crossing turned red and he had to stamp on the brakes to stop the car, such was his preoccupation. Dan swore to himself and forced his mind back on to the drive.

All would soon become clear.

At Charles Cross, he'd found Adam in a buoyant mood. 'It looks like the High Honchos might get their wish and see the case cleared up by tomorrow,' he said. 'Then we can all have a Happy Christmas – apart from our newly exposed murderer, of course. He gets to rot in the cells while we all eat turkey.'

They chatted a little more about the scientists' findings, then Adam said, 'Yep, you're right, we're going to have to demolish the alibi, but I reckon that's not beyond us. In fact, I'm hoping for a quick confession and an early resolution. We might even be able to celebrate with a couple of beers tonight, if you're up for that. I always like to toast the successful end of a case. Are you ready to go?'

Dan had grabbed his satchel and followed Adam and Suzanne down the stairs.

'I always like to make the arrest in a big case,' Adam said, as they walked. 'Some of the other chief inspectors steer clear of this bit. They think it's a little tawdry and leave it to the troops. But I reckon it's a senior officer's prerogative.'

Suzanne had driven them, as methodically and carefully as she carried out her investigations. She didn't once exceed the speed limit and fed the steering wheel through her hands in a way that would make a driving instructor nod with pleasure. They were at their destination by a quarter to five, and there, just around the corner and out of sight, they parked and waited.

'We just need to get the call to say we're good to go,' Adam said. 'That should come through in the next few minutes.'

A couple of sizeable, uniformed constables were waiting around the back, just in case their suspect should make a run for it. All was in place for the arrest.

The next few minutes passed more slowly than any Dan could remember. He tried to distract himself with thoughts of Christmas. Rutherford and his smiling face as he smelt the turkey roasting in the oven. El, his malt whisky and whether there was any way to get a snap of the scoutmaster, and Kerry, and what she would make of her present.

He even wondered what Claire, the dark haired detective, was doing over the holiday time. Whether she was celebrating with a boyfriend. Or if she could perhaps be single.

None of these thoughts had any chance of taking hold. All Dan could think of was the man, at work in the office around the corner, oblivious to what was about to unfold, and how he could possibly have murdered Edward Bray.

Adam eased his seat backwards and stretched out. He was as relaxed as a holidaymaker who'd journeyed for hours to finally reach the promised beach, complete with comfortable lounger and cold lager. Suzanne worked through her notes.

Cars and vans drove past, even the odd cyclist, despite the weather. The rain continued to pound down, drumming relentlessly on the roof. It was dark in the car, only a distant streetlight casting a faint amber glow.

Dan took out his mobile, fiddled and fussed, changed the screensaver, then decided he preferred the original version and changed it back again.

Slowly, the clock turned around to five.

Adam's mobile rang. He listened, then hung up and said, 'Right, that's it. Julia Francis has gone home. He won't be able to call her now. He's all ours. So let's go.'

They pulled on their coats, dodged the growing puddles, jogged around the corner and up to the door. Adam took the lead, then Suzanne, Dan hanging back a little.

The man standing by the filing cabinet turned, a professional smile ready for the newcomers. It faded fast when he saw Adam, and the expression on the detective's face.

And it died entirely at the words, 'Gordon Clarke, I arrest you on suspicion of the murder of Edward Bray.'

The scientists had not found the Holy Grail of detective work, no flakes of skin, hairs or fingerprints on the gun which would give them an instant means of identification of the killer. They concluded whoever had brandished it had worn gloves, as they had expected, but also probably some kind of coat, or overall, with a hood, tightly drawn around his or her head, and perhaps even a hair net. It was an increasingly common technique amongst the more intelligent criminals, and further evidence the killing had been thoroughly researched and planned.

But what they had found were some minute fibres, near invisible to the human eye, stuck in a crack between the stock and barrels of the shotgun. The conclusion was that the weapon had probably been placed on, or into a piece of plastic sheeting, and put in the boot of a car after the murder. But the movement of the vehicle on that journey to the edge of a farmer's field had shaken it loose.

The killer was, unsurprisingly, in a hurry to leave the lay-by and thus had done a poor job of wrapping or securing the gun, so the theory went. He probably drove quickly, cornering at speed, and the weapon had slid around in the boot.

During that process the tiny but telltale fibres had become attached.

The scientists' view was that whoever had then taken the gun from the boot had realised the potential danger and made another hasty attempt to sanitise it. But once more he was in a hurry, fearful of being seen. It was dark and wet, and the fibres were so very small. He had not been thorough enough.

That was the investigation's golden break, the beam of sunshine of progress through the bank of dark cloud.

The thin black curls of material, no more than mere shavings, had been isolated, analysed, and the information fed into a database. Then, it was just a question of waiting, only a short period, but one which felt very long indeed.

The wait had been worthwhile. The results came back within half an hour and they were definitive.

The fibres were from a batch of materials used to line the boots of BMW three series saloon cars, made for the British market between late 2003 and mid 2004.

The owner of one such car was Gordon Clarke.

Clarke didn't say a word for the whole of the journey back to Charles Cross. He sat in the back of the car, alongside Dan, and stared at the falling rain picked out in the passing streetlights. Occasionally, he would glance at Adam or Suzanne, and shift position in his seat, but otherwise he was still.

One search team was going through his house, another his office. The High Technology Crime, or Square Eyes division as they were known, were searching his computers, looking for any evidence he may have been planning a murder. Forensics officers were examining his car for any traces of Edward Bray's blood, and its boot for evidence the shotgun might have been carried there. It was an extensive and expensive operation, but the High Honchos had willingly authorised the overtime.

The final draft of their beloved annual report was on hold, ready for some new and proud headlines.

At the police station, Adam booked Clarke into the custody suite. Even then, the businessman spoke only to confirm his name. He was asked if he wanted a solicitor and allowed to make his call to Julia Francis's offices. They were closed until the morning. Just as Adam had hoped, Clarke didn't have her home number.

He was offered the duty solicitor, but refused. For the first interviews, Gordon Clarke would have no lawyer to shield him.

The plan was working.

Adam held a quick discussion with a Crown Prosecution Service solicitor, a young but effective man called Richard, to consider the evidence they had against Clarke. It was a ruthless dissection of the case and a forthright exchange. The eventual verdict was that the evidence was suggestive, but in truth only circumstantial, by no means yet sufficient for a charge of murder and certainly nowhere near to being strong enough to convince a jury.

Clarke had means and motive, but it was the opportunity which was the problem. They could show he hated Bray with a raging passion, and they could speculate that it wouldn't be difficult to get hold of a shotgun. But in his visit to Bristol the man had an alibi, one which had yet to be properly punctured.

Even the trump card in Adam's hand had a weakness, and one which would be fatal to any case. The fibres on the gun might match those from Clarke's car, but they would also match similar BMWs from an eight-month period of manufacture. The database had no precise answer as to how many cars that would be, but the estimate was at least several thousand.

At that point in the discussion, Adam went quiet.

The conclusion of the case conference was that they were still some way short of securing sufficient evidence to consider the killer of Edward Bray identified and caught.

And so the strategy for the evening changed. Adam had been keen to interview Clarke as soon as possible, pile the pressure on him and see if he could be pushed to make a mistake and incriminate himself. But now he decided to wait, to see what the search teams and the Square Eyes turned up.

They needed more evidence. As Richard put it, with the case they currently had the Crown Prosecution Service would be most unlikely to be able to find a barrister willing to argue it before a court. Even if they did, he estimated the jury would scarcely need to retire to consider their verdict before pronouncing Gordon Clarke not guilty.

There was another advantage to letting the evening run. Some quiet and solitary minutes inside a small, cold and uncomfortable police cell might also prompt Clarke to consider his position and make him more inclined to talk.

So wait was what they did.

It was hardly the way Dan expected to spend the night before Christmas Eve.

He sat on the windowsill in the MIR and watched the people passing by. Despite the rain the city was busy, hundreds making their way between restaurants, bars and clubs. Most were obscured from his view and only apparent by the procession of colourful umbrellas they carried.

The room was silent. Adam was standing, arms folded, staring at the green boards, rapt in thought, Suzanne sitting at a desk working through some files.

The mood had changed. The breakthrough had become

tarnished with reality. The euphoria of earlier had evaporated fast. The results from the search teams had come back. They had turned both places inside out and there was nothing incriminating in either Gordon Clarke's home or office. All that remained was to wait for the Square Eyes to report their findings.

'It's just about our last hope,' Adam said quietly. 'If they don't come up with any evidence we've got nowhere near enough.'

'Clarke still might talk when we interview him,' Suzanne said, although her voice sounded anything but hopeful.

Adam snorted. 'Fat chance. He's not daft. He'll soon realise we haven't got anything. He'll just stay silent until the morning, then get that solicitor to come and release him. And we won't have anything to stop it. There's no way I'll get a magistrate to let us keep holding him over Christmas on the evidence we've got.'

A couple of sharp phone calls from the High Honchos, demanding updates, hadn't improved the detective's mood. His usually impeccable tie was hanging low on his collar and he looked jaded.

It was almost eight o'clock and growing colder in the MIR. Dan pulled his jacket around his chest. He comforted himself with the thought that at least two outstanding issues in his life had been resolved. Earlier, he'd asked Adam how long it would be before anything happened this evening, been sullenly reassured he had an hour or more, and had driven home to feed Rutherford and give him a quick run around the garden.

'Sorry for neglecting you old fellow,' he called to the dog, as he cantered around the garden in the rain, 'but the investigation's at a crucial phase – or at least I hope it is. We will have Christmas together though, I promise you, and I will get you that turkey.'

Dan drove back to Charles Cross via El's flat. He picked up the photographer, as they'd arranged earlier, and did his best to calm him. It wasn't easy. El was like an excitable child at the best of times, but given the prospect of what might be about to happen he was a blur of agitation. Yes, Dan soothed, he was sure it would work – well, almost sure anyway. Whatever, it was certainly worth a try. El might have to wait for a few hours, hidden in the footwell of the car's back seats, but it would happen.

Dan just hoped the photographer was at his surreptitious best. There would be more than a little explaining required if he was caught. He'd said he would try to tip El off if it looked like the opportunity for the picture was about to arise, but he couldn't be sure he'd have the chance. The photographer would have to be ready.

Dan had left El hunched down in the car, burbling to himself and preparing a rhyme, ready for if the plan should work.

The phone rang, loud in the quiet of the MIR. Suzanne answered it, listened for a few seconds, then hung up.

'The Square Eyes,' she said, shaking her head. 'They didn't find anything incriminating at all on either Clarke's home or work computers. If he has been researching murder he's been smart and done it in some internet café somewhere.'

Adam nodded slowly. 'Then it's down to us, isn't it? Our questioning and our wits. If we don't get anything, we don't have a case. Come on then, let's go and do it.'

Chapter Twenty-one

ON THE WAY INTO the custody suite, they passed a sergeant who was escorting a chubby, balding man outside. Dan fumbled surreptitiously in his pocket and hit a couple of buttons on his phone. He gave it a few seconds to ring, produced an unconvincing coughing fit, then cut the call.

'What are you up to?' Adam asked, over his shoulder.

'Me?'

'Yes, you.'

'I'm just – err … turning my phone to silent. I don't want to interrupt this, do I?'

'Is that all?'

'That's all.'

The detective turned and gave Dan a knowing look, but didn't reply.

Clarke was waiting in Interview Room Two. He was sitting at the table, upright, his arms folded. Down here in the dim depths of the police station it was even colder than the MIR. Rain spattered on the tiny window and the odd thud of heavy feet passed by.

Adam introduced them for the tape recorder. He and Suzanne sat opposite Clarke, Dan took his customary place by the door.

On the walk down the stairs, Dan had again asked whether he should be here at such a sensitive moment, what might well be the culmination of the case.

'Still yes,' Adam grunted. 'You want to come join an inquiry, you get the whole deal. There's no copping out when things get tense.'

'And how are you going to play the interview?'

'The usual way. Go for his pressure points. Mix the questions up between Suzanne and me, to try to keep him guessing. Just watch and learn. But I'm not going to mess about. We don't have the time. I'll go straight in and aim right between his eyes.'

And the detective was very much true to his word.

'Mr Clarke,' he began, 'We have reason to suspect you were responsible for the murder of Edward Bray.'

The businessman stared at him, but didn't reply.

'What do you say to that?' Adam asked.

'No comment.'

'We have evidence to implicate you in the crime.'

'No comment.'

'Well, maybe this will change your mind. As you may have seen on the news, we've recovered the murder weapon. We've got it safely in the labs here, and do you know what?'

Adam paused, waited for a reaction, but Clarke gave him none. He just sat, staring straight ahead.

'It's been telling us a little story. It's not like an informer, spewing out what happened, but it's been telling us nonetheless.'

Another pause. But still no reaction from Clarke.

Now Adam's voice changed, from hard to conversational, almost friendly. 'Do you know, it's amazing what our scientists can find. It's an unfortunate fact of modern policing that killers are clever these days. They know all about DNA and hairs and fibres. They know how to cover their tracks – or at least how to try. But the problem is these little bits of evidence can be devils to get rid of. There's nearly always something left behind, if you look hard enough.'

Adam leaned forwards, so his face was close to Clarke's, and lowered his voice.

'We looked damned hard. And guess what we found?'

The businessman didn't reply.

'Fibres!' Adam spat. 'Little tiny telltale fibres. They came from the boot of a car. And here's the punchline, Mr Clarke. Guess whose boot they match?'

No reaction.

'Go on, have a guess.'

Clarke's eyes were widening. A quick hand flicked up to itch at his ear.

'Yours, Mr Clarke. The fibres on the gun are an exact match for the boot of your car. Now, isn't that a remarkable coincidence? Is there anything you'd like to say about that?'

. Clarke gulped. 'No comment,' he said finally.

'No comment?'

'No comment.'

Adam angled his head. 'You know, I thought you might say that. But comment or not, I'd reckon you're in a bit of bother, Mr Clarke, wouldn't you? We can show you had a motive, the means and, with some work, the opportunity to kill Edward Bray.'

'No comment.'

'We know you hated Bray.'

And this time, Clarke looked as though he was going to say something more, but after a couple of seconds replied only, 'No comment.'

Suzanne opened a file on the desk, sat back and leafed through it. Clark eyed her nervously. He was sweating now, despite the cold. Outside, in the corridor, a cell door banged.

'That's a sound you'd better start getting used to,' Adam remarked, casually.

The silence returned. Suzanne kept flicking through pages. Adam's attention was set on adjusting his cuff. The strip lights buzzed.

At last, Suzanne looked up and in a kindly voice said, 'Was it love? Or infatuation?'

Clarke sounded surprised. 'What?'

'Love. For Eleanor Paget. That prompted you to kill Edward Bray.'

'No comment.'

'We know you hated Bray, but then so did many people. You hated him for a long time. But it was when you fell for Eleanor, and you thought Bray was in the way of you having a relationship with her, that was what finally spurred you to murder – wasn't it?'

Clarke lowered his head and massaged at his temples with unsteady fingers.

'No comment,' he muttered.

'We're going to have to keep you here unless you talk to us, you know,' Suzanne added.

'No comment.'

'And that's not going to be good for your business. I wonder how it'll cope without you.'

'No comment.'

'Our accountants tell us it wasn't doing well anyway.'

The businessman's face was reddening. 'No comment.'

Now Adam spoke, opening a new angle of attack. 'What was it that forced you to put the killing off?'

'What?'

'From the week before. It was all planned for the Monday before, wasn't it? But you had to put it off.'

'I have no idea what you're talking about.'

'I think you do.'

'Well, I don't.'

'It would be easier on you if you talked to us.'

'No comment.'

'It would weigh in your favour with a judge.'

'No comment.'

'At your trial.'

'No comment.'

'For murder.'

'No comment.'

'A cold-hearted, premeditated, ruthlessly plotted and planned murder.'

'No comment.'

'It would be likely to get you a substantially lighter sentence if you cooperated with us.'

'No comment.'

Adam leaned back from the table. 'I'll give you one more chance tonight, Mr Clarke. Before we leave you to your little cell and an opportunity to reflect on whether it might just be in your interests to talk to us.'

'No comment. I don't intend to say anything to you until my solicitor is present.'

'And that's it?'

'That's it.'

'Then this is your last chance. Before we leave you to your cell and we all go home, to our lovely warm houses, eat our tasty dinners, have a beer, put our feet up and look forward to Christmas. Things you won't be doing, not for a very long time.'

Clarke tapped a finger on the table, then said, 'OK, if you're so sure I killed Bray, charge me then. Charge me now.'

Adam hesitated. 'All in good time,' he said, but not quite quickly enough.

The two men stared at each other. Then Adam got up, called the sergeant, and Clarke was taken back to his cell. In the doorway, he paused and looked back. It was difficult to be sure in the dim light, but the expression looked very much like a smirk.

'He knows,' Adam said, as they sat in the MIR. 'He knows we don't have anything like enough on him.'

'I think you're right, sir,' Suzanne agreed. 'And it's also clear that he's not going to talk to us. He'll suffer the night in the cells, then call his solicitor first thing in the morning.'

'And when she gets here, we're stuffed,' Adam agreed. 'We'll try a few more questions, she'll know the only evidence we've got is the fibres and that they could have come from thousands of cars, and that'll be it. He'll walk free.'

'We'll get him sir,' Suzanne said, with an unconvincing attempt at reassurance.

'Will we?' was the grunted response.

Adam paced back and forth in front of the boards, the leather soles of his shoes clicking on the floor. Outside, the rain was sweeping in harder, waves of falling water pummelling the windows. It reminded Dan of the times he'd been in a storm at sea.

'I know it was Clarke though,' Adam said. 'Or if he didn't actually pull the trigger, then he was involved. It's just too much of a coincidence otherwise. And it's bloody frustrating, knowing it but not being able to prove it.'

He kicked out at some imaginary debris on the floor.

'Come on then, what do you make of it?' Adam said, turning to Dan.

'Err, me?' he said, surprised.

'I appear to be talking to you,' came the petulant reply. 'You've been conspicuously quiet. That's not like you. What do you reckon?'

'I've been quiet because I'm a hack, not a detective,' Dan bridled. 'And I don't know what I reckon. If you can't work out what happened, what chance have I got?'

'Come off it. You've been in on the case since the start. You've met all the suspects. Tell me what you think. You've got a decent brain and a reasonable insight.'

Adam clearly wasn't in the mood to rise even to the heights of damning with faint praise.

'Well,' Dan said slowly, 'if you're really interested, my "decent" brain and "reasonable" insight agree with you. Clarke has to be involved. But as to how, when he's got an alibi that he was in Bristol, I don't know.'

Adam didn't reply, so Dan looked over to Suzanne. He expected the usual rich helpings of scorn and contempt, but she was nodding.

'It's a pretty decent alibi, without ever actually proving he was in Bristol,' she said. 'There's the phone trace, the CCTV, and the cashpoint.'

'And those text message to his secretary,' Adam pointed out. 'She was sure they came from Clarke, a hundred per cent certain, and there's not a hint of suggestion that she's lying. The messages were about all the ongoing business deals and gave her exactly the instructions she'd expect about what to do. That would be powerful evidence for him in court. And that's the problem, isn't it? He doesn't have to prove he was in Bristol. We have to prove he wasn't.'

No one replied. Adam pointed to the pictures of the six suspects on the boards and ran his hand along them. Arthur Bray, Penelope Ramsden, Eleanor Paget, Andrew Hicks, Jon Stead and Gordon Clarke himself, all stared out into the MIR.

'The answer is in that lot somewhere,' he said. 'But we're not seeing it.'

Another wave of rain lashed at the window. Dan's stomach let out a loud rumble and he clutched at it and muttered an apology. In all the excitement of the evening he'd forgotten he was hungry.

'Last thoughts for the night then, before we all go home,' Adam said.

'What about if Clarke lent his car to someone else?' Suzanne ventured.

'Go on.'

'He goes to Bristol to give himself an alibi, while someone back here does the deed.'

'OK then, that points us towards someone who doesn't have a car. And who's that?'

'Hicks doesn't,' Dan said quickly. 'And he hates Bray as much as Clarke. And they're mates.'

'Now you're talking,' Adam said, his voice stronger with fresh hope. 'So we're looking at a conspiracy.'

'But,' Suzanne interrupted, 'I hate to put a damper on the idea, but Hicks and Stead were fishing, and then in that shop, buying bits of food and smashing a milk bottle.'

'But the timings of their alibis aren't exact. They would have had time to get to the lay-by,' Dan said.

'Which means Stead would have to be involved too. And he's too much of a mouse, isn't he? He's got a young family too. He's got too much to lose. He never struck any of us as someone who'd go for a murder plan.'

Another silence settled on the room.

'Well, what about our other suspects?' Dan asked, but without any conviction. 'What about a conspiracy between Clarke and Arthur Bray, or Eleanor Paget, or Penelope Ramsden?'

Suzanne shook her head. 'How? On what grounds? What could bring any of those three together with Gordon Clarke? In their ways they've all got reasons to dislike him.'

'Ramsden's in hospital after her crash. That could have been a suicide attempt, because of the guilt at what she'd done.'

'Or it could just have been a car crash.'

Dan nodded. 'Yeah. It could. Sorry, I was just clutching at straws.'

Adam let out a long yawn, then said, 'And interesting though all that speculation might be, it brings us right back to the same old problem, doesn't it? The lack of any real evidence.'

The door opened and a cleaner walked in, bid them a cheery good evening and began emptying bins.

'And I reckon that's our cue to call it a night,' Adam added. 'We'll reconvene in the morning and have another go at Gordon Clarke, but it won't be long before his solicitor gets here and we're stuffed.' He paused, then added in a tired voice, 'You know, if we're honest, I have to say I fear this one's getting away from us.'

It was getting on for ten o'clock when Dan finally got home. He'd had to drop El off first, and resist the photographer's manic entreaties to go for a celebratory drink, or more likely several.

The paparazzo had got his snap.

In fact, that was more than apparent from the moment Dan opened the car door in the police station car park. The scrunched up bundle of untidiness which was El's idea of lying low was giggling madly to itself and repeatedly burbling a rhyme.

"A naughty pervy scoutmaster,
We'll turn his face alabaster,
With El's little splash,
He'll suck up the cash,
As over the papers the pictures, he'll plaster."

'Blimey,' Dan said. 'Alliteration and using a word like alabaster. You surprise me.'

'I may be sleazy mate, but I'm not stupid,' came the chirpy reply.

In the canteen, on one of his missions to fetch teas and coffees, Dan had overheard an interesting conversation. The Scoutmaster smoked, but the law forbade anyone doing so in the police cells. And so as not to breach his rights, which obviously included the important constituent of poisoning himself, the man had to be allowed outside regularly for a cigarette.

With so many criminals smoking it was a common enough problem for the police, and one which they had resolved by constructing a metal cage around the back door of the police station. It was open at the top, but the walls were high and bedecked with razor wire, quite sufficiently secure to allow a prisoner ten minutes for a smoke.

And the cage was visible from the car park.

For El, it was just a case of waiting, something he knew well how to do. He had a good idea what his target looked like from the photos of when the scoutmaster was a younger man, and a long lens, ready to shoot his snaps.

Dan's coughing fit had tipped the paparazzo off nicely, and he was now gleefully in possession of half a dozen fine photographs of his victim, which would be hawked around every paper that went to press. Christmas was traditionally a quiet time for news, so there would be no shortage of bidders. In fact, the rights to the images were likely to reach that dizzying height of the paparazzi's delight, an auction.

For El, it was a lucrative payday. And combined with the snap of the shotgun being recovered from the ditch, it had turned into a lottery winner of a week.

So great was the chubby buffoon's excitement that it took Dan a good quarter of an hour to calm El down before he could get away. The whisky he would be sampling on Christmas Day would now be the finest money could buy. Or, at least, the finest the local Plymouth supermarkets could provide, which was highly unlikely to be the same thing. But, as was often said with Christmas presents, it was the thought that counted.

Back at the flat, Dan just about found the strength to make himself some beans on toast, and sat on the great blue sofa, Rutherford at his feet, watching the rain's relentless attack on the bay window. Too tired even to get up and turn on the television, he finished the poor substitute for a meal and made the fatal mistake of laying back and closing his eyes just for a few minutes.

He woke again with a start and a cricked neck half an hour later and forced himself to get up and start getting ready for bed.

Rutherford sat in the middle of the hallway, looking pointedly at the airing cupboard where his lead was kept.

'You dropping hints, dog?' Dan asked him. 'I am more than a little tired, if you hadn't noticed.'

Rutherford angled his head and produced his "never been loved" look.

'And it's raining – hard. In case you hadn't noticed that either.'

The dog pawed at the carpet.

Dan couldn't help smiling. No matter how low his mood, how leaden his body, that daft dog could always be relied upon to lift his spirits.

'All right then, just a little run, a couple of laps around the park. I suppose it'll probably do me good too.'

The rain was pounding down, filling the air with a barrage of hurtling droplets. Dan pulled on a coat and jogged over the road to the park. The grass was soaking, churned to mud in patches, and the planned run duly became a brisk walk.

'Health and safety, dog,' Dan explained over the din of the downpour. 'I'm taking full advantage of one of the curses of modern life. I wouldn't want to damage myself just before Christmas.'

Rutherford never worried about the weather and went sprinting off across the park to sniff at the myriad of fascinating scents the visitors of the day had left behind. Dan strode hard, felt his heart picking up with the effort and his head clearing with the rush of pulsing blood. The wash of the rain was refreshing, even exhilarating.

The houses at the far end of the park were all bedecked with Christmas lights, each competing to outdo the others in strings and weaves of flashing colour. It was a sight to delight an electricity company shareholder and outrage an environmentalist. The roads were quiet now, only the odd bus and taxi flitting past.

A white Christmas was off the agenda, but a wet one looked likely. It was by no means as romantic, but far more British.

Dan walked automatically and found himself thinking

through the inquiry once more. He wasn't surprised to suffer a welling disappointment. He had never considered that the first murder case he'd worked on, had become such a part of and been so fascinated by, would remain unsolved.

All that work, all that thought, and all for nothing. It was like receiving a surprise package, pawing and picking at layer upon layer of wrapping, the excitement and anticipation building, only to find there was nothing in the middle.

Still, at least there was Christmas to look forward to. He was due a few days off and would spend tomorrow evening with Kerry and much of the day itself with El. They would sip at the fine whisky he had been promised, watch old films and swap yarns.

Rutherford ran back and jumped up, prompting Dan to dodge from his filthy paws.

'Too quick for you, my old rogue,' he said, 'I know you far too well. Right, one more lap then and we'll get home. I could do with some good sleep.'

Dan pulled the hood of his coat tighter and walked on, blinking hard against a swirl of wind and rain. Across the park he noticed another figure, bent beneath a large umbrella, also accompanied by a dog. So, he wasn't the only idiot sufficiently devoted to his canine friend to bring him out on a night more resembling a mid-Atlantic squall.

Dan squinted through the gloom. It looked like Jim, a man who lived a little further along Hartley Avenue, and who walked his Labrador, Firkin, around the park. The dog was one of Rutherford's few friends and would often join him in running laps together.

But this time Rutherford had begun barking and snarling.

'Hey, idiot, what're you doing?' Dan called to him. 'Calm it down, it's only Firkin.'

The other dog ran over and started barking back. The two animals circled each other, both growling and baring their teeth.

Dan stumbled into a run. A dog fight, an injured Rutherford for Christmas and some expensive vet's bills he could well do without.

'Rutherford!' he yelled. 'Heel! Come away! Now!'

The dog ignored him. The other figure was hurrying over too. Dan grabbed for Rutherford's collar, missed, tried again and this time caught it and pulled him back.

'Hey, Jim, what's the matter with Firkin?' he said. 'I've never seen these two behave like that ...'

He stopped suddenly. Staring at him wasn't Jim, but a middle-aged woman with a face as furrowed as a pickled walnut.

'Oh, sorry,' Dan muttered. 'With the rain and your big coat and umbrella I thought you were someone else.'

'So I see,' she said sniffily. 'Come along now Beatrix,' she told the dog. 'Let's leave this nasty rough beast and be getting home.'

Dan scowled and was about to find a suitably sharp rejoinder when the beautiful moment came. Its power rendered any speech impossible. In just an instant the park, the beating rain, the cold, the blackness of the winter night, all rushed away, receded in his mind. He stood, soaking, just staring.

The only thing Dan could see was Edward Bray, climbing out of his jeep, a dark figure waiting, hidden in the gloom, levelling the barrels of a shotgun and squeezing the trigger.

And now he knew just who that person was, and how the crime had been committed.

Chapter Twenty-two

DAN STUMBLED BACK HOME, his mind a spin of thoughts. A taxi blared its horn as he wandered across the road, hardly even seeing the speeding headlights. The wash from a long puddle drenched him further, but Dan didn't notice. At the flat, as he fumbled the key into the lock, he reached for his mobile, then, with an afterthought, hesitated.

It was coming around to midnight. Not perhaps the ideal time to make a phone call.

Dan forced himself to wait and think. He grabbed an old towel, dried Rutherford, then patted some of the rain off his own face and hair. He didn't even comprehend that he was using the same towel.

All he could see was that evening, ten days ago, what he was now certain had happened then, and in the hours and days leading up to the moment of murder.

He filled the kettle, made himself a cup of coffee and wrapped his hands around the mug, only then realising he was cold. Dan dumped his wet clothes on the bathroom floor, turned on the shower, stood in its pummelling heat and let his mind ricochet through the case.

If he was right, there was only one way to solve it, and just one opportunity. It would have to be done tomorrow, and before nine o'clock in the morning.

There was no choice. He'd have to talk to Adam now.

He sipped at the coffee and flinched. He'd forgotten to put in either milk or sugar.

Dan wrapped himself in a towel and made the call.

Adam answered within three rings.

'I'm sorry if I woke you,' Dan began.

'You didn't. I was sitting up. Thinking.'

'About the case?'

'Yep.'

'Get anywhere?'

'No.'

Dan hesitated at the absurdity of what he was about to say. He was a television reporter, with a grand total of ten days experience of police investigations, and he was about to attempt to tell a Detective Chief Inspector how he thought a murder had been committed and then covered up.

'Get on with it,' Adam prompted.

'What?'

'As it's almost midnight, I suspect it wouldn't be my most brilliant deduction to assume you haven't just rung for a friendly chat. I can hear the excitement in your voice. In fact, it sounds like you're being strangled. So come on, out with it.'

'Well, now I'm talking to you it feels daft ...'

'Just get on and try me.'

Dan swallowed hard and did, blurted it all out in a rush of thought. He hardly took a breath in the whole monologue.

There was a silence on the end of the line.

'Hmm,' came the eventual reply.

'Hmm?'

'Hmm.'

Rutherford nosed his way into Dan's legs, bit and tugged at the towel, but he eased the dog away. This was no time for games.

'It could certainly explain much of the case,' Adam said at last.

'Much?' Dan ventured mildly.

'Well, most.'

'All, even?'

'Possibly.'

The line clicked and buzzed.

'If your theory is correct,' Adam said slowly, 'And I say – if, then there's still one big problem. The same one we hit earlier. The one I suspect we're always going to come up against.'

'Proof?'

'Yep.'

'Well, I think the answer is still the same as earlier. If we can't find the evidence we need, then it'll have to be a confession.'

'Yep. And in order to have any chance of that ...'

250

'We'll have to act now. Or first thing in the morning, at least.'

'Yes,' Adam said thoughtfully. 'And if that's to be the case, it'll take me a few hours to organise what we'll need.'

'So – what do we do?'

'We get organising. Or, at least, I do. You get some rest, tomorrow looks like being quite a day. Set your alarm for five a.m. I'll call you then with the details.'

Dan noticed his voice was suddenly unsteady. 'OK.'

'See you in a few hours then.' Adam paused, and then added, 'Oh, and Dan?'

'Yes.'

'Bloody good thinking.'

Sometimes, sleeping is simply impossible. Whether it's as a child on Christmas Eve, or an adult the night before a big job interview, driving test, wedding or whatever, the excitement and nerves can never free your mind and leave the blissful space for delicious release.

Before the epiphany moment in the rain and wind and darkness of Hartley Park, Dan had felt tired. But no longer. He tried lying in bed, breathing deeply, imagining relaxing visions of long summer walks across Dartmoor with Rutherford, or paddling in secluded sun-blessed bays on the Cornwall coast.

But try as he might, he couldn't rest.

He looked for another distraction, began to work on Bonham's riddle again, screwed his eyes closed and imagined the characters floating in the darkness.

992 619U

And now something came. A vague thought at first, but fast building momentum. A dusty memory from college days. Of a lecture theatre, overly warm and dimly lit, rows of hundreds of baffled young faces. An exposition of organic chemistry, an aged professor extolling the virtues of carbon.

'This element ahead of all others we should hold high,' the rather eccentric man had extolled, waving a ferrule like a wand. 'For without it, you, me and all around us would not be here.

Behold the mighty Carbon, sacred number six in the atomic scale!'

Dan tumbled out of bed. He strode into the lounge, flicked on the light, squinted at the bookcase and grabbed an old chemistry text book from one of the shelves. Rutherford padded in to see what the fuss was about.

Fast the pages turned. Dan flicked to the back of the book and found the chart he was looking for. It was the foundation stone of so much of science, the familiar shape of the twin columns at each end, the lines of boxes arrayed between them. After some scrabbling Dan found a piece of paper and a pen on the dining table in the bay window. He traced his way along the block of tiny rectangles and wrote down the letters which corresponded to the numbers.

And there, staring at him in smudgy blue ink, was the answer to Bonham's riddle.

So simple, and yet so smart.

And so offensive.

What an extraordinary night it was turning out to be. One of revelation upon realisation.

Dan's first thought was to find his phone and call Adam again. But this was hardly the time. Plus, the detective would be far from impressed with the solution.

Rutherford yawned, turned, and headed back for the bedroom. Dan took the hint, placed the book back on the shelf and followed.

He tried once more to sleep, but of that there was now no hope whatsoever. The thought about what could come to pass in the next few hours in the Bray inquiry, along with finally finding the answer to Bonham's riddle meant sweet unconsciousness was a hopeless prospect.

At around half past two he admitted defeat. Dan got up, and sat on the great blue sofa, the duvet wrapped around him, listened to the late night radio and tried to read a book.

And as is often the way with sleep, the moment you start ignoring it, it takes offence and decides to come calling. Dan must have dozed off, because he was startled awake at just after five by the ringing of his mobile.

It was Adam, telling him to be at Charles Cross by six.

The preparations were laid. The plan was in place.

The car park of the police station was as busy as Dan had seen it. There were two large police vans, teams of officers milling around, chatting as they strapped on their protective gear. Four police cars were also lined up and ready to go, their headlights on, directed to illuminate the vans. The relentless rain drifted in the white beams and long shadows shifted across the tarmac as the men and women prepared for the raids.

A Tactical Aid Sergeant was giving a briefing, but it was short and less than informative.

'As you know, we've had no time to do any reconnaissance or intelligence work on these houses, so we can't give you much idea of what you'll be up against. These are ordinary members of the public you're grabbing, so we don't expect too much trouble, but bear in mind this.'

The rumble of conversation died, and the man waited until he was sure he had everyone's attention, then added, 'You're dealing with people who may have committed murder, and while we think it's unlikely there will be weapons in the houses, be ready for anything. Good luck.'

The teams continued donning their clothing, heavy boots, shin and knee pads, stab resistant and bullet-proof vests and helmets. A woman was checking the equipment in the back of a van. A small red battering ram with the words, "The Enforcer" handwritten on it in white paint, which she patted affectionately. Metal bars, mini fire extinguishers – which one officer had explained were used to calm angry dogs – and taser electric stun guns.

Dan caught a sight of Claire, bunching up her bob of hair, ready for the raid. Her figure was backlit by a headlamp, empasising the silhouette of her lips.

His long and lascivious stare was only broken by a heavy hand on his shoulder. Adam.

'Impressive, eh?' he said. 'Without being overly melodramatic, I always think of it as like the troops getting ready for battle.'

Dan nodded, but didn't speak. Adam peered at him. 'This your first time on a raid?'

'Yes,' Dan managed, his voice thin.

Adam gave him a look. 'Without being rude, given my experience of you over the last ten days, I wouldn't say you're the bravest of men – are you?'

Dan shook his head and opened his mouth to speak, but words were proving elusive.

'Well, don't worry,' the detective continued. 'We'll ride with the troops, but they're going in first. We'll just watch and wait until it's all sorted. OK?'

Another nod.

'Look, are you sure you want to come along?' Adam asked.

Dan hesitated, but then nodded once more.

'You'd better,' Adam said. 'Because all this is down to you and your little moment of inspiration. I just hope it's right.'

It was only a short drive from Charles Cross, no more than ten minutes or so. Dan sat right at the back of the van, squeezed between the wall and a police officer who was large in both height and girth.

The man kept clicking his knuckles in a less than reassuring way.

The banter which had flowed on the first part of the journey faded as they neared the target. The expressions of the men and women changed, grew implacable, focused. The windows of the van began to steam up with their steady breath.

Adam sat in the front, giving directions to the driver. The van lurched around one more corner and pulled up in the shadow between two streetlights. A police car drew up behind.

A glowing clock on the dashboard said the time was 6.15.

'Right,' the sergeant whispered. 'Final time checks. We hit at 6.20 precisely.'

There were two entry teams, Adam had explained earlier, one for each house. The raids would be carried out simultaneously, to eliminate any chance of either of their two targets being able to call the other.

Because, as they now understood, it was a conspiracy they

254

were trying to crack.

The clock turned.

6.16.

The teams would smash their way through the front doors and rush into the house. They would flood each room until they found the people they were looking for. They would be arrested on suspicion of murder, given a few moments to dress if they were still in bed, then taken straight to Charles Cross for interview.

Time was vital. They had only until nine o'clock, perhaps a few minutes more if they were lucky, but not many. Nine was the deadline they had to work to.

The digits of the clock flickered and changed.

6.17.

Dan noticed his chest felt tight. He tried to breathe easily, think about what he and Kerry would do tonight. They could go out for a drink, but all the pubs would be packed with Christmas revellers and he wasn't sure he would be up to it after the lack of sleep and what might come to be an extraordinary day.

The day the Edward Bray murder case was solved.

Much of it down to him.

Or so he hoped.

What a ridiculous way to spend Christmas Eve.

6.18.

Adam had made his calls as soon as he and Dan had finished their midnight conversation. First, to the Deputy Chief Constable, who agreed the raids may be a little excessive, but given that they could serve to frighten and intimidate their suspects, and perhaps help to make them talk ...

No further discussion was needed. The decision was made.

Then it was to a magistrate, for a warrant, or three warrants in fact. The woman had been unphased at the awakening call, listened carefully to the evidence and duly granted the police permission for their raids.

'Three warrants?' Dan asked, surprised. 'Surely just two.'

'No,' Adam replied, enigmatically and annoyingly. 'Three. I'm a detective too, remember? I've been working on a little idea of my own about what might lie behind the murder of

Edward Bray. And funnily enough, I think it could just fit in with your inspiration about how the killing was carried out.'

Dan persisted in trying to find out what Adam was talking about, but he would say no more except that all would become clear later in the day.

The final task on the detective's list was to ring the Tactical Aid Group, to alert them to what would be required. They were entirely used to such calls and the arrangements were duly and quickly made.

Then, it was a few hours restless sleep.

Which brought them to now.

6.19.

The officers began climbing out of the van.

A woman took the lead. They jogged after her, two abreast, at the front the men carrying the "The Enforcer", Dan and Adam at the back.

The street was classic suburbia, a line of neat terraced houses and parked cars, the streetlights on, the pavement shining with the rain. They passed a postbox, a bicycle propped against it, a couple of puddles splashing with their footfall. A white van rumbled past, trailing diesel fumes to taint the freshness of the early morning air.

They rounded the arc of a corner. The street was narrower now, gently sloping downhill to a cul de sac. The woman stopped by a low metal gate, pointed both arms to a dark and silent house. 'Number 23, that's it.'

For the home of someone involved in murder it was absolutely ordinary. A paved path cut through a tidy lawn, a well-trimmed hedge, a dark wooden front door with a brass knocker, curtains drawn tight over the unlit windows.

The men pushed past, strode up the path, hesitated at the door and looked back. Adam checked his watch and gave a nod. They swung the battering ram.

There was a crunch, crack and thudding creak, violent metal on wood. The door splintered and buckled, but held.

Another swing, another heavy pounding impact and it gave,

smashing back into the wall and juddering on its hinges.

The search team tumbled inside. Shouts echoed in the darkness of the hallway. 'Police! Stay where you are!'

Two went left, towards a lounge and kitchen. Lights flicked on. Two more clambered upstairs, their boots pounding on the wood.

'Police! Keep still! Do not move!'

From above came a woman's voice, a scream, and angry, muffled yelling.

Adam waited at the door, held out a hand to bar the entrance. 'This is far enough. We don't need to go inside. We'll just get in the way.'

Dan had made no move whatsoever to enter the house. 'OK,' he gulped.

They stood sheltering from the rain, squinting inside. More voices from upstairs, calmer now, but the words were unintelligible.

A ginger cat sprinted out of the door, making Dan jump back. Adam shook his head, but didn't say anything.

Two of the search team walked past, back outside. 'The downstairs is secure sir,' one said to Adam, and began taking off his helmet.

The police van pulled up outside the house. A couple of people had already gathered on the pavement and were watching curiously, despite the rain. Good gossip from an eyewitness angle was always worth a soaking.

Adam's mobile rang. He answered, listened, then said, 'OK, we're almost done here too. See you in a few minutes,' and hung up. 'Suzanne,' he explained. 'At the other house. They've got him. He's on his way back to Charles Cross.'

A milk float trundled by, the accelerating whine of an electric motor accompanied by the cheerful clink of bottles. From upstairs came the woman's voice again, loud, then turning to a cry. A baby started wailing.

A man's figure appeared at the top of the stairs, silhouetted in the light behind. He began walking slowly down, step by hesitant step. His arms were held behind his back and as he passed Dan saw he had been handcuffed. The face was familiar from their previous meetings, but the expression very different now. His mouth was a little open, his eyes blank, his skin colourless, almost bleached.

It was a look deeper than disbelief, more utter incomprehension.

Two police officers led him to the van, opened the back doors and pushed the man gently inside.

'OK,' Adam said. 'That's Stead safely in custody. Suzanne's team have got Hicks. That's part one of the plan successfully sorted. Now comes the tricky bit. Let's get back to the station, start talking to them and see if we can crack this case.'

From upstairs came again the woman's voice, breathless and stifled, sobbing and rising to a shrieking crescendo as it mixed with the baby's wailing cries.

Chapter Twenty-three

IT TOOK MORE THAN an hour before Hicks and Stead had been booked into custody, assessed, and were ready to face questioning. Adam harassed and chided the poor custody sergeant as the man filled out his forms.

The reaction of the two men to their arrests was very different. In one cell, in the far wing of the custody block, Stead sat quietly on the thin blue mattress which covered the stainless steel ledge that passed for a bed. He was hunched forwards, hands on his knees, staring silently at the concrete floor.

Even the offer of a cup of tea or plastic beaker of water went unanswered. Stead just shook his head, a movement so slight as to be almost undetectable, and returned to his miserable trance.

As he waited for the sergeant to finish his work, Dan couldn't resist taking a tiptoe walk along the cell block. It was a feeling he suspected was akin to his ancestors going to a public hanging, one of pure, inhumane fascination and schadenfreude at the sight of the condemned, but it was no less tempting for knowing that.

At the tiny peep hole to Stead's cell, he stopped, waited and watched.

It was a good three or four minutes before the man moved at all. And when he did, it was only to reach out a hand, extend a couple of fingers and touch the bare, whitewashed brick of the cold, confining wall. He pushed at it and then did so once again, disbelief filling every pitiful motion.

Hicks by contrast was a boiling kettle, a caged animal, railing against his incarceration. He paced back and forth, kicked out at the flimsy mattress and pounded his knotted fists on the unyielding steel of the cell door, beating out a relentless boom. He would lean back against the wall, then launch himself forwards, arms flailing, voice screaming obscenities, the words echoing along the hollow corridors of the police station.

It was the manner of a man who could be a murderer. And Dan was sure he would have thought so, had he not known otherwise.

Or perhaps, in truth, the word was suspected.

Last night, in the safety and security of his flat, he had been so sure of how the killing of Edward Bray was carried out, who had pulled the trigger and who had helped to foment, plan and then cover up the crime. But now, faced with the men themselves, the suspicion of what they had done and what might now happen to them, and with the denouement of the case approaching, the doubts were crowding in, whispering their sly, corrosive toxins into his mind.

There was another delay as the sergeant called the police doctor to check Hicks and Stead were well enough to be questioned. The behaviour of both raised obvious questions about their stability.

'For Christ's sake!' Adam exploded. 'I don't have enough time as it is.'

'I'm sorry, sir,' the sergeant replied, 'but there's no choice. And as you well know, if you question them and we haven't checked they're up to it first, anything you get will be chucked out of court straight away. It's in both our interests to make sure they're OK.'

Adam swore and issued a vehement restatement of his oft-repeated position about criminals having far too many rights, but stalked off to the MIR, tetchily beckoning Suzanne and Dan to follow.

'Right,' he said, as soon as the door clicked closed, 'let's talk tactics. It's vital we get this right. How do we do it?'

Suzanne ran a hand over her chin and said, 'We don't have much time, so how about you do Hicks and I'll question Stead? We give them both half an hour, then regroup to see what we've got.'

Adam nodded. 'Seems fair enough. It's logical. It maximises our time and resources.'

'Err ...' Dan began, then stopped himself.

'What?' Adam snapped.

'Sorry, I didn't mean to interrupt, I was just thinking ...'

'Yeah, right. I know what that means. Your thinking can be dangerous. Come on, out with it. What exactly were you thinking?'

Suzanne's hostile eyes were on him. Dan thought about what was happening downstairs, the men who were currently being examined by a doctor, but who, in the next couple of hours could be charged with their parts in a murder. They could spend tomorrow, Christmas Day, in prison, and many more such days to come.

And he was a TV reporter. A child in an alien land. Where the fun of the game of the last ten days had suddenly become very serious.

How sobering could be the ruthless impact of reality.

'Nothing,' he muttered. 'It was nothing.'

'Well, don't waste our bloody time then,' Adam growled. 'We're not exactly blessed with much.'

'Hey, hang on!' Dan heard himself say. 'If it hadn't been for me we wouldn't be here now. Who cracked the bloody case?'

Adam took a step towards him. The detective's hair was uniquely wild this morning, spraying in patches of dark tufts and his face was creased and shiny with sweat.

'We've cracked nothing yet,' he said ominously. 'Not – a – bloody – thing. All we've got is a theory. That's it. And unless we get on with finding something to back it up we're stuffed. So come on, that's enough sodding about. Let's get down to questioning them.'

He turned to go, but Dan reached out a hand and grabbed his shoulder. Suzanne's mouth slipped open. It was as if he had touched a sacred object, a heretic condemned in the eyes of a believer.

'What the hell are you doing?' Adam barked.

'I think you're wrong.'

'What?'

'You wanted to know what I thought. Well, this is it. I reckon it's wrong, splitting up and seeing them both at the same time. We'll get nothing from Hicks, I can guarantee it. He's too tough. He's delighted in Bray's murder all along. Stead's our only chance. He's the weak link in all this, the quiet one. We should concentrate on him, go at him until he cracks, all three of us.' Dan paused, then added quietly, 'Well, you two, anyway.'

Adam hesitated and glared at Dan. He wiped a sleeve across his forehead. There was a silence in the room, a long, loud and resonant silence.

'Suzanne?' Adam said finally.

She shrugged. 'It could work. It's a gamble, isn't it? It's got to be your best guess, sir.'

'Down to me then, is it? As ever.'

No one replied.

The detective drew himself up and stared out of the window at the grey, creeping dawn and the sullen, spattering rain.

'OK then, Stead it is,' he said at last. 'Let's go.'

It was just after half past seven on the morning of Christmas Eve. Downstairs in the cells were Andrew Hicks, Jon Stead and Gordon Clarke, the three men who Dan believed had plotted together to kill Edward Bray.

All three had named Julia Francis as their solicitor. Her offices opened at nine. At that point the messages on the phone would be played, and she, and doubtless some equally well trained and similarly ferocious colleagues would hurry straight to the police station to represent her clients.

As ever with Francis, the word was a masterpiece of euphemism. It might equally be used to describe the way the Royal Air Force represented their country and dealt with the Luftwaffe during the Battle of Britain.

With the evidence they had, in the face of committed and informed legal resistance, Adam said they would not be able to justify keeping the men in custody. Against Hicks and Stead they had essentially nothing, merely some circumstance and a theory, in effect, pure supposition. Against Clarke, at least they had the fibres from the car boot, but it wouldn't take Francis a great deal of research to find out they could have come from thousands of boots.

The men would walk free within minutes.

The only hope remaining was a confession, or for one of the men to let slip something which could incriminate them. And they had an hour and a half.

Adam's view was that it was probably now or never. If they couldn't build a case today, he thought they were unlikely ever to have sufficient evidence to charge anyone with the murder of Edward Bray.

They would always believe they knew what had happened, how the killing had been carried out and by whom, but never be able to prove it.

The faltering pulse of justice would suffer another wound.

The detective's mood wasn't improved by the phone call he received on the way down the stairs to the cell block.

'Yes sir,' he said wearily. 'Yes, I know this is probably our last chance. Yes, I'm aware it's a huge case. No, I haven't forgotten the annual report. Yes, I know it's important to you. Sorry, sir, yes I do mean extremely important. Yes, I know you're relying on me. Yes, I will call as soon as I have any news. Thank you sir.'

'Deputy Chief Constable?' Dan ventured.

'Well deduced,' Adam grunted. 'You really are showing a flare for this job.'

The sergeant swung open the thick, metal barred gate which marked the entrance to the custody block. The police doctor, Silifant, an ageing crab of a man, had pronounced Hicks and Stead fit for questioning, saying they were only showing fairly typical reactions to arrest.

A doctor more used to dealing with the factory line of fresh corpses which it was the police's lot to process, Silifant's less than endearing habit was to award the newly deceased marks out of ten for efficiency of dispatch. It had become a trait well known and much commented upon in Greater Wessex Police.

'As you didn't have any dead bodies for him this time, he wanted me to pass on that he gives you nine out of ten for getting him out of bed unnecessarily,' the sergeant said, with a thin attempt at a grin.

Adam didn't smile, hardly even seemed to notice the man's words. He was too intent on the cell door ahead, the name "Jonathan Stead" written in chalk on the board beside it.

'Nice and nasty?' Adam whispered to Suzanne.

'Yes, sir. As ever.'

'You ready?'

They waited for a few seconds outside the door, then Adam nodded and Suzanne opened it.

Jon Stead was still sitting, staring at the floor. He looked up, then quickly back down again.

'Mr Stead, can you come with us please?' Suzanne asked pleasantly. 'We need to talk to you and we've got somewhere more comfortable where we can chat.'

The man didn't move, didn't even look at her.

'Mr Stead?' she persisted. 'Please?'

Still no reaction.

'Stead!' Adam barked. 'Either you get up and come with us or I have you carried.'

Suzanne slipped a gentle hand under the man's arm and led him down the corridor. She walked slowly, giving him plenty of time to take in the raw, whitewashed brick, the row of steel doors, the light catching in the distortions of their pits and dents, the metal bars and the grim, echoing coldness.

It was a precursor of the taste of prison. And it was making its mark. Stead's frightened eyes darted around as he walked. At one point he stumbled and half fell, but righted himself again.

From behind, Adam watched carefully.

At the end of the cell block, the sergeant let them through the gate, making sure, just as he would have been told, to take his time and jingle the thick and heavy keys in the indomitable lock. The man could have been a jailer from medieval times.

And Stead stood and stared, his thin frame looking even smaller in the white glare of the electric strip lights.

Suzanne pushed open the door of Interview Room Two and guided Stead to sit down at the table. He lowered his head and stared once more at the floor. Adam and Suzanne settled opposite. Adam made a big play of turning on the tape recorder, introducing them and emphasising that they were conducting an interview with Jonathan Stead, a man who was a suspect for murder.

264

And after that final, lingering word, he left a long silence.

Even Dan, standing over by the door, arms folded across his chest, innocent and set apart from the scene though he might be, felt himself swallow hard.

'Right Jonathan,' Suzanne said, at last, in a friendly voice, 'Let me try to help you. We know how you and Andrew and Gordon worked together to kill Edward Bray. But we also know it wasn't your idea and that you didn't do the actual killing. But, nonetheless, I have to be honest and fair with you and tell you that you are part of a murder conspiracy, and that means you're in very serious trouble. We want to help you make it as easy as possible for yourself. So, it's probably best if you tell us in your own words exactly what happened.'

Stead didn't reply.

'We know about the switch of identities,' Suzanne persisted, 'and the phone call you made, to be sure the timings worked for all your alibis.'

Still no reply.

'We know about you swapping your mobile phones ...'

She waited, but there remained no reaction.

'And how important the weather was to you that day, and why.'

Stead shifted a little in his seat, but said nothing.

'In short,' Suzanne said, 'we know everything.'

She sat back on her chair and looked at Stead. He didn't move. His eyes were still set on the floor.

Suzanne glanced at Adam. He was studying the man, waiting for his moment. When the silence had ticked on, he barked, 'Stead! I don't think you realise how serious your position is. You played a significant part in a murder. The judge will see that in exactly the same way as if you'd pulled the trigger yourself. You'll be sentenced to life – that's life – in prison – to serve a minimum of fifteen years or so, maybe even more. That baby son of yours – little Joseph – will be a young man by the time you get to see him again.'

Adam waited, but there was still no response from Stead.

The detective slapped his hand on the table. 'That's if you ever get to see him again at all! Some kids disown their parents, you know. They're so ashamed at what they've done. They can't live with it. Joseph might well feel that way. And as for that pretty young wife of yours ...'

Adam lowered his voice, to a sly whisper.

'... how do you think she's going to cope, not having you around? And do you really think she's going to wait for you? They always say they will, I've seen it often enough. But come on – they never do. She'll be off with someone else and she'll forget all about you. It won't take long. One of those letters will arrive in your cell. You know the sort of thing – "Darling, I don't know how to say this, but ..." And you'll have nothing to help you through those fifteen long and lonely years in that prison cell. And nothing and nobody will be waiting for you when you come out – that is – unless ...'

A wave of rain sprayed on the tiny barred window.

'Unless, you talk to us, so we can tell the judge you were forced into what you did – that you went along with it because Gordon and Andrew pushed you to. And that will mean you'll get a substantially shorter sentence.'

No reaction.

'Which will mean you do get out in a reasonable time. And you do get to see your wife and son again. And you've got some chance of a future.'

Still no response.

'Mr Stead!' Adam barked. 'Are you listening to me? I'm trying to help you!'

The man looked up, but only briefly. His eyes quickly slid back to the floor. And there they stayed, despite the questions, threats and cajolements Adam continued to rain down upon him, an armoury of pressure and persuasion built up over the years of the detective's experience.

The time was a quarter to eight. They had seventy-five minutes left, and so far they'd made no progress.

Nice and nasty had quickly turned to not so nice and noxious. But whatever they tried, it still wasn't working.

Stead shivered occasionally, squirmed and shifted in his seat once or twice, but stared resolutely at the floor and would not answer the questions.

'Jonathan,' Suzanne said quietly. 'We want to help you. But we can only do that if you talk to us.'

Then, still without lifting his head, and in a faltering voice, Stead said, 'I have nothing to say to you until my lawyer is here.'

Suzanne and Adam exchanged glances. The words came like a schoolchild reciting something drilled into them in long and repeated lessons, learned by rote and repeated by instinct.

Adam got up and stalked out of the door.

There are different forms of silence, and in that dawn hour they heard three. Stead's was nervous and frightened, Hicks's smug and Clarke's arrogant, but all were steadfast and effective, and none of them were any use as evidence.

And they were fast running out of time.

It was half past eight and they'd trudged back upstairs to the MIR. Adam stood at the felt boards, Suzanne by a desk, Dan next to the windows. After last night's sleeplessness and the busyness of the last ten days, the tiredness had started to creep up on him. He'd tried perching on a desk, but then stood back up again. This was no time for sitting down.

He would have a rest tomorrow, Christmas Day, but not before.

'The bastards,' Adam hissed. 'They've planned this damn well. Not just the cunning of the bloody killing, but what to do if we got close to them. They know staying silent is the best way to frustrate us. They must have agreed beforehand and drilled it into each other, not to say a thing.'

'Yes, sir,' Suzanne agreed. 'I think you're right. And I don't know what we can do. We've tried just about everything. Unless you've got any other ideas?'

It was a measure of the growing desperation of the moment that she even glanced at Dan, but neither he nor Adam replied. There was nothing to say. They'd used up an hour of precious time, and had got nowhere. In perhaps a little over thirty minutes Julia Francis would arrive and fleeing quickly before her would be any hope of solving the case.

After talking to Stead – or trying to, as the case might more accurately be described – they'd had Hicks brought to the interview room. The moment he walked in the door it was apparent they would get nothing. The man was smirking.

Adam stood over him, said simply, 'We know what you did. We know all about your switch of identities.'

'No comment.'

'We know about your little away day.'

'No comment.'

'We know about Bristol, the phones, the cashpoint, the texts, the lot.'

'No comment.'

'You might as well admit it. We've got you.'

And now the smirk became a smile.

'No comment.'

'You're going to be charged with your part in murder and you're going to prison for many long years.'

The smile grew, and the scorn in the voice with it.

'Really? No comment.'

'I hope you've got something more convincing than that to say when you're standing in the dock, before a jury.'

And now Adam succeeded in forcing the longest response in the series of interviews he'd carried out this morning, but it was by no means any more helpful.

'You're not getting this, are you?' Hicks said, sarcastically. 'Then let me spell it out for you, nice and simply. I have no comment to make. I will not be saying anything until my solicitor arrives. Is that clear enough?'

Finally they had tried Clarke, all the while aware that it was hopeless. As they were now sure, he was the ringleader, the brains behind the plan and the motivator. Of the three, he was the least likely to crack.

Still, Adam and Suzanne did their best. Not get on though they may, Dan had to admit her opening question was a stinger.

'How does it feel to be a murderer, Mr Clarke?'

But the only reaction she got was a look of amusement.

'Funny is it?' Adam added. 'Killing someone? Taking their life?'

Now the look changed to contempt.

'No comment.'

'We know what you did. How you hid in that lay-by. How you waited for Bray to arrive. How you shot him, right in the heart, how you kicked him in the face afterwards and watched him die and how you dumped the gun in the field.'

'No comment.'

'How you planned the crime and how you covered it up.'

'No comment.'

'How you did it because you thought it gave you a chance with Eleanor Paget. So, what chance do you think you'll have with her when you're charged with murder and sitting in a cell, waiting for your trial?'

Clarke shook his head contemptuously. 'You can try whatever you like, but I won't be saying anything until my solicitor arrives.'

And nor had he. Clarke gave a long and very pointed yawn, folded his arms on the table, rested his head on them and ignored every other question that was put to him.

The interview was finally concluded when the businessman started emitting melodramatic snores.

By this time, Adam's neck was red and throbbing, and two more conversations with the Deputy Chief Constable had only frayed his temper further. Dan too had received an unwelcome call of his own. It was Lizzie, it was Christmas Eve, there was nothing happening in the world of television and she wanted a story.

'Every selfish sod is out having fun rather than creating news,' she said. 'So I want a report on the Bray case, I want it exclusive, I want it good and I want it by lunchtime.'

Dan had tentatively raised the question with Adam as they walked back up the stairs and been surprised by the reaction.

'You'll be getting a story OK,' he grunted. 'It'll be – "pissed-off police admit defeat and give up on trying to find the killer of Edward bloody Bray".'

The clock laboured around to twenty to nine.

'So,' Adam said, heavily. 'Last chance. We've got twenty minutes. Any thoughts? What do we do?'

Suzanne shook her head. 'We've tried everything. We've

got nothing left to throw at them.'

'Dan?' Adam prompted. 'Come on, you've come up with some decent ideas. I'll take anything at this stage.'

'I have to say, I agree with Suzanne. I reckon we've tried everything. I thought Stead was the most likely to break, but he's been too well trained. He's been conditioned into saying nothing.'

'So that's it? We're done? We're beaten? Is that it?'

Sometimes a silence can say much more than mere words.

The clock ticked on. A quarter to nine.

'Let's try Stead again,' Dan heard himself say. 'I still reckon he's the only hope. Let's give him anything we can think of. It must be worth a go.'

Adam shrugged. 'Yeah, why not? What else have we got?'

Chapter Twenty-four

A MANNER OF WALKING can give away a great deal. As they headed back down the stairs to the Interview Room, Dan thought how very different Adam's gait had become in just a couple of hours. Before the raids he was moving fast and upright, full of purpose and energy. Now he walked slowly and with a weariness befitting someone who expected only defeat.

It was as if the passage of only a short time had sapped a disproportionate degree of spirit.

A couple of young, uniformed cops bid them chirpy good mornings as they passed on the stairs, but Adam only grunted in return.

All the way down to the custody suite, Dan searched the recesses of his mind for a way to get Stead talking. Adam was convinced that if they could just get a few sentences out of the man, break through his conditioning of silence, he would open up and the case would be cracked.

There had to be a way. His was the most fragile of the defences they faced. It could be breached. It was surely only a question of how.

There was just the one possibility teasing Dan's thoughts. He let it linger and grow, then felt the weight of reality come to bear and dismissed it. It was far too ridiculous a way to try to tempt a man to admit to his role in a murder.

Anyway, it was hardly his part, at this most crucial moment of the investigation, to start chipping in with his own far-fetched ideas.

The professional detectives, Adam and Suzanne would handle the final questioning, as so they should. He would play the part he had been given from the start. He would watch and learn.

But Dan stored the thought, just in case, like a desperate gambler with a last card.

They reached the entrance to the custody suite and were about to head for the Interview Rooms when Dan said, 'Hold on.'

'What?' Adam replied. 'Come on, we don't have time to mess about.'

'Why don't we talk to him in his cell?'

'What? How does that help?'

'Psychology. Let him see the reality of what he'll face in prison. Metal bars and cold brick, surrounding him.'

'Bit wild, isn't it?'

'I'd take any possible advantage at the moment, wouldn't you?'

Adam rolled his eyes, but headed for the cells. Suzanne, though, nodded and said, 'Good idea.'

Dan was too surprised to reply.

They walked along the corridor, passing the steel doors, one by one, heading towards Stead's cell. The hard soles of Adam's shoes beat harsh and loud in the narrow space. From behind one door came the sound of a man being violently sick.

It was ten to nine.

One of the lights towards the end of the corridor was fading and flickering. The smell of strong disinfectant lingered in the still air.

The shadow of a mouse slipped around a corner.

They reached Stead's cell.

Adam hesitated, then opened it.

The man was still sitting on that thin blue mattress, staring at the floor. In his face, as he looked up, there was an expression of hope.

Adam saw it and leapt upon it. 'No such luck I'm afraid. No one's come to free you. And no one will be coming. You'll be spending a very long time in prison, unless you start talking to us.'

Stead returned to his study of the ground. They edged into the cell, fanned out around him, Dan and Suzanne to each side of Adam. They were packed together, side to side. The tiny space now felt chokingly claustrophobic.

'This is your last chance, Mr Stead,' Adam said. 'If you don't talk to us now, I'll have no choice but to charge you with murder. I know you didn't do the actual killing, but I'll have no

272

evidence to prove it wasn't you. And that means a long time in prison.' He waited, then spelled out the words again.

'A – very – long – time – in – prison.'

Stead was shaking his head, slowly, but still he didn't speak.

'This is what you'll have to get used to,' Adam continued, gesturing to the confines of the cell. 'A tiny little, cold, miserable home. In fact, even that's not the truth of it. This is luxury compared to what'll happen to you. Prisons are dreadfully overcrowded these days. You'll be sharing a cell this size with a couple of other men. You'll hardly have the room to breathe. And they're unlikely to be the sort of people you'd want to share a country with, let alone a little cell. Hardened criminals ... gangsters ... murderers ... rapists ...'

The detective waited, then his voice changed, became more chirpy. 'Mind you, they do let you out of the cells occasionally. I suppose that's something to look forward to. You'll probably get – I don't know, say ... maybe half an hour a day for a little walk around the prison yard.'

As a note of optimism, it was beautifully and effectively discordant.

'And there's something else I should mention,' Adam went on. 'You're probably imagining that you'll be in a prison somewhere near here, so whatever's left of your family – whoever still wants to know you, if that's anyone at all – can come and visit. Well, I'm sorry to have to say, that's not going to happen either. We don't have any prisons fit for newly convicted killers anywhere close to Devon. Most murderers get taken to a jail miles up north. You'll be lucky to see a friendly face twice a year.'

And now another change of tone, more sympathetic. 'I don't envy you for what you're having to cope with, I can certainly tell you that. All this – and at Christmas too. When the rest of us are looking forward to going home and being with our families and having some good food and drink and enjoying ourselves, and you'll be sitting in the cells. Your so-called mates Gordon and Andrew have really dumped you in it, haven't they?'

Stead raised his hands, clamped them over his ears. Adam

leaned forwards, so his mouth was just a few inches from the side of the man's head and said, 'Still, let's look on the bright side. At least it'll give you time to get used to how the next fifteen years of your life are going to be, eh?'

He took a step backwards, into the doorway of the cell.

'Last chance, Mr Stead. If you talk to us now, I promise you I'll tell the judge it wasn't your idea to kill Edward Bray and that you were dragged along by the other two. And that'll mean you'll get out of prison much more quickly. Your – choice ...'

Adam waited expectantly, his eyes fixed on the thin, hunched figure sitting in the miserable cell. But Stead didn't move, didn't even react. And now Suzanne stepped forwards and sat gently next to him, her voice that of a kindly and favourite aunt.

'We can help you, Jonathan. Let us help you.'

Stead flinched, shifted a little away from her, but on the tiny bed there was nowhere to go.

'Let us help you,' she repeated, kindly. 'And perhaps more importantly, let us help your family. That poor wife of yours, imagine how she'll feel when you're locked up for life. How's she going to cope? And what about your son? It's poor Joseph I feel for the most in all this. He's going to grow up without a dad. What's your wife going to say when he starts asking questions about where you are?'

'I couldn't imagine not seeing my son growing up,' Adam added from the door. 'Every day is a joy. That's the point of fatherhood, isn't it? You'll miss out on all that. Bizarrely enough, knowing what little I do of you, I think you might have made a good father. And of course, when he gets a little older, he's going to need his dad, to help him through the troubles of adolescence. And where will you be? In a prison cell, rotting away.'

'So,' Suzanne said. 'Let us help you. None of that needs to happen. If you just talk to us.'

Stead pushed himself further against the cold bricks of the unyielding wall and clamped his hands harder over his ears. They were white with the pressure. He was muttering to himself, repeating, 'No, no, no, no,' over and over again.

Adam and Suzanne exchanged looks, nodded to each other. The tiredness had left Adam's face. He looked keen, alert, his eyes bright.

There was a crack in the fortress. They were close to the breakthrough.

But it was five to nine.

'Come on, Jonathan,' Suzanne said. 'Just talk to us. It wasn't your idea, any of this, was it? It was Gordon's. Andrew got caught up in it and pulled you along too. I know you think they're your friends, but look what they've got you into. You don't owe them a thing. They told you that you couldn't possibly get caught, didn't they? And now look what's happened.'

'You're sitting in a police cell,' Adam continued. 'On Christmas Eve, when you should be with your family. And you're looking at a life sentence for murder.'

Stead was rocking now, just a little, back and forth, his hands still clamped to his ears, his lips mouthing unintelligible words. He'd shrunk into himself, as if to try to escape this place of torment.

'So talk to us, Jonathan,' Suzanne said. 'And we'll look after you.'

Adam glanced at his watch. It was almost nine o'clock. They had minutes, if that. Julia Francis and the other solicitors could be on their way here, even at the police station's front desk, demanding to see their clients.

Suzanne was leaning forwards, had laced an arm around Stead's shoulders. He didn't react, didn't even seem to notice. Adam was staring intently, his fists in tight knots.

They were so close.

The scales were balanced. Just another little ounce of pressure would do it.

Dan nudged Adam. The detective's head snapped round. Dan leaned over, whispered a couple of words in his ear. Adam's brow furrowed. The disbelief was clear. But then came a slight nod.

Stead let out a low whine, his feet twisting on the cold concrete floor.

Dan swallowed hard, found his voice. It felt breathless and hollow and he had to concentrate hard to form the words.

'You know what I'd miss most about being locked up for so long, Jonathan?' he said. 'I think it'd be my hobby. Every man needs his little passion, something to get lost in and love. I'd be desperate without mine. I go walking with my idiot of a dog. We hike across the moors, around the coasts, anywhere really. I love the sense of space and nature and escape from the everyday world. I suppose, in a way, yours gives you the same sort of thing. With you it's fishing, isn't it?'

Stead's feet stopped their continual shifting. Dan could have sworn the man's hands lost some of their pasty whiteness as they released a little of the pressure on his ears.

So often in life, words don't come remotely close to being able to describe a feeling. They can be as solid as clouds. And to Dan, this was just such a moment. Absurd, idiotic, ridiculous, any one of a range of similar descriptions didn't have a hope of doing it justice.

He was trying to trap a man into confessing to his part in a murder by talking about fishing.

But Stead was listening. He was sure of it.

And so he went on. There was nowhere else to go.

'I used to go fishing,' Dan continued. 'When I was a kid. Freshwater fishing, not in the sea like you. I loved those summer days when the sun beat down and the river just slipped by and occasionally you'd get a bite. I think it was the excitement of not knowing what it was you were about to reel in. That's the fun of it, isn't it? Knowing that at any moment the big one could bite.'

Stead straightened a little, his eyes flashing up from the floor.

It was working. Dan had no idea how or why, he just knew the words were having an effect. Perhaps it was because his was a different voice, not the stern and intimidating sound of the law that was Adam, or the false friendliness of Suzanne, but someone else. Someone who was not a part of this new hell into which Jonathan Stead's life had been transported.

Or perhaps it was the vision of a favourite escape, a

treasured pastime, a way to be free from the confines of the cell and the threat of many more years of incarceration to come.

But whatever, it was working.

Adam was nodding hard.

But the clock was ticking ever on. It was now a couple of minutes past nine.

The tannoy crackled and boomed.

'Mr Breen, you have a visitor in reception. Urgent.'

Adam's eyes widened. Francis was here. Their time was almost up.

He nudged Dan with a sharp elbow.

'You know,' Dan said, wondering what else to say, but just aware that he should keep going, 'I used to like doing fishing stories. When I covered the environment I did quite a few, it's such a popular hobby. I used to like going out and talking to anglers and reporting on what they were up to. I suppose it took me back to my childhood. Mind you, that was before my job got changed. I do miss it sometimes.'

Stead had raised his head, was almost looking up. His eyes were unfocused, as if he was lost in his imagination.

The tannoy boomed again, the voice more insistent now.

'Mr Breen, you have an urgent call to reception. Please respond.'

Adam stretched out a foot and eased the cell door closed.

'You fish in the Sound, don't you?' Dan continued. 'I did a story there last year, about how the water company kept releasing polluted ...'

'I know.'

The words were only thin and soft, but they stopped Dan in a second. Stead was looking up at him, nodding gently. Adam, Suzanne, both were frozen, as if frightened to break the moment.

'You gave us the news,' Stead said softly. 'You told us. They tried to keep it quiet, but you told us.'

Dan nodded, but found he hardly knew what to say. 'Yes. Yes, I did. I thought you deserved to know. Is – is the Sound your favourite place to fish?'

'No. I like the river, but Andrew...'

Stead stopped. Something unpleasant had intruded on the vision.

And Dan saw the opportunity.

'You don't like him, do you?'

Stead raised a hand, bit at a fingernail.

'No. I used to, but …'

'He started to tell you what to do?'

'Yes.'

'Bullied you?'

'Yes.'

'Him and Gordon?'

'Yes.'

Dan swallowed hard, could scarcely breathe so tight was the tension in his chest.

'And they – they forced you to do … they pushed you into what happened with Edward Bray?'

A slight hesitation, but then came the beautiful word.

'Yes.'

Stead's eyes were shining now. Suzanne put her arm back around his shoulder.

'Tell us all about it,' Dan said quietly. 'Just tell us everything and we'll sort it all out.'

Chapter Twenty-five

CHRISTMAS EVE TRADITIONALLY COMES with a knocking-off early, if indeed work has the temerity to intrude at all, a few warm-up drinks as a prelude to the day itself, and a general spirit of a time to relax. Dan did get to enjoy the drinks, eventually, but it became a day of very little relaxation and plenty of work, both in the service of his official job, and even more in what he had secretly come to think of as his second, secret, and far more exciting role.

In the early part of the morning alone they had solved the case, and in the greatest tradition of thrillers and dramas, the kind aired annually at this holiday point of the dying year, only just in time.

It was indeed Julia Francis in reception, burning with a stellar legal ferocity and harassing the desk sergeant ever more with each passing minute. She must, she insisted, be allowed to see her clients at this very instant, or she would bring thundering down upon the police all the mighty force of hundreds of years of statute, case law, natural justice, human rights, and whatever else she could spout from the vast gamut of legal gobbledygook.

Suzanne escorted her, first to see Andrew Hicks, then Gordon Clarke. By the time she got round to Jonathan Stead it was too late. He had been interviewed, and recorded, in sane possession of his faculties and happy to dispense with the services of a lawyer. In a catharsis of release he had described in detail exactly how Edward Bray had been killed, who by, how, why the plot began and how the murder was covered up.

Under stern advice from Francis, Clarke and Hicks would say nothing, apart from denying the allegations against them. But Adam was content that with the wealth of circumstantial evidence, the detail of the fibres on the shotgun and most importantly Stead's confession, they had plenty to secure a conviction.

The police also found a way to give themselves an early

Christmas present. The parking around Charles Cross is limited to an hour. Julia Francis had far more work to do than that, and so with the assistance of an understanding traffic warden she was duly given a ticket.

It was petty, yes, Suzanne admitted, perhaps juvenile, or arguably even small minded, but it most enjoyable nonetheless. And no one disagreed.

Dan would have his story, it would make the lunchtime news, it would be an exclusive and it would be good, just as the insatiable Lizzie had demanded. Adam reckoned by the time all the allegations had been put to Hicks and Clarke and they had the chance to rebut them, as the law required, the time would be around noon. The two men would then be charged, just nicely in time for the half past one bulletin.

Sitting in the MIR, Adam raised a cup of coffee, and Suzanne and Dan joined in the sober toast.

All that remained was to go through Stead's statement and check that what he had said tallied with how they believed the murder had been committed.

Adam sipped at his drink, was about to speak, then turned to Dan.

'It was a defining moment in the case. So, why don't you do it?'

'What?'

'Tell us how it was all done, and how you realised.'

'Me? But I'm just a hack, and ...'

'It's your first time, so call it beginner's privilege,' Adam said levelly. 'Just get on with it please.'

And so Dan did.

Edward Bray had been, if not the author of his own downfall, as the old saying goes, then certainly the instigator.

The story began when Clarke, Hicks and Stead met at court on one of the days given over to cases brought by Bray. They had their shared passion in hating the man, they supported each other and they got on well. The friendship continued and grew.

The mutual grudge against Bray had often been discussed and nurtured, even to the extent of the now infamous "Kill Edward Bray game", as played out in the Red Lion.

'But,' said Dan, 'at that point, I think it was only fun. However sick, it was just drunken friends having their idea of a laugh. There was no real intention to harm Bray. But then however, things change. Eleanor Paget comes on the scene.'

At that point in Dan's narration, Adam did something strange. His face became thoughtful and he nodded slowly and said, 'Yes, indeed she did,' but he wouldn't say anything else, instead prompted Dan to carry on with the story.

Gordon Clarke took a fancy to Paget, and it grew fast, into a fascination and then perhaps even an obsession. There were the endless flowers and that ill fated date, but most importantly in the chain of events was her time-honoured excuse for why she couldn't get involved in a relationship.

She was too busy with work, particularly dealing with, and fending off, the relentless demands of Edward Bray.

'And that was the catalyst for all this,' Dan explained. 'First, Clarke becoming infatuated with Eleanor. Then, she says she can't reciprocate any feelings because of Bray. And now Clarke has another reason to hate the man. This time it's fresh and new and all the more powerful for that, enough to shift his thoughts from fantasy to fact. He starts to actively plot how to get rid of Bray.

'And so the plan grows. Clarke does some research on methods of killing and the best ways to evade detection, probably using an internet café so there are no traces left on his own computer. He finds that a shotgun is good, as the pellets can't be definitely linked back to the weapon itself. Plus they're easy to get hold of. He might have bought it second hand, maybe even stolen it, but he gets himself one, and in such a way that there's no link back to him.'

Dan paused, thought his way through the case. 'Now I'm on less firm ground, as I don't think we can prove this, but it's my guess at what happened anyway.'

'Go on,' Suzanne said. 'You're doing fine so far. We'll pick you up if you get too creative, don't worry.'

So Dan went back to his story.

'Gordon Clarke probably spent a great deal of time trying to work out how he could kill Bray, but still have an alibi which would free him from suspicion. He would know that his past, his threats against the man, the website he set up to attack Bray, all that would soon have the police knocking at the door. But he couldn't find a way to distance himself sufficiently from the crime. The only possible method was to have an accomplice, to enter into a conspiracy. He needs someone to help him. And he realises in fact he has two possible candidates, Andrew Hicks and Jon Stead. So, he comes up with a plan which includes them both.

'They know enough about Bray's way of working and the property business to set a trap. They lure him to the lay-by with that appointment and talk of a lucrative parcel of land nearby. They know too that Bray's always punctual, so they can set their timings to give them all decent alibis.

'Clarke's the ringleader, and he's going to do the actual killing, so he needs the strongest alibi of all. Hence his visit to Bristol. He was on the train coming back to Plymouth when Bray was murdered, the mobile phone trace puts him there. We've got CCTV of someone who looks like him going into the station, his cashcard being used in Bristol, texts to his secretary containing information only he could know. It's not conclusive, but it's not far off. Except – except that he wasn't in Bristol. He was in Plymouth all day, and then, later, at the lay-by, waiting for Bray. Which raises the big question. How could that possibly be?'

Dan paused, his mind flying through what had happened. It was a remarkable story. He wondered how much of it he would be able to report. The entire tale would probably only come out at the trial. But it would be well worth waiting for.

'This is what they did,' he said, finally. 'They switched identities, to give them alibis. Clarke didn't go to Bristol. Hicks did. The two men have similar builds and they used that. Hicks took Clarke's coat and umbrella and went to the station. He was carrying Clarke's phone, so the location trace would check out. They knew we'd look at that. In Bristol, he used Clarke's card to get some cash – he'd been given the security number. And as for the texts to Clarke's secretary, I'm guessing Hicks and Clarke had both got themselves another untraceable pay as you go mobile. When Hicks needs to know what to put in a message, he texts Clarke to find out – he wouldn't want to risk speaking on the train. The answer comes back and he sends it off, using Clarke's own phone. To the secretary it would have seemed just like Clarke answering.'

Adam nodded. 'Go on,' he said. 'And the other details?'

'Clarke's car was parked up by the river. I'm guessing he'd got some false plates to confuse the number plate recognition system. As you said, that's easy to do, and it fits with the pattern of events. This was a well-planned crime. The gun is in the boot, hence the fibres we found. Clarke spends the day fishing with Stead, or at least pretending to. When it's time to go, they pop into the shop and deliberately drop that bottle of milk, then make a fuss about helping to clean up so the woman will remember them. They know the CCTV's not working. I suspect they'd already researched that, maybe asking her some throwaway question about it weeks ago, so she won't remember when we investigate. She's short sighted, and they're in disguise, anyway. It's raining and they've got big coats on with their hoods up. She gives the two men their alibis, as they know we'll think it's Hicks and Stead and from there they can't get to the lay-by in time to carry out the killing as they don't have a car. But in fact it's not Hicks, it's Clarke. Into his car he gets, off to the lay-by he goes, and ...'

Dan's voice tailed off.

'A shot through the heart for anger, revenge and passion, and a kick in the face for good measure,' Suzanne said quietly

There was a silence as the ghost of Edward Bray drifted through the room.

'The missed appointment,' Adam said, at last. 'Tell us about that, the one from the week before, when they first planned to kill Bray. As we always thought, it did turn out to be the key to the case.'

Dan sipped at his coffee. 'Indeed it was. And here's the golden reason the appointment was cancelled. We overcomplicated that, looking for some personal reason in our suspects' lives why they might be forced to put off a meeting. In fact it was far simpler. It was all down to the bane of the

British – the weather. The week before, the forecast was for a fine day, and that's exactly how it turned out. I remember it well, it was remarkably mild for December. I took Rutherford for a walk on the beach that evening, it was so warm. And, of course, for the disguises of Hicks wearing Clarke's raincoat and sheltering under his umbrella, and Clarke wearing the big fisherman's coveralls, the weather had to be nasty. So when they saw the fine forecast they postponed the killing. Even murderers can be let down by the weather, it seems.'

The attempt at humour raised no smiles. It wasn't that kind of a morning.

'You know,' Dan went on, 'it was thanks to Rutherford I realised what had gone on. My little moment in the park when I mistook that woman for a neighbour. That was when I suddenly saw the one very obvious advantage that bad weather gives you in terms of dressing for it. It's a handy excuse for a good disguise.'

'And all that you've said about the men fits in with what we know about our conspirators,' Suzanne observed. 'Clarke takes the leading role with the murder. Hicks does the next most tricky bit by going to Bristol. Stead more or less tags along, carried by the other two.'

'He does do his bit though,' Adam said. 'It was he who took Hicks' mobile phone and dropped it off at his house, under a bin in the back yard as it happens, before going home himself. That was an important detail, to make sure their two mobile traces would lead back to their houses. And he made the call, the muffled one, to tell us about the body. To make sure we knew exactly what time the killing happened, so their alibis all worked out.'

In his earlier interview, Stead had pleaded that he shouldn't be charged with conspiracy to murder. He said Clarke and Hicks were adamant the idea was to injure Bray, not kill him, just to teach him a lesson. He would never have gone along with a murder plan he said, was shocked when he heard Bray was dead. But by then he was too bound up in the plot to do anything about it.

Adam looked dubious. He asked whether Stead had any

evidence to support that and was pointed to the call he made to report Bray's body in the lay-by. He had clearly said "body", as opposed to dead body.

Adam nodded, clicked his tongue, but said a matter like that would have to be for a jury to decide.

Hicks had been in tears when they left him, pleading to be allowed to see his wife and son. That, Dan reflected, would be a reunion he would never want to witness.

'So, that's it then,' he said slowly. 'Case closed.'

Adam walked over to the felt boards, ran a hand along the line of faces looking out there. He stopped at Eleanor Paget, clear eyes and inscrutable expression, and tapped the picture.

'Not quite,' he replied. 'I think there might be one more loose end to tie up. Or if not tie, then at least give it a little tug to let it know we're well aware of it.'

Dan dashed back to the studios to cut a story for the lunchtime news. A man had been charged with murdering Edward Bray, he reported, two more with conspiracy to murder. He named all three and gave a little information about them, that they had known Bray for several years and had business dealings and disagreements with him, but couldn't go into more detail.

The laws of contempt in Britain are both strong and fierce, designed to prevent any possibility of prejudicing a trial, and with a lawyer like Julia Francis on the men's side, caution was advisable. She would be looking for any excuse to have the charges against them dismissed, and Dan didn't want to provide her with the amusing irony of helping to crack the case, then wrecking the trial.

Still, it was a fine splash and pushed Lizzie as close as she came to contentment and a hint of festive cheer.

'Not bad,' was the verdict from the rabid newshound. 'I'll consider that my Christmas present. I'll have more of the same for tonight, and if there are no developments you may just be permitted to go sloping off to make an unwarrantedly early start on your barely deserved break.'

Lizzie had never quite got the hang of humour. It hardly suited her, but at least she had the decency to put on a semi-

285

smile to make it clear she was teasing.

Although Hicks and Stead had been charged with the same crime, Adam made it clear that Stead was going be treated more leniently. The trial would be told he had cooperated with the police, had helped to bring the case to justice, and that detectives believed he had acted his part under pressure from the other two men.

He would still go to prison, but the sentence would be substantially shorter and arrangements would be made for him to serve the time in a jail as close as possible to home.

There was one more piece of news about the case. Penelope Ramsden had regained consciousness and was said by the doctors to be improving well. She was going to be OK. A detective had been to see her, only briefly and under medical supervision, but had the answer to a couple of questions Adam asked him to put to her.

Despite Bray's death, the hospice would still be cared for financially, for the foreseeable future at least. Bray was a rich man, with substantial investments. He had altered his will in recent weeks to make sure St Jude's would receive a large sum if something should happen to him.

At this news, Adam nodded slowly.

The other detail of information was that it hadn't taken long to conclude Ramsden's crash was nothing more than an accident, caused in the main by her anguished state.

At least, Dan reflected, one person had loved Edward Bray on the day he died. It wasn't much of an epitaph, but it was better than none.

He set off down the stairs to return to Charles Cross. This afternoon, Adam said they had one final visit to make before he would consider the case to be truly resolved.

Eleanor Paget welcomed them into her office and offered them tea or coffee. Adam declined, politely as ever, but also with an edge in his voice. He'd greeted Paget stiffly and formally, with no warmth or pleasure, most unusual for someone Dan had already come to think of as a gentleman detective.

His manner made it clear this was going to be a brief and

businesslike visit, very different from those which had gone before.

Adam settled in his chair, opened his case and found a file. He began reading, but didn't speak.

Paget studied him, but also said nothing. She tapped an elegant fingernail on the desk and waited.

And Dan was left in a familiar position, one which he had come to know well at the start of the inquiry, but had hoped he'd now worked his way out of. He was wondering what was going on. This strange, silent scene had the atmosphere of a volcano about to erupt from beneath calm and easy waters.

Dan eyed Adam, managed to take in a quick glimpse of the file. It was titled, "Eleanor Paget", and beneath were rows of type, but the words were too small to make out.

A puzzle had joined a mystery.

On the drive to the hospice, the detective had hardly spoken. He sat, staring at the raindrops sliding down the windscreen.

Once, when they stopped at some traffic lights, Dan said, 'Care to enlighten me?'

'About what?' came the gruff reply.

'About what we're doing? Why we're going to the hospice? This loose end you're going to tug?'

'No. You'll see. In a few minutes.'

Just ten days ago, Dan would have kept quiet and driven the car. Now though, whether it was his role in solving the case and the polishing of his ego and self confidence it had bestowed, the improvement in his relationship with Adam, or perhaps just the welcome sensation of Christmas creeping up, he felt sufficiently emboldened to challenge the detective.

'I'm sorry, I don't understand.'

'What?'

Dan sighed. Monosyllabic was clearly the theme of Adam's conversation this afternoon. He tried again.

'I don't understand why you're feeling grumpy. You can have some time off over Christmas now?'

'Yep.'

'You're still spending it with Annie and Tom?'

'Yep.'

'And looking forward to it?'

'Yep.'

'And happy about it?'

'Delighted.'

Three syllables. By comparison with what had gone before it was almost an oration. They were making progress, albeit painful.

'You've made your arrests.'

'Yep.'

'One murder charge, two conspiracy.'

'Yep.'

'The High Honchos have been on the phone, congratulating you.'

'Yep.'

'It's all over the media, very good for the force's standing.'

'Yep.'

'The case is done.'

'No.'

One little word can have a remarkable impact. It felt like a stone shattering the windscreen. Dan found himself recoiling.

'But we've got our killers.'

'Yep.'

'So, what's going on?'

'Just wait, will you! You'll see in a minute.'

Dan decided it was time to be quiet. He drove them to the hospice without another word.

'So,' Paget said finally, in a friendly voice, which didn't quite work. 'What can I do for you, Chief Inspector? It's Christmas Eve, but I don't expect you've just come to pass on your best wishes for the season, have you?'

'No,' Adam said grimly. 'That I haven't.'

Another silence. He leafed though a couple more pages, then closed the file and put it back in his case.

Adam folded his arms, stared right into the woman's eyes, and slowly let his mouth form the words, 'I know.'

'Know what?'

'What you did.'

The words hit their target. She sat upright, and there was a hint of fear in her reply.

'"What I did?" What is it I am supposed to have done?'

Adam bent forwards so he was leaning across the desk.

'I debated long and hard with myself about how to handle this, but you don't need to worry, Ms Paget. I'll never be able to prove it. In all honesty, I'm not even sure you've committed a crime. I know you won't say anything and I also know you won't have left me any evidence. I did consider having the hospice and your office and computer searched. I even got a warrant for it, but I decided not to in the end. It wasn't worth it. It'd just upset your guests, cause a huge fuss and I know I won't find anything anyway. Gordon Clarke isn't saying a thing either, and even if he did talk to us I doubt he'd realise how he was set up.'

And now she was clearly flustered. 'I … I don't know what you're talking about.'

'I'm talking about justice, Ms Paget. Or, at least, the nearest I can get to it. And I think this is it, this little chat we're having. Or – that we've had.'

She didn't reply, just stared at him, her face flushed. Adam got up from his chair, reached for the door.

'I just wanted you to know,' he said, before he left. 'Just so you don't think you got away with it completely, and to warn you that if anything like this happens again, and you're in any way a part of it, I'll be coming straight for you.'

If Paget did have anything to say, it was lost in the way Adam quickly pulled the door shut behind him. He strode back out to the car, leaving a baffled Dan mouthing questions and struggling to keep up.

Chapter Twenty-six

IT WAS CLOSING IN on midnight, the first such celebrated shadow between Christmas Eve and the day itself that Dan could recall spending on his own, but some things simply feel right. He had much to think about, and needed to go through it all and try to come to terms with it.

How life had changed in the last two weeks.

It wasn't as though he had to be alone. He'd had a couple of offers about how to spend the night, it was just that he didn't fancy either.

El was out in town with some other hacks, photographers and assorted members of the disreputable club of the media. Dan had received a loud and largely nonsensical phone call from the paparazzo, which, after some translation, had probably said he was awash with cash from selling his photographs of the Scoutmaster. He'd established a form of celebratory base camp in a bar, it was very busy, he was intoxicated, fully intended to become even more so, and would Dan, old buddy, good pal, top mate, etc., care to join him?

Dan, old buddy, etc. thanked him kindly for the considerate offer, but declined. He would see El tomorrow – not too early, naturally – to partake of the promised single malt and some yarning of tales from the year which had passed. As ever, there had been mishaps and misdeeds aplenty, all candidates for amusing recap.

He also made a mental note to take some headache tablets for his friend.

The evening with Kerry had gone well enough. Dan got a taxi to her house, no easy task given the busyness of the night, and had taken along his little Christmas gift. They sat in her living room and exchanged presents over a glass of wine.

She'd bought him a beautiful shirt from a very fine designer, sky blue in colour, impeccable in tailoring and extravagant in expense. It could be worn for work or play, fitted him perfectly and suited him more. She'd even got Rutherford some dog biscuits and a new ball to chase, chew and eventually lose, a familiar fate which befell all such offerings to the recalcitrant canine.

The nagging voice of guilt began to carp away in Dan's mind.

'The shirt, well ... how did you know – like, sizes and styles, and taste and all that?' he found himself stammering. 'I'd never have a clue what clothes to buy for you. It took me long enough to find any sort of present.'

'It's a girl thing,' she replied, and held out her hands for her own gift.

It was untidily wrapped with a couple of patches that didn't match the mainstay of paper, running out as it had at a critical point, and so perhaps resembling a small harlequin. But Dan thought she was pleased with the new hair drier he had bought. She certainly laughed enough.

They walked down to her local for a couple more drinks and a chat. It was a decent place, still with some original wooden beams and stone flooring, even better a couple of good ales and mercifully only one fruit machine and no jukebox. Even the Christmas decorations didn't look forlorn, not the usual pub type, their cheap glitter worn away by years of dutiful festive airings. The pub wasn't too busy either and they found a corner to sit.

Dan noticed he had to concentrate hard to hold a conversation, and even then it flowed like a river in a drought. His mind was too full of the day and all that had happened.

'Are you OK?' she asked, at one point.

'In what way?'

'You seem a bit – distracted.'

Dan put down his pint. 'In truth, I am. It's been a hell of a few days and it won't leave my mind. I'm sorry, it's nothing to do with you, it's just sometimes I get a bit lost in myself.'

She smiled, squeezed his knee and talked about tomorrow, her family, and their traditions for Christmas Day. They would open their presents early, over a breakfast of smoked salmon and champagne, sit and chat, then have a feast of a lunch and afterwards go for a walk to try to ease the assault of the armies of calories. In the evening they would play cards for pennies.

If, as Dan suspected, it was a final attempt to lure him along, it sounded as appealing as an invitation to an astrophysicists' party.

They walked back to her house and had another glass of wine while Dan waited for a taxi. He'd deliberately asked to visit her rather than have Kerry come to the flat. It was always easier to make an exit yourself than to try to usher someone else towards a door.

'Are you sure you don't want to stay?' she asked gently, cuddling into him as the car drew up outside.

'No and yes,' was all Dan could say in reply. 'But I just don't think I'm up to it. Sorry.'

She smiled understandingly, they kissed goodnight, he gently freed himself and made his way to the waiting cab. She stood on the doorstep and waved until he was out of sight. Dan wondered what she'd be thinking when she got back inside.

The evening had been dry, but on the short drive home the rain started to sweep in again. The season just wasn't the same without the snow Dan could have sworn was far more common in the distant days of his youth.

If the song had been written, "I'm Dreaming of a Wet Christmas" it would never have been a hit, he thought.

Back at the flat, Dan let Rutherford out into the garden, then settled on the sofa with a glass of whisky. So many thoughts were careering through his mind that he had to take out a pad of paper and pen and try to marshal them into some form of order.

The clock slipped past midnight. Christmas Day had arrived. Across the city, fireworks showered their colours over the dour night sky and a cacophony of horns blared. But Dan noticed none of it. It was only after half an hour's uninterrupted writing that he looked up from his pad.

'We've got one thing in common, Gordon Clarke and me,' he told Rutherford. 'We were both set up. Subtly maybe, but undoubtedly nevertheless.'

After that final interview with Eleanor Paget, Dan had driven back to the newsroom. He had a couple of sentences to add to the end of the report from lunchtime, that Clarke, Hicks and Stead had been remanded in custody by magistrates. Despite the pleas of their lawyers for bail, the seriousness of the charges meant the men would be spending Christmas in a prison cell.

Even with Dan's repeated and increasingly irritable inquiries, the enigmatic Adam still wouldn't talk about what the interview with Paget meant. He said he needed to do a little more work on his suspicions, but that Dan should come back to Charles Cross later for a final discussion.

He had been left with a couple of hours to kill, and wandered around the newsroom, chatting to a few colleagues, finding the strength and forbearance to wish most a happy Christmas, and even filling out an expenses form. It was one of his personal definitions of boredom. When he felt the need to do some paperwork he knew life was far from its pinnacle of excitement.

He took the sheet of paper and its attendant envelope full of receipts into the management office. Louise, Lizzie's cheerful and loyal secretary was away from her desk, so he left it on her chair to ensure she wouldn't miss it and would appreciate the urgency of the matter. He was owed hundreds of pounds. Dan was about to stroll down to the canteen to get a coffee when a piece of paper caught his eye.

It was the letter of complaint, the one which had seen him summoned to Lizzie's office, rebuked, and told his employment would change or would rapidly become extinct. He could hardly miss it, those moaning capital letters describing his behaviour;

"DISGRACEFUL ... DISGUSTING ... APPALLING ... SCANDALOUS ..."

And now he knew where he recognised the handwriting from. It was Louise's.

Dan took a quick look around. The office was empty and there was no sign of anyone returning. He shifted the letter to see what was underneath. There was just one more piece of paper, a note from Lizzie.

"Good spy work, thanks. The "complaint" gave me just the pretext I needed. But better shred it now."

Dan stood, staring at the note. He thought back to that late afternoon, the rain pounding down and his interview with Rose, the prostitute. There had been a car parked opposite, he was sure, and it had driven off, just after he handed over the money.

And then had come the showdown with Lizzie, which had seen his job change and all that had grown from it, a true turning point in life.

Wessex Tonight, by common consent, needed a new Crime Correspondent. He'd been asked, but had refused.

And then he'd been cornered. In just the way which someone who knew him well, who had been forced to deal with many a complaint about his ways in the past might readily anticipate. Lizzie could be sure he wouldn't come back to the newsroom without the story and all the constituents needed to make a good report.

Dan swore loudly, forced himself to walk downstairs, get that cup of coffee, and take it to the Quiet Room to think.

His first instinct was to confront Lizzie, but it didn't take long to reconsider. Fighting the news demon was something you did out of necessity, not choice. Perhaps it was better to file away the advantage, ready to use sometime in the future, a buried weapon to unearth when he really needed it.

And of one thing he was sure. Given the vagaries of his life, that day would come.

Plus, if he was honest, there was something else. Inadvertent and unexpected though it might have been, could Dan Groves, sitting here on this comfortable chair, excited apprentice in a new world, going back over the remarkable events of the last ten days, really deny that he was enjoying this job he had never asked for? Perhaps even delighting in it?

Dan nodded to himself, finished his coffee and set off down to Charles Cross to see Adam.

The detective's spirits had improved markedly. Dan wondered whether to ask if he wasn't the only one who suffered with depression and mood swings, but decided against it. It might prompt an argument, or perhaps just a discussion, but certainly a delay and he very much wanted to hear what Adam had to say about Eleanor Paget without any unnecessary interruptions.

It was the case's final mystery.

'Don't get comfortable,' Adam said, as Dan walked into the MIR and began taking off his coat. 'Let's go and have a pint.' He got up from the chair, patted Dan on the shoulder.

'It's Christmas Eve, and after all, a decent beer in a pub is pretty much how you managed to worm your way into the sanctum of my confidences.'

'I'd say it has a certain symmetry, yes,' Dan replied.

On the walk, Adam talked about how much he was looking forward to Christmas, a few days off and time with Annie and Tom. He would be spending the whole of Christmas Day with them, and perhaps, maybe, just possibly, if he played it right ... Annie had said to bring his overnight bag.

As hints went, it was as subtle as a drum roll with a cymbal crash added for good measure.

Better times lay ahead. It was an old cliché, but often true. The advent of another year did prompt people to consider their lives and think about a new start. Or, in Adam's case, a new old one.

The detective was smiling once more and looked much less tired than earlier. He even pointed to some newspapers racked up outside a supermarket. The picture of the Scoutmaster smoking away in the cage at the back of the police station was on the front of each.

'Anything to do with you, that?' he asked, airily.

'Pleasant evening, don't you think?' Dan replied.

'I don't want you thinking you can get away with anything, whatever kind of understandings we might occasionally reach.'

'Christmas is great, isn't it? I'm looking forward to a few days off. A bit of excessive eating and drinking, taking Rutherford for a good walk.'

It felt like a verbal version of those Red Arrows displays, when the pilots approach each other at right angles and only just miss colliding.

Adam walked on in silence, then said, 'Well, just so long as whatever scurrilous tricks you might get up to are good for the police and the public.'

'You mean like getting a picture of a paedophile published? So all the local parents will know?'

'He is an alleged paedophile. He hasn't been convicted of anything yet.'

'But the evidence is pretty strong, according to what "senior police sources" have told me.'

'There is that.'

'And you're a father yourself.'

Adam didn't reply, just began humming a little tune. A couple of women passed, one stopping to thank the detective. He had investigated a prowler on the loose in her neighbourhood five years ago and got the man sentenced to twelve months in prison. She was evidently extremely grateful. The kiss she planted on Adam's cheek was long and lingering.

And he didn't look in the slightest abashed.

At risk of denting his mood, Dan asked again about Paget, which prompted a shrug. 'I've been thinking about it all afternoon,' he replied. 'I can't honestly say to you that she's committed any offence, not legally speaking anyway. Morally maybe, but not legally. I think she's certainly been devious and manipulative, but if they were crimes ...'

'Then all our politicians, leaders, most senior managers, business people and the like would be in prison by now,' Dan added.

'Not to mention journalists,' Adam concluded.

And Dan didn't demur.

At the double doors to the chosen bar Dan quickly studied each and picked the right one, shiny as it was with wear. The place was filled with a group of office staff, their work clothes all askew, and one of whom, a young man, was attempting to perform a pole dance. The cheering and clapping was quite out of proportion to the skill and dexterity on show, and even more so the sexual allure, but then it was Christmas Eve and the group had clearly been here for a while. Dan and Adam watched for a couple of minutes while they waited to be served before retreating to a table at the back of the bar.

'Cheers!' Dan said, holding up his glass.

Adam clinked it. 'Cheers!'

They each took a deep draw at their beers, then Dan produced his best expectant look.

'Are you alright?' Adam chuckled. 'You look in pain.'

'I was trying to prompt you to tell me about Paget.'

'I'm aware of that. Subtlety isn't your strongest suit.'

'I don't suppose you've ever heard of the dubious art of delayed gratification?' Dan countered, with heavy irony.

'I may have done. I might even confess to practicing it occasionally.'

'So then?'

'So what?'

Dan sighed. The burgeoning desire to throttle the maddening detective was back. 'Tell me what you know about Paget, and what that little scene in her office was about?'

Adam leaned back on his chair, took another sip of beer, and finally he did.

Eleanor Paget was not all she seemed, or certainly not quite the person she liked to present herself as. Her commitment to the hospice was not in doubt Adam said, but as so often with people, there was a subtext, an agenda or way of working hidden beneath the fine public face.

Her history had been examined and a series of interesting events revealed. Several years ago, probably as her initial move into the world of business, she had run a successful interior design company. It was a relatively small business, but still employed a dozen people, was well thought of and appeared set for considerable expansion.

Then had come a problem. The company's major customer went bust and the cash flow faltered markedly and dangerously. Paget struggled to keep the business going. She had done well from it in just three or four years, to the extent she had a lovely house on which the mortgage had been paid, and a fine car.

The bank had offered to refinance the company to keep it going, but the price would be Paget's home as security.

She closed the business and made the staff redundant.

'OK,' Dan said. 'So she's ruthless. She protected herself. But so what? It was her company. That's a tough stance, but it's a judgement call and entirely defensible. Isn't being tough part of the brief if you're in business?'

'Listen on,' Adam replied calmly. 'I'm only just starting to build up the picture for you.'

Paget had taken a couple of other jobs at companies, one as a Marketing Manager, one as a Development Executive. At this stage, her CV had a sense of someone treading water, dabbling in work to keep busy and solvent while she waited for the next opportunity to come along. But then, what plans she had were knocked off course, in a way familiar to anyone who has walked the surface of this earth and breathed the planet's air.

Relationship troubles.

The man she had been living with in that fine house, a Stephen Wicks, had been seeing another woman and decided to leave her. But, although the house was in her name and they didn't have children, he had been working, contributing to the upkeep of the place, supporting her in her career, and thus in the view of the lawyers was entitled to a share of the property. Naturally they weren't going to be living together any more and she didn't have the money to buy him out, so a sale was mooted.

At this point, the story of Eleanor Paget became markedly more interesting.

She got involved with a new man, and one of no fine repute. Jimmy Masters was a local lad, good looking enough, but not averse to stepping on to the wrong side of the law to make a living, and even less concerned about settling a score with his fists.

The view of her friends was that Eleanor was upset, a little unbalanced by the break-up of her relationship, and that this was just a fling, one which would help to restore her self-confidence. She would soon be back on track and move on.

Then came the sting in the tale.

Masters met Wicks in a pub one night, and there was a fight. Wicks came off very much the worse, courtesy of a swinging bar stool to the head. He was put in hospital for several months, before beginning a slow recovery at his brother's house. Masters was charged with grievous bodily harm. He was sentenced to a year in prison.

The only one who emerged from the episode well was Eleanor Paget. With Wicks out of the way she was able to raise the money to buy him out of the house. Anyway, he was hardly in a state to want to make an issue of it. And while Masters was in jail, Paget found herself another man and on her life moved.

'OK,' Dan said. 'So things got nasty. They sometimes do in relationships.'

'Indeed,' Adam replied. 'So let's continue. Let me tell you a little about Masters' trial.'

The sentence the man had been given was probably on the lenient side, and much of that put down to the eloquent pleadings of his barrister. Jimmy Masters, he said, had been blinded by love. He'd fallen deeply for Eleanor Paget, held out great hopes for a future with her, and it was, in Masters' view, only Mr Wicks who stood in the way. Paget, it was alleged, had told poor Jimmy she could never commit to a future with him so long as she was locked in such a bitter dispute with Mr Wicks.

Dan almost spat out his beer.

'Bloody hell,' he said. 'That sounds more than a little familiar.'

Adam nodded hard. 'Doesn't it just? For Jimmy Masters, read Gordon Clarke. It took us a long time to find that info. It was all down to a very fine up and coming detective called Claire Reynolds, an officer I tend to send on some of the more tricky inquiries as I know I can trust her entirely. Because obviously Paget wasn't mentioned in the charges, only at the trial – where she refused to appear as a witness, by the way – it wasn't on the police computer and so took quite some digging out. That case was where I'd recognised her name from, and gave me the nudge to look into her past a little more.'

Dan swirled his drink and tried to concentrate on the information he'd just heard, rather than the word "Claire". It wasn't easy. It was echoing through his mind like a harp solo played by a virtuoso angel.

'OK,' he said, finally. 'It sounds interesting, to say the least. But being Devil's advocate here, that Jimmy Masters business still doesn't necessarily mean anything. It could all just be an unfortunate coincidence.'

'Yes, it could,' Adam said, with a raised eyebrow of scepticism. 'So let me continue with the story.'

Then came the next revelation. St Jude's Hospice was in secret talks with a large healthcare firm about a takeover. It would still be run largely as it always had, but now charges would be introduced. The trustees were seriously considering the proposal, as it would ensure there was unlikely ever again to be a cash crisis which could threaten the hospice's future.

Eleanor Paget was in favour of the takeover. The business case, she had concluded, was compelling. The current guests would not be affected by the change, only new ones. There would be minimal disruption to the hospice, if indeed any, but maximum financial security in being part of a far larger empire.

Adam said he thought that was probably a genuine position, that she really was passionate about protecting St Jude's and believed it to be the best way.

There was though one other little fact which shouted its doubts.

Paget would stay on as Chief Executive, with an enhanced salary package and also lucrative share options. Ironically for such a driven businessman, a free-market thinker to the core, Edward Bray had been vehemently against the move. Adam suspected that was probably because of his emotional attachment to the hospice and his desire to see it continue to run just the way it always had. He had been resolved and resolute in his determination to fight the takeover.

'Hell,' Dan spluttered. 'Another reason for her to want him out of the way. This is getting worse. I need some more beer.' He got up to head for the bar, then stopped, turned back.

'But wasn't the hospice going to be OK anyway? It had Bray to fund it – when he was alive, at least – and when he died, his will provided for it.'

'The will he'd only recently changed,' Adam said meaningfully.

'At the request of Eleanor Paget, by any chance? On the off chance, extreme as it might be, that something untoward could happen to him.'

'We'll never know. But a dreadfully suspicious person like yourself might well think that.'

Dan bought them another couple of pints. The pole dancing had ceased, happily, but a strip tease act had replaced it. Given his physical qualities, the only explanation for the man performing the divestment was that he had been drinking heavily, and quite possibly of large measures of true absinthe.

'Are you ready for the final detail of Paget's little story?' Adam asked, when Dan returned.

'Hang on, I might need this first.'

He took a gulp of beer and listened, as Adam continued.

'Being the suspicious sort I am, I had another look at those reports of when Paget and Clarke met at that business lunch. What I wanted to know wasn't in there, so I sent Claire out to do some more inquiries. How's life with that woman of yours, by the way?'

'What?' Dan asked, thrown by the conversational tangent. 'Err, well, I'm seeing her later.'

Adam chuckled into his beer.

'What?' asked a piqued Dan.

'Your tone. It was like – later, I'm going to be washing my underpants, then ironing them. If I feel daring enough and the mood takes me, I might even do some hoovering too.'

'OK, fair enough. I'm not exactly overwhelmed with passion, but I'm trying to give it a chance. So, why the sudden interest in my love life?'

'Just asking. Just wondering. Just that – I reckon you'd like Claire. I might even have a tiny suspicion you think so yourself.'

Dan felt his face growing oddly warm. 'Then I'll look forward to being introduced to her another time,' he said determinedly. 'Now, aside from the matchmaking – Eleanor Paget.'

'Eleanor Paget indeed. So, her meeting with Gordon Clarke.'

There had been about thirty people at the lunch. It didn't take the fabled Claire and her detective powers long to track down several who had noticed how Clarke and Paget first met. And their view was uniform.

Paget had made the first move. She'd plotted a vector straight for him and made a point of talking to him, with a beaming smile, a willing laugh and a general and very obvious sense of fascination. And understandably enough he had reciprocated.

Now Dan swore again, but this time at the ultraviolet end of the spectrum's blue. Adam produced a fatherly look of disapproval.

'Would she have known in advance who was going to be at the lunch?' Dan asked.

'Yes. A list was circulated.'

'So, she had plenty of time to do some research on the other guests. Just as we might expect of a diligent businesswoman like her? To maximise the networking opportunities.'

'Yep.'

'And look up Clarke, and you find the links to – if not exactly love for – one Edward Bray.'

'Yep.'

'And an idea sparkles. A re-run of what happened with poor Mr Wicks and Mr Masters. If fortune favours her, if Clarke should fall for her and if the situation is handled and fomented nicely.'

'Yep.'

'It all adds up.'

'Yes,' Adam said emphatically. 'I would say that it does.'

The two men sipped at their drinks. The office party and its amateur stripper and pole dancer constituents were heading out of the door, arguing about where to go next. It was like a travelling circus. An older man walked in with a woman holding his arm.

Dan nudged Adam, whispered. 'That's Joseph McCluskey.'

'Who?'

'The famous artist. You know, the one who's dying. The one who says he's going to set that riddle in his last paintings. It's all over the media, you must have heard of it. The puzzle of The Death Pictures, the papers are calling it. I might have a go at it myself. I've always liked riddles.'

Adam stared at the man, without showing much in the way

of interest. But Dan had been awaiting his opportunity and added, 'Talking of riddles, I think I may have an idea what the answer to Bonham's is.'

Now he did have Adam's attention. 'What? Really?!'

'Yes, really.'

'What – who his other victims were and where their bodies are hidden? He's never said anything about them. In prison he's always refused to answer any questions about who else he killed.'

'I'm not surprised.'

'Come on then, don't mess about, tell me. Is it because he murdered loads more people?'

'Not quite. Not exactly.'

Dan rummaged in his satchel and found the piece of paper he'd printed out earlier. It was a copy of the periodic table. He wrote the characters from Bonham's riddle beside it.

992 619U

'Right,' Adam said, with impatience which would impress a five-year-old. 'So?'

'I don't think I should just tell you what it says. You might take offence. It's better if you work it out yourself. Match the atomic numbers with their elements. It helps if you look at the puzzle in a slightly different way.'

Dan wrote:

9 92 6 19 YOU

The detective groaned and shook his head, but started working through the numbers. One by one, he wrote the corresponding letters in the margin by the side of the table. It took less than thirty seconds to decode a riddle which had stood for more than fifteen years.

When Adam had spelled out the word he sat back, swore and stared.

'The bastard,' the detective added at last. 'So it was all a bloody taunt. There were no other victims.'

'I think you're right. That riddle was just his little game to have some small way of getting back at the police and the justice system.'The two men sat in silence for a good couple of minutes. A barmaid dropped a glass and it smashed on the floor, but they hardly noticed.

Eventually, Dan prompted, 'What do you do about Paget then?'

'What?'

'Come on, leave Bonham behind. He's the past. This is more important – Paget.'

Adam blew out a lungful of air. 'What can I do? I reckon I pushed it about as far as I could with what I said in her office earlier. It's doubtful whether she's even committed a crime. All she's done is manipulate. As far as I can tell she hadn't directly told, or even asked Clarke or Masters to go and carry out an attack. I'm guessing, from her reaction she had no idea Clarke would kill Bray. I suspect she was hoping he'd just have a fight with the man, or renew their vendetta, or something like it, something to distract Bray from the hospice for a while so she could get on with sorting out the takeover. Given where the negotiations had got to it wouldn't take that long. By the time he was back on her case the deal would be done.'

'Yes,' Dan said thoughtfully. 'And Bray was very much against it. It sounds like perhaps he wasn't quite such a bad sort after all.'

They finished their drinks and headed back to the police station. Adam wanted to get an early night to be fresh for Annie and Tom tomorrow. Dan had his date with Kerry, which he had now performed dutifully and satisfactorily, if not, in truth, actually enthusiastically.

He sat back on the sofa, yawned hard and debated whether to have another glass of whisky, but decided against it. He was tired out and a good long sleep would be very welcome. Sometimes oblivion could be such rich bliss.

As Dan got up and readied himself for bed, he thought about what Adam had said as they stood on the steps of Charles Cross and wished each other a Merry Christmas.

'It's turned out OK, having you around. Better than I expected, anyway. You were even quite useful at times.'

The detective had clearly studied at the same school of praise and compliments as Lizzie.

'Thanks for the glowing tribute,' Dan replied, with a grin. 'In return I can say that it was pretty much OK, being around.'

They shook hands, Adam headed for the police station doors, then stopped and over his shoulder said, 'You know what? It surprises me to say this, but I'm going to anyway, as it's Christmas and all that.'

He hesitated, then added, 'I reckon we might just benefit from having you join us again sometime – if you're up for that.'

Dan nodded hard and noticed his grin growing. 'You know, I think I just might be,' he replied.

Also by Simon Hall

The Death Pictures

A dying artist creates a series of ten paintings "The Death Pictures" which contain a mysterious riddle, leading the way to a unique and highly valuable prize. Thousands attempt to solve it. But before the answer can be revealed, the painter is murdered.

A serial rapist is plotting six attacks. He taunts the police, leaving a calling card counting off each victim.

Dan Groves covers the stories and is drawn in by the baffling questions. Why kill the artist when he would soon die naturally? Could it be connected with the rapes? He crosses the line from journalist to investigator, forced to break the law to try to solve the crimes.

ISBN 9781906125981
Price £ 6.99

Evil Valley

A psychopath is out to teach the world a shocking lesson and the clock is ticking. Can the police crack his cruel riddles and stop him from committing the ultimate crime? Chief Inspector Adam Breen and crime-fighting TV reporter Dan Groves are reunited in the hunt for a masked man who boasts of plans to commit a crime so evil it will shock the nation.

ISBN 9781906373436
Price £ 7.99

The Judgement Book

*We all have our shameful secrets and one of our greatest
fears is seeing them revealed.*
The Judgement Book – just a pocket diary, but festering
with so much sin.
A faceless criminal, seeking not money, but revenge.
Secret after secret of the prominent and powerful is
revealed… sordid sex, corruption and murder… and
suicide, scandal and humiliation follow.
And then crime fighting TV reporter Dan Groves and his
detective friend Adam Breen discover they too are in The
Judgement Book…

ISBN 9781906373733

Price £7.99

About the author…

Simon Hall

Simon Hall is the BBC's Crime Correspondent in the south-west of England. He also regularly broadcasts on BBC Radio Devon and BBC Radio Cornwall.

Simon has also been nominated for the Crime Writers' Association *Dagger In The Library* Award.

For more information please visit Simon Hall's website

www.thetvdetective.com

A

For more information about our
books please visit
www.accentpress.co.uk